LOCKED IN

LOCKED IN

A Department Q Novel

Jussi Adler-Olsen

Translated by Caroline Waight

DUTTON

DUTTON

An imprint of Penguin Random House LLC
penguinrandomhouse.com

LIBRARY OF CONGRESS CATALOGING-IN-PUBLICATION DATA
Names: Adler-Olsen, Jussi, author. | Waight, Caroline, translator.
Title: Locked in / Jussi Adler-Olsen; translated by Caroline Waight.
Other titles: Syv m² med lås. English
Description: [New York]: Dutton, 2024. | Series: Department Q; 10
Identifiers: LCCN 2024033144 (print) | LCCN 2024033145 (ebook) |
ISBN 9780593475690 (hardcover) | ISBN 9780593475706 (ebook)
Subjects: LCGFT: Detective and mystery fiction. |
Thrillers (Fiction) | Novels.
Classification: LCC PT8176.1.D54 S9813 2024 (print) |
LCC PT8176.1.D54 (ebook) | DDC 839.813/74—dc23/eng/20240719
LC record available at https://lccn.loc.gov/2024033144
LC ebook record available at https://lccn.loc.gov/2024033145

Printed in the United States of America
1st Printing

Dedicated to Louie,

our beautiful ball of energy

LOCKED
IN

PROLOGUE I

2005

"**Again with this** crap?" Anker flung open the passenger-side door and reached one arm across the windshield. "Can't see shit when they put it at that angle."

"Let me guess," grunted Hardy from the back seat. He looked at the sticker Anker was waving. "Okay, that's a new one," he went on. "'The Three Musketeers.' Our colleagues at the station are getting creative."

"They're just jealous the three of us make such a good team, Hardy," said Carl from the driver's seat. "Hey, look over there." He pointed across the street. "Those two guys standing back from the road. The one on the left, isn't that the knifeman we're after?"

Hardy leaned forward, between the two front seats. "Nah, that's his brother. Means he'll probably be along in a minute, though."

"Well, if we're the three musketeers, I'm sure as hell not going to be that sanctimonious twat Aramis, even if I am the shortest," said Anker dryly.

Carl shook his head. "Why not? Aramis was a bit of a charmer too, you know."

"Nah, that was the big one, the drinker," interjected Hardy. "Which would be me, obviously."

The two men in the front seat started chuckling. Hardy and the female sex—that was its own can of worms.

"Hey, come on. You think I don't know what I'm like?" Hardy groaned. "Women! It's enough to drive you nuts."

"It's not like you actually have anything to complain about, though, do you?" asked Anker. "Minna's gorgeous."

Carl kept his eyes on the road, trying not to react. It wasn't the first time Anker had said exactly what Carl was thinking.

"Yeah, she is, and she knows it."

There was sudden yelling from the pavement opposite, and Hardy rolled down the window a fraction. "I'm sick of Minna flirting with every Tom, Dick, and Harry who comes her way. You two included."

Anker turned to look at him. "Aww, boo hoo, poor little Hardy. You've got it made. Not like me and Elisabeth. Pretty sure I'll be needing to borrow a sofa at a friend's place any day now."

"You know you're always welcome at mine, right, Anker?" said Carl.

"Or at ours," Hardy added.

Anker gave Carl's shoulder a squeeze. "Thanks, lads. Now that's hospitality for you!"

"I think that's him now," Hardy said.

"Are you kidding? That's his missus. Probably never seen a woman in trousers before, have you?" Anker teased. "Okay, Carl, tell me," he went on, "how long have you and Vigga been separated? You must be getting a divorce soon, surely?"

Carl stifled a laugh. Vigga was the most puzzling creature on Earth. No man with an ounce of common sense could argue that she was till-death-do-us-part material, but to let go of her completely—that might be a step too far.

"So you're hoping to be a free agent again, eh, Anker?" said Carl. "Or do you already have another iron in the fire?"

Anker smiled lopsidedly. "Always! I've met somebody. Proper wild one, full of surprises. I think you know the type?"

Carl nodded. Surprises were Vigga's specialty as well.

Anker gave an exaggerated wink. "Let me tell you, this one certainly knows how to make a man an offer he can't refuse. She'll be the death of me, if I'm not careful."

Hardy shook his head at him and opened the door. Something had caught his attention.

Oh really? Carl thought. That particular piece of information from Anker was new to him, but it was always like this when the three of them were on duty together. The only difference between them and teenage boys with bulges in their trousers was age. No other team at the station got on as well as they did, that was for sure.

"She sounds dangerous," Carl said. "Very intriguing. So who is she, Anker?"

Anker seemed to drift off for a moment, as though he was already in Paradise, nearing the forbidden tree.

Then he smiled the smile that brought down almost every woman's defenses. "You already know who, Carl!"

Abruptly, Hardy took off running. "Come on, lads, we've got him," he yelled, sprinting across the road.

PROLOGUE II

Saturday, December 26, 2020

"**You got the** balls to repeat what you just said, Eddie? Do you, you little shit?"

Eddie Jansen lowered his gaze, trying not to provoke the man, but the blow came anyway.

"We had an agreement, didn't we? So how about sticking to it?" the man said, as the whine in Eddie's ear rose to a screech.

Eddie nodded cautiously. He sincerely hoped he was hiding his desperation, because the last thing he wanted was to get on the wrong side of the people running the operation—or their representative, the man currently sitting opposite him with the two different-colored eyes.

He had to stick to the deal, said the man, as though Eddie didn't know that. The truth was he had no choice, unless he wanted things to take a very nasty turn indeed.

That fucking deal!

For years he'd been dazzled by the size of the bribes, and who could blame him? The salary of a detective on the Rotterdam police force was a drop in the ocean compared to what these powerful men had offered him for his services and information. Eddie had jumped at the chance, and, as expected, it was easy money. It had paid for a cushier life: gifts for his girlfriend and later for their daughter, payments on the summer cabin, installments on the boat and the cars. From that point on, there'd been no more money worries, no more anxious nights.

And yet, the moment of reckoning had come. Of course it had.

He had been dithering for some time over the job the man opposite was now demanding he finish. Compared to the other stuff, there was something indisputably uncompromising about this one. It was on another level. And although God knew he'd been lax over the years, sloppy, he had always muddled along, and his employers' demands had seemed to be lessening. So what, he'd thought, was there to be afraid of?

Eddie tried to steady his trembling hands. Was the real problem that he'd gradually lost the courage to carry out his orders? No, it was no good—his hands continued to shake uncontrollably. This could cost him everything.

He took a deep breath and almost whispered, his eyes still downcast, "We . . . no, I mean, *I* promise I'll get him. It'll be just like we agreed, you can count on it."

Raising his head, he found himself looking straight down the barrel of a gun, which a second later was pressed to his forehead.

The tall man held the gun firmly. His face was expressionless, his voice ice-cold. "You've been sitting on this for thirteen years, and then just when our product turns up in a suitcase in the man's attic, you aren't ready. Now you tell us the man's been arrested, acting like it's no big deal that he's in the custody of the Danish police at this very moment. Do you have any idea how dead fucking serious this is going to be for all of us if he suddenly decides to get chatty?"

"Yes, but—" The click as the trigger was pulled made Eddie's body jerk.

The man laughed. "Bit of a shock, eh, Eddie? Like the Chinese fellow I heard about in a story: they put all the prisoners on their knees in a row, lined up waiting for a bullet to the back of the neck, and this poor bloke jumps clean into the air when the man next to him gets shot. Not a very nice thought, I know, but you could end up the same way, Eddie. That's the reality now. If we're ever in this situation again, you're not going to know if there's a cartridge in the chamber or not, you follow me?

So. Get off your arse and show us what you can do. We're not taking any chances about what Carl Mørck knows—or what he might decide to do next."

Eddie looked out the window, gazing across the darkened city of Schiedam and Louis Raemaekersstraat, where the traffic lights at the bottom of the high-rise block had turned green. In a few minutes, his wife, Femke, would be back in their apartment with their little angel, having spent all day with Siri, a former colleague. She would smile at his guest, and afterward Femke would ask Eddie who he was, this man who had come to visit so late. But she could have no involvement in that part of his life. None.

"Yes, of course! I understand." He nodded, gingerly nudging the barrel of the gun away from his face. "I'll make contact with the Danes tonight."

1

CARL

Saturday, December 26–Sunday, December 27, 2020

The predicament in which Carl now found himself reminded him of childhood, of the moment when its haze of innocence had been cruelly and definitively lifted. When, for the first time, he had come to see everything a little too clearly, to feel the sting of lies. It was the experience of injustice burning itself into his cheek after an unearned slap. Of his younger years, when his love was unrequited, or later in his adult life, when a lover's betrayal loomed suddenly and without warning.

All these emotions came rushing back the second his most valued colleague, Chief of Homicide Marcus Jacobsen, clicked the handcuffs around his wrists—a lot tighter than necessary. They pressed harder still as he was dragged away from Mona and shoved into the waiting patrol car, while she signaled to him from the top of the steps that he wasn't alone.

Cold comfort.

Things went from bad to worse when the officer in the front seat instructed the driver to head not to the police station but directly to Vestre Prison.

"Hey, no, what are you doing? That's not right. Why aren't you driving me to the secure unit at the station?" he asked, but received no answer. He heard only mutters from the front seat, as well as Marcus Jacobsen's name mentioned several times.

Carl leaned gingerly forward between the front seats, trying to find a position where the cuffs behind his back weren't cutting off his circulation. It was blindingly obvious now that although he'd worked like a dog at the station for decades, solving difficult—almost impossible—cases, from this point on, he could forget about receiving any support from his colleagues.

What had he expected, really?

How many times had he escorted someone in custody to that bleak mammoth of a prison? And how many times had the tear-choked detainees in the back seat fought desperately to defend themselves with everything they had . . . or didn't have? Innocence, remorse, a family left behind—always in vain, mind you. The disgrace and humiliation simply had to be endured until the preliminary hearing. Pastoral care wasn't his job. He was just there to get them from A to B. At this point in the process, you were guilty until proven innocent.

Now, the day after Christmas in 2020, as the car drove down dark and frozen streets decorated with now-redundant wreaths and snowflakes, Carl tried to imagine what defense he could possibly muster.

What am I even defending myself against? he wondered. He had been arrested just as they had solved the Sisle Park case and freed Gordon. But had he actually done anything to feel guilty about? How had things gotten this far? Was it his reluctance to investigate the nail gun murders? His naivety when it came to the activities of his colleague Anker Høyer? His suspicion that Anker himself had been using drugs? Or was it that he'd stupidly done him the favor of storing that suitcase without asking what was in it? Left it sitting up in his attic all these years, never giving it a second thought? The suitcase, as it turned out, had been crammed full of hard drugs and a dizzying amount of cash in various currencies. God, if only he'd broken it open before the others got there, he could have handed it in. How silly of him to believe so blindly that when push came to shove, nobody would suspect him, loyal detective that he was, of criminal activity. That was practically a mortal sin in and of itself. And now he didn't have a clue what to say in his defense. All he knew was that his colleagues in the patrol car had no interest in protestations of innocence or invocations of abandoned families. What did that have to do with them? They would listen only to remorse, to confessions and repentance—but they weren't getting that. So Carl said nothing as they drove through the prison gates, nothing as he was escorted toward the intake officer, winter-pale and weary-looking.

The accompanying paperwork handed over by one of the police officers was examined carefully through matte-framed glasses, and the guard glanced up to confirm that they were not requesting protective custody. This seemed to surprise him, since the prisoner in question was a high-profile police officer.

Carl too was taken aback. No protective custody—what did the man mean?

"Hey, listen," he said. "I'm pretty sure that a lot of the people in here are locked up because of me. So—"

"You'll take what you're given," the guard interrupted.

That didn't bode well. And as Carl was led away and asked to strip, his colleagues didn't nod goodbye.

The wizened guard conducting the search eyed Carl with the same contempt as Jacobsen had when reading him his rights.

"Well, well, well! The revered Carl Mørck. Well, well, well," he repeated, tossing the clothes into a pile. "I'd say there are a few lads on the wing who are going to enjoy this. Doubt there's a single inmate in this whole establishment who'd want to be in your shoes right now," he went on, dumping a change of clothes into Carl's arms.

Although Carl had been anticipating them, the words still hit harder than he'd have liked. Perhaps he'd been expecting some magical portal to open up and drop a solution into his lap? But none seemed to be forthcoming.

As he was led down the familiar narrow, colorless corridors and past peeling bars into the East Wing itself—an imposing jumble of stairs, railings, safety netting, and countless cell doors—and toward cell 437, his last protective layer of armor fell away, and Carl began to sweat. He knew for a fact that any naïve remnant of a sense of justice he might have had would vanish the moment the heavy door slammed behind him with its irrevocable click.

Carl's eyes darted around the large, sterile prison wing, which was lit coldly from above, before he was led into the cell and the key was turned on the other side of the door. He'd seen hundreds of prison cells in his time, of course, but never before had a narrow black mattress like the one before him been *his* bed. The bed where he would have to try to get some rest without Mona by his side. Where he would not be woken early next morning by his daughter crashing into him headlong, would not wake up hoping that the dawning day would hold good things in store for him.

Carl surveyed the damaged gray noticeboard above the bed, reading the words a former inmate had written in pen, the letters gradually fading.

All of them depressing. No small light in the darkness.

He had just drifted into a kind of sleep, having spent most of the night racking his brain over what was going to happen next and what he ought to do, when someone hammered on the door and a rough male voice yelled that they fucking knew who he was in there, that they were going to get him. Then the voice fell silent, evidently due in part to a couple of guards bundling the aggressive man away.

But the words could not be unsaid: "We're going to get you, pig."

Propping himself up on his elbows, Carl took a deep breath. So. The harassment had begun, throwing reality on the inside into sharp relief. "Get" meant "kill." "Pig" meant he deserved it. From now on, being him was deadly. As he thought back to all the times he'd seen things go badly for an officer on the inside, he swallowed a lump. His only hope now was to get a court-appointed lawyer who could yank him out of the firing line, either by getting him released after the preliminary hearing or by obtaining protective custody, which surely he had a right to as a police officer.

Plus he'd have to find some way to talk to Rose, Assad, and maybe also Gordon, if the poor guy wasn't still too shaken up by the nightmare that had unfolded over Christmas, when he'd been held captive for several days and come within a hair's breadth of being executed by the serial killer Sisle Park. The three of them would have to knuckle down and uncover the truth behind the nail gun murders, now that things had so suddenly and radically gone into overdrive. Finally, it was crucial that Mona, in her capacity as a police psychologist, be given permission to visit him more often than was normal for close relatives.

The case they seemed to be trying to pin on him was rooted fifteen years in the past. The chief witness—also the prime suspect, his former colleague Anker Høyer—had died in Amager in 2007, and another colleague, Hardy Henningsen, had been paralyzed during the same incident by a bullet through the spine. So who was left to testify, then, apart from the third person involved in the shooting—Carl himself? Could Hardy? Would he? Was he even on Carl's side?

Carl sank back onto the thin mattress, feeling the weight of his powerlessness. A bullshit case, that was what this was, and all roads led back to Anker Høyer, the man who had once been a good friend and colleague. If it wasn't for Anker, Carl wouldn't be lying here now, he was sure of that. Anker had been one of those cops who didn't see himself in the same role as Carl and Hardy for the rest of his life—that much had been obvious even then. He had ambitions, and for Anker, Anker and Anker's needs always came first. It was the reason why his wife had kicked him out, why he was always on the lookout for opportunities to climb another rung up the social ladder. To Anker, social climbing meant getting his hands on money, and lots of it. Why hadn't Carl foreseen that that might eventually become a problem? Still, the idea that Anker was corrupt, that he was complicit in drug dealing—and worse—it had never crossed his mind. Nor that it would lead to Anker's death in some godforsaken hovel in Amager. And now here he was, suspected of being his accomplice. The truth was, Carl couldn't remember a damn thing about almost anything that had happened back then.

He had never wished more fervently that his old friend Hardy was by his side, so that together they could try to figure out what had happened in 2007, in what everybody had called "the nail gun case." Carl sighed again. He knew perfectly well that it was wishful thinking. Hardy was currently undergoing several months of alternative and probably pointless rehab in Switzerland. There wasn't much chance of his getting involved.

In the hours that followed, Carl took up the fragments of the past and tried to piece them together. When he looked at them arrayed like that, he realized what an idiot he'd been. He'd kept Anker's stolen goods hidden in a suitcase in his attic. He and Hardy had allowed themselves to be lured out to Amager, ignoring Anker's erratic behavior. He had neglected to delve further into what had happened afterward, when those mechanics in Sorø were killed with a nail gun in exactly the same way as an uncle of one of them, Georg Madsen, the old man in Amager. Neglected to take sufficient interest in what the victims had actually done, given that their lives had ended so ignominiously, with nails buried in their skulls.

Carl fixed his gaze on a spot on the ceiling and tried to hold it steady as he marshaled his excuses. First and foremost, that Anker's death and Hardy's terrible injuries had almost destroyed him. He'd had two breakdowns in succession and a bad case of PTSD, which he obviously hadn't wanted to admit. And on top of that he'd just been so fucking gullible, even though that wasn't usually like him.

On Sunday morning at eight thirty a.m., after a miserable night, Carl was driven to court in the city center and placed in a holding cell. Barely fifteen minutes before the session was due to start, he was led up to a side room where his unknown defense counsel was waiting.

As soon as he set eyes on the man, Carl sighed. One quick glance at his shabby green overcoat and unshaven face was enough for Carl to know he couldn't expect much help from that quarter. Clearly one of those court-appointed lawyers who had abandoned hope of a glorious career as a star defense counsel, the sort of trajectory crappy TV series led law students to believe awaited them after university. Still, what else did he expect? No doubt there wasn't exactly a huge selection of lawyers who were both available and highly motivated, not two days after Christmas. And on a Sunday, to boot.

"Has my wife been informed that my preliminary hearing is up first today?"

The lawyer shrugged. "I don't know, actually. Seems like it's only just been decided." He smoothed his glistening hair. "Name's Adam Bang," he said, gripping Carl's hand. "I have my two kids with me this weekend, three and five, and I had to twist my sister's arm into coming over to babysit. So you'll have to excuse my appearance." He tried to straighten his crooked tie. "Didn't even have time for a shower, actually."

Nice of him to admit it.

In the courtroom where the preliminary hearing was being held, Carl realized from a single sweeping glance that none of his relatives or friends from Department Q were present. There were, however, ranks of journalists from the Copenhagen dailies, as well as the police officers who had been present at his arrest. Among them, presumably, were members of the Police Complaints Authority, or PCA. They would be the ones responsible for the investigation going forward, since the assumption was that Carl, like Anker Høyer, had broken the law during his time on the force. Carl scanned for friendly faces among the black chairs in the public gallery but found only one, Sergeant Bente Hansen. She caught his eye and nodded quickly at him with a cautious smile, but Carl dropped his gaze awkwardly. He was genuinely touched to think that she was there for him. Maybe he should tell Rose that the Q team could count on her for a helping hand.

"What the hell is going on?" he whispered to his lawyer. "Why are there journalists here? We need to get rid of those hacks. Do you know how they found out about my arrest?"

Carl leaned toward Marcus Jacobsen, who was sitting behind him in the front row of the gallery. "Is this your doing, Marcus?" he asked, nodding in the direction of the already scribbling journalists.

The chief of homicide shook his head. "No, I'm afraid that's just the grapevine for you. I heard the information came from Vestre Prison. Regrettable, of course." He couldn't even bring himself to look Carl in the eyes or say his name. The room was freezing, as though filled with broken ice. Carl had never seen such glaring disappointment.

But he wasn't letting him off the hook that easily. "Oh really? Then why the hell didn't you keep me at the station last night? This whole circus could have been avoided."

Marcus turned to the narcotics boss, Leif Lassen, nicknamed "the Sniffer Dog," who was sitting next to him. Lassen whispered something into his ear.

"The remand center at the station is only for foreign nationals these days, that's why," he said curtly, when they finally made eye contact.

That made the second time in twenty-four hours that Carl could have punched him.

Then the prosecutor came in and sat down. It was clear that he, at least, hadn't skipped his morning shower. The man seemed to be walking in a cloud as perfumed as a waft of the beauty department at Magasin du Nord.

The judge who strode in and took a seat at the bench while everybody else stood was as unknown to Carl as the public defender and the prosecutor.

The session was brief. The prosecutor was as dry as gravel on a summer's day, gabbling through his statement like he was practicing for the Danish rap championships. Carl barely had time to reread what the text put up on the display to his right said about custody before the statement was over. His lawyer stood very slowly, straightening his back with as much authority as his rumpled coat allowed him to muster, and requested a closed hearing. No press. The judge eyed him for a moment, then Carl, and finally shook his head as though they'd called for champagne and a bowl of caviar. He did, however, issue an injunction prohibiting the media from publishing the name of the accused, which prompted most of the reporters to stand and leave the room amid a stream of hungry and vociferous protests. What was the point of stopping them from printing his name when the news was all over town already anyway, and what good would it do to throw them out? Wasn't it in the interest of the accused to have people covering the case fairly and objectively?

Their protests did them no good. Given the concerns around this high-profile policeman's safety, it could not be otherwise.

Carl gave the judge an appreciative nod, and the prosecutor, in a clear voice, began to lay out a case that made Carl's jaw drop. He was charged with murder—or aiding and abetting a murder—corruption, theft, and drug dealing. Carl couldn't make sense of any of it, although each of the charges was accompanied by a justification. He looked back at the chief of homicide, who was observing the proceedings coldly.

Carl shook his head and leaned in toward his counsel. "That's a bald-faced lie from start to finish. It's all been grossly distorted," he whispered, but the lawyer hushed him with a gesture, trying to concentrate on what the prosecutor was saying.

"My client pleads not guilty on all counts," he said, without conferring with Carl first. So far, however, the two of them were on the same wavelength. Obviously he wasn't guilty. He patted his lawyer cautiously on the shoulder, clearly enough for Jacobsen behind him to see it, and then he was remanded into custody for four weeks.

Darkness gathered. Even half the charges presented might be enough to put him in prison for at least five years, and if they couldn't be disproven, he could end up being sentenced to much longer than that.

He glanced again at the information on the display. It appeared that several passages from Section 762 of the Administration of Justice Act were being cited in reference to the charges.

Carl was trapped.

2

EDDIE

Sunday, December 27, 2020

"**Yep, he went** straight back to prison after the preliminary hearing, and right now he's in a private meeting room with his lawyer. From what I understand, the police have already questioned him briefly."

"Fuck's sake, Eddie, that's really not good. Is he in protective custody?" asked the man with the strange eyes over the phone.

"Nope." Eddie grinned to himself. "From what I've been told by our man on the inside, he'll be brought back to cell 437 after questioning and the consultation with his lawyer, but I'm sure it won't be long before he's isolated from gen pop, maybe as early as this afternoon."

"Who told you that?"

"One of the guards. We've had him on the payroll for a few years now. The man's worth his weight in gold, and he's on shift today."

"On our end we're thinking the price for murdering a policeman should be about a hundred thousand euros. Sound good to you?"

"Yup!"

"Right, so what's the plan?"

"It's going to happen when the lunch trolley's being taken around. Our guard has made a deal with an inmate. He's a bit dim-witted, bit simple, but he's got nothing to lose, and this is a way to provide for his family."

Eddie turned to look at his colleagues on the Sunday shift at Rotterdam Police Station, each of them hunched and struggling over their reports. There were still a few decorations up, but there was no trace of
Christmas cheer: criminals didn't take time off on Sundays and holidays.
There was plenty of work to be done.

Eddie had been working with international informants in the drug
world for twenty years. He spoke English with them, and nobody questioned that. Every officer had their own informants—it was the best way
to protect their sources—so Eddie had no trouble running his little side
hustle.

"How's he going to do it, this guy you've selected?" asked the man on
the phone.

"Knife straight to the heart!" Eddie nodded, pleased with himself. In
a couple of hours, he would be able to go back to his employers and tell
them the final loose end in this piece-of-shit case was tied up.

He hung up, unlocked the cabinet in his desk, and took out a drawer
of hanging folders. The case file was archived under the year 2003, but
it contained entries all the way up to the present day, seventeen years
later. Lists of dates when people had been given a little nudge into the
afterlife, dates when drug shipments had been disrupted, and of course
the dates when Eddie had been called to act.

To an outsider it would have been encrypted gibberish, but to Eddie
these notes were his insurance policy, his way of making sure that if
things went tits up, he could always testify, make deals that, if they
didn't save his job and reputation, might at least save his life.

Eddie had gotten himself embroiled in the whole mess in 2003, the year
the bank foreclosed on their summer cabin at Bergen aan Zee and sold it
off at auction. Femke had been devastated. She had inherited the somewhat run-down, debt-laden, but beloved cabin from her parents. They
had been on the verge of losing it when Eddie had gone to the bank to
beg for more time so that they wouldn't have to sell the place for far
below what they believed it was worth. But it was futile. There weren't

many bidders at the auction, but the man who won just so happened to bump into Eddie in the lobby of the bank, and he wasn't the type of person Eddie wanted to see take over their private sanctuary. He spoke Dutch but obviously wasn't really from the Netherlands—perhaps he had roots in the Dutch Antilles.

Moments later the man left the bank, leaving Eddie shamed and empty.

So it was a bit of a shock when, five minutes later, he was stopped on the street by a hand on his shoulder and saw the man who'd just bought the house smiling at him.

"It's a lovely cabin, Eddie," he said, a bit too chummily, as he swept off his sunglasses to reveal two different-colored eyes. One brown and one blue. "There aren't many of them with such a beautiful view of the dunes. You must have loved that place."

He was rubbing salt into the wounds, but not in a way that allowed Eddie to react angrily.

He nodded, trying to decide which of the man's eyes to focus on. The cold blue or the warm brown?

"Yeah, we did. We're very sorry to lose it."

"Hmmm! Who says you have to lose it, Eddie?" The tanned man stepped closer. "Come on, there's always a solution."

A wave of confusion. What did that mean?

"I can't imagine how. We couldn't afford to keep up with the payments, that's just the reality of it. My wife and I both work in the public sector, and money doesn't exactly grow on trees."

"Well, perhaps we can find a solution to that, eh? Why don't we head into that coffee shop and have a little chat?"

At first the man hadn't wanted much in return, just information. And since Eddie's job with the police afforded him a lot of latitude, all he really had to do was adjust an entry or two in the occasional case file. It wasn't until the man suggested they forget all about the purchase price of the summer cabin *and* also write off the payments that things got too tempting—and a lot more intense. After a visit to a notary, Eddie found himself the owner of a company in Switzerland in exchange for only a few hundred euros, and suddenly he and Femke owned not just the summer cabin but a couple hundred thousand Swiss francs, freely available in the company bank account.

Eddie decided not to tell Femke what he was being asked to do in return, so he claimed he'd won the lottery. She'd run around with her hands in the air, whooping with joy.

After that, the demands grew heavier and more dangerous.

Now, without knowing any names, Eddie thought he had an idea of who was behind the whole thing: probably a mix of wealthy businesspeople with roots in Surinam and Curaçao. He knew it would be no easy matter to back out and stop doing them these special favors. He was already ankle-deep in a very dubious quagmire. Their organization had long been in his colleagues' sights, but the Dutch police didn't have much detail, only that its activities included drug trafficking and possibly also murder.

Eddie had gotten restive and tried via the middleman to explain that he couldn't directly be party to any criminal activity carried out by such unscrupulous individuals. Then, out of nowhere, the money in the Swiss bank account had tripled, and ambitious architectural plans to extend the summer cabin landed in his mailbox. Only then did he realize they had him definitively cornered, that he had no choice but to follow the rules of the game. Within a year or two he was the organization's most important informant, supplying intelligence of all kinds and keeping them in the loop about ongoing police investigations. That way they could always redeploy or replace their drug couriers.

After a while, they had Eddie himself doing handovers of money in his patrol car. And later, when the quantities of product and cash got too big, he acquired an eight-seat SUV for the purpose, which also happened to suit his family pretty well.

When he first got wind of the executions being carried out, he had protested vehemently, but the result was merely that the noose tightened still further around his neck: "If you pull out now, we'll pin it all on you, Eddie. Trust me, we've planted evidence that could be used to incriminate you, and your life will be over."

And so, despite all his protestations, Eddie had become privy to the series of nail gun murders ordered by the gang.

3

MALTHE

Sunday, December 27, 2020

At school they'd called him "the Sausage." They weren't wrong: the fat was deposited symmetrically around his body, effective camouflage for the bundles of muscle around his torso. He was a head taller than his classmates and pale as a maggot—people used to turn and glance at him on the street or whisper in corners. But Malthe was a simple, good-natured boy from a loving home, with a younger brother and sister and two overprotective parents who didn't have the heart to tell him how malicious other people could be.

So, quietly and placidly, Malthe put up with the nickname, as well as a couple of others, like "the Pickle," "the Spring Roll," and "Lurch," until one day, when a kid in one of the classes above—famously fond of provoking people—expanded the range of nicknames to include "Fatso" and "Shithouse." Malthe smiled at him and nodded. He'd heard worse. But when the boy, who was three or four years older, not only didn't smile back but hocked a large gobbet of spit onto Malthe's shirt before shoving him hard in the chest, something in his brain short-circuited.

His friends tried to warn him that the kid did martial arts and apparently had a black belt, but Malthe gathered all his strength and threw a single punch, hitting the older boy in the face so hard that he broke a vertebra. The black belt never got back up.

From that point on, Malthe's path was laid before his feet, taking him through a series of residential institutions and eventually youth detention centers and prisons, a predictable tale of ever-spiraling degeneration, poor decision-making, and an endless train of assaults and mutual violence.

By the time Malthe turned twenty-five and had spent a couple of years in Vestre Prison for yet another incident that had ended in brutality, he knew that things were never going to change. He made peace with his situation and on the whole was a good-natured, friendly inmate. After a while he was given extra responsibilities on the wing, one of which was to make sure the various meals were ready on rolling trolleys for the other inmates. The door of his cell was kept unlocked during the day so that he could carry out his other chores—cleaning, odd jobs—and Malthe was quite happy to be located in the East Wing, where new prisoners on remand were admitted.

When his father got cancer and died after a brief and violent struggle, it became a point of honor for him to send home every hard-earned penny he made as an inmate to his mother and two younger siblings. His little brother had been seriously ill for a few months, and the public hospitals were hesitant to admit him for emergency treatment because of the expense and the COVID pandemic. Malthe was convinced his little brother would die if he wasn't sent to a private clinic in Germany.

Then, that very morning, a prison guard he knew well had made him an offer: "We can help you. We can make sure your little brother gets treated in Germany, Malthe. But you have to do something for us in return."

"Really?" Malthe couldn't believe his luck. "What do I have to do?"

"You have to kill the prisoner in cell 437. They'll be bringing him down in a bit," he said. "And you'll have five hundred thousand kroner for your family."

At first Malthe was shocked, but then the cogs began to turn. Killing a fellow prisoner would add at most fifteen years to his sentence, but with good behavior he would still be out by the time he was fifty or so, and his brother would still be alive. What was there to think about?

Since he was the one preparing the trolley, getting hold of a sharp implement that could be used to kill was child's play. Malthe filled the trolley as usual with sausage, remoulade, tomatoes, chicken salad, bread and butter, and plastic cutlery, including a fork that had been sharpened at one end like an awl.

When the inmate was led down, Malthe would offer him lunch, and the second he approached the trolley, Malthe would jab the makeshift awl diagonally underneath the sternum and straight into his heart. He'd heard that to pull off a killing like that, you had to shove the awl in all the way to the base, and if the prisoner was very big and heavy around the waist, he'd have to bang hard on the end of it with his fist. Frankly, it sounded pretty simple.

Unfortunately, however, the prisoner in cell 437 didn't come down before the food trolleys had been wheeled away, so Malthe simply loitered in the corridor afterward, waiting.

"What are you doing out here?" asked the highest-profile prisoner currently on the East Wing, William Bastian. It wasn't the first time they'd crossed paths. Bastian was known as "the Jackhammer," because his specialty was getting into relationships with wealthy women, then dumping them when their bank accounts were empty. But that wasn't all the Jackhammer was good for: if there was trouble brewing on the wing, you could be pretty sure he had a hand in it somewhere. William Bastian called the shots in this wing and had done so for as long as he'd been an inmate there. He'd probably done the same at the other prisons he'd been transferred to in the past.

"Me? I'm not doing anything. I'm just hanging around. What are you doing?" Malthe said.

"That's no concern of yours. Some of us have got privileges, you know. But I'll ask you again: What are you waiting for?"

"For the guy who's going in there," said Malthe, pointing at cell 437.

"Oh, are you now? Getting friendly with the cops, are we? What are you expecting to get out of it?"

"The cops?" Malthe shook his head. "Why do you say that?"

"Why? Because the man in cell 437 is Carl Mørck. Don't you know anything, you fucking half-wit?"

Malthe had no idea what he was talking about.

"Clearly not. He's a copper. One most of the lads in here wouldn't mind seeing get fucked up."

Malthe held his breath for a moment. It was a good thing Bastian had added that last part—everything would be fine, then.

"Right, yeah, well. Since you say so . . . look, okay, that's why I'm waiting for him." Malthe smiled. It couldn't hurt to tell him, after all.

What happened to the Jackhammer at that moment Malthe couldn't quite fathom, but all the furrows in his face contracted, as though he were blinded by the sun.

"What did he do, do you know?" Malthe asked.

"You're planning to stick him with that, are you?" The Jackhammer pointed at the clenched fist that hung at Malthe's side.

Malthe looked down at his hand. Was it really that easy to tell?

"How much are you getting for it?" the Jackhammer asked.

"I don't think I'm supposed to say."

"Well, well! Who should I be asking, then?"

Malthe glanced down the corridor. His prison guard was obviously staying far away.

"Aha. One of the guards, then? Must be Joensen. Peter Loudmouth, am I right?"

How did he know that?

When Malthe hesitated, the Jackhammer nodded. "You'll be getting a million for it, I suppose?"

Malthe shook his head. "No, no, nothing like that much."

"How much, then?"

"About half that, I think."

Bastian laughed. "Wonder how much old Loudmouth is getting. You know what, Malthe? I think I'll take half of what you're getting paid. Two hundred fifty thousand kroner to me, or I'm warning that policeman in cell 437."

Malthe shook his head. Why should he give the Jackhammer anything at all? He was the one ordered to do it. He was the one doing the dirty work.

"No, William, I can't do that. I have to have the whole lot or it's not enough. I'm going to use the money for my brother—he's really sick."

The Jackhammer turned his head slowly toward the level above them, looking at a few prisoners leaning over the railings. Several of them nodded. They'd heard the whole story.

"I think I'll have a word with Loudmouth and explain to him that we need a million. Then your cut can be, oh, I dunno, let's say four hundred thousand kroner. How about that?"

Malthe thought about it. Four hundred thousand was probably about what the clinic in Germany would charge. "But will that work?" he asked. "I don't think you can pressure Loudmouth into doing anything, can you?"

The Jackhammer looked up again at the floor above, where several inmates were waiting to be locked inside their cells. They laughed.

"Malthe, he's already fucked up by giving you the job, hasn't he?"

There were shouts from above, and Malthe wrinkled his forehead.

"He's halfway up shit creek as it is—he won't want to end up without a paddle as well," the Jackhammer continued. "We'll just give him a few hours to negotiate with whoever wants the cop dead. All right, and Loudmouth can have an extra fifty grand from my share, for the inconvenience, and you lot up there can have some too, why not. I'm feeling generous."

Silencing their noisy enthusiasm with a wave, he turned his head toward the door at the end of the long corridor and listened.

"They're coming. What do you say, Malthe? I give the game away here and now, or we'll have a chat with Loudmouth and you give me half at least?" He interrupted Malthe before he could reply. "And listen, hey— don't even think about screwing me over, or I'll make sure your days are fucking numbered."

Malthe was utterly confused. He didn't like it when things got changed or moved too quickly. He wanted to stab the man now, that was the plan, but the Jackhammer hadn't had time yet to speak to the guard who'd arranged it all—so what should he do?

"But, okay, that means I have to wait, right?"

The Jackhammer nodded, first at Malthe and then, with a crooked smile, at the policeman being escorted past them to cell 437.

4

CARL

Sunday, December 27, 2020

Carl registered each movement in an instant. The fixed stares from the level above, watching him attentively. The big, baffled-looking man near the empty food trolleys and that idiot they called the Jackhammer, who was known to pretty much every officer in the wider Copenhagen area. Carl had never arrested him personally, but he and Assad had testified against him in a couple of cases when his criminal activities had impinged on Department Q's investigations. Ages ago, just after the turn of the millennium, the guy had been suspected of murdering an elderly woman whose bank account he'd emptied, but he was never actually charged, because they caught the guy who did it using his footprints.

The Jackhammer was a career criminal, plain and simple, always up for a good scam, doomed to spend his whole life serving endless sentences. Carl knew that.

It was the lopsided smirk the man gave Carl as he was escorted past that gave him misgivings. It wasn't the kind of smile intended to send a concrete signal—it was the inscrutable type, the type you really had to watch out for.

Carl glanced up once more at the men above him, their elbows resting heavily on the railings. He got the sense they'd been standing there awhile, waiting. But for what?

"You look like a fucking dickhead with that pussy red hair, Carl Mørck," one of them yelled, and Carl nodded. The bastard was right. Why the hell had he thought dying his hair red would keep him under the police's radar while he was investigating the Sisle Park case? He'd better wash out the last of the dye as soon as possible.

As he took the last few steps into his cell, Carl drew closer to his guard. "You lot need to put me in solitary tonight; otherwise there's going to be trouble here. You know that, right?"

The guard nodded. Carl knew him, a broad-shouldered, decent, good-natured chap who'd been working at Vestre ever since Carl first arrived at the station.

"I heard, they were talking about it in the guard room. Maybe—"

"Frank, listen to me. You saw the way those dickheads up there were looking at me. Why are they even out of their cells? It's not enough to talk about it; it *has* to happen. Please can you make sure my lawyer knows there's something about to go down? Believe me, it'll happen before we even know about it."

Frank nodded, then he unlocked the door and escorted Carl inside.

Two hours later, Frank returned with the message that they still hadn't confirmed protective custody, that the prosecutor had insisted on all visits being supervised and all letters inspected, and that Carl's wife had just arrived with his lawyer. From now on, meetings like this one would be conducted in the presence of an officer. The only person allowed unsupervised visits was his lawyer.

Mona had come, thank god, but Carl was uneasy at the thought of leaving his cell, and the whole way to the visitors' room his nervous system was on high alert. Every step he took, every tiny sound or movement, a fresh dose of adrenaline shot into his bloodstream, and as they neared the family room, every muscle in his body was wound up to defend himself.

They're not getting me, he thought, and his mind was already rehearsing it: kick his assailant in the crotch, strike the carotid artery with the edge of his hand, roar like an ox, and then just start kicking—throat, eyes, kneecaps.

So, when the door opened and his little girl came rushing toward him for a hug, he wasn't himself.

Jesus, what's happening to me? he wondered as his heart pounded wildly and little Lucia clung to his leg.

Mona saw immediately how he was feeling and softened the situation by pulling him in close, with their daughter between their legs. The officer by the door protested, but Carl ignored him. When he looked into her eyes, he knew something was badly wrong.

"Good morning, Detective Mørck," he heard a woman's voice say from somewhere near the wall behind him.

He turned in surprise toward the woman. She was elegantly dressed and immediately recognizable, smiling at him—if he could call it a smile—with carefully drawn red lips.

"Oh. Molise, it's you. But where's my lawyer?" he asked, withdrawing from Mona's embrace.

"I'm afraid that's why I'm here. We have some rather bad news for you," the woman said. "I'm sorry to tell you this, Carl, but two hours ago your court-appointed lawyer was run over by a car while on his way to meet you. It happened just outside the prison. A vehicle suddenly went up onto the pavement and rammed straight into him."

Carl frowned, swallowing a few times. "Outside the prison, you said? Was he badly hurt?"

"He was killed instantly," she said.

A few seconds passed as Carl tried to get his head around it. How could he?

"Killed?" He looked at Mona, who was shaking her head while Lucia tugged at her dress. "I don't understand. Are you telling me he was run over on purpose?"

Mona took his hand. "There was only one witness. One of my colleagues is treating her for shock, but she had the presence of mind to get the license plate. She described what happened as clearly deliberate, because when the vehicle mounted the pavement, it was still far enough away from the pedestrian to easily avoid a collision. Instead, it accelerated—the poor man didn't even have time to jump out of the way."

Carl looked down. This was madness. And it seemed his lawyer was the first to pay the price—although Carl had no doubt that the message was meant for him. He shook his head. What had started yesterday as a farce was now rapidly spiraling out of control. This was sheer nightmare, and like all nightmares, now that it had started, it was escalating quickly.

"Poor guy, I can't even remember his name. Do they know who did it?"

"There's no trace of him. The car was stolen from one of the carparks just behind the prison on Vestre Kirkegårds Allé, and barely an hour later it was found illegally parked halfway onto the pavement opposite Vesterbrogade 144."

Carl looked at Molise Sjögren. He knew she was one of the highest-profile defense counsels in the nation. "And that makes you my new lawyer," he said without much enthusiasm. If anybody was going to be able to help him, Molise was an exceptionally good bet, but she'd gotten several criminals acquitted when he and the rest of the homicide squad had worked hard to have them arrested and charged, so he wasn't exactly happy about it, despite her indisputable talents in the courtroom.

"I tried to get in touch with Molise yesterday, but I only got through today," Mona said. "That was when she told me you already had a lawyer and that you'd been to a preliminary hearing this morning. They didn't say a word to us, Carl. Jacobsen didn't even let your colleagues at Department Q know about it until the hearing was over. I know they've been trying to come and visit you, but I suppose Marcus must have put the kibosh on that. I know all three of them filled out the form to request a visit, but maybe Correctional Services was told to stonewall, I don't know."

Blood began to whoosh in Carl's veins. If Lucia hadn't pulled him down onto the chair and started clambering around on his lap, ruffling his funny red hair, he would have lost it.

"Well, I can of course see how you're feeling, Carl. Naturally, I dropped everything when Mona called and told me what had happened to Adam Bang."

Carl shut his eyes. "Adam Bang, was that the lawyer's name? That poor, poor man."

The rest of the meeting was a blur of emotions and concrete instructions, and Lucia cried because he couldn't come home. So did Mona.

He signed a piece of paper making Molise Sjögren his defense counsel. They agreed she would contact the Police Complaints Authority and familiarize herself with the case before they met again the next day in the room a little farther down the hall.

5

CARL

Sunday, December 27, 2020

Frank, the guard, brought him a couple of soggy sandwiches in his cell and announced apologetically that the directive from above was that he would spend one more night in cell 437. A final decision on his request for protective custody would not be made until the following day.

Carl forced back the curses rising to his lips, but they remained hovering there. This was outright malicious.

His eyes swept across the dingy wall toward the half-open shutter and the bars between him and the world outside the window, where voices and jeers bounced across the walls.

"Pig!" yelled a few men into the dark, and he knew it was aimed at him.

Frank gave him a nod. There was no doubting the seriousness of the situation. "I don't know . . . Maybe you'll be transferred to another prison, at least I think that's what your lawyer is working on," he said, adding that both Carl's lawyer and wife would be returning in the morning. Whether they'd be coming together he didn't know.

Afterward Carl lay gazing at the grubby walls, where previous inmates had scrawled their primitive musings in childish block capitals. All told, it was a pretty sorry testament to the social underbelly. To powerlessness. Why the hell didn't they just paint over it?

He tried to organize his thoughts. He had to get hold of some paper so that he could summarize his response to the charges against him during the interviews with the PCA. Then Mona needed to get in touch with Rose, so that he could explain to her what he wanted her and the others to do next.

He was brooding. He couldn't help it, because the diminutive TV on the table didn't work and he couldn't quiet his mind.

When he tried in vain to recall a complete picture of what had happened since that day in 2007 when Anker was killed, he knew the trauma of that day had changed him, that there were still some walls, irritatingly watertight, which were inaccessible to reason and memory. Sometimes it felt as though he were looking into the past through a spider's web, vague episodes and images dancing behind it. Now, tonight, it seemed almost as though Anker stood before him in a fog, speaking to him, but the words were slurred and made no sense.

He stared obliquely at the floor, brow furrowed, and tried to concentrate. If only he could remember, could pin down, at least something of what had happened, but nothing came to him. Right now all he could really recall was that he, Anker, and Hardy had driven out to Amager, and then there were a few clearer seconds immediately before the shots were fired. In the period since the incident, his memories had been colored by what other people had told him.

Carl's fingers tingled, a clear warning that right now he needed to be careful about his thoughts—and was it any wonder? The whole thing was surreal; it was driving him nuts. A year or two after the shooting, he had experienced a few instances when the accumulated unease had brought him to the brink of collapse, and he certainly didn't need that happening again, not now.

Carl tried to recall Lucia's soft cheek against his, her damp breath and reedy voice. For a brief moment it helped, and then the hazy jigsaw puzzle of memory came rushing back full force.

It had been raining that day in Amager, many years ago, when Hardy, Carl, and Anker had reached the dilapidated shed where the neighbor had found the old man, Georg Madsen, with a nail in his skull. The rank stench of the corpse had washed over them as they opened the door in their white coveralls. The man was seated in a chair, blisters on the grayish-green skin of his face and a waxy sheen to his dead eyes. Not a pretty sight.

The neighbor had said it was the smell that had alerted him, so Hardy had opened the window. Carl remembered that now. Good old Hardy, tall as a lighthouse and reliable as a diesel engine. He always did the right thing.

And Hardy, who was also something of a handyman, noticed at once that the nail in the dead man's head was a Paslode nail, and that the nail gun was on the table next to him. Carl wondered at that, he recalled. Why hadn't the criminals taken the murder weapon with them? Anyway, it had to be worth something, surely.

Carl swallowed a few times. Unease was creeping over him again. *It's because you're thinking solely about the shooting itself, Carl,* Mona had said once, and she was probably right. A few seconds after the shots were fired, the reality was that it was all over. Anker had been struck in the middle of the chest, lying apparently lifeless on the floor, and a short distance away Carl was knocked to the ground by a glancing shot to the temple. Hardy had been hit in the back.

Why couldn't I react more rationally, for Christ's sake? thought Carl. But now that he pushed himself to remember more precisely, he knew it was because Hardy had been shot a second after him and collapsed on top of Carl, pinning him underneath his massive bulk. Carl had lain there as though paralyzed, but who wouldn't have, he thought now. He had glimpsed an upright figure in a red-checked lumberjack shirt through the door to the room at the front, and that was all he'd seen. Moments later, the perpetrators were talking in the hall, and then a badly wounded Anker had suddenly twisted his body toward the strangers and tried to draw his gun, yelling at them to freeze.

It was the last thing he said before they shot him in the heart.

Later, Carl was asked many times what the killers had said to one another, but he hadn't been able to make sense of the muttering.

When, some years later, the Dutch police had theorized that the case might be connected to similar drug-related incidents in a suburb of

Rotterdam, he had reasoned that perhaps he hadn't understood the killers because they were speaking Dutch.

Carl sighed. What was he supposed to make of the situation with the
Dutch? During the hearing it had been confirmed that a kilo and a half
of cocaine and heroin and a whole lot of foreign currency had been found
in the suitcase in his attic, the one Anker had asked Carl to keep for
him—though the prosecutor expressed his doubts about this—and Carl
was now under serious suspicion of both trafficking and dealing drugs,
as well as possibly being an accomplice to murder. It was also alleged that
Anker had made contact on several occasions with people associated with
a drug ring in Holland. The Dutch had apparently found strong evidence
to support this, and Carl frankly had no idea about it one way or the
other—so perhaps Anker really had been involved? But had he also been
connected to the mechanics in Sorø? A couple of months after the shooting and Anker's death, two men involved with drugs in Sorø had also
been killed with a nail gun, in the same way as the old man in Amager,
who had turned out to be the uncle of one of them. But what did any of
it have to do with him?

Thinking about it now, he should probably have made more of an effort over the years to be more closely involved in the investigation around
the nail gun case, but there was a potential conflict-of-interest issue, and
he'd had more than enough on his plate. Besides, by rights it was his colleague Terje Ploug who'd been responsible for the case for all those years.

There was a metallic clang from the prison corridor outside. Not much
sound penetrated through the thick door, but the sharp noise of metal
falling to the floor could cut through almost anything.

Carl drew back against the wall, sending yet another glance toward
the window, the open air. Armored glass on one window and bars over
the other—that was what he saw when one shutter was pulled back. But
what kind of a view was it anyway? Tall fences and barbed wire, that
was what kind. The yells outside had gradually died down.

Carl shut his eyes.

What was the next step in the case? He simply had to think about it,
try to approach it as a detective.

He and Assad had driven down to Sorø so that Carl could identify whether the lumberjack shirt one of the murdered mechanics had been wearing was the same type as the one he'd seen when he'd been shot in Amager.

He smiled for a moment. That trip to Sorø was one of the first times he and a very inexperienced Assad had been on assignment together. Sitting at the wheel, he'd been thinking he would have preferred Hardy at his side, but with the clarity of hindsight he was no longer so sure. And of course he hadn't known Assad then the way he did today.

The light in the cell switched off, so only a faint glow fell through the bars of the shutter, tinting the walls. Probably about ten o'clock, thought Carl.

A couple of days after the visit to Sorø, the local team had arrested a suspect in the murder of the two mechanics, a guy who used to hang out at their garage. But the evidence was apparently shaky, and he was released. Carl couldn't remember now what had happened to him. Had he been questioned to find out how much the mechanics knew about the one's uncle? Maybe Rose and the others should see if they could locate the man and lean on him a bit.

Carl took a deep breath. Immediately after the arrest in Sorø was announced, he had had his first panic attack, to his immense surprise. Jesus, what a horrible fucking experience that had been, losing total control of his own body. Unable to breathe. Living with the moment's realization that this must be how it felt to die. Still, there must have been some greater point to it all, because that was what ultimately led to his meeting Mona.

More metallic clangs echoed from the corridor outside, so he sat up in bed and listened intently, leaning against the wall.

Then, silence again. The prison guards were never idle, even late at night, he supposed. After all, you couldn't exactly schedule toilet trips.

When he looked back at that day in the shed in Amager, there were several things that gave him pause. According to the coroner, Georg Madsen had been dead for eight to ten days by the time he, Hardy, and Anker arrived on the scene. Why hadn't the killers cleaned up after themselves? Removed the nail gun, hidden the body, the whole caboodle—they'd had more than enough time. And even if they hadn't, they could have just set fire to the place. It would have burned to the ground in ten seconds flat. Was it possible the police were *meant* to find the scene? And, following that train of thought to its logical conclusion, was Anker, Hardy, and Carl's team also meant to be there? Judging from the prosecutor's brief statement that morning and the questions put to him by the PCA, it was certainly a hypothesis they were exploring, and frankly that made sense. How else could the killers have arrived on the scene with such conveniently perfect timing? Had they been tipped off? Were they keeping the place under observation? No, they'd been tipped off, he could see that now. And who had been the target? Anker? Were he and Hardy merely collateral damage?

And what about the body found buried in a crate under Georg Madsen's place when it was torn down three years later? A crate that also contained false evidence against Anker and Carl, which could be dated to a few years before the shooting. How did that fit into the case?

Something hit Carl's cell door with a bang. He had a bad feeling about this. Carl got out of bed and stood still in the middle of the room. Was there some sort of punch-up going on outside? It sounded that way.

Carl took a deep breath and held it for a moment, until he heard a key scraping in and around the lock.

Doors in prisons opened inward, which was convenient for staff but not great for the prisoner waiting in his cell. There was nothing effective to barricade the door with, and at the same time he had to assume that anybody trying to get in at this time of night probably didn't have his best interests in mind.

Carl stared intently at the door. He had two choices. Stand by the far wall, covering his back, or the opposite: take the initiative and resist immediately. He chose the latter.

The door swung open a little too carefully—the intruder was

probably wary of the person inside lunging at him. Shifting his full weight onto his left leg, Carl kicked out at the door with his right, with a force that made his knee crunch.

The result was loud swearing followed by a thud, which could only mean that whoever had unlocked the door was now on the floor—hurt.

When Carl sprang through the half-open door, he found the Jackhammer standing in front of him, holding the sharpened end of a plastic fork poised to strike at Carl's stomach.

But as the man tried to pounce, Carl parried so that the sharpened end went through his palm instead, and then he twisted his hand to break the fork in two.

For a moment, the Jackhammer stood irresolute. He had just lost the tip of his weapon—and, with it, his plan—but he plunged the blunt end hard against Carl's belly anyway. A spot of red blossomed on his white T-shirt, but it was nothing compared to the blood that started gushing out of the Jackhammer when Carl yanked the tip of the fork out of his palm and slammed it into his attacker's shoulder in two fast jabs.

The Jackhammer fell back a step or two, screaming as though he'd never tasted defeat in his life. Now Carl saw that, apart from the man on the floor—who didn't seem like much of a threat in his current condition—there were two more prisoners as well. They exchanged a glance before vanishing up the stairs to the next floor.

Only then did Carl call for help.

The story they went with afterward was that one of the prisoners, possibly during a visit to the toilet, had attacked prison guard Peter "Loudmouth" Joensen, who was on a twenty-four-hour shift, taken his keys, and let out a couple of other prisoners. But Carl had seen the officer wincing as he lay on the floor a little farther down the corridor, and he had seen his theatrical attempts to get up when his colleagues came rushing in and called a halt to the whole performance. It was a ridiculous, dilettantish bit of playacting. Carl had seen better at one of the annual school plays at Skolegade Primary in Brønderslev. There would, of course, be an official investigation, and counseling would be offered to all the members of staff on duty that night—that was procedure—but Carl was pretty sure Peter Loudmouth would get away with his part in the attack and might even finagle himself a couple of sick days into the bargain.

But Carl knew now he was dealing with a corrupt prison guard, and from that moment on, he would be constantly having to look over his shoulder, like a hunted antelope with a pack of hyenas after him.

Carl's injured hand throbbed. He barely closed his eyes that night. That made the second in a row, and the lack of sleep was already beginning to grind him down.

6

ASSAD

Monday, December 28, 2020

It was a rare sight to see the chief of homicide in police uniform, stepping out in front of Copenhagen Police Station and taking in the assembled crowd with a sweeping stare. At least fifty journalists and cameramen had turned up, shuffling their feet in the cold, gusts of warm breath turning the air white.

At the very front stood Assad. He was freezing, but then again, he was always freezing at the beginning of winter. *Where are the palm trees when you need them?* he thought, laughing inwardly. He looked at the clock. It was precisely ten. Neither Rose nor Gordon was anywhere to be seen.

"I appreciate so many of you coming at such short notice," Marcus Jacobsen began, nodding in the direction of the outstretched microphones.

"As you will be aware from our press release, a significant number of the most heinous crimes committed during the last three decades have now been solved. A network of killers led by one of the nation's most prominent businesswomen, Sisle Park, has been broken up, resulting in several arrests and the death of Park herself. It is not feasible at the current time to go into all the details of the case, but I can tell you that a number of deaths going back many years, deaths that had previously been declared accidents or suicides, have now, thanks to some skilled police work, been revealed as murders. These include the case of Palle Rasmussen, the well-known politician, as well as the abductions of Birger von Brandstrup and most recently Maurits van Bierbek, whom we are now sorry to announce is also deceased."

A forest of hands went up explosively, everybody yelling over everybody else, but the chief of homicide waved off the questions and tapped the microphone in front of him until silence grudgingly descended once more.

"I will not be taking questions about individual cases or the investigative work at the present time. We will, however, be releasing a list of the crimes over the coming weeks. Please remember that we have the victims' families to consider—they must be properly informed before we make anything public."

He gazed out over the crowd, not lingering on Assad's face, although at that moment it looked like he'd just drunk a glass of vinegar mixed with freshly squeezed lemon juice.

"The homicide department in Copenhagen is aware of certain irregularities in some of these cases, and it is only thanks to the tireless efforts and high ambitions of our investigators that these old cases have finally been solved. As you know, there is no statute of limitations on murder in Denmark, but the same goes for unanswered questions. When someone takes a life, that must never be forgotten—and it cannot be allowed to go unpunished."

"Who cracked the cases?" a voice shouted at the top of its lungs.

"Was it Department Q?" another added.

"Department Q was involved, yes," Jacobsen replied, and took a short pause. "But first and foremost we have ourselves to thank for the thoroughness of our records and reports and our careful documentation of evidence, which enabled us to find a pattern and draw connections between seemingly separate cases."

"Who else participated in the investigation apart from Department Q?" the first voice yelled again, but Jacobsen only smiled.

"You'll have plenty to write about soon, don't worry," he said. And with that, the black uniform was already on its way back into the building.

Assad cast a heavy glare after him. That wasn't the chief of homicide he knew, the man he owed a debt of gratitude. The man who, only a few days ago, had gone out of his way to help him, protecting Assad's family when their loyalty to the police was under scrutiny.

He was still sighing when a hand was placed on his shoulder. "When did you lot get involved, Mr. Assad?" asked a blond man with a friendly expression. He held out a hand. "I'm from the *Venstrepressen*. Benny Falck Olsen," he went on, as Assad shook his hand.

Assad lowered his chin, surveying him from underneath his bushy eyebrows. "You know what, Benny Olsen," he said, "I think you should be directing that question to the chief of homicide."

"Okay! Your partner, Carl Mørck, doesn't seem to be here. Is he still in prison?" Olsen asked as the throng of journalists around Assad jostled closer.

"What do you mean?" asked Assad. As if he didn't know the press were still under an injunction not to mention Carl by name. He was supposed to be keeping his mouth shut.

"Okay, well, if he isn't here, then where is he?" another journalist tried, but Assad still didn't take the bait.

"Hey, it's Monday morning," he said, enjoying the confusion on Olsen's face. "Some camels are a little late to the water trough. Think about it."

Olsen was too baffled to respond immediately, and Assad seized the opportunity to barge his solid body away from the rabble.

Rose called fifteen minutes later. She and Gordon had been standing at the back of the horde of journalists, and before the reporters could spot them, they'd headed off toward the city center and were now sitting in the basement of Restaurant Nytorv across from the courthouse.

"Marcus, that stupid bastard" was the first thing Gordon said when Assad stepped into the basement. Department Q's youngest team member didn't look too good. Still pale, still clearly affected by the terror of coming so horribly close to death during the period of days when Sisle Park had held him captive, executing one of her victims by lethal injection before his very eyes. If it hadn't been for Carl, Rose, and especially Assad, she would have stuck him with it too and emptied its contents into his bloodstream. Barely two days ago the doctors at Riget Hospital had been pulling the tip of a hypodermic needle out of him and pumping saline through his veins—the fucking hospital chaplain had been there, for God's sake, trying to make him feel better about witnessing his fellow captive suffer and die a terrible death. What he really needed now was sleep. Sleep would help him to move on. Because although everyone was begging him to, Gordon sure as hell wasn't taking any leave. He was going to fight for Carl tooth and nail, just like the other two.

"Marcus didn't say a single word about Carl or the rest of us, not one. It was so humiliating," Gordon went on. "It was us who solved that case, nobody else. Not to mention, the boss knows there's a good chance we could all be dead right now."

Assad nodded. "A couple of journalists were asking me where Carl was today. I could tell they knew perfectly well where. But maybe we're being a bit hard on Marcus; maybe he's just trying to protect Carl from public scrutiny."

Rose patted his disheveled hair. "It's really nice of you to think that, Assad, but I doubt it. In fact, I reckon we should be keeping a pretty good eye on Marcus right now, because he's not on Carl's side. It's obvious he's deliberately withholding information about how shittily he's being treated. Can't let Carl benefit from any sympathy right now, can he?"

Assad shook his head. "Benefit how? What do you mean?"

"Can't let it help him! Carl's still not in protective custody, and last night was a very close call. Some of the other prisoners tried to kill him. You didn't hear?"

The sinews in Assad's throat went taut. "Wait, what? That's not true—is it?"

She nodded slowly.

"Just tell me who the prisoners were. I'll show them how you kill somebody!"

"I don't know who, Assad, and anyway, I don't think that's a good idea. All I know from Mona is that some prisoners tried to force their way into his cell and stab him, but Carl neutralized them. One of them, that guy they call the Jackhammer, is currently in the hospital wing. He'll be charged with assault."

"I like the word 'neutralized.' Sounds like it hurt." For a moment a glimpse of a smile appeared through Assad's stubble, but then Gordon broke in.

"I'm afraid that's not all, Assad," he added. "Carl's court-appointed lawyer was run over by a car yesterday right outside the prison— deliberately. Pretty astonishing it hasn't reached the press yet."

Instantly, Assad's face darkened and contracted. "Run over? On purpose, you're saying? Do we know who did it?"

Rose shook her head.

"I don't get it. Who's coming after Carl like this? Isn't there anything we can do?" asked Assad.

"Not much, I'm afraid. The Police Complaints Authority are running the investigation now. Marcus called me yesterday and gave us strict instructions not to meddle. Then he added that if we had any intention of defying that order, we might want to think twice, because we've just had about twenty files land on our desks, and in the boss's eyes all of those cases are higher priority. If we start looking into Carl's, he'll take us off active duty on the spot."

"Marcus can't do that!" Assad was shaken. He'd been seriously considering lately whether he should find something else to do with his life, and this wasn't helping. Right now, however, what mattered was Carl. He always came first.

"Now, I'm just going to come out and ask this," said Rose. "Do you two think there's any way Carl could be guilty of what they're accusing him of? Because if so, we need to keep our hands off this case."

"He's about as guilty as the cat my wife feeds on the front step every day, that's what I say," Assad cried, slamming the flat of his hand down onto the table.

"Yeah, why in the Himmel and Hell are you even asking that? Do you have any reason whatsoever to doubt his innocence?" asked Gordon.

"I mean, 'innocence' may be putting it a bit strongly. We all know Carl—can't say he's not prone to the occasional controversial decision. But is he innocent of these charges? That's what we have to ask ourselves. Murder, drug dealing? It's a hell no from me. Carl hates that shit, and he's certainly no killer. So, innocent of that, yes. As for the rest: How much did he know about what Høyer was up to? How much did he know about the stacks of drugs and money in that suitcase in his attic? Only he can tell us that. Personally, I think Carl has been extraordinarily naïve and perhaps irrational as well, and I'm very much hoping that's his only crime."

"All right, then, innocent. I think so too," Gordon agreed.

Assad merely nodded. Of course they believed that. They had to.

"So. What now?" Gordon leaned back in his chair as a plate carrying an unusually substantial sandwich was placed in front of him. Perhaps a trifle overwhelming in his current condition.

"We've got to find out who put that Jackhammer guy up to this— who's behind the attack," said Rose. "As far as I'm aware, there was no beef between him and Carl. Then we should gather together all the files on what we call the nail gun case and make sure we know them inside out."

Gordon poked vaguely at his smoked salmon sandwich, as though it might fling itself into his stomach of its own accord, then gave up and put down his cutlery. "The guy who knocked down Carl's lawyer, can we find him?" he asked. "And is there any way we can get the PCA lot to help transfer Carl out of Vestre?"

"Yes, but I reckon we should be a bit cautious about sticking our necks out, or we could end up in the PCA's sights as well, you know. Un-authorized official investigation, it's called, apparently. Since we're close colleagues, there's a conflict of interest," Rose said.

"Then we'll just have to tread as lightly as possible," replied Gordon.

Rose nodded. "As long as the PCA and Marcus don't get wind of it, we'll be fine."

"Which prison did you have in mind? One without bars, I think," said Assad.

"Well, not sure if we can quite manage that, but something along those lines. I'm thinking Slagelse Remand Center. Lots of the inmates there are in temporary custody, and West Zealand isn't so far away that we can't drive down there once in a while," Rose said.

Slagelse? Assad tried to picture it. Hadn't he and Carl been down there once to interrogate an inmate? Yes, that was right. A year ago, maybe? And who was it? The only thing he really remembered was the cake— dry, but not the worst for dipping in coffee.

"Oh, and one of us will have to be in the office at all times. We should probably futz around a bit with the cases Marcus gave us, just for appearances' sake, so he doesn't get suspicious," Rose continued. "Most importantly, though, whoever's in the office has to make sure they're up-to-date on the case and can do research for the rest of us."

"'The rest of us'? So you're not the one who'll be stuck in the office, eh, Rose? Then who? Assad?" Gordon asked.

Rose's lips curled into a kind of smile. "You're quick on the uptake, Gordon. Of course it'll be you. You have legal training, and you're fantastic at dealing with complex, interrelated cases. Anyway, we don't want you out in the field until you're back to your old self, do we?"

He nodded reluctantly, and Assad patted him on the shoulder a fraction too matter-of-factly.

"What about you, then, Rose? If you're going to be bumbling around with the rest of us, just remember that when the blind are leading the blind, they generally both end up in the pit."

Gordon didn't look too thrilled at the idea.

Assad laughed. "Well, you'll always have me to drag you out again."

Rose looked down. She was miles away. "Gordon, I think you should dive straight into what we'll call Carl's case. Begin at the beginning. Also, try to get some information on the car that ran over the lawyer."

She turned to Assad. "What about you, Assad? Where can you be most useful, do you think?"

His worn face crumpled, killing the smile he'd just mobilized. "You know what? I was just thinking about the first time Carl and I were out on assignment together. We drove down to Sorø, where those two me-chanics were killed—Carl and I didn't do it, by the way." He shrugged. It was obviously a joke. "The local police did come up with a suspect, eventually, but he was released for lack of evidence." Assad nodded to himself. "Anyway, I think I'd better call my wife and tell her not to wait for me before she digs into the dawood basha, despite how delicious they are. Then I'll try to find out what happened to that suspect, pay him a friendly visit."

"And you, Rose, what about you?" Gordon asked. He slid the plate toward himself and took a bite of salmon after all.

"Me?" She hesitated. "I'll try to have a word with the people at the PCA."

"And if you can't?"

"Then we'll have to seriously consider if it's worth threatening to go to the media and telling them what Department Q went through with Sisle. Might give us and Carl a bit more public support. We can't have Marcus calling all the shots around here. Whatever the cost."

7

EDDIE

Monday, December 28, 2020

On Monday morning, Rotterdam had woken up to an entirely normal weekday—except Eddie Jansen.

The message from his contact in Denmark said that Carl Mørck was still alive and kicking despite the well-planned attack in his cell last night, and that the authorities were apparently considering a transfer to another prison.

Until ten minutes ago, Eddie had thought he was the only one in possession of that information, but a phone call had disillusioned him.

One of his colleagues at the station had noticed how pale he looked immediately after the conversation and asked if he was feeling sick. Eddie shook his head with a smile. But he was. Sick down to the marrow, because the gist had been unambiguous.

"You're juggling a lot of plates right now, Eddie," said the man with the different-colored eyes on the phone. "We have four things to say to you. One, the contact's now demanding twice the money for this job after the absolute shitshow that went down last night—we've approved the request, but we're not planning on actually following through, of course. Those arseholes are going to regret being greedy, I can promise you that. Two, there are now several individuals in that prison who are aware of the plan, including, unfortunately, some who aren't happy about murders being committed on their cell blocks. So we can expect some pushback there."

At this point he took a small, contrived pause, which Eddie had come to learn meant nothing good. "Three, our contact on staff at the prison has now been brought in for official questioning, which means we have to resort to contacts on the outside. We can't risk losing him. He's too useful to us. You following, Eddie?"

Eddie mumbled that he was. But why the hell didn't he already know all this?

"And last but not least," his tormentor continued, "we're really running out of patience with you, Eddie. There'll be no more taking it easy after this, I can tell you that. We're assuming, as we have done all along, that Mørck is fully aware of Høyer's activities and contacts."

Eddie nodded to himself. If it was true that Mørck knew everything, then his back was up against the wall as well.

"The money and drugs Høyer stole from us have been in Mørck's attic all these years. He's a sly one, this Mørck. Patient, clearly. He wanted to wait until the time was right and he was retired before dipping into the treasure chest. But Mørck doesn't have the money or the drugs in his possession anymore, so believe you me, it won't be long before he starts negotiating with the prosecutor in Denmark to get his sentence reduced. He'll be singing like a canary, give the whole lot of us away. The prosecutor's throwing the book at him—accomplice to murder, the whole caboodle—so he has every reason to put up a fight, if he wants to go home to his wife and child before he's an old man."

"I promise he'll be dead before you know it."

"Well, that's good, Eddie. Because if not, we'll be coming for you *and* your family—just so you know we mean business."

Afterward, Eddie sat staring blankly into space. No wonder he was pale. The Christmas holidays would be over soon: his daughter was starting kindergarten, and Femke would be back at her new job as a secretary at NIRAS in Rotterdam.

He just didn't have the first idea what the hell to do. Judging by what he'd heard from Denmark, it might be a while after this before they got another shot at the policeman, and certainly not until he'd been transferred. But as Eddie saw it, they did still have one last chance of making the current plan work. But it wouldn't be easy, because that left them with only one opportunity—tonight—and Mørck would no doubt be kept in isolation from gen pop. His daytime exercise was guaranteed to be a solo performance, and his meals would be taken directly to his cell by prison staff, who would also accompany him to the toilet.

Those were the odds, as Eddie saw them.

So, all in all, if tonight's attack failed, he'd have to get his family somewhere safe, just to be sure.

There was no way Eddie could tell his wife what was brewing. She still blindly believed that her husband had won the lottery and made some smart investments with the money. So smart, in fact, that for a while they'd been talking about both taking early retirement.

That said, Femke was far from naïve. He had met her at the police station in Rotterdam, where she had made herself indispensable as a secretary pretty much from day one. She had grown familiar with all sorts of cases and all types of criminality, so that now she viewed most of the people around her with the kind of distrust that precluded deep friendships. That was why she'd had to switch jobs. So how was he possibly going to fool her?

If he couldn't come up with a plausible explanation for moving his family somewhere safe, Femke's suspicions would bubble up like boiling lava, and if he knew his wife, he couldn't expect much support. She was so obsessed with doing the right thing—she was bound to send him packing. He wasn't sure if she'd actually go so far as to report him, but he didn't want to test that scenario. Either way, his whole life would come crashing down around his ears, leaving him with a walk in the woods with his service revolver as the only real way out. He'd often thought it might be.

Then, however, he turned and saw the empty desk chair behind him. And in that moment, a way out presented itself.

His colleague Gerd Bakker had been sick with COVID for two weeks, and the station had just been told he had gone into intensive care, struggling with severe breathing problems. He'd been sniveling for a few days before taking sick leave and had been visibly sweating. After fiddling with something in his desk drawers for a while, he'd suddenly jumped up with a handkerchief over his mouth and bolted out of the room. Apparently he hadn't infected anybody else, but could they know that for sure? Not necessarily.

Eddie glanced around. Most of his colleagues were out in the field, and the ones doing paperwork were lost in their own worlds.

Slowly rising from his seat, he edged around Gerd Bakker's desk and bent over it, pulling out a drawer.

Bingo.

People are still getting COVID all the time, thought Eddie, reaching for the two used rapid-antigen tests at the top of the drawer.

Shit, he thought, realizing that the two revealing lines were now no longer particularly visible. Still, he pocketed the tests and sat back down in his chair.

If Carl Mørck didn't die tonight, his employers' patience would run out, and that would not end well for him. He'd seen it before, how efficient they could be when their underlings showed weakness. He had been warned.

I have to make sure I'm ready to disappear with my family, he thought. *I need time to gather ammunition against the people who want me out of the way. Time to make a deal with the prosecutor's office.*

Yes, come what may, that goddamn virus *had* to be the solution to this impossible situation.

Putting his hand in his pocket, he checked that the tests were where they should be. They were the first and most logical step toward getting himself and his family out of harm's way while still ensuring Femke was none the wiser. He would infect himself, her, and their little one with COVID, then go into isolation somewhere safe. The summer cabin wasn't an option, of course, but he had other places.

But how could he be sure they would contract it? Everybody on the street was wearing masks. Even if he drove to the test center and got ahold of the swabs used for PCR tests, he still couldn't be sure any of them carried the virus. So where, then?

After ten minutes' deliberation, he finally got up from his chair and explained to his colleagues that he had an interview in Dordrecht. Then he drove straight for the ring road and on toward Zorgboulevard, where the Maasstad Ziekenhuis hospital was located.

Eddie was familiar with the procedures and strict requirements for entry. Nobody would be allowed to enter the ward where the worst-affected COVID patients were kept, including him, even though he was a colleague of Gerd Bakker's—who had been admitted there—and could document that he needed to speak to him on official business.

He scanned the area. Maybe there was a side door he could sneak through. Maybe he could come up with a cover story to say that, as one of Bakker's colleagues, he needed important information.

He inhaled cold air through his nose, trying to give his brain a little extra oxygen. But a plausible solution came to him only when he set eyes on a woman hacking and coughing, clearly ill, walking down the path toward him. She briefly lifted her mask to blow her nose into a tissue, which she threw into the bin she was shuffling past.

Eddie waited for a second or two, then went over to the bin. Apart from some plastic and other debris, there were at least ten tissues in there. He grabbed them all hurriedly and returned to his car in the parking lot.

There was no doubt that the tissue into which the woman had blown her nose was the one still damp and slimy from her nasal secretions. Eddie brought it to his nose and inhaled forcefully. Once he'd done that several times, he repeated the procedure with the rest of the used tissues. When he was finished, he threw them all into the footwell of the passenger seat.

If there wasn't COVID in at least one of those used, disgusting snot rags, you could call him whatever the hell you liked.

8

CARL

Monday, December 28, 2020

You're an animal in a cage, Carl, he thought. *A poor moth-eaten creature that nobody else wants to touch. A pariah among living beings, that's all.*

"Stand still," the guards said as they cuffed him to take him up to the visitors' room, and it wasn't for safety reasons. It was out of disgust. The staff who had come on shift had already judged him—he could see it on their faces.

When they entered the visitors' room, one officer uncuffed him and stood by the wall, staring contemptuously at Carl until Mona was led in.

"I can only be here until the PCA comes to interview you again, but that's okay, because Matilde can't pick up Lucia today," Mona said. "And, Carl, I've requested that you be immediately transferred into one of the isolated cells, but they say that won't happen until tomorrow morning. They say there aren't any available."

"You heard what happened last night, didn't you?"

She nodded, with a cold glower at the guard. "And it won't happen again, will it?"

The blameless statue by the wall didn't move a muscle.

"I'm well aware that everybody in here hates cops. But why are they trying to kill me? It looks like a hit, Mona. Tell that to the chief of homicide."

Mona shifted back in her seat, and Carl saw clearly how shaken she was. He reached for her hand. "It was close, Mona, they came within a hair's breadth of stabbing me. But no, there won't be a second time."

"No touching," the officer said coldly.

Mona narrowed her eyes and gripped Carl's hand tightly. "What do the people trying to take you out think about you, Carl?"

"That I know too much, I reckon, and maybe I do, I just can't remember it! It's all so long ago. But how the hell am I going to convince the people trying to kill me? I don't even know who they are, and if I did, I'd hardly be negotiating."

"I had a quick word with your caseworker here. She's busy at the moment, but she'll visit you this week, she said. She told me you've been suspended, but that's no surprise, and apparently you'll be on two-thirds pay until a verdict is reached."

Carl sighed. There was always something. "Find out how much you can transfer to me, Mona, and how you do it. It's always a good idea to have a bit of money on you in here."

She nodded. She knew that better than anybody.

The door clanged, and a tall, slim man stepped into the room. Carl didn't recognize him, only the person with him. It was the fellow from the Police Complaints Authority who had questioned him briefly yesterday.

The first man held out his hand. "PCA. Head of Investigation Noah Rommel. No relation to the German field marshal, in case you were wondering." He smiled. "I'll be leading the investigation into your case, in collaboration with Senior Detective Laust Smedegaard, whom you met when you were taken into custody yesterday. We're permitted to use the visitors' room, since your wife is already here, and there's more space than in the little conference room."

Carl nodded to them both.

"I'm sorry I couldn't come earlier, but I've had a few hospital appointments recently, and I'm afraid they've kept me a little busy."

"Of course." Carl nodded. "When sickness comes to the house, piety

has to take a back seat, as an old Jewish man once said on the Sabbath,"
he said. Evidently only Mona and Rommel understood what he meant.

"We'll have to ask you to finish your conversation with your husband, Mrs. Mørck."

"You'd better look after him," she said, looking like the authority she
was. "And, Carl." She got up and stepped in front of him. "No matter
what obstacles Marcus puts in your way, your friends at Department Q
are working overtime—you need to know that." She turned to Noah
Rommel and Laust Smedegaard. "So please, just let Carl's colleagues do
what they can to help, all right?"

The head of the PCA shook his head slightly, and Carl knew what that
meant. The investigation was the PCA's alone, and nobody else was going
to meddle in it.

She bent down to Carl and kissed him, ignoring the protests of the
guard. "You'll be out soon, my love," she said.

A minute went by, then he was alone with the two detectives.

"We're talking about a case that goes back many years, Mørck, so it
demands a lot more resources than our usual investigations. For that reason, I'm afraid I can't tell you much except that it will take some time and
that it's possible you may be on remand for several months. But I assume
you already know that."

"Yes. And I take it the Dutch police and the narcotics squad have
overwhelming evidence, or you'd be releasing me on the spot?"

"I should perhaps remind you that the PCA doesn't have access to police data systems. We are independent. We run our own investigations,
and then we send our reports to the public prosecutor's office. You heard
the charges yourself, and now it's our job to make sure they hold water."

"Or the opposite, I hope, because I'm innocent. I have nothing to do
with this case. Except that I worked with Anker Høyer, and he asked me
to hold on to a suitcase for him. A suitcase I believed contained his private
possessions. Clothes, things like that."

Noah Rommel's partner nodded. "Oh yes, everyone is innocent until
proven guilty," he said dryly.

———————

He couldn't see them, but it felt as though a hundred piercing eyes rested on him from the windows above as he was led down to the yard after the interview.

"Nah, you're not going in there," said the officer as they neared the pen where the exercise equipment was kept. "You're going to the solitary yard, in the Cake. I'll come and get you in twenty minutes," he continued, letting him into one of the twelve slice-shaped cages arranged in a circle.

Carl narrowed his eyes and folded his arms across his chest, watching as blasts of his own icy breath powdered his nose. They could at least have given him a jacket—it was forty-one degrees Fahrenheit at most, and the rain was pouring silently down. But perhaps they wanted him to freeze to death.

Carl began hopping from foot to foot on the spot, going over what had just happened in his mind.

Given the seriousness of the situation, Noah Rommel had been disconcertingly pleasant during the interview. If Carl had been in his shoes, he'd have gone straight for the jugular, but Carl had never worked at the PCA, and it had dawned on him only gradually that these new people were employed solely to try to establish, step-by-step, what each party had to say before they drew any conclusions. Carl, at this point, was merely one piece of the puzzle: guilty or not guilty, he was a witness just like everybody else.

"I certainly can't say we know all the facts at the present time, Mørck. But we intend to question your colleagues, as well as everybody else with an opinion on this case. First, we'd like to know if you have any comment regarding the prosecution's claims?" Rommel had asked.

He had said, of course, that he denied all the allegations against him. It was true that he'd unwittingly stored a suitcase full of money and drugs for Anker, and it was also true that he'd suspected Anker was using drugs himself, because Hardy had told him so. But he knew nothing about the body that had been found in a wooden crate under Georg

Madsen's house in Amager or why, of the two foil-wrapped coins in said corpse's pocket, one had Anker's fingerprints on it and one had Carl's. That—and a lot else—was a mystery to him. Was he the victim of a conspiracy?

This investigation is going to take months, they had said. But what if it took even longer than that? What if it ended in a prison sentence?

He looked up at the heavy wall and its many glowing windows, from which sporadic taunts were hurled down at him.

Could he even survive a prison sentence—one that might last years?

Even if I do make it, Mona and I will be past seventy by the time I get out. Lucia will be a grown woman, he thought.

Step by step, he tried to imagine her growing up. The baby years, the first day of school, her confirmation, a slender young girl with bright cheeks.

Then he had to stop.

Abruptly he ceased shifting from foot to foot. What could he do to prevent that scenario?

A bunch of keys jangled, and a second man was brought in and left immediately outside his cage. Then the guard turned and walked off toward the other side of the yard.

"Hey," yelled Carl at the guard's retreating back. "What's this guy doing here? Shouldn't he be locked into one of the slices like me?" No answer. "It's freezing out here. I want to go back inside."

The officer showed no sign of turning, not for a second. Perhaps he couldn't hear him. The situation felt extremely unsafe.

Carl saw through the bars that the man on the other side had come closer. Did he have a weapon out? Was he about to be shot with a silencer, or would the man let himself in and stab him? Carl withdrew to the far wall, calling yet again for the guard.

He stopped when the prisoners above began cackling at him from the many-windowed wall.

"The guard's just tired, and when you're tired you get stupid, like most of the people in here," said the man outside the bars. He stood motionless.

Carl nodded. It was probably true.

"But not as stupid as you, eh, Mørck!"

Carl tilted his head and looked directly at the man. Carl didn't know him, but he was a good-looking man, his skin and hair a little too well groomed, wearing a strong citrus-scented cologne that was definitely way out of Carl's price range. Maybe the same cologne Morten had once caught a whiff of in a toilet in Hellerup, where he'd spent the night with a stockbroker. This guy didn't exactly fit the prototype of the standard jailbird.

"Okay. And you've learned this at the University of Iron Bars, have you?"

"Mørck, we need to be completely sure you keep your mouth shut. Otherwise this won't end well for you. Understood?"

Okay! A direct conversation! But who the hell was this guy?

"Keep my mouth shut about what? About what I think of scum like you? Please, enlighten me!"

The man took hold of the cage bars, his hands wet with rain, and leaned toward Carl.

"There are people out there who think you know too much, Mørck. You saw what happened to your partner Anker Høyer, and he was lucky enough to die pretty quickly. In your case, you get to choose what happens next. Can I go back and tell my employers they've got nothing to worry about? If so, maybe you and your family will live to see another day. Your beautiful wife, your lovely little daughter, she—"

The man took a step back as Carl lunged forward and slammed his fists against the bars in front of his face. "You're not threatening a policeman, and you're definitely not threatening his family, are you? Because if you are, you're the one in deep shit." He pointed at the man.

"Threatening? I'm not threatening you. I'm just warning you that there are forces out there greater than you can hope to overcome." He smiled crookedly. It looked like the slimy citrus-scented bastard had already gotten his answer. But what was Carl supposed to shut up about?

"Your employers, who are they?! Who sent you?"

The man laughed. "We'll squeeze it out of you, you can be sure of that."

"In here? I think you'll find that a challenge." Carl nodded slowly, trying to sound self-assured. As though he had any reason to be confident.

Then the man drew back and gave a brief whistle.

A minute or so, and then the door opened at the top of the steps leading to the prison entrance, and the pomaded man took a key out of his pocket and let himself out of the pen around the Cake.

On the steps by the door, he turned back and looked straight into Carl's cage. "You won't see me again. I was only visiting, Mørck. Too bad you didn't have anything I could take back with me." Then he glanced up at the windows in the wall.

"Open season, lads," he yelled curtly, and vanished through the open door.

9

ROSE

Monday, December 28, 2020

Come on, call me back, Gordon, thought Rose after the phone rang out for the third time. He was great as support staff at the office, but when it came to improvisation and fobbing people off with on-the-spot lies, he still had a lot to learn. They couldn't let anybody at the station—or anybody outside Department Q—suspect they were digging into anything remotely connected to Carl Mørck's current predicament. That might mean duty reassignment, perhaps even suspension, and then who would Carl have to back him up?

She had just decided to head back to Teglholmen and speak to Gordon one-on-one when the phone finally rang.

"Hey, sorry, Rose, I saw your calls. Look, I'm literally in the toilets at the Investigation Unit right now—I have to be, because Jacobsen's put one of that new lot into our office to spy on us. They've also completely sealed off Carl's office, so my hands are completely tied. I can't talk on the phone, Rose, and I can't bring anyone in here to talk to them. And as if that wasn't enough, the spy keeps asking where you and Assad are. *Mein Gott*, it's impossible." Gordon sighed. "What the hell am I supposed to do?"

"Okay, Gordon, I get it. Look, pick up one of the cases we've been given, then call us and tell us in broad strokes what it's about and what you think we should do next in our fictional investigation. Tell your spy we're run off our feet with all the cases Marcus has suddenly dumped on us and that we've decided you'll coordinate from the office while Assad and I will be working in the field for the foreseeable future."

"Nobody here is going to buy that."

"They will, because when you're on the phone with us, just say 'right' and 'aha,' like we've already got cracking with the fieldwork. Add in 'Yeah, I think you probably should,' or whatever, while really reading up on everything about Carl's case. Look at Assad's PC; he copied the files ages ago. Send them to yourself, then the idiot sitting near you can't work out what you're up to. Call me a couple of times a day so he can see you're doing it. And when the guy goes home at four, call us up again and tell us what you've found out about Carl's case. Meanwhile I'll do my best to look into the murder of Carl's lawyer. Wish me luck."

Rose found the silver-gray Passat abandoned halfway across a cycle path on the corner of Amerikavej and Vesterbrogade. For some reason the police hadn't removed it for further analysis after Adam Bang's death, instead cordoning it off with plastic tape so that the crime scene techs could search for evidence around the car. Two officers stood behind the window of the copy shop next door while the man they were speaking to kept shaking his head. Presumably they were unlikely to get a description of the driver out of him.

White-clad techs were padding around the car. A few of them Rose had occasionally flirted with at crime scenes, and they acknowledged her with lopsided smiles or raised eyebrows. That was the effect she had on people. They hesitated, though, when she lifted the tape and slipped underneath, but when she stopped a short distance from the car, they left her alone.

Aside from a couple of dents, the front of the Passat was largely undamaged. If it hadn't been for the blood and grayish flecks on the license plate, which she presumed were the dead lawyer's brain matter, she would have thought it was a harmless accident. The kind a few hours at a repair shop could erase completely.

Looking again at the license plate, she memorized the registration. "And the driver?" she asked.

"The vehicle was reported stolen around the same time as the collision, but we're trying to establish whether the owner of the car might be involved in some way."

"Wasn't he in the carpark behind the prison when he reported the theft?"

"You'll have to ask the officers in there."

"So you found no fingerprints apart from the owner's?"

"Oh no, plenty. We're thinking they're maybe his wife's, his brother's, his kids', and also his passenger's—we're still determining that."

"His passenger? Were they with the owner when they came back to find the parking space empty?"

"Yeah, I think so. Again, you'll have to ask those two. The passenger was putting flowers on his wife's grave, your colleagues checked and confirmed that, so I'd assume he's a reliable supporting witness, but it's all still up for investigation."

"We're reasonably sure the car was fished, just so you know," said the other tech.

Fished? Rose hadn't heard that term before, and they could tell immediately.

"The Passat was keyless, so they must have fished the signal from the owner's key in order to open the door. We think so, anyway, because there's no sign of a physical break-in."

Rose was as mystified as ever.

"The owner says—and the witness confirmed this—that after parking the car, he stood still by the road for a moment while a passerby asked him if it was free to park there, and that's actually all the time you'd need."

"I don't understand." Rose's dimples carried the next question. "Time for what?"

He smiled back. "To fish the signal. If you're standing close enough to a person locking their car with a smart key, you can clone the signal and transmit it to someone else, even up to several hundred meters away.

They grab the signal with a similar device, and then they can fool the car into thinking the button has been pressed. The car unlocks, and the thief can simply get in and drive away."

"Okay, but if that's your theory, and the witness is reliable, then you can't suspect the owner of the car."

"Sure, I mean, right now we're checking everything, but I don't think we'll get anywhere. The killer probably bought the device online, which is easy to do. It doesn't cost much either, and since there's no shortage of places selling them, your colleagues probably won't have much luck that way."

Rose shook her head. It was a good thing she still had her old banger of a Renault. Yes, it could be stolen with a crowbar, but who'd want to drive it?

"Are there any usable footprints around the car?"

"The driver jumped straight onto the cycle path and across Vester-brogade, I think, so no. The ground is only partially wet here, as you've probably noticed."

"Do you have the name of the owner?"

"You'll have to ask your colleagues. Why haven't you checked all this yourself?"

Rose shrugged, going to stand at a slight distance when the first officer emerged from the copy shop.

"Hello," she said. "Did they see anything useful in there?"

The officer looked at her with the sour animus Rose herself used when curious onlookers got too close. So he didn't recognize her, then. Rose was about to take her ID out of her pocket when she changed her mind. She didn't want to end up in a report that might land on the chief of homicide's desk.

"Hello, this is Gordon, in my office chair," Rose heard when Gordon picked up the phone.

"Thanks for the information," she said. "I think you should just say your name. The rest of it sounds a bit weird."

She explained what she'd been doing and gave him the vehicle registration number.

"The man's name? Okay, I'll try. Sounds straightforward enough."

Afterward she called the lead detective at the PCA, Noah Rommel, who answered her call with all the cooperation of a hardened criminal asked about his precise activities. Friendly but distinctly dismissive.

"Well, who am I supposed to go to, if not to you lot at the PCA? Aren't you even remotely interested in making sure the person you're investigating actually survives his time in detention?"

"Protective custody for Carl Mørck, you say. And you think we have the authority to make that happen? Look, frankly, you probably shouldn't be getting involved in this anyway."

Rose ignored that. "Of course you have the authority. You can interrogate him somewhere more convenient for you than Vestre Prison, if you want. We're thinking Slagelse Remand Center might be a good bet. Wouldn't that be easier for you anyway, since you're driving all the way up from Aarhus?"

He grunted a few times, and the conversation didn't last much longer.

Then her phone rang.

"Gordon here, I'm in the toilets again. Listen, Rose, if you ask me, I don't think we'll get anywhere with the owner of that car. It belongs to someone by the name of Jess Larsen, who lives in Smørum, and he explained he was just giving his boss a lift. Apparently the guy asked Larsen to take him to the cemetery, because he'd lost his driver's license. The boss wanted to visit his wife's grave and lay some flowers, which he did. That's all there is to it."

Rose sighed. It had been almost too easy.

"Who gave you that information?"

"Who do you think? Lis, of course."

Rose nodded. Homicide's omnipresent secretary, one of the department's very few Carl Mørck fans.

"Is that everything you have for me?"

"No, Morten called. He and his boyfriend, Mika, are on their way home from Switzerland with Hardy. They arrive in Copenhagen this evening. Hardy's had chips surgically implanted in his brain, and now he wears an exoskeleton to get around."

"An exoskeleton?"

"A sort of shell that keeps him upright. Sounds like they've turned him into RoboCop."

"Jesus, does Carl know?"

"I called Mona half an hour ago."

"Can you put me through to Lis?"

A moment passed, then there was a chirrup at the other end. It almost sounded as though the secretary was talking to three or four people in the front office at once, and she probably was.

"Yes, sorry, Gordon, I just had a couple of other inquiries to deal with first."

"This is Rose, Lis. I know you've just given Gordon information. Would you mind repeating some of it for me?"

"I'll try," she said in an undertone.

"The man whose car was stolen, the car that was used to run down the lawyer out by Vestre, do you know the name of his boss?"

There was silence on the other end.

"Are you there, Lis?"

"Hang on. Marcus is just heading out."

Rose could picture Lis smiling as her boss walked by.

"Right, he's gone now," she whispered. "I hate him for what he's doing to Carl!"

"Arresting him, you mean?"

"That too. But he's also going out of his way to prevent us helping Carl. If he knew I was talking to you and Gordon, he'd blow a gasket. And when new information comes in, he makes sure the rest of us don't find out about it. Still, we do get wind of a few things."

"He's a stickler for the rules, Lis, we know that. He's not allowed to obstruct the PCA's investigation."

"Hmm, maybe."

"What did he tell you to keep quiet about?"

"I can't say."

"So you can't tell me the name of the car owner's boss?"

"No, maybe because his name is Dutch."

Rose frowned and thanked her for the clue. "And you've heard from Morten and Hardy?"

"Yes, isn't it wonderful? Mona's already explained everything to them, so they know Carl's in Vestre. If he hasn't already been transferred, Hardy and the others will try to visit him one of these days. I don't think Marcus minds that."

"Why not?"

"Because Hardy's been dropping hints that he suspects there was something dodgy going on with Carl and Anker Høyer. Maybe Marcus is hoping he can get Carl to open up a little."

10

PELLE / MONA

Monday, December 28, 2020

Pelle Hyttested was gloating. As a journalist at the tabloid *Gossip*, there was only one thing better than being able to present a juicy story to drive up circulation, and that was a juicy story about one of his archenemies. On various occasions over the years, Pelle had had the very great pleasure of dragging their names through the mud, but nothing got his blood boiling more quickly than when his victims retaliated—most notably, the time when that idiot Carl Mørck had made him a laughingstock. So when a colleague from one of the major dailies had let slip while blind drunk that Mørck had gotten himself in hot water, that he'd been arrested and brought to a hearing on Sunday morning, at which point he'd been remanded in custody, Pelle felt as though the potential headlines—garish yellow, boldface—were raining down over him in an endless stream.

A policeman in custody—*Carl Mørck*, no less! It was a hell of a story for a gossip rag that operated in the gray hinterland, accustomed both to reprimands from the Press Council and to substantial fines.

The front page was ready in an hour, and the story posted on the website.

"Hero Policeman Banged Up," read the headline, with the subhead: "Serious Charges at Closed Hearing."

He had nothing concrete to say in the article, of course, but blurry images of an angry Carl Mørck plus a few bars and handcuffs always went down well.

The entire editorial staff came to pat him on the back. All the other sordid stories about famous people drinking, whoring around, double-crossing their nearest and dearest, and generally getting up to no good were immediately swept off the table and into the corner. The editor in chief was called in, and the briefing he gave to the journalists and photographers was short and precise.

"This is the story of the year. A policeman like Carl Mørck—everybody knows who he is, his department has cleared one case after another, he's someone many of his colleagues probably look up to and try to emulate—is currently in jail for four weeks, which could mean anything. There's been a closed hearing, ladies and gentlemen, there has been an injunction, meaning that all your esteemed colleagues were chucked out. Taken together, that may well mean he's being charged with a serious crime here. Could it be corruption, bribery, tampering with evidence? Or perhaps even homicide, negligent or otherwise? Is this finally something that could bring an entire team of investigators to its knees? We don't know. The journalists were only allowed to hear a brief account of the charges, just the relevant legal clauses but no details, so we've got our work cut out for us, dear friends. I'll deal with anybody who comes whining that we've"—here he drew air quotes—"'violated the injunction.'" He smiled broadly, and a wave of braying laughter rippled among the journalists. Injunctions were the bane of their profession.

"All right, I want you putting the thumbscrews on all the police, prison staff, and prosecutors you can get your hands on. Why has Carl Mørck been arrested? What did he do? How serious is it? We want details, got it? The minute you get anything at all, you take it straight to Hyttested."

A finger was raised in the air, and the editor in chief pointed at the person with the question.

"If we're going to fill this edition plus the next few, why don't we cram in a load of old stories about police who broke the law and ended up in prison? I'm happy to go to the archives and dig up some old photos."

The editor in chief nodded and pointed at the next person.

"I'm thinking we collect a bunch of Mørck's cases and run them one after another, add in a lot of pictures and commentary on what happened. There's no shortage of pretty spectacular cases that ended up with the main suspect getting killed for one reason or another *before* the case went to court."

At this point several people began to clap. This was going to be one of the best winters in the tabloid's history.

"Now, is there anybody here who wants to tackle the wife?" asked the editor in chief. "If anybody knows something, it's her. Anyway, she works for the police as well, as far as I know."

A couple of the female journalists held up their hands.

"Good. Then that's a start. I don't want you going easy on anybody, all right? Including yourselves. If you get the combined circulation and number of hits on the website above 250,000, there'll be bonuses for everyone."

• • •

Mona sat facing the chief of homicide. He was practically seething, but it was nothing compared to the volcano of rage boiling inside Mona. Everybody was talking about the latest online edition of *Gossip*. The whole of Denmark now knew what was going on, but what could Marcus Jacobsen do about it? Help prize the doors of the closed hearing open slightly? God forbid. That was probably the last thing Mona wanted, because the report from Vestre Prison about the attack on her husband spoke for itself. Carl had been left high and dry, and now he was under fire on all fronts. The situation was deadly.

"Marcus! Do I really need to remind you of everything Carl has done for you and this department over the years? Do I actually need to *say* that you owe it to him to get him in protective custody right now, before the injunction is lifted and before the details of the case become public knowledge? His name's already out now, and believe me, it won't be long before every inmate in Vestre knows who he is, not to mention the people outside who are trying to harm him."

Jacobsen drummed his fingers on the table, trying to avoid eye contact. "I'm sorry, Mona, but you know as well as I do that there are procedures for this sort of thing. It's Correctional Services' job to solve this problem, not mine."

"Can't you call them now and insist that Carl be assigned specially selected guards until he can be isolated or transferred?"

Marcus tried to look unmoved as she slammed her bag onto his desk. He merely stared at her, brow furrowed, and shook his head. She wasn't about to force him into anything, clearly. When she did it a second time, however, overturning his half-full cup of coffee over the mess of papers on his desk and screaming that he was a shit boss, that she would go straight to the chief of police and demand Marcus be taken to task, he fumbled for his phone and began to dial.

11

MALTHE / CARL

Monday, December 28, 2020

Tensions were escalating in the corridors and in the yard, where the inmates stood in groups exchanging dark scowls. With each second that went by, more and more of them knew that the reward for the murder of Carl Mørck had risen to a million kroner.

That open season had been declared on the prisoner in cell 437.

"Open season," which meant that Malthe was no longer the only one on the job, even though he was the one the unknown string-pullers had asked to do it. A million kroner was enough to tempt anybody, he could see that, and it certainly tempted him.

With a million kroner, Malthe could do everything he wanted to do for his little brother. He could make life easier for his whole family.

In the exercise yard that afternoon, however, he was cornered by a couple of the skinheads from the first floor, whom he'd always been at odds with.

"Listen here, moron. You're not involved in this anymore," one of them said coldly.

"You fucked up, didn't you, you ugly twat? So the bosses have decided you're out—from now on, you stay away. And you'd better keep your mouth shut, because if you don't, it'll be your family that pays the price. There are people out there who know where your mum lives, your brothers and sisters, and it'll be child's play to have them killed. A can of petrol and one little match, and the whole place'll go up in smoke. Understood?" the other man said.

Malthe understood, but he was also seriously fucking pissed off, so he swung his gigantic fists and knocked them both to the ground. As they lay there gasping, their faces smeared with blood, he decided they must be thinking that threatening his family might not be such a good idea after all. For a second he was triumphant—he didn't notice the four or five men behind him, who suddenly grabbed hold of him tightly while the inmates howled and hooted from the windows. "Fuck him up!"

"You're too thick to be in here," yelled one of the attackers, while a couple of the others pressed lit cigarette butts hard against the back of his hand, until the cold air was spiced with the acrid stench of burning hair and flesh.

Then Malthe relaxed.

He could take the pain, and he'd gotten the message.

And he knew he'd pay them back, when they least expected it.

Everybody knew that the failed attack the night before had nothing to do with Malthe. The blame rested squarely on the Jackhammer's shoulders, so no one felt sorry for him ending up in the infirmary or that he would soon be standing stoop-shouldered in court as his additional sentence for attempted murder was read out.

Malthe heard the whispers on all sides as he doled out food, so he knew for certain now that he couldn't help his little brother. Although his heart ached with grief, what he mostly felt was rage. Twenty-four hours ago he had believed his brother was out of the danger zone, but then the Jackhammer had come along and stolen his only lifeline. If Malthe ever got the chance, that would be the last time the Jackhammer messed with his family.

Malthe stared at the door of cell 437. Inside it was the man who should have been sacrificed for his brother's sake. Malthe didn't know him, but he had learned over the course of the day that it was a mystery how the man had ended up in Vestre. Some people said he was the sharpest detective in the country. Anybody who tangled with him would have their work cut out for them dodging a conviction, they said.

When Malthe looked around at the inmates coming up to him and the food trolley with their plates outstretched, he couldn't help but be amused. Most were cold-blooded bastards who bragged about their crimes and the lousy job done by the police. In their eyes, cops were just a bunch of arseholes and pussies who could be twisted around their little fingers. And if they were unlucky enough to be caught, it was always someone else's fault.

But then how come the policeman in cell 437 was so feared that somebody was willing to pay a million kroner to have him killed? How come everyone in here knew who he was, and they were all whispering about him like he was the most dangerous of the lot? Malthe was curious.

The people who wanted the man dead would get hold of the key to his cell, that was for sure, but Malthe had no idea how. Only that it might already be hidden in one of the skinheads' cells, waiting to be slid into the keyhole of cell 437 so that they could kill the man during the night and claim the reward Malthe had been promised.

"Can't let the bastards do that," he promised himself, observing the activity in the corridor.

The question was, how could he stop them? Were there any guards he could confide in? He'd noticed that the guard they called "the Barn Door," the one whose real name was apparently Frank, had looked out for the policeman. The two of them seemed to respect each other, so if he could find a way to do it, maybe he could stop those bald pricks by having a little chat with the fat guard.

"Do you know where Frank is right now?" he asked a pale prison guard who had just strolled onto the wing. He hadn't seen the man before.

The guard shrugged. "He's left for the day. His shift's over."

Malthe grabbed his wrist and was a split second away from being rewarded with a blow from the man's baton. "They're planning to kill the guy in cell 437 later today. You've got to isolate him."

"Carl Mørck? He's nothing to do with me."

"Fine, but just pass the message up the chain, all right!"

Later, when they locked the door to Malthe's cell and he sat down on his bunk, it struck him that perhaps telling the guard hadn't been the smartest move. After all, Loudmouth had been indirectly involved in the first attempt on Carl Mørck's life. And although Loudmouth himself wasn't a threat tonight, since he'd been sent home for a few days, the pale officer he'd spoken to might be like him. *Too much money corrupts even the most trustworthy among us,* his dad had always said.

Malthe tried to picture how much a million kroner actually was. He couldn't really wrap his mind around it, only that a sum like that would be life-changing for most people and that being a prison guard probably wasn't the highest-paying job in the world.

• • •

Carl had said goodbye to Frank late that afternoon in a gloomy tone of voice.

"Tell your colleagues to be on the lookout, Frank."

The big man nodded. He said he would, and then the door slammed between them.

Again, Carl lay with his eyes fixed on the ceiling, trying to puzzle out the charges against him. The drugs charge was actually pretty straightforward, because they didn't have a shred of evidence. They knew, obviously, that Anker had been addicted to coke and that he'd asked Carl to store a suitcase for him, which turned out to contain drugs and several million kroner's worth of cash. But they couldn't prove Carl had had any involvement with drugs.

The murder and attempted murder charges, however, were based on a series of facts he couldn't fully get straight in his head, let alone understand.

It had all come back to Georg Madsen, that poor sod they'd found with a nail buried in his temple. Then, three months later, Madsen's nephew and the nephew's business partner had been murdered the exact same way. The two younger men had connections to the Netherlands, and a few of their lot had also been found with nails rammed into their skulls.

One victim was named by an anonymous source as Pete Boswell, so at first that was what the detectives had called him, and apart from the fact that he'd been found in a wooden crate in the ground under the shed where Georg Madsen sat dead in his armchair, there had been no immediately obvious connection to the other victims.

Nevertheless, it was this particular corpse that worried Carl the most, given the link to Carl and Anker Høyer that had been established by the discovery of those two carefully packaged coins bearing Carl's and Anker's fingerprints, respectively.

The fingerprint-laden coins, his old involvement in the murder case of Georg Madsen, and the infamous suitcase in Carl's attic were the basis for the case against him, the case that the PCA were currently assigned to investigate.

"Shit!" he said out loud, thumping his head with his fist. Why couldn't those goddamn brain cells help him out? Why couldn't he recall those memories when he needed them most?

And then, in the next seconds, three sounds wiped all thought from his head.

The quiet click of a key being slid into a lock and turned.

Himself tumbling off the bed.

And finally his heart, which began to hammer so hard the blood was whooshing in his ears.

12

ASSAD

Monday, December 28, 2020

Assad lay on his prayer rug, trying with all his might to shut out worldly thoughts as he prayed, but it was difficult.

His mind was full of sadness about Carl, but he was equally preoccupied with troubles on the home front. His son, Afif, was going through a very challenging period, bringing the mood in the house down to zero. It seemed as though all his senses were torturing him and that his only defense was either to scream inarticulately or to do the total opposite: to isolate himself completely from the rest of his family. Both Assad and Marwa had sought help many times, trying to understand what was going on inside the boy's head, but so far nothing had worked.

Afterward, as Assad rolled up the rug and apologized to Allah for his faltering concentration, he felt nonetheless that prayer had done him good. An hour ago he had dusted off the name of the man who had been released in Sorø after the nail gun murders, and just now, in his meditative state, he had recalled that he'd stumbled across the name in another context too.

The name Niels B Sørensen did not, in and of itself, strike him as anything special. There were probably a thousand Niels Sørensens in Denmark, so under normal circumstances it most likely wouldn't have rung any bells. But it was that little B in the middle, the one without a period, that reminded him of the story of why the American presidents John F. Kennedy and Franklin D. Roosevelt had a full stop but Harry S Truman didn't. In the first two cases, the full stops indicated an abbreviation of their middle names, Fitzgerald and Delano, respectively, whereas President Truman's *S* didn't stand for any one name.

This had also been the case for Niels B Sørensen, whom their highly respected colleague Terje Ploug had brought in for questioning some years ago as part of a peripheral case. Afterward he had come into the canteen laughing, telling them all about the idiot who'd tried to make himself a bit more interesting by adding a letter to his very ordinary name. It had led to discussions about borrowed plumage, people who called themselves "von" without a smidgen of aristocratic ancestry, and the ones who glued two names together with a hyphen.

"Terje, do you remember bringing a Niels B Sørensen in for questioning, that guy who'd just stuck a B onto his name?" Assad asked.

Terje Ploug grunted his acknowledgment on the other end of the line. What was this about? he asked. Not the nail gun case?

Assad hastened to say it wasn't. Oh no, they weren't allowed to touch that. The man just so happened to be a suspect in a different case.

Assad knew a detective of Terje's caliber would hardly accept that at face value. Which case? he would ask. He might even want to know how the name had popped up on Assad's radar. He obviously couldn't explain that he'd spotted it in an article about the Sorø nail gun murders in the *Zealand Times*, that Sørensen was the suspect who'd been cleared. And sure enough, Terje paused, the kind of pause that made it clear he had seen through Assad's amateurish bluff.

"Yes, I remember that case well!" he replied at last.

Assad breathed a sigh of relief. Terje was on his side. Good!

"What do you want to know, Assad?"

"I can't find the case in the digital archive—can you give me a quick rundown?"

"It was a case in Sorø, so that's why you can't find it. Niels B Sørensen was reported to the police by the company he worked for, after a co-worker died under tragic circumstances. Our techs reviewed what happened, and they determined that the death was strikingly similar to another accident that had taken place at the company a few years earlier, before the suspect, Niels B, had started working for them. Unfortunately for the company, the Working Environment Authority and the police launched a joint inquiry that ended in a conviction for gross negligence, and the company had to pay a pretty eye-watering sum of money to the two victims' next of kin in compensation. They ended up going bankrupt. Obviously, I had nothing to do with that." He laughed for a moment, a chuckle that felt misplaced. "Anyway, I remember the man very well. Textbook megalomaniac. What do you want to know?"

"Oh, I just need an address for him, but I suppose you don't have one? I mean, since there wasn't a report filed on him. The police in Sorø have given up as well. Finding this guy is like finding a needle in a haystack, I'd say."

At that, Terje laughed again—Assad didn't quite know why.

"Well, Assad, it's funny you should ask, because you wouldn't forget this guy's address in a hurry." Terje Ploug laughed once more. "No, he was an ordinary man but a massive snob. An ignorant one, though—he wouldn't stop boasting that he lived on Slotsgade, which is hardly the fanciest address in the city."

"Slotsgade? Oh, Castle Street. In Nørrebro?"

"Yeah, at number one or something—his lucky number, anyway."

"When was this? The case, I mean?"

"Ohhh, let's see, maybe nine or ten years ago? I'm not sure."

"So the man could have moved ages ago. He could be in Ebberød or Thisted or Ølsemaglegård or . . ." He tried in vain to think of other funny-sounding names he'd come across in Denmark.

"True, and a guy like that might easily have changed his name to something flashier, I reckon."

Assad sighed. He'd been down this road many times before. There were at least four dusty registers he had to check through, and that was assuming the whole thing wasn't a wild goose chase.

Slotsgade in Nørrebro was a street in the Sorte Firkant neighborhood, where brand-new monstrosities and gorgeous old buildings were nestled cheek by jowl.

Assad stood at the Baggesensgade end of the street, scratching the back of his neck as his eyes swept across the façades. Even though this was one of the shortest streets in the area, and quite a few of the properties had been knocked down in favor of carparks, there were still far too many numbers to choose from. The task had, at first blush, seemed simple: check all the apartments and ask if anybody knew a Niels B Sørensen, but Assad didn't have that kind of time. He didn't even know what information he would get out of the man if he found him. Gordon had been no help, because Sørensen didn't have a telephone number registered to an address on Slotsgade—or anywhere else in Denmark, for that matter. That meant he might be dead, or he might have immigrated to Scotland; he might have changed his name, he might be living on the streets, or he might simply not have a telephone.

Maybe he should just go back to the office and find something else to do. The nail gun case was a complex one, after all, and Gordon could probably do with a bit of help chasing down all the different leads.

Assad took a deep breath as he crossed Baggesensgade in the dim light. A couple of speeding cyclists yelled at him to watch where the hell he was going, which resulted in their being pursued all the way to the corner by a barrage of curses in a foreign language.

Assad glanced at the buildings. Terje Ploug had said that Sørensen's bore his lucky number. On one side of the street were the numbers 2, 4, 6, and 8, and on the other 1, 3, 5, 7, 9, and 11. Assad's own lucky number was 22, from his military days, but what the hell would Niels B Sørensen choose as his? Assad's wife's was 5, the size of their family. Rose's was 1, as far as he knew, and he'd never really paid attention to anybody else's.

He called Gordon. "Who owns the houses in Slotsgade? You know, owner-occupied, rentals, shared ownership?" he asked, and two minutes later he had an answer.

Pulling up his collar around his ears, he got to work.

When at last he reached the other end of the street, emerging onto Nørrebrogade, he had checked all the names on the intercoms and was still none the wiser, so he went to stand on the corner in front of a Netto grocery store, took out his ID, and stopped everyone who turned down Slotsgade.

"Hey, excuse me, do you know a Niels B Sørensen who lives on this street?" he asked, again and again.

Most people were nice and shook their heads politely. A couple of the rougher-looking types glared derisively at his ID and strode on without a word. They too were chased on their way by a couple of Arabic swear words—there were plenty to go around.

After he'd been standing there for forty-five minutes, his private parts shrinking in the cold, a man walked by. Like the others, he didn't reply, but for a second he stopped short, and—more significantly—he darted a fist out reflexively toward the wall, as though an invisible hand had pushed him.

"Stop, hey, you," Assad shouted after him, but to no effect, even when Assad ran up to him.

"I can tell you know something," he said, jogging as the man sped up.

"Nothing that concerns the police."

"You might be who I'm looking for—Niels B Sørensen. Do you have any ID?"

"You're a sharp one, eh, Paki? Got cotton between your ears? You don't even know what the guy looks like? Anyway, why should I believe that shitty plastic card you're waving about? You got a score to settle with him? You might be one of the dealers he goes to? You come to beat him up?"

Assad lifted his chin. "All right. Now I could arrest you for calling me a Paki, or I could give you a knock in the head with this." He raised his ice-cold fist. "Which would you rather?"

At last the man stopped. "What does he look like, this guy you're after?"

Assad dug around in his back pocket and took out the copy to show the man. "Maybe now you can figure out why I don't know what he looks like today."

The man bit his cheek. "Fucking hell, that's what he used to look like? How old is that photo?"

Assad sent up silent thanks to the almighty. So the man did know something. "This is from about 2007, so it's nearly fifteen years old. And you do know who he is."

He nodded.

"Do you know where he is now? He doesn't live on this street anymore, does he?"

The man glanced across the street and pointed at number 5, one of the newer blocks, which according to Gordon was owned by a popular apartment rental agency. Niels B Sørensen's name had certainly not appeared on the intercom.

"He lived right there at number 5, but that was a while ago. And he certainly isn't called Niels B Sørensen anymore."

The man put down his shopping bag outside his front door and motioned for Assad to follow him.

As they walked around the carpark, Assad heard a few croaky voices trying to drown one another out at the far end.

"Talk to that lot over there. If you've got money on you, wave that around instead of your plastic card. It won't get you very far with them."

He vanished back around the corner before Assad could ask what Niels B had changed his name to.

Four seedy-looking guys, all of whom had seen better days—a very long time ago—glared at him immediately with red-rimmed eyes as he wound his way toward them through the cars.

"Oy, you! This is a private area, this is. Why don't you fuck off back where you came from?" snorted the largest of them, while the rest broke into scornful laughter and jeers.

Down-and-outs of a certain age tended to arrange themselves in a hierarchy: the person who had pissed himself the least and still had a bit
of welfare money to spend was top dog, whereas the one at the bottom
of the heap just lurked in the background.

It was this man, the weakest, whom Assad made a beeline for.

"You don't recognize this man, do you?" he asked, sticking the photo
of a fifteen-years-younger Niels B Sørensen directly into the skeletal little
man's line of sight.

The top dog, unable to countenance such a subversion of rank, barged
forward and tore the photo out of Assad's hands. For a moment he stared
at it, then a rumbling began to well up from the depths of his ailing
lungs.

"Haha," he laughed, coughing loose chunks of ancient tar, "take a
look at this, that's Niels."

The others huddled around, nodding, each trying to outdo the other
with the vehemence of their expletives.

"Jesus," said the guy with the highest number of tattered jackets
worn one on top of another in the damp, chilly air. "Niels didn't look too
good back then either."

Assad reached into his pockets. "Listen! I'll give you a few bottles of
wine if you help me find him."

"What wine are you talking about?" asked the top dog without hesitation. "We never touch a drop on Mondays."

The whole group burst into raucous, sound-barrier-breaking laughter.
Assad could see these were the things that kept them together.

"What can you get for three hundred kroner?" Assad replied.

They stared incredulously at the two notes. *The whole shop* was written all over their faces.

"What do you want with him?" asked one of the others. Perhaps he
was the one who knew Niels B Sørensen best.

"I just want to give him a nice surprise. Is he okay?" Again, Assad
replied in a tone of voice that confused them.

"What the hell does 'okay' mean, mister?" sniveled one of the underdogs. "Do you think homeless people just stand around in the cold for fun? You think we're okay, do you?"

Assad looked down at the ground and shook his head. "Is Niels homeless too, then?"

They exchanged a look. This was the moment when they might either clam up completely or start talking the hind legs off a donkey.

Assad raised his eyes. "Look, as I'm sure you've realized, it's been a long time since we were last in touch. I just wanted to see him again, so please, don't tell me it's too late."

"Then shut your trap," said the top dog. "You lead the way, Bubba. But check first and make sure Niels isn't high as a kite."

They stopped outside two green garage doors not far away, and Assad's guide grabbed him and pushed one of the doors ajar.

"Are you in, Niels?" he yelled into the dark room.

"Yeah" came a dry response.

The guy beckoned Assad in after him, and he found himself face-to-face with the man who had once looked like the person in his photocopy.

"Hi, Niels, good to see you. I've been looking for you."

If it wasn't for the stench of a chemical toilet in the corner of the garage, the humble, ill-lit space could just about be mistaken for a home. There were a couple of worn chairs and a matching sofa draped in a jumble of quilts, surrounded by some wooden crates littered with empty bottles of booze and dried scraps of food, while all manner of discarded junk, from torn posters to shiny sheets of copper, had been put up on the walls. The man was sourcing his electricity from an improvised plug in the ceiling. It powered the single spiral hob in his makeshift kitchen, where a large container of water drained via a tube into a tub, evidently providing him with the means to cook hot meals.

"Reminds me of a place I once lived in the Middle East, Niels," said Assad after a few initial pleasantries.

"This is my castle," said the man, straightening his back. "As befits my name, I call it the Palais Bourbon." He pointed at a coat of arms, which depicted a royal crown and an ermine-trimmed cloak adorned with a sword-wielding dragon. It hung on the far wall, surrounded by small diplomas and other evidence of the nobility he had bought for himself. Nothing less would do.

Stepping closer, Assad realized the man was now calling himself Niels B Marquis de Bourbon, of all things.

That must have been expensive, thought Assad, *but I guess he's finally who he always wanted to be*. He tried to look impressed.

"I'm sorry, I didn't realize you came from such a noble lineage. How should I address you? I should have brought a bottle of champagne for the occasion," he said.

The man tried to hold his head up high, but it looked wrong. "Give me some dope instead. I'm not an addict, you understand, but still."

"All right, but first you tell me who reported you for the murder of those two mechanics in Sorø," he asked, holding up some cash.

The man snatched it like a chameleon catching a fly. "You can just call me Niels in here, otherwise it's 'Your Excellency.' And if I knew who and why, I wouldn't be here."

"Who are you afraid of? Has anybody threatened you?"

"I'm not afraid, just cautious. I bought drugs off Nick and Jake. The mechanics. At first the police thought I'd killed them, because that's what the anonymous tip said, but I couldn't have. The police figured that out, and then they thought I knew who'd done it, but I didn't know."

"Cautious, you said. Why so?"

"When they let me go and I got home, I found a couple of long nails in my bed. So I kept myself to myself for a long time after that."

"Was it a warning? Did you know anything that might be dangerous? Is that why you're living here now?" Assad waved another note. He'd better get an answer this time, because that was his last one.

"Maybe, I'm not sure. But somebody was looking for something valuable, and I think they suspected I had it."

"They?"

"That Dutch-Danish guy who used to hang out at the workshop every once in a while."

"Who?"

"His name was Rasmus. That's all I know."

"Was he selling drugs to the mechanics?"

"He was selling something, that's for sure, because there were always more drugs around after he'd stopped by."

13

MALTHE / CARL

Monday, December 28, 2020

The second Malthe lay down on the bed, his thoughts began to race. In the darkness, images from his former life appeared before his mind's eye, and all the good times felt clear and safe. Memories of a time when he and his little brother had been close. Happy. Memories from before his father died, before his little brother got sick and Malthe had gone to prison for the first time. All those things had chipped away at his family, broken it down. And although Malthe tried his best to shape another reality out of the dream, one where everybody was still happy and together, he had to open his eyes for only a moment and see the bare white walls and the locked cell door for reality to come flooding back. The muted noises from the corridor outside weren't his brother's footsteps. The faint voices weren't someone asking him to play. They were anything but.

It must have been almost midnight when Malthe heard the key being put into the cell door and turned.

Guess it's my turn now. Let them come, he thought, drawing himself up to his full height. He could always yell and hope someone would come and help him before it was too late.

Feet apart, he assumed a solid stance with the duvet wrapped around his left arm, ready to parry an attack with a knife. And there he stood for several minutes, until he realized the door was in fact already open.

Only a millimeter, not even letting in a strip of light, but in Malthe's world, a millimeter might mean everything.

He crept warily forward and gave the door a slight tug so that he could look through the crack. Nothing moving in the corridor. A few muffled snores from the other cells, like always, but otherwise the place was silent.

Malthe's mind began to whirl. What were they up to? And who were "they"? Was it the prison guard he'd confided in who'd opened his cell door? Or one of his colleagues? And why? Did he know too much? He probably did. Should he be bracing for an attack?

The latter sounded like a reasonable enough conclusion to draw, so he pushed the door back to its original position and assumed the same stance he had before.

More time passed, and eventually Malthe's patience thinned. He had just sat back down on the bed when a new sound reached his ears. Again he leaped into a defensive stance, standing there for a moment until he realized what was going on. He wasn't the target at all—it was the policeman in cell 437.

They didn't pass on my message to management, he thought. *Somebody wants me to get involved. Bet I'm supposed to make an idiot of myself and die with the policeman so they can pin the blame on me. They'll say they overpowered me and neutralized me, but it was too late for him.*

Malthe flashed a grin. He'd never been able to work out something that complicated before, but the sounds he could hear now were very telling. Creeping steps, whispered voices. Men preparing for something.

When the click from cell 437 reached his ears, he was still deliberating. Should he intervene or not? What did he stand to gain?

• • •

Carl opened his eyes at the very moment of the click, when the attack was already a reality.

All his pleas had been ignored. He'd not been moved into protective custody, and the impending consequences were certain to be brutal.

If you're scared, Carl, then you're not thinking clearly. And if you're not scared, your body won't be ready. The thought flitted across his mind as he flung himself toward the door like last time. But the men outside were ready for it now, and they hurled themselves against the door so fiercely that Carl couldn't keep it closed.

Carl knew intuitively that he couldn't reach the alarm or take his attackers by surprise, so he had to kick and punch a path through the doorway to get out. Once he was in the corridor, he could shout, maybe try to get away from his assailants.

But Carl wasn't going anywhere. There were far too many legs and hands hitting and shoving at him, until he lost his balance and his shoulder came down so hard on the floor of his cell that the pain momentarily paralyzed him.

Staring up at his attackers, he recognized one of them from the cluster of haggard, ugly faces that had glowered down at him from the railing on the floor above earlier in the day. The others seemed equally determined to get it over with in a hurry, stamping repeatedly on Carl's chest and stomach. One of them smashed his shoe into Carl's larynx, and a whistling burst of pain escaped his throat.

They picked him up resolutely, four or five men, and although he kicked out in all directions, they forced him backward to the cell window and put a noose around his neck.

"You got sick of all the accusations against you, Mørck, and you were man enough to end it all—that's how this is going to look," said one of them as they lifted him up and tied the end of the rope around the handle of the closed shutter.

Two of them grabbed Carl's wrists, twisting them back so he couldn't use his arms, while two others pulled as hard as they could on his legs.

Very slowly, Carl felt the noose tighten and dig into his throat. He opened his eyes wide, limbs thrashing, staring straight into the face of the man giving the others their instructions.

Executioner, he thought. And as he felt the oxygen dwindle and the fog descend upon his brain, he said goodbye to the world, to Mona and his beloved child.

His vision was beginning to go dark when he registered bellows and pandemonium by the cell door, then the bang as it was hurled open. He noticed too that one of the attackers had loosened his grip on his right arm and that the men pulling on his legs had stopped.

Instinctively he raised his free arm to the handle and pulled himself upward, bracing his legs against the floor so that the rope slackened around his neck. His temples throbbed, but a tiny jet of oxygen made it through his nostrils, and he managed to loosen the knot a fraction.

The bedlam in the room was spreading, and the other man now let go of his left arm and began thumping him hard in the stomach, making his knees buckle again, although his fingers were still under the rope.

Carl kicked out at his attacker several times until he finally connected, planting a hard instep kick between the man's legs. The prisoner doubled over with a deep groan.

Now, at last, Carl wrestled himself out of the noose, and for a second he stood there gasping as the fight before him came into focus.

The heavyset young man Carl had noticed by the food trolley was hurling punches at his assailants without pause or hesitation. Three were already on the floor, apparently unable to get back up on their own, and the yowling from all five of them was in stark contrast to the giant's utter silence as he kicked and hammered at the two still on their feet.

It wasn't until all five were on the ground that they heard the running footsteps of the guards.

14

EDDIE

Monday, December 28–Tuesday, December 29, 2020

Eddie and Femke made love like wild things that night. Afterward, as they lay entwined in each other's arms, exhausted and satisfied, Eddie felt certain she was infected with COVID as well, sure as the devil lived in hell. Oddly enough, he felt no shame at playing such a mean trick. He, Femke, and their little one were all healthy enough, he hoped, to withstand the virus, even if they got seriously ill, and at least now he had his alibi for getting them all somewhere isolated. The question was simply whether they could wait until he got the good news from Denmark that Carl Mørck had been killed.

But then, in the middle of the night, the call came in. Disaster had become reality.

Yet again, the attack on Mørck had failed. Not only was the man still alive, but all five of his attackers had been incapacitated and were now facing interrogations and additional years added to their sentences. If Eddie had screwed up before, he'd done so royally now. And as if that wasn't bad enough, it was the man Eddie had initially hired to kill Mørck who had saved him.

They'll be coming after us now, he thought, gazing in despair at his unwitting, sleeping wife.

He waited a few hours, then pretended to cough weakly, half waking Femke.

"I'm sorry, Femke," he said, showing her the used tests. "You were wonderful last night, but I shouldn't have risked giving it to you."

"Giving me what?" she asked drowsily.

"I'm positive for COVID. I've probably been contagious for a couple of days. I took these two tests earlier, and the lines on them are pretty unambiguous."

"Oh no, Eddie. What should we do?"

He coughed again a few times, trying to make it sound like he was bringing up phlegm. "I've been thinking about it for the last hour, Femke. We need to isolate. We can't risk you and bubs passing on the infection at work and nursery. I thought maybe we could make a little holiday out of it while we recover."

She sighed. "The summer cabin gets pretty cold this time of year, Eddie."

"I know that. That's why I booked this."

He showed her the picture of the apartment he'd found in Valkenburg. They could drive down there in just a few hours.

15

MONA / ROSE

Tuesday, December 29, 2020

"**I've seen it,** Mona, I know it looks bad. Please, just take it away." Jacobsen waved off Mona's outstretched hands, which were holding out a photograph of Carl's neck taken by the doctor at Vestre Prison. The deep, fiery-red abrasions around her husband's neck spoke volumes, testifying to how close Jacobsen's best detective had come to losing his life. "He'll be transferred to Slagelse in half an hour. I hope you're happy," Jacobsen said.

It was so pathetic. He couldn't even bring himself to say Carl's name. If Mona had ever felt any affection toward the legendary chief of homicide, she realized now that even the most positive emotions could have an expiration date.

"Damn right, Marcus, and so will the inmate who risked his life to save Carl, yes? If it hadn't been for him, think about the position you'd be in right now. You didn't even lift a finger to keep Carl safe."

He held up his hand to ward off another attack. "Listen, Mona. The five men who attacked him have all been brought into the station, so we'll interrogate them thoroughly and get them processed back into the legal system ASAP. I promise you they're going to pay for this—they'll all get more years added to their sentences for attempted murder. At least six each."

She eyed him, thin-lipped. "We've all seen the way you dismissed the very significant risks Carl has been exposed to over the last few days. He should have been put in protective custody the minute he set foot through those doors. You're just lucky you aren't complicit in his death. But tell me, how do you intend to protect Carl in Slagelse?"

"At Slagelse he can be put in protective custody any time he requests it. It's just about the cushiest place in Denmark to keep someone on remand."

"This is twice in the span of barely a day or two that someone has tried to liquidate Carl." Mona paused for a moment. What a terrible word, "liquidate." When she thought about it, it was hard to hold back the tears, but she had to. Somebody had to keep a clear head, and once Mona gave in to her emotions, it usually ended badly.

"Look, it's been a while since Carl was in combat training, and he's not a young man anymore. Nor are you. How long do you think *you* could hold out under pressure like that, Marcus?" She got to her feet. "All you have to do is pick up the phone and request that Correctional Services move that young man, Malthe, to Slagelse with Carl. Tell them that from this point on they need to be particularly mindful of Carl's safety, especially given that the whole country is now aware he's been arrested. Am I getting through?"

All day long, Mona felt shaken. It wasn't just Marcus's betrayal or the gravity of Carl's situation, and it wasn't just that his former colleagues had turned their backs on him or that his friends at Department Q had been forbidden from touching Carl's case. She was shaken by the Danish people and their deafening lack of support.

There hadn't been a single social media post in support of her husband. All the posts, news bulletins, and status updates on Instagram, Facebook, and Twitter had been deluged with hateful comments from users, and although the charges against Carl had not been made public, people seemed quite happy to cast aspersions without a single shred of proof, accusing him of everything from misconduct, corruption, violence, and untrustworthiness to police brutality, while commenting on his supposedly "dubious" and "ruthless" pursuit of a higher clear-up rate. Nobody was talking about the complexity of his investigations or how killers had been thwarted and labyrinthine mysteries untangled. Overnight, Carl Mørck had become a synonym for duplicity, for sheer evil itself, and she couldn't let that stand. She had to make sure her husband got credit for everything he'd done, and she had to see to it that people didn't jump to conclusions about him—that, gradually, they might even be brought over to his side.

Gordon wasn't alone in the office when she went in, still seething with rage. She nodded curtly at a new detective who sat a few feet away from Gordon, staring at Mona as though she were releasing toxins into his own personal atmosphere.

"Where is Rose, Gordon?" she asked.

Gordon's eyes wavered. "Uhh, she's . . . We've got this case up in . . . ! She might be in a bit later today, I'm not sure."

Then he poked four outstretched fingers cautiously above the edge of the desk.

She nodded. He didn't need to say anything else.

After four o'clock she'd try again.

• • •

All the windows of the apartment were dark, so maybe Jess Larsen, the owner of the car that had been used to run down Carl's first lawyer, wasn't in. Rose was standing motionless for a second or two outside the block when a janitor came hurtling around the corner on his electric sweeper like he was preparing the footpath for a time trial at Formula 1.

"You don't know if Jess Larsen's home, do you? I called his work and rang the bell, but nobody's answering."

"Oh yes, he's home. I spoke to him an hour ago when he got back from the supermarket," the janitor said as the machine idled. "You can't judge by the windows; it's always dark in there. Jess is home now—you can see him, actually, right there."

He pointed up at the story high above them, where Rose glimpsed a figure moving behind the glass.

"He said someone stole his car. Apparently a man was run over. Nasty story."

Then he tugged at a handle and continued his rumbling pursuit of a snowflake or two.

Rose had to ring the bell three times before he opened the door, and the look he gave her was almost as dark as the apartment. He was obviously still very much affected by what had happened on Sunday.

"Why are you home during working hours on a Tuesday?" she asked, after she'd introduced herself and been shown into the living room.

He frowned. "Maybe you police officers don't take Christmas holidays, but at my company we do. Anyway, it's not exactly easy getting to work when forensics haven't finished with my car. How long can it take?"

"Why don't you drive the company car? I can see there's a Mercedes registered to the company you work for. DKNL Transport."

He nodded.

"You drove your boss to Vestre Cemetery on Sunday—why was that?"

"As you can probably see, the company car is out of commission at the moment. My boss lost his driver's license six months ago. Personal reasons, you know. So I'm driving him."

"Yes, so I read. There were traces of drugs in his blood, and not for the first time."

He looked surprised. "Then why aren't you talking to him? What do you want with me? I've given a statement to the police. I was driving him because he wanted to put flowers on his wife's grave."

"Yes, I read that his name is Hannes Theis and he'd been having trouble with substance abuse since his wife's death. Isn't that right? I can also see he runs an import-export company. But what do you import and export? It's not immediately apparent. I phoned the company number, but nobody picked up."

Jess shrugged. Evidently he was in no hurry to offer up that information.

"But, Jess, I can find all that stuff out if you don't want to tell me," she went on, sitting down uninvited on a sofa that took up half the living room. "It can't be something that requires a lot of manpower, because you're the only employee, aren't you?"

"We work with forwarding agencies that transport goods directly from the suppliers to the purchasers. Most of what we do is paperwork."

"Maybe you can give me a list of your forwarding agents?"

"That's up to Hannes. I just work there. Are we under suspicion of something? I thought this was just about my car being stolen."

· · ·

Rose, Assad, and Mona arrived at the Investigation Unit in Sydhavnen a few minutes apart, and Gordon's keyboard was practically glowing as he tried to input all their statements into the system. Clearly it had been a day that opened more doors than it closed.

"Would you mind recapping the basic facts, please, Gordon," Rose said.

He flushed slightly and cleared his throat. "All right, well, Assad met Niels B . . ." He glanced at his screen. "Niels B Marquis de Bourbon, formerly just Sørensen." He suppressed a laugh. "And if we believe him, the two executed car mechanics had a regular supplier, a Danish-Dutchman by the name of Rasmus, who Assad believes could be one Rasmus Bruhn. I've certainly got good reason to remember him. For the time being, though, until we can investigate further, let's just call that a fact."

"To me that's better than a fact, it's *facts*!" said Assad, scratching his beard.

Gordon looked bewildered. Then he turned to Rose. "And Rose has spoken to Jess Larsen, owner of the vehicle that knocked down Carl's first defense lawyer, Adam Bang. There are several points of interest that emerged from that conversation. The company Larsen works for is an import-export company that has no physical warehouses. There are only two permanent employees, and one of them is the owner, Hannes Theis, who we're currently unable to locate. He has been given two suspended sentences three years apart for driving while under the influence of drugs, and he is also of Dutch descent, which is interesting. Moreover, Rose found it odd that he suddenly asked Jess Larsen to drive him to his wife's grave on a day that, according to my research, isn't the anniversary of her death, or her birthday, or their wedding anniversary. The date seems random—unless the intention was always that Jess Larsen's car would be involved in the murder of Carl's lawyer. That last bit is me speculating."

"Anything is possible," interjected Mona.

"Yes, and you, Mona, have spoken to Marcus—and it doesn't seem like you feel well disposed toward him," Rose went on.

"I think it's safe to say that, yes. If I could have throttled him and gotten away with it, I would have done it on the spot."

Only Gordon laughed. "I know, Mona, but still—Carl has been transferred to Slagelse today with that Malthe kid who helped him during the attack, so something's been done after all. And then you paid a visit to that tabloid, didn't you? What should I write about that?"

The newsroom had been a hive of activity when Mona arrived, but the minute she stepped through the door, it went deathly quiet. Photographers fumbled for their cameras, journalists drew close to their screens so she couldn't see what was on them as she walked past, and at the back of the room stood Carl's archenemy, Pelle Hyttested, scowling at her like someone being dragged very deservedly to the scaffold.

They locked eyes without warmth as she strode past him, heading for the office of the editor in chief.

Torben Victor, the head honcho at *Gossip*, to use the phrase generally applied to him in conversation, had always been the kind of stupid bastard the industry both envied and loathed. He had an unerring eye for a sordid story, and the number of copies sold during his tenure was approaching several of the major dailies' combined circulation. If that meant flouting the occasional injunction, especially when it involved the police—well, that was just part and parcel of the job.

Torben Victor, like many of the journalists on the editorial staff, was utterly indifferent to the Press Council's decisions and criticism, and to the daily stream of fines he was gradually accumulating. But the editor in chief also had a practical side: he was perfectly willing to scrap an existing story if one that had more legs appeared to take its place.

"We both know what you're working on here, Victor," Mona said without preamble.

The oaf gave a bow and thanked her. This was not a man afraid of hurting people's feelings.

"And it's a rotten story that will end up coming back to bite you in your wrinkly arse, let me tell you."

"Indeed. We make a living from the social rot—your analysis is entirely correct. You're Carl Mørck's wife, if I'm not mistaken?"

"And the person you're spitting on right now is an innocent man. Perhaps you couldn't care less about that, but if you pursue this, you'll end up laughingstocks. I'm offering you a different story, one with a bit more meat on its bones, and I can promise you even higher sales."

He smiled the kind of skeptical smile that revealed a certain curiosity. "That all sounds very promising, but promises like those tend to be empty, especially when they're coming from a close relative of the person who's made an unmitigated arse of himself."

Mona kept her middle finger in check, holding up her forefinger instead. "I can give you a story with enough spin-offs to fill more editions of this magazine than in your wildest dreams, Mr. Victor."

He didn't raise so much as an eyebrow. But Mona was used to dealing with men whose buttons had to be pressed just right, and this guy was practically begging for it.

"For one thing, I can tell you what Carl has been wrongly accused of. I can also point you in the direction of who might be interested in hanging him out to dry. On top of that, I can give you all the gory details of the major case the chief of homicide just outlined at the press conference. He deliberately neglected to mention, by the way, that it was solved by Carl and his team, despite the fact that Carl was being hunted by every police officer in the country for most of December and Christmas. Because Carl is a detective who prioritizes his job above himself. It's probably one of the juiciest murder mysteries a smutty little rag like yours could ever hope to come across. Once in a lifetime. Do you understand me, editor in chief Torben Victor, or do you need me to repeat it for you?"

He stuck out his bottom lip and shook his head slightly. "Sounds thrilling," he said. "And what will it cost me?"

"You'll need to do a complete one-eighty on your current editorial line. You need to take Carl's side. Put Hyttested on a leash, and if he continues his crusade, pack him off to Greenland to report on sled dog attacks and the icecaps slowly melting, okay?!"

Victor stood up, shut the door to the newsroom, then leaned back in his chair. "You'll have to give me something very concrete to go on before I agree to this."

Mona looked around at the most loyal supporters Carl could ever expect to have.

"So did you reach an agreement?" Gordon asked, as though they were nearly at the end of an exciting podcast.

Mona nodded. "I was in there for hours. They'll stop the smear campaign against Carl in return for access to his case and the specifics of all the Sisle Park killings. In tonight's online edition of *Gossip*, they'll be revealing everything Carl has been through in the last twenty-four hours."

Rose frowned. "Are you completely sure this is wise, Mona? It's going to start a media feeding frenzy. There'll be journalists hounding you day and night to get an exclusive like the one *Gossip* is getting."

"Well, I think if anybody is going to bear the brunt of that, if it happens, then it should be me."

"They'll go after us too, Mona," added Gordon. "And we're not allowed to say anything."

"Exactly. You're not allowed to, so that gives you a free pass. Whether the same goes for Jacobsen is another matter. *Gossip* will be releasing a list of the charges against Carl tomorrow, and there'll also be a teaser for the print edition coming out on Thursday, which will publish the first part of the Sisle Park case—the stuff about the salt and the repair shop in Sydhavnen. Then they'll follow up with the subsequent murders in future issues, so you'll be kept pretty busy feeding them, Gordon. You'll have to make a start this afternoon, actually, so you can give them the facts about the woman who recently committed suicide and who lost her baby when the repair shop was blown up. They'll be making it clear from the very first article that it was well-known businesswoman Sisle Park who was responsible for the brutal murders. Plus *Gossip* will get all the information on the victims; the methods used in the killings; Sisle Park's team of deranged, vengeful women; and the way you and Carl all fought tirelessly to solve the case, despite the fact that Jacobsen's officers were hunting Carl. Which didn't stop him, of course. We can't let people forget that Carl handed himself in."

A lump appeared in Mona's throat. If she could just get the message out, maybe people might see Carl in the right light. She sincerely hoped so. She gazed at the others apologetically, but there was no doubt they knew what she was going through.

"And *Gossip* will be getting that material for as long as Carl is in custody," she went on. "At the same time, Carl will also have opportunities to report on his situation in jail, either through me or through his lawyer. And if you find anything relevant to his case during your investigation, they'll print that too."

In a heartbeat, the atmosphere in the room shifted. Gordon and Assad turned their faces to Rose, whose expression was suddenly grim. That last part might not be such a good idea.

Rose took Mona's hand. "For the most part, that's fine by me, and I think also by Assad and Gordon."

The two men nodded, thank god.

"Even though you can bet your life Jacobsen will be grilling us about how *Gossip* obtained such in-depth knowledge of the Sisle Park case."

She squeezed Mona's hand. "But this stuff about publishing the results of our investigation into Carl's current predicament—you can forget about that, Mona. If we reveal anything about what we're working on, we'll be suspended on the spot. We *have* to keep our hands off his case—you saw the guy in the office earlier today, spying on us. Both he and Marcus are capable of putting two and two together, Mona. So I'm sorry, but our names absolutely cannot be linked to the information you're passing on to *Gossip*. We're happy to let you know when we find something new, but only if we have your full discretion. Can you promise us that?"

16

CARL

Wednesday, December 30, 2020

It had been twenty-four hours since they'd transported both him and the big prisoner, Malthe, who had intervened during the attack and saved him, to Slagelse Remand Center.

Carl had tried to thank him in a voice that was still strained and hoarse during the fifty-five-mile journey from Vestre Prison in Copenhagen to the center in Slagelse. But Malthe had kept silent at the other end of the vehicle, and since then they'd been kept apart.

Slagelse Remand Center was located in the middle of the town, and from the outside it looked like anything but what it actually was. A gorgeous redbrick building dating from the latter years of the First World War, it had elegant sash windows and an imposing judges' chamber on the first floor, which had been abandoned for some time and simply left as it was. From the outside, it was easy to assume the center was a harmless, almost pleasant place to stay, but once you'd driven through the gate to the right of the building, you realized it was no bed of roses. There was only space for thirty inmates, and now Carl and Malthe had joined them.

Carl had been there many times before on police business and had always gotten on well with the day-to-day management and other staff. They were a friendly lot, and from Carl's perspective they seemed to live an entirely normal civilian existence, far away from the pressures and

bustle that Copenhagen and its surrounding areas often imposed on people. Ordinary, decent men and women, easy for visitors to talk to, who
operated on the principle that flexibility and a positive tone were the
best approach to the inmates.

So both he and the officers doing the intake were equally baffled as
to how to tackle the unusual situation. Carl Mørck was the reason why
dozens of inmates had arrived at Slagelse over the years, so he'd visited
regularly to conduct interrogations. Days when he'd mostly sat in the
guard room with the staff, exchanging bad jokes and eating soft pastries
with his coffee.

But this time there were no jokes, no chitchat over coffee. Only procedures and more procedures. The transport officer removed Carl's waist
restraint and cuffs and handed over the paperwork. They searched his
body, his clothes, and the few personal effects he'd brought with him as
thoroughly as they would for any other inmate and briefed him on what
he could expect and his daily tasks. The whole process didn't take long.
He and a prison guard then crossed into the main corridor, which was on
the ground floor, and he glanced briefly upward at the safety netting and
the stairs leading up to the other two stories, recognizing the mahogany
ceiling at the top, before he was led directly toward the gray door of cell
6, where there were towels, dishcloths, and bed linens laid out ready on
the blue bed.

"They requested that you be placed in voluntary isolation, but right
now we've got a couple of pedophiles who don't want to risk going into
gen pop. But you know what the difference is, don't you, Mørck? Your
cell will be kept locked, and we'll only unlock it if you ask us to. Anyway, we'd be sorry to stick you in a cell with a padlock hanging sym-
bolically on the door, like we do with some of the pedos, don't you agree?"

Carl nodded, taking in the tray on the narrow desk, the steel cutlery
on ordinary plates, a mug, a sponge, toothpaste, and a fresh toothbrush
in a plastic bag. Names were written in pencil on the wall, and unlike at
Vestre the messages were relatively harmless. *Fuck the guy who drew our
prophet*, read one of them. *Fuck the police*, read another, which in his situation was a little more concerning. The shelf above the desk was empty,

and the window was so high up that he could only see the treetops, the tower at the fire station, and the sky beyond the netting and bars. The double-glazed windows were opened inward, airing out any odors that may have been left behind by the previous inmate, and below them a little flat-screen was mounted crookedly on the wall. Despite the relatively limited programs on offer, television would probably be his most reliable source of comfort in the months that lay ahead.

The fridge was empty and lukewarm, and in his doorless wardrobe was a coat hanger and a large swastika drawn on the back wall. There was also a noticeboard with a printed calendar, so that inmates could mark off the hopelessly long processions of days in 2021 with small, perfunctory crosses.

Next to the calendar were the words "Tony from Ringsted is a son of a bitch" and other feebleminded scrawls that Carl had no intention of supplementing. Maybe at some point he could persuade the staff to give him a brush and a bucket of paint, which he would pay for himself, and he'd soon have it all painted over. After all, as things stood, he was going to be in here a while.

At one o'clock he was led into the visitors' room, where a man from the PCA he hadn't seen before was waiting.

It was a bright and colorful space, with walls covered in childish imagery—hot-air balloons, the back end of an elephant, a bear, and so on. The children's chairs and table were decorated too, and if he ever had to wait, he could always flip through a picture book or "boil potatoes" on the tiny pretend stove.

Carl sighed. Next time, Mona would be bringing Lucia, and it was a good thing the visit was happening here. She would get a small woolly teddy bear to take home as well, but still—his heart ached. How was he going to live with seeing his daughter so rarely?

"The charges against you include the murder of the individual found dismembered in a crate under Georg Madsen's shed in Amager," said the man from the PCA, after introducing himself. "However, we have discovered that the body in the crate and the items found with it may have been intended to throw us off. It's possible the man's death was tangential. We are now convinced that the photograph also found in the crate with the corpse, in which you, Anker Høyer, and the murdered man are standing side by side, has been faked. A good one, mind you, but we've established that it was composed from two different photos in which the pixels were of a similar size. We also believe that the coins on which we found your fingerprints and Høyer's were falsified for this specific purpose. They were clearly eager to package them so that the fingerprints would remain identifiable, and that in itself is quite striking."

Carl took a breath deep into his lungs. He'd assumed as much all along, but it was still a relief to hear it. He'd been about to insist on his lawyer being present, as was his right, but after that bit of good news, he didn't actually care.

"We don't know where the prints came from, but they're remarkably clear, and Senior Detective Laust Smedegaard believes they may have been pulled from something made of glass, possibly a bottle or something similar, where the prints tend to be sharp, before being transferred to the coins."

He finished the sentence by looking down at his paperwork, and Carl breathed a sigh of relief. A relief that momentarily pushed out all gloomy thoughts, until the man looked up again.

"We haven't gotten to the same stage in our investigation of the other charges, which naturally must be taken seriously, so the remaining points still stand."

Carl lowered his head. How long was this going to take?

"You may not realize this, but unfortunately the gutter press has started to meddle. They've been poking around in your case. You don't have many friends in the judicial system right now, or at the PCA. If you'd like to proceed, I'm ready to interview you."

An hour and a half later, the man was ready to go back to his office in Aarhus.

Poor guy, driving that far in this weather, Carl thought.

All the other charges remained in effect, he'd said. Accomplice to murder, trafficking in hard drugs, tax evasion, and official misconduct of the worst sort. The prosecution wasn't pulling any punches. But now, for the first time, Carl felt reassured that the case would take its natural course: as long as the PCA were leading the investigation, any sort of bias was out of the question, he was sure of that. They would leave no stone unturned, and until they found hard evidence to the contrary, they would pursue his case in parallel with any other potential accomplices of Anker Høyer, taking an impartial view of the charges alleged by the senior legal counsel at Violent Crimes.

In their world, thank god, Carl was entirely innocent until proven guilty, and no matter how small or how far-reaching the case, they would find the resources to get to the bottom of it.

We're lucky in Denmark to have neutral investigators who step in when police officers are accused of criminal activity, he thought.

"I'd like to speak to my lawyer in the video room—can that be arranged?" he asked a little later, addressing the corrections officer escorting him to the toilet.

"Of course," said the guard. "There are time slots available tomorrow around one o'clock."

Carl frowned. That was nearly twenty-four hours away. "I heard there have been some articles written about my case. Do you know anything about that?"

The guard shook his head. "I'm sorry, but talk to your lawyer" was his only response.

17

MALTHE

Wednesday, December 30, 2020

There were one or two officers on staff at the remand center grumbling under their breath that Vestre had sent them yet another detainee—they were running short on space as it was. And if it hadn't been for Correctional Services' decision that this Malthe lad was currently a kind of designated bodyguard for Denmark's highest-profile prisoner, they would have immediately bounced him to another remand center.

Now they were telling him that if they'd had two free cells next to each other, Malthe would have been put next to Carl on the ground floor in cell 7, but for the time being, he was getting the cell directly above Carl's. If they both opened their windows, they could communicate that way.

Malthe was pleased. It might create some kind of solidarity and trust between them, although Malthe was pretty sure Carl Mørck already thought the best of him. It had seemed that way, at least, from what he'd said during the transfer to Slagelse.

But then, that morning, he'd been given the awful news that his brother's condition had worsened and that Malthe shouldn't expect him to live much more than a month or two. If this German thing was going to work out, it had to happen fast. There were suggestions that a specific and incredibly expensive operation and course of treatment might buy him some more time, but even that wasn't certain, he'd been told. And it wasn't offered in Denmark.

The whole way to the remand center, Malthe could think of nothing else. His little brother, Hansi, was the sweetest, most loving person he had ever known. He was also the only person who never failed to leap to Malthe's defense.

"It's not Malthe's fault. It's the rest of them, they provoked him," Hansi had always said. And when Malthe was in court, Hansi had sat in the public gallery, smiling at him as he was led in and out. In the last six months, however, Malthe hadn't seen Hansi even once, because the disease exhausted him, and it upset Malthe that he couldn't be there for his brother.

When he and Mørck were seated close to each other during transportation, Malthe had turned away from him. He didn't want to let Mørck see him getting emotional, and anyway, it would be wrong. Mørck was now Hansi's only chance of survival, which meant Malthe would still have to kill him the first opportunity he got. *Keep your distance and watch out for your emotions*, his mother had always drilled into him.

You don't pet the pig that's on its way to slaughter, she used to say. But Hansi had pet it anyway, and not just that. He comforted it right up until the moment its throat was slit and it stopped howling. There was no way Malthe could do that, absolutely no way, so he didn't meet Carl's eyes all morning, not even once.

The question now was how to communicate with the people who were going to pay him for the murder. He'd spent a few months at Slagelse a year or two ago, but he had never been close with any of the staff, and he highly doubted he could persuade them to pass messages to CO Peter Loudmouth at Vestre Prison. If he only knew the man's real name, he might have stood a chance. He could have asked, for instance, if someone would call Loudmouth and thank him for his help with the transfer to Slagelse, and say that he was also pleased to find that he and Carl Mørck would be seeing each other regularly, and on the same terms. Loudmouth would understand and would be able to pass on that information to his paymasters.

Malthe glanced around his cell, then he lowered himself to the floor, where there was space for his sizable bulk, and did his usual two hundred push-ups with both arms, then fifty quick one-armed ones. When Malthe got to the point when his heavy body made his arms tremble with fatigue, he thought about all the people who had wronged him, and it gave him the energy to do another set.

Afterward he lay down on the bed and exhaled, staring up at the ceiling.

He had to wait before killing Mørck, until Loudmouth had received the message and given him the go-ahead. Whether it was a million kroner or only the five hundred thousand he had originally been offered, Malthe didn't care, as long as he was assured the money would be paid into his brother's bank account, and soon.

Once that was settled, he would grab Mørck from behind and snap his neck before he could react. The story of the murder would spread like wildfire or ripples in a pond across the whole of Denmark in no time, he knew, and Malthe was ready to take the punishment without a murmur.

If he showed suitable remorse and could convince them that Mørck had tried to attack him, that it was self-defense, then hopefully he could avoid ending up somewhere they might never declare him fit for release. Still, even if it came to that, his ruined future would at least give his little brother the chance to get his life back.

"Sorry I didn't talk to you during the transfer, Mørck," he shouted down a couple of times when he'd opened the windows wide, but Carl didn't reply.

When he repeated it five minutes later, a voice came echoing from one of the other cells: "What the hell, arsehole, are you and the cop bunk-buddies or what? You'd better shut the fuck up, unless you're looking for a slap in the exercise yard."

Malthe frowned. It was only occurring to him now that everybody else could listen in.

"You just try it, you little shit," he yelled back.

The reaction was completely unexpected, and a chorus of guffaws and jeering rippled along the windows.

"Little shit, haha! You haven't seen who you're up against!" another voice yelled.

And there was another roar of laughter that rattled the windows of Slagelse Remand Center.

Malthe didn't reply.

He was going to have to earn some respect around here.

18

EDDIE

Wednesday, December 30, 2020

It had been a day and a half since Eddie exposed himself to infection, and he still couldn't feel anything. Maybe a slight dryness of the throat, maybe a faint tickle in the nose, but that could have been anything. It was probably just because the holiday apartment was freshly painted and still had some drying to do.

"It could be that we're in for a relatively easy ride," Femke suggested. "Maybe you're the only one infected. You've been working day and night lately, Eddie—you need to learn to take better care of yourself."

"I've put my phone on airplane mode, Femke, isn't that a step in the right direction?"

That wasn't strictly true. He had paid a month's rent off the books for the apartment in Valkenburg, and it was more than big enough for the three of them to have their space and do their own thing. Femke loved pottering around with their little daughter, so when Eddie wanted to communicate with the outside world, he fished his ancient prepaid phone out of the back of the toilet cistern and used that.

Now that the second assassination attempt on Mørck had failed, he had to make sure he couldn't be traced, so he was getting his information directly from his Danish contact. The contact told him that Mørck had been accompanied to the new prison by the man who'd saved him during the second attack, who—as Eddie reminded himself—was also the person they had originally hired to kill Mørck.

They were now sending a man to the remand center southwest of Copenhagen to find a solution that would satisfy the bosses in Holland. Maybe this time they would succeed. But since Eddie had failed to carry out his instructions, the Danish contact advised him not to put his head above the parapet until the whole thing was over, and maybe not even then.

As if Eddie didn't already know. Over the years he had shown great loyalty and willingness to serve, and in many ways he'd been a useful man to have on your side. At the same time, though, he knew a little too much about too many things, and foot soldiers were always expendable— he'd seen it happen time and time again. Notably to Rasmus Bruhn, who had overseen the direct transportation of narcotics from Holland to Denmark and the rest of Scandinavia.

Eddie shuddered at the thought of Rasmus Bruhn's fate, and he felt even worse when his man at Vestre told him that the guy known as the Jackhammer had come out of the prison hospital and almost immediately been unlucky enough to "fall" down the first-floor stairs, breaking his neck.

Was Eddie next?

He thought of his colleague Hans Rinus, who had been in charge of the investigation into the nail gun murders in Schiedam. He'd come perilously close to figuring out that Eddie might have had something to do with the whole thing. But he wasn't the brightest bulb, thank god, and hadn't kept it to himself. His death a short time later was met with deafening silence, because policemen choking to death on their own vomit after a drunken binge wasn't exactly something people shouted from the rooftops. After that, the case had been closed, which spoke volumes about how ruthless and tenacious his employers were. In a way, Eddie wasn't afraid for his own life—by now he was thoroughly sick of himself anyway—but he was afraid for his family. How could the bosses be sure he had managed to keep Femke ignorant of everything? That she was still unaware of where all the money suddenly in his possession had come from? They would almost certainly assume she must have figured out he hadn't come by it honestly. She was an intelligent woman, after all, and they were bound to be aware of that, the bastards.

But then why don't I turn myself in and face what's coming to me? Is now the time? We've had a few good years together, haven't we, since I joined those arseholes' payroll?

Eddie's stomach began to ache. What would happen to Femke and the little girl? Would everything they owned be confiscated? Would they end up poorer than before the whole thing began? And the humiliation, the scandal, the disappointment, the rage—how would she deal with that? Would she still have feelings for him once the truth came out?

He rested a hand on his belly and did breathing exercises as the discomfort eased, only to be replaced by nausea that brought him to the verge of throwing up.

Pull yourself together, Eddie, you're panicking. You're here now, and you'll stay here for as long as people infected with COVID are supposed to. And in the meantime you'll have to put together enough dirt on the bosses to save all our skins.

He opened a Word document and began to type. All of this was going up into the cloud. And when the time was right, he'd bring it crashing down.

19

MONA

Wednesday, December 30, 2020

Mona had not been in contact with Carl since his transfer to Slagelse Remand Center twenty-four hours earlier, which was worrying. She comforted herself, however, that he was with that giant man Malthe, and surely Malthe had demonstrated—by putting his own life on the line—that nobody was going to mess with Carl.

So she hoped he was safe. Last night's headlines on the *Gossip* website had set the cat among the pigeons, and there was now tremendous attention focused on Carl. On the one hand, there was a chance it would get the public on his side, but on the other, everybody who hated him now knew where he was located and how vulnerable he was.

And the headlines were coming thick and fast, constantly adjusted and updated online all morning.

"Denmark's Best Detective in Prison."

"Assault by Fellow Prisoners."

"On the Verge of Death."

"Mørck Denied Solitary—Disowned by Colleagues."

"Why Is Carl Mørck in Prison? The Case in Detail."

And, as Rose had already foreseen, it had unleashed tremendous pressure on Mona. Her phone had been ringing all night, to the point that

Lucia had been woken up and had started to cry, but Mona didn't dare switch it off. What if it was Slagelse calling?

Her phone had buzzed roughly twenty times in the early hours of that morning, journalists introducing themselves and their intentions, and every time she'd turned them down, saying that she had no comment at present, that they had to speak to the chief of homicide, who had been responsible for Carl's incarceration and transfer. But they were persistent.

Then the doorbell started ringing every five minutes, and when she didn't open up, they knocked and yelled they knew she was still in there. They were almost as bad as the British press, and when she drove Lucia to nursery, she had to squeeze her way through a wall of shouts and outstretched microphones, first outside her front door, then at the carpark, and then again on her way in and out of the nursery. Lucia was inconsolable and terrified, and it cut Mona to her core.

You're the one who poked the hornet's nest, she reminded herself, biting her tongue. This was simply a stage she had to get through.

Later that day she drove to the station in the city center, where she had sessions with two foreign inmates in the jail.

She had just twisted herself away from some reporters who had driven after her and leaped out of their cars to confront her, and was hurrying past the guard at the gate when they stopped her with a message: she was to go straight to the chief constable's office.

There she was met not only by the chief constable in full, imposing uniform, a hard glint in her eye, but by Marcus Jacobsen as well, obviously seething at the earful he must have just been given.

Please just let her be on Carl's side. Our side, Mona thought naïvely.

But the chief constable tilted her head—not a good sign. "I hope you both realize that I need to take a very serious view of the media storm we're in right now."

The chief constable fixed her bare eyes on them. Clearly she hadn't had the time nor the energy to apply her usual slick of mascara.

"Marcus denies having anything to do with the current press coverage," she went on, "and I've just been hauling him over the coals for not taking better care of Carl."

Mona almost burst into applause, but Jacobsen looked away. He very obviously didn't give a flying fuck about being told off. It was clear he'd never been more disappointed with a colleague in his life.

"So, Mona, I'm turning my attention on either you or the three detectives in Department Q. Clear? Now I'm going to ask you straight out: Did any or all of you give this information to the press?"

Mona looked at the chief constable with restrained calm. "Okay, you're asking me, but first, since you're both so upset that the case is spiraling out of control, you should be asking your chief of homicide why *he* doesn't come forward and explain things to the press."

She turned to Marcus Jacobsen, who looked older than ever. Perhaps he'd already been too old when he returned to the station. Perhaps this particular case was the straw that had broken the camel's back.

Mona held his flashing gaze. "You should be going out there and telling them everything about the Sisle Park case and Department Q's extraordinary police work, Marcus. And you should tell the public what's really going on with this case against Carl. If *you* don't do that, you'll both just have to deal with the media fallout."

"I'll consider that option, Mona," said the chief constable. "But you haven't answered my question."

Mona noticed that the polish on the chief constable's fingernails was chipped and that her unwashed hair was held precariously in place with various bobby pins. Clearly, she'd been in a rush this morning. She'd probably been sitting in her dressing gown scrolling through the news headlines when the gravity of the situation dawned on her.

"Who leaked those stories? Was it you four?" the chief constable continued.

Mona sat up straighter. "I'm outraged that you would even ask me that, actually. Think about the situation I'm in and how frightening this is for me and my family. Carl was very nearly killed as a result of police negligence, and now you're trying to lay all this at my door. Not to mention, I think you should remember that the detectives down in Department Q have more than enough on their plates right now dealing with all the cases Marcus's other officers have been unable to handle."

She gave the chief constable a terse nod and rose to her feet. "If you're going to be questioning everybody you suspect, then there are quite a number of journalists who—unlike myself and Carl's colleagues—were given the opportunity to attend the preliminary hearing when the charges were read out, so you'll be kept pretty busy asking them. You really don't think any of them sniffed out a few details, closed hearing or no closed hearing? Besides, think how many people at the PCA must be working on this case. Now, I'm certainly not suggesting we suspect them, but their activities will have been kept under pretty close scrutiny since the hearing, wouldn't you think? Then there are our own people here on the force—I'm sure one or two of them have had pretty sizable 'consultation fees' waved under their noses so that *Gossip* can get a leg up on the competition."

The chief constable's stubby eyelashes were practically dancing the fandango as she tried to get her head around all the possibilities. She had a carefully rehearsed way of sighing almost imperceptibly, and she used it now to full effect as she turned her shapely body toward the window.

"And as for Sisle Park," Mona carried on, "Department Q's activities during the investigation into several of those cases that ended disastrously—including the brutal murder of a woman on Amagerbrogade not long ago—weren't exactly discreet. The press is always working, and if you ask me, you should try to get a bit of credit for Department Q solving the Sisle Park cases. Let Carl's colleagues in Department Q release the information—if they can find the time, that is, given how complicated the cases are, after all."

She left them both in total silence, nodding briefly to the chief constable's secretaries as she strode out of the office.

She had no idea what the consequences would be, but hopefully she'd covered her back.

———————

She just had time to skim *Gossip*'s latest online article before she was escorted into a session with some bastard who'd killed his wife.

"Park Killed at Least Twenty," it read in huge letters, and the subheading—"Get all the details on serial killer Sisle Park," announced a line in the bottom corner—was no less thrilling. "Read the New Year's Eve issue of *Gossip* tomorrow for the latest on Department Q's investigation into the sadistic murders."

Marcus and the chief constable were in for a shock—as were all the journalists who hadn't gotten the scoop.

Mona pictured her commute home: it would be a gauntlet all the way to her front door.

20

GORDON / MONA

Wednesday, December 30–Thursday, December 31, 2020, New Year's Eve

On Wednesday at ten past four, the chief of homicide stood in the office of Department Q and looked around.

"Where's Petersen?" he said, referring to the man who'd been keeping an eye on what Gordon was up to.

"He leaves every day at four o'clock on the dot," Gordon replied.

Jacobsen frowned. Going forward, he'd have to put a stop to that.

"Hm. Well, he's supposed to be here when you are, to make sure you don't try to pull anything. Actually, you know what, I think all three of you should drop what you're doing. I'm sending you home over the New Year."

Jacobsen seemed unusually calm and cold, as though it were an instruction like any other, but underneath his black leather jacket, the adrenaline was pumping. It wasn't a suggestion, and it wasn't up for discussion—that much was clear.

Gordon was, as usual, the only one in the office, and he replied with the same superficial calm that unfortunately they were too busy at the moment to knock off work early. He offered no further justification but simply got to his feet—legs shaking underneath him—and went over to the whiteboard, where he began to write. It was total gibberish, of course, but he hoped it looked relatively plausible.

"QUESTIONS 12-30-2020!" he wrote, with his back to the chief of homicide.

"Witch's Tree! I'll take that myself!"

"Committed alone? I'll take that one too!"

"Enoksen, Witt, Dennis Larsen? Assad!"

Then he paused and thought for a moment before he continued:

"Hostages or accomplices? Rose to ask around at Vesterbro Square?"

Then he turned back to Jacobsen. "It would be nice to have a few days off, of course, we appreciate that, but as you can see, we've got a lot going on."

Jacobsen rubbed his forehead. Was he about to explode, or would he retreat into his office to brood over what had just happened?

"Enoksen, Witt, and Dennis Larsen, who are they?" he asked, brow furrowed.

Gordon looked at the board. Good thing he hadn't asked about the "Witch Tree." How the hell would he have explained that? Bloody stupid thing to make up.

"Oh yeah, we've already interviewed them, actually, but I just wanted to confer with the others to make sure we all agree they can be eliminated. They're not significant, I don't think." He cleared his throat a couple of times—he was almost choking on his own breath—but Jacobsen didn't pursue the point. The truth was he had only the haziest grasp of Department Q's methods. They knew that.

"So which case are you working on, then?" he said, pointing again at the board.

Oh god. Cornered.

He pointed at the whiteboard with a crooked finger. "Those are the three cases we're exploring right now. They're all ones you gave us. We're still dealing with a lot of unanswered questions at the moment, as you can see. It's like pulling teeth, but I'm sure we'll get to the bottom of them soon."

And then Jacobsen left.

He wasn't stupid, but according to Mona he'd had a rough day with the chief constable, so maybe he was just keen to go home and put his feet up on the coffee table.

Gordon stood there for a while, smiling sheepishly. It was better than sinking to his knees in terror, after all.

Gordon called the PCA several times after Jacobsen had left, but the only answer he received was that he had to stop. There had to be a strict separation between them and the Investigation Unit in Copenhagen until such time as their own detectives had questions or comments, they told him.

Rose walked through the door at that very moment, and for a second she stood open-mouthed, staring at the whiteboard.

"What the hell does that mean, Gordon?"

"No idea. I wrote it for Jacobsen's benefit."

"That's a dangerous game, Gordon. What on earth did he say?"

"Not a lot. But I think one of these days he's going to send us home."

Rose sat down heavily. "I wish Carl was here. Maybe he could figure out what the heck DKNL Transport actually transports. The owner, Hannes Theis, isn't home, and his employee Jess Larsen couldn't tell us any more than 'he's probably in Holland.' I'm thinking Theis is reporting to somebody down there, maybe planning some sort of retreat, or best-case scenario preparing the next shipment to Denmark."

"You seem pretty sure the DKNL Transport is involved in the drug trade."

"I reckon there's a good chance, but as things stand, there's nothing we can do about it. I'm wondering if maybe we explain to narcotics—" He broke off and nodded at Rose. "I know, I know, these days it's the Organized Crime Unit, but I'm not hopping on that bandwagon. Anyway, either way, they should consider searching the company's registered address. I mean, it's their department, isn't it?"

"Well, then you'll just have to tell them a little birdie told you." Rose cupped his cheeks and shook them gently. "Not so daft after all, my little Gordon!"

• • •

On New Year's Eve they all met up at Mona's. She had invited them over for coffee so they could agree on what they thought about the case.

Carl's lawyer and Assad could stay for only a few hours because they had family at home, but Gordon and Rose, who would otherwise simply be sitting at home alone, agreed to spend the evening with Mona and Lucia.

"I video-chatted with Carl a few hours ago," said his lawyer, Molise Sjögren. "He looks all right, and it seems like he's in good spirits. One of the guards was kind enough to lend him his copy of today's *Gossip*, and apart from a couple of photos Carl didn't think were suitable, he was happy with information being released about the Sisle Park case. He sends his love to everybody but especially to Mona and to you, Gordon, for having briefed *Gossip* so well."

The pale man's cheeks reddened. "It's really good to hear that. Several of the old cases I'm sharing with *Gossip* are from before I joined Department Q, so it was a bit tricky, actually."

"What about Carl's safety? Should I be nervous?" Mona asked Molise.

"Carl seems pretty confident, to be honest. He's having his meals brought to his cell, and he's been to the toilet a couple of times, as well as into the exercise yard—duly escorted by a few decent officers. The PCA came to interview him yesterday, and Carl asked me to say that the visitors' room reminds him of Lucia's nursery."

Mona smiled. "What about the guy who was transferred with him?"

"Yes, Malthe is in the cell above Carl's, but Carl doesn't know what's going to happen with him. I spoke to the guards, and they told me Correctional Services were pretty upset the attacks on Carl were made public, but that they'll soon find a solution."

Mona twisted her wedding ring a few times. "Correctional Services were upset they were made public? They should be more upset they couldn't take better care of their inmates. Carl's safety was their responsibility, after all."

Bright voices and chortling laughter drifted in from Lucia's room. She'd had a friend over for a couple of hours, and Mona cast a stolen glance in that direction. She and Lucia were alone now, and soon the new year would begin. What would it bring but more bad luck? She could scarcely bring herself to think about it.

"I have been informed by the PCA that they no longer suspect Carl had anything to do with the body found in the crate in Amager," continued Molise. "They didn't have to tell me that, so it was nice of them, but they also confirmed that he is still under investigation for aiding and abetting in drug trafficking and murder. They couldn't tell me what the worst-case scenario might look like, if he was convicted of all the charges, but they did say we could be looking at upward of twelve years, and unfortunately I would tend to agree—if the worst happens."

She reached for Mona's hand, which had begun to tremble. "Look, don't worry, Mona. None of the avenues they're investigating right now have led anywhere. This whole thing may be just a ploy to try to get Carl to voluntarily confess his role in the crimes, make a play for a reduced sentence."

"For what?" said Mona, her voice quivering. "I *know* he hasn't done anything illegal."

"Well, yes, that's why we're having this meeting, Mona. We're all on the same page there." Molise turned to the others. "So. Has anybody made any progress?"

Assad shifted in his seat. "First, I should just say something that might come as a bit of a shock. I invited Hardy and Morten—they'll be here in half an hour, and they'll be bringing a specialist to help keep Hardy's exoskeleton working properly. The guy only speaks French, apparently, but he and Hardy manage to chatter away just fine. I remembered you had a lift, Mona, so I thought it might be all right."

It was as though all the air had been sucked out of the room. Mona gasped for breath, while the others sat frozen. It had been sixteen years since Hardy was shot in the back, essentially paralyzed from the shoulders down. How were they supposed to act when he arrived?

Rose shook her head. "I think you should have given us a bit more warning, Assad."

"Yes, I know. I found it a bit weird too when I met him, but Hardy asked me not to. I was only allowed to tell Molise, then share it quietly with the rest of you later on. He can't cope with a whole lot right now, if you're thinking of showering him with . . . I think 'pity' was the word he used. Anyway, he can't stay long, but he wanted to see us and answer any questions as best he can. He thought New Year's Eve would be a good day to start moving on with his life."

"How, Assad? What are we about to see?" Gordon was, if possible, even paler than usual. "I've got a really bad feeling about this. Have you seen him?"

"Yes, I spent about an hour with him this morning. He was in a wheelchair, so I haven't seen him walk."

"How is he getting here?" Rose asked.

"He'll be driven to the front door in an accessible vehicle."

Rose looked out the window. There wasn't a single journalist or photographer to be seen on the street, thank god. Otherwise it might have been quite the show when Hardy turned up.

"Okay, but, I mean, what are we going to see, Assad?" Gordon asked again.

Assad folded his hands and brought his knuckles to his mouth. Mona understood why he was hesitant to answer. Surely they were all equally moved by Hardy's fate and what he'd had to go through over the past few months and years.

Then there was Morten and his boyfriend, Mika. They deserved all the respect in the world for supporting him so tirelessly in Switzerland. Sponsoring his stay, taking care of the treatment—all while trying to keep his spirits up throughout his agonizing journey.

"You'll see that Hardy has two devices surgically implanted in his brain, which control his colossal exoskeleton," Assad said, pulling himself together. "I saw it myself a few hours ago, but it's not as RoboCop as I thought. The suit he wears looks almost like those evil space soldiers in *Star Wars*, the ones who go running around in white costumes and can't hit anything with their laser blasters."

Mona tried to picture Hardy in the suit. He really was a very tall man, and the living room wasn't exactly huge.

"Maybe we should move the chairs around a bit," Rose said, and immediately set about doing exactly that. "We don't want him tripping over anything."

At this point Molise Sjögren broke in. "Now, obviously we have no idea who the prosecution will call as witnesses, so we need to make sure Hardy is on our side. And by that I mean during the trial itself, most importantly—if things get that far."

Mona shook her head almost imperceptibly. "Hardy can't be manipulated one way or the other. But we could get his version of the story, perhaps. That might be interesting."

"I'm not talking about manipulation, Mona. I'm talking about what a man like Hardy might say about a person like Carl, who welcomed him into his own home and gave him back the will to live. Gratitude is powerful stuff, wouldn't you agree?"

A ripple ran through the living room when the intercom finally buzzed. And while the elevator worked its way up, their minds raced. What would he be like? Was he the Hardy they knew? What did he think about all this? Would he stab Carl in the back?

It was Morten who stood immediately in front of Mona when she opened the door. Behind him, a head and a half taller, towered a mountainous man, upright as the pyramids and strapped firmly into a chalk-white hulk of an exoskeleton. Mona tried to control herself, but her jaw dropped and her lips began to tremble. It was a shock to see him—and to see him like that. She turned her head toward Assad with an expressive look. Had he been equally as moved, as shaken, when he first saw Hardy earlier that day? she wondered.

The small muscles around Assad's eyes quivered when he caught her gaze. Of course he had, and the others all felt the same.

Slowly, with a heavy tread that echoed in the stairwell, Hardy moved forward.

The upper part of his torso was held firmly to the back of the exoskeleton with broad straps that were gathered into a cross over his chest and shoulders. Behind his head was a neck pillow, and like a halo above him there was a hoop, like a headset positioned too high up. *That must be the thing connected to the two implants in his skull*, thought Mona. Bit creepy, actually.

Hardy grinned at the little gathering like a child who had just ridden his first few yards on a bike without his dad behind him, while they all collectively tried to wrap their minds around the surreal sight. The once powerfully built man now had thighs as thin as a teenager's, and his face had grown narrow and creased. A well-groomed gray beard gave the illusion of renewed vitality, but it was obvious the slight movement had cost Hardy most of his strength. And yet, he had stood up.

Nobody said a thing. The words were stuck in their throats.

"Well, look at that. You've got a ticker tape parade waiting for me—without the ticker tape." He smiled, indicating the passageway Rose had created with the dining chairs on either side.

Close behind him trotted an anonymous man who kept a tight grip on a strap on Hardy's back, and behind them both was Mika. Like Hardy, he had lost a significant amount of weight along the arduous road leading to this moment.

Hardy stopped and looked around. Parts of the living room were inaccessible—and no wonder, because the plates under his shoes increased his height to about six foot eleven: exactly the same height as the glass arms of Mona's Venetian chandelier. For a moment he seemed dizzy, as though he might smash everything in front of him if he lost his balance.

"It might be best if I sit in your chair, Assad. It looks wide enough."

He began to sit down with immense slowness after Assad had gotten up, then let himself fall heavily the last couple of inches.

It was a macabre sight: arms and legs strapped into the exoskeleton, which melded symbiotically into the black leather. He looked almost like a prisoner about to be executed in the electric chair.

"Phew!" he said, as though to lighten the mood, motioning to his carer to loosen the straps around his chest a little.

"Yeah. It's not the kind of suit you wear to a carnival or a party," he said, smiling with a tact Assad and Rose had never seen in him before.

"Can't believe I actually get to sit here with you all in this lovely living room," he said, sounding genuinely moved, and the atmosphere eased a little.

Then he fixed his eyes on Mona and offered his sincere condolences for what had happened to her and Carl. "I imagine you'd like to hear what I think about all this, wouldn't you? I'll be honest, it's difficult for me. Today is my very first day out in the real world for many, many years, and my brain's racing in a million different directions. It's getting me confused and making me mix things up. But what I can tell you is that I have no concrete memories of Anker dragging Carl into this."

Molise squeezed Mona's hand, and she began to cry. Whether it was relief or despair she wasn't sure, but the moment was interrupted by two little girls who suddenly appeared in the doorway, looking like they'd run smack into a wall.

The girl who'd been visiting Lucia gave a howl, and Lucia herself began to sob, her eyes darting from her crying mother to the enormous man who sat like some strange robot in the middle of the room.

"It's all right, girls," Mona said, as she stood up and wiped away her tears. "It's just Hardy. He's wearing a suit because he can't walk very well without it. Go back to your room and I'll bring you something yummy in a minute, okay?"

While the girls scampered delightedly back to their room as though nothing had happened, she went over to Hardy and embraced him. It was obvious he wanted to lift his arms and return the warm hug, but instead he pressed his cheek against hers.

"Thank god you're back, Hardy," Mona whispered. "Thank god."

———————

For the next half hour, they let Hardy talk about whatever he felt like.

Since he and the others had gone to Switzerland several months ago, during breaks between the treatments and the pain, he had thought of almost nothing but the nail gun case.

"I've got to admit, for a long time I suspected Carl might have been more involved in Anker's shady dealings than he let on." He looked apologetically at Mona. "I don't think so anymore. And I've only grown more sure about that since his arrest."

"You've spoken to Ploug, I know," Molise said. "But he's the person who's been running the investigation into Carl's case here in Denmark, so how does this all fit together? Was he even willing to discuss it?"

"This stays between us, all right?" He glanced at the tech, who unhesitatingly took out a bottle with a straw and put it in Hardy's mouth.

Hardy thanked him, then continued. "Ploug and I have always been good friends, and he told me the Dutch now believe several of the charges against Carl may have been set up, and that he and the PCA have come to the same conclusion. I mean, if you murdered someone and put the dismembered body into a wooden crate under Georg Madsen's house, wouldn't you make sure nothing led back to you as the killer? In which case, why did they find coins with Carl's and Anker's fingerprints on them—coins, moreover, that were painstakingly wrapped to preserve the fingerprints? And would you really overlook a coin from 2006 in the corpse's pocket, when it's obvious the date would reveal the year the body was buried? Anker and Carl were both too smart for that. Basically, who the hell would be that dumb, unless they wanted to be linked to the murder? It's a deliberate attempt to muddy the waters. Somebody has tried to frame Carl, to pin the murder on him, plain and simple."

He saw everybody nod.

"On the other hand, I have no doubt whatsoever that Anker was guilty. For years before the shooting in Amager, I watched him getting more and more coke-happy, with more and more cash to splash around.

To this day I fucking hate Anker for what he did, because in a lot of ways, he's the reason I ended up like this . . ." He trailed off for a moment.

Then Morten stepped forward and put a hand on his shoulder. "Is this getting too much, Hardy?"

The big man's eyes wandered for a moment, then he shook his head.

"Three things, okay, now pay attention," he went on. "The body in the crate and the faked evidence aren't particularly interesting in and of themselves. The key thing is who they point back to, who made them and buried them, and why. We need to figure out who could have had a direct interest in harming Carl and what their motive might have been. Then we need to show that Anker was part of a bigger setup. It was Anker who dragged me and Carl out to Amager, where we found Madsen's corpse. Now, under normal circumstances Anker was *always* the first one into a crime scene, but not that day. No, that day he went straight to interview the neighbor. Fuck that! If you ask me, he already knew Madsen was dead."

Hardy's gaze crossed swords with Mona's. She shrugged, not understanding.

"What I'm asking, Mona, is how does this all fit together? We've got to work that out. And *if* the hypothesis is that Anker Høyer was guilty of everything he's been accused of, then it stands to reason that other people were involved as well—just not Carl."

"That sounds about right, but it's also a pretty tall order, Hardy. It's been years," Rose said.

"You don't think I know that better than anybody? In fact, it's an even taller order than I first thought, because I've come to the conclusion that we can't work this case back to front, so to speak, and get Carl declared innocent for lack of evidence. We'll have to go the other way, find the real perpetrators ourselves. Figure out who the masterminds are, the go-betweens, and the people running things in Denmark, then get Carl acquitted based on that."

"You know Marcus will do pretty much anything to prevent us from investigating the case like we want to?" Rose asked.

"Yeah, I know it's a PCA case, but fuck him."

Several brows furrowed. Had Hardy really just said that?

Hardy nodded. "Yeah. I mean it. Almost makes me wonder if Marcus is involved himself, he's so keen to make life difficult for Carl. But we've got to let that go and remember he was away from the station for a few years while his wife was sick, and that the department has never run more smoothly than since he got back."

"So you don't think Carl had any idea what was in that suitcase? The one Anker asked him to keep?" Mona asked.

"Carl took me in and looked after me for a few years, and he could easily have used some of the money in the suitcase to improve the situation for all of us, so no, I believe Carl. About everything. Anyway, an intelligent man like Carl wouldn't have left it in the attic after he moved in with you, Mona. It would have been way too risky. He'd forgotten about it, it's as simple as that. I mean, you would, wouldn't you, if you didn't know what was in it? Cocaine, heroin, millions in cash! So now the detective in me is wondering: Where do we start?"

Hardy took a heavy breath.

"Just a minute, Hardy. Is something too tight?" Morten asked.

"I'm having a bit of trouble getting enough air," he replied very faintly.

Morten and Hardy's tech exchanged a nod. "I think that'll have to be enough for today, Mona. Maybe we can pick it up another time. After all, this is the first day Hardy has—"

"Wait." Again, the weak voice. "Could I have a little sip of the coffee on the table?"

Assad, Rose, and Mona all leaped up at the same time, but it was Assad who got there first.

"Two or three spoonfuls of sugar?" he asked, ladling it in without waiting for a response.

He put the rim of the cup to Hardy's lips, tipping it a little too quickly, so that coffee ran out of the corners of his mouth.

Hardy swallowed a little laboriously, and suddenly his eyes widened. "Jesus, Assad, you don't hold back, do you? If I was diabetic you'd have killed me." He laughed dryly as his carer wiped his mouth. "So, what have we got? Where do we go from here?"

"Just before Assad told us you were coming, Molise asked if we had anything new to report," Mona said, "and we never got around to answering that question. Do you have anything, Rose?"

"Yeah, I'm confused, and I don't like it. I've been doing some digging into the death of Carl's first lawyer. You heard about that, right, Hardy?"

He tried to nod, and Rose understood.

"The vehicle used to run him down belongs to a man who is the sole employee of a company called DKNL Transport. As the name suggests, it's an import-export company that operates exclusively between Holland and Denmark. The owner of the company is one Hannes Theis, and he's Dutch. He's currently in his home country, as far as we can tell, but we don't know why or where."

"Aha!" Gordon broke in. "You see, once again, it just goes to show how important the Dutch connection is to the nail gun case. I mean, obviously we know the Dutch police are on this and that two men over there were executed with a nail gun."

Rose still looked confused. "But, given that this guy Hannes Theis has such an obvious connection to Holland and that he transports all sorts of goods back and forth to Denmark, why on earth would he risk going anywhere near the murder of a lawyer outside Vestre Prison? If there really is something shady about him, I mean? Or could it be just more misdirection? Perhaps the car genuinely was nicked by some third party who used it to kill the lawyer? The whole thing is bananas."

Hardy cleared his throat. "Whether it's misdirection or extraordinary stupidity, we still have to pursue it. I mean, it's the most obvious lead we've got, right?"

Assad raised a cautious finger, but it was Gordon who spoke.

"Well, I've certainly got plenty that needs investigating," he said. "I'd like to know how it's possible that Carl was attacked in his own cell at Vestre. How did the inmates get access to the keys? I think the prison guard—Peter Loudmouth, they call him apparently, the guy who was supposedly knocked out before the first attack—may well be up to his eyeballs in it, so I'm digging further into that. Also, you may remember that detective in Schiedam, Hans Rinus, who was working with our very own Terje Ploug on the nail gun case?"

"Yes, Carl didn't have a tremendous amount of respect for him," said Mona.

"Nor did the rest of us," Rose laughed. "He died in the middle of the investigation, and I must say it was pretty convenient for any potential suspects in the case for the lead detective to choke on his own vomit. Maybe someone got him out of the way? I agree with you, Gordon, it's fishy!"

"Well, anyway, his replacement, Wilbert de Groot, is a lot sharper, so I think we should get in touch with him," Gordon added. "I'd like to go to Rotterdam to see if I can find out anything new, do some investigating on the ground there, if the rest of you don't mind."

"Uh, Gordon, you're not exactly fighting fit yet, are you? You look to me about as pale as a corpse that's been kept in a fridge," said Assad, demonstratively placing his arm on top of Gordon's thin white tubes of macaroni.

The others smiled cautiously, not wanting to offend him.

"I'm fine. I didn't even take the elevator on the way up when I got here. Did you hear me getting out of breath?"

No comment.

"Anyway, I'm just saying. Every thread we pull in that case, it always seems to lead us back to Holland," Gordon concluded.

Here Assad interrupted Hardy, who had been about to say something. "I spoke to the man who was initially arrested for the double murder in Sorø, Niels B Sørensen. He's calling himself Niels B Marquis de Bourbon these days. The man's an addict and he's sleeping rough in Nørrebro, but he gave me some information I'm sure is significant. He said he was suspicious of a Dutch-Danish man by the name of Rasmus and believed he had something to do with the arrest. Rasmus always had drugs on him and only entered the country every now and then. Niels B went to ground before he was arrested, hiding from Rasmus and whoever shot nails into the heads of the two mechanics. When he got back home, he found Paslode nails in his bed, so you can understand his concerns and why he got the hell out of Sorø."

Hardy nodded. "Dutch-Danish! Yeah, hang on, didn't Hans Rinus also mention something about a Dutch-Danish guy?"

"Well, that was certainly what Niels B called him," Assad said. "Probably a courier of some kind, since he only came to town occasionally and always had drugs on him, Niels B said. And the man called himself Rasmus. I think it was Rasmus Bruhn."

"Just to be on the safe side, you did get a description, right, Assad?" Rose asked.

Assad looked a little hurt by the question. Of course he'd gotten a description.

"Yes. He was in his late thirties at the time, always wore a gray suit, a bit on the tubby side—pudgy, as though he lived off fried food."

"That's Holland for you," Molise interjected. "A dangerous place to live if you love fries, mayo, and croquettes."

"Bingo, Assad. That's him. It's Rasmus Bruhn," Hardy exclaimed. He looked pleased, as though he'd been waiting for input on a topic he knew something about already. "Now he's directly linked to Sorø, where the two mechanics were killed, and we know from the Dutch that they found the gun used on me, Carl, and Anker in Amager during a search of Bruhn's home in Holland."

He looked at them one by one.

"Let's do a quick recap, shall we? Mona and Molise probably don't know about a lot of this stuff, I'd imagine. Was this Rasmus Bruhn even mentioned in the charges against Carl?" asked Hardy.

Molise shook her head.

"So the PCA team almost certainly aren't aware of the connection either, then?"

"I'm not sure. They may have spoken to the Dutch already, when they were up here to present charges against Carl."

"Okay. But let's work on the assumption that the PCA will need to be informed somehow."

Molise nodded.

"Good," continued Hardy. "So, very briefly. His name was Rasmus, last name Bruhn. We can be pretty sure he worked as a drug courier, but he was also a freelance journalist who wrote travel books and articles under the pseudonym Pete Boswell. It's since turned out that the corpse was actually a drug courier by the name of Gérard Gaillard, originally from Haiti, but that's another story."

Gordon sat open-mouthed. He'd obviously forgotten all about it.

"Rasmus Bruhn was tortured and killed in 2014 in a park outside of Rotterdam, as far as I recall, so about six or seven years ago now."

Rose nodded, and Gordon looked as though a glimmer of memory was slowly dawning.

"That's right, yep, 2014," Hardy went on. "What you don't know is that at the time I remembered Carl having a confrontation with Bruhn in 2005. I remember the year because Anker, Carl, and I were at a restaurant in Copenhagen, Parnas, for a sort of commiserative drinks after Vigga— Carl's wife at the time—had left him. Bruhn showed up out of nowhere. Not sure if it was a coincidence, but Anker and he evidently knew each other, because Anker said his name. He was aggressive and drunk, and he and Anker started getting into it. They argued—we never figured out what it was about, because the guy was slurring his words—and then all of a sudden Anker socked him right in the jaw. No idea why. Carl got between them, and if he hadn't done that, we probably wouldn't be sitting here today."

"Why haven't we heard about this before?" Rose asked.

"Carl could barely remember it himself when I told him about it later. But either way, he wouldn't have mentioned it to anybody else, since the guy was dead, and Carl had nothing to do with him anyway."

"But *you* think it's significant?" Rose went on.

"Yes, I do, because it didn't stop there. After a waiter came over and helped Carl throw Bruhn out into the street, he started threatening to gouge Carl's eyes out with his car keys. But he didn't know who he was dealing with—Carl grabbed his keys off him in a split second and told Bruhn in no uncertain terms that he'd have to take a taxi home. He could pick up the keys from the restaurant some other time."

Assad sighed. It occurred to Mona that perhaps he'd heard something about the incident after all.

"Anyway, then the idiot punched Carl right in the eye, which just escalated the whole thing. Carl grabbed his arm and twisted it around, then yanked Bruhn's wallet out of his inside pocket. You should've seen the look on that guy's face when Carl took his driver's license out and set fire to it with his Ronson lighter."

Gordon smiled. "Good old Carl. Sounds like the guy deserved it, even if it was a liiiittle bit over the line."

"I remember it as though it was yesterday, Bruhn's parting shot. He said, 'I'll remember that for next time, Carl.' He called him by name, which took me by surprise, because it hadn't been mentioned at the table."

A dark cloud had settled over the gathering, and Mona felt an ache that ran deep into her soul. Petty bullshit like that, some miserable barroom brawl—could it really destroy the lives of good people?

"Is that what this is really all about?" she asked. "Some stupid dickhead wanting revenge on Carl? But how? How is it all connected to the situation Carl's in right now, Hardy? Do you have any ideas about that?"

"No, but Bruhn had the gun used to shoot us down in his possession. Was he the one who used it, or was it planted at his apartment? He was part of a brutal world. And who knows what was going through his head when they finally caught up with him in that park outside of Rotterdam and he was begging for his life. He probably blurted out all sorts of names. Why not point to Carl, someone he thought of as a thorn in his side?"

"So that's our current hypothesis? The people behind all this believe that Carl is involved, especially since the police found all the money and drugs in his attic. So they want him eliminated?" Rose asked.

"Yeah, I think that sounds about right, Rose. Maybe they believe he knows more than is good for him. It's a pretty ruthless organization we're dealing with."

"Surely we can explain this to someone, Hardy," Gordon said.

"You can try to find out more about Rasmus Bruhn if you ask around in Schiedam and Rotterdam," Rose said.

Gordon smiled. He'd already mentally bought his plane tickets.

"Sure, and I'll see what I can find out about Bruhn's activities here in Denmark," said Assad, already getting to his feet. It had been a while, but the spark was back in his brown eyes.

Hardy gazed blankly into space. Clearly something was bothering him.

"And . . ." He paused, breaking into a few short bursts of shallow coughs. "Perhaps in the meantime I can try to arrange to see Carl."

"Well, if you do, it'll give the photographers and journalists standing guard outside Slagelse something different to take pictures of," said Mona.

21

ROSE

Friday, January 1, 2021

There wasn't much sense of festive cheer at Rose's place. For one thing, she'd drunk too many gin and tonics and had gone to bed at six, short-circuiting all the synapses in her brain and putting them out of commission. For another, the relentlessly depressing situation was starting to get to her. And to top it all off, she'd started sniffling. Not surprising—it had been extremely cold when she went home.

She realized how shitty she felt the minute she woke up, head pounding, to the sound of unfamiliar voices calling her name from the carpark outside.

As always, unless she'd invited some random man up for a one-night stand, she was alone in the apartment. But the bare walls of her bedroom had rarely felt more crushing and accusatory.

Carl was gone, so it was up to her now to lead the troops, wasn't it? To find some way for her, Assad, and Gordon to secretly pull off the impossible. To keep Jacobsen and his mob at bay. To make all the photographers and reporters currently gawping up at her kitchen window from the carpark piss off. To help Department Q solve the case when not even the chief witness, Carl Mørck, could shed any light on it.

She tumbled out of bed without even the energy to shower. The mere thought of having to change her underwear put her off.

The clock on the wall stared at her reproachfully, but she wagged a finger at it. "Hey, don't start with me, okay? It's January first, and I don't give a shit if it's three o'clock. I—"

The doorbell rang.

Trudging barefoot down the hall in her Sloggi underwear and nothing else, she put her eye to the peephole.

Outside stood a man she didn't know, and behind him another man, trying to hide his camera behind the first.

"Fuck off! I'm getting my beauty sleep," she yelled, glancing sidelong at the full-length mirror, which mercilessly reflected back her hangover and the slumping curves of her figure. The bags under her eyes were locked in a battle with the wrinkles traitorously beginning to form in parallel from the corners of each eye to the sides of her mouth. If her face hadn't still been slightly swollen from sleep, smoothing out the worst of it, she would have been in for a shock. Instead, she planted her fists against her hips and contemplated the life-or-death struggle currently going on between breasts, stomach, and gravity.

It was quite a sight. She almost wanted to open the door just so she could scare them off.

Instead, she flung herself onto the sofa and blew her nose a couple of times. Let them ring the bell as fervently as they liked. She was going to call narcotics and give them something to think about.

"This is Rose from Department Q," she said with a snuffle. "I've received an anonymous tip suggesting we should get a search warrant for a company by the name of DKNL Transport. The man who called me suspects that they're involved in a large-scale drug-smuggling operation, and he said we should take a closer look at the owner, Hannes Theis. Pass that on to the Sniffer Dog."

But she wasn't getting off that easily.

"How did you receive this tip?" asked the officer on duty.

"Um, it was a phone call this morning."

"Great, then you can give me the number of the guy who called you."

Shit! She wished she had her brain back.

"You can't. Sorry, I don't have it."

Then she slammed down the receiver.

"Okay, time for some hair of the dog," she said, lurching into the kitchen.

She had just taken a sip when the doorbell rang again.

All right, that's it. Now they're in for a shock, she thought, as she moved toward the front door. For a moment she paused, the tips of her fingers on the latch, then she twisted it and opened the door with a bang.

A well-dressed woman with a few streaks of gray in her hair took a few steps back, trying not to look at Rose's naked upper body.

"Ohhh, sorry, love, I'm afraid you're too late. They picked up all my empty bottles this morning," Rose boomed, and was about to shut the door when the woman jammed it open with her foot.

She's asking for a slap, thought Rose for a second, until the woman shouted that she was there to help Carl, if she could.

"My name is Merete Lynggaard," she said, stepping back.

Rose frowned. Merete Lynggaard, really? They'd never actually seen each other in the flesh, but so what? Was there anybody who didn't know about the woman who'd been kept trapped in a pressure chamber for six years before Assad and Carl finally got her out?

"Why don't you let me in? Otherwise there'll be a stampede. One of the journalists outside recognized me, even though it's been quite a few years since I was in the public eye."

Rose's guest nodded appreciatively as Rose entered the living room five minutes later wearing a kind of kimono and carrying two mugs of coffee.

"I'm sorry to come barging in like this, but I know a few people at the station and I'm aware that Department Q has been prevented from investigating Carl's case. It was my contacts who gave me your address. I hope that's all right?"

Rose nodded. She tried to recall the face of the woman who had been front-page news for a long time, some years ago.

Merete Lynggaard had to be over fifty now and was a far cry from the woman Rose remembered. Well preserved, her features still soft and elegant, but there was a veil over her former beauty that suggested a life less than perfect.

"I know what you're thinking. But the years take their toll." Merete put her hand up to her hair and smoothed it slightly. "Carl isn't the only one who's been through the wringer. I've just buried my wonderful younger brother, Uffe. He was only thirty-nine. Died of cancer on Christmas Eve. Do you remember him?"

Rose nodded. It was Uffe who had turned mute after his older sister was kidnapped.

"He was doing well after we were reunited. We loved each other, and he actually adjusted pretty amazingly. He got a job at an electronics company, and after he moved out of my place ten years ago, he got himself a girlfriend and a little daughter, whom I'm very fond of. I looked after her for several years after his girlfriend left him, and now I'm all she's got."

Rose was trying to keep up. She had joined Department Q a year after Carl and Assad had investigated the Lynggaard case, and thanks to her blood alcohol level and the ruthlessly pounding headache, the pieces were taking their sweet time falling into place.

"How can you help Carl? Can you tell me that, and slowly, so that I can follow?"

"I lost interest in politics and parliamentary work in 2007, after Carl and Assad got me out of that horrible pressure chamber where I'd been imprisoned for six years, so I didn't go back to that world. The insurance company paid out some money that kept me and Uffe afloat for a few years, and after that we moved to England. The thought of living in Denmark frightened me, so I got a job consulting for lobbyists."

"Okay, yeah, I can imagine you knew a lot about that too." Rose nodded, trying to look focused while the idiots in the carpark downstairs continued trying to drown each other out.

Merete Lynggaard nodded. "I met a man who owned what you'd probably call a security firm. A man I married, and who helped the authorities when British citizens got into trouble abroad, if they were kidnapped in Colombia, for instance, or Mexico or the Middle East. We had been together for some years before he died during a mission, and then I took over the company."

Rose took a sip of coffee, which tasted like shit, to put it mildly. Even Assad could have made a better brew.

"We currently employ more than two hundred people, and things are going swimmingly. So if there's anything I can do to help, I can make those resources available for as long as it takes."

"Help how?"

"I read that Carl has been assaulted twice in prison. Perhaps I can help make sure that doesn't happen again."

"How the heck are you going to do that? I doubt you can get him out of Slagelse; he's only just arrived."

"Leave it to me. And I could put a couple of my people on this, try to figure out who's behind it all."

"Sure, that's fine by me. Do you have my number, or Assad's or Gordon's? We'd like to be kept in the loop, ideally on an ongoing basis."

She nodded.

"But why you specifically, Merete?"

She smiled. "You know why! Without Carl, so many people like us wouldn't be alive today. Call it a debt of gratitude—or justice. That's why we want to help."

"We?"

"Yes. Ever since they got me out I've been keeping an eye on many of Department Q's cases, and I've met several of the people you've helped. A lot of names you'd recognize. And each and every one of them owes Carl a tremendous debt."

"Who?"

"Kenneth, for example! Do you remember Mia, the young woman who was held captive underneath moving boxes?"

"Yes, of course, the message in a bottle case! Wait, remind me, who was Kenneth again?"

"The soldier who rescued Mia. They got married, and he works for me now. There's nothing he wouldn't do to help Carl."

———————

Merete Lynggaard left as abruptly as she'd arrived. She'd be in touch again in a day or two, she said—she was looking forward to seeing Assad again.

Rose glanced out the window at the horde of journalists, who pounced on Merete Lynggaard as she stepped out of the apartment block. She had assumed that the burly men who surrounded Merete were there to help her barrel through the crowd and into the waiting car, but evidently she was mistaken. It looked more as though their job was to make sure each reporter got a brief interview with Merete. After each one, the journalist jogged over to his or her car as the cameras flashed incessantly.

After fifteen minutes, Merete Lynggaard had passed through the mob of hungry journalists and was finally alone with her security team. Then they too drove off.

No less than Merete Lynggaard wants to help Department Q—is that what she said? Bit bloody surreal, thought Rose. Carl would be genuinely touched by this, she was sure, and so would Assad.

Rose blew her nose and knocked back a final gulp of tepid beer as she considered her next move.

She was just about to call Assad and tell him what had happened when her phone buzzed. She didn't recognize the number but picked up anyway. If it was one of those arsehole newshounds she would give him a piece of her mind.

"This is Leif Lassen," said a dry voice, as though Rose gave a flying fuck what his name was.

"Great, and who exactly do you write for, if I even want to know?"

"Leif Lassen. Do I really need to say it again? Superintendent of the Copenhagen Narcotics Unit, you moron!"

Oh, fuck. The Sniffer Dog. That twat, she thought, with one eye on the empty beer bottle. She was considering hanging up and grabbing another.

"Do you think we're a total bunch of clowns, Rose? I've already in- formed your boss that you're conducting an unauthorized investigation well beyond the scope of your authority. You're looking at a suspension here."

"Okay, well, thanks for the warning, Your Holiness. But what makes you think I'm doing that? If you're referring to the anonymous phone call I received earlier today, I didn't ask for that. I just thought it should be passed on to the relevant—"

"Don't bother. The man who owns DKNL Transport is Hannes Theis, who was sitting in the car used to mow down Carl's lawyer. That's straight from the mouth of the driver, Jess Larsen. Did you think we didn't know? Or maybe you think we can't put two and two together, Rose? Now, you listen to me. You're investigating Carl's case and you've been caught with your pants down, and because of that you'll be hearing from Marcus Jacobsen. I'll say it again: he's suspending you!"

A few choice expletives popped into Rose's head before she regained her composure.

"You got a tip-off because I'm a good colleague, and that's that. Are you searching the company or not?"

"We run constant checks on transport companies like Theis's. It's been a few months since the last time we paid them a visit, before all this happened, and there was absolutely nothing to find. Their business is totally aboveboard. Now stop pulling this shit." Then he slammed down the phone.

By then, Rose had long since sobered up.

She drove straight to Jess Larsen's address in Smørum, and this time she leaned on the bell until he opened up.

"Sorry, Jess, but I need answers to some additional questions I've been mulling over," she said to Larsen, who was swaying slightly. Evidently she'd woken him up. He must have had a boozy New Year's Eve as well. "Has DKNL Transport ever had a visit from the Copenhagen Narcotics Unit?"

He nodded.

"And they searched the company?"

"Well, I wouldn't exactly call it a search. They just came in and went through some paperwork and asked a few questions. Nothing major. Why? That was ages ago."

"Do you have the keys to your offices?"

His brow furrowed, and he slowly shook his head—clearly a lie. He didn't want to get dragged into any of it, that much was obvious.

"Heard anything from Hannes Theis?"

Again, that inscrutable shake of the head. Was the man on something? she wondered.

"Look, I'm sorry, but I'd really like to talk to him. Is he still in Holland?"

At last he answered in the affirmative. "Yes, he is. Why? Has he done something wrong?"

She smiled a little too widely. "Oh no, no. But he might be able to help me with a couple of things. And I do have one more question." She tried to catch his eye and give him a suggestive look, but it bounced off him. Might as well cut right to the chase, then.

"Why were you at Vestre Cemetery the day your car was stolen, Jess?"

He considered this for a moment, gazing out the window. "Yeah, it was a bit weird. Hannes got a phone call saying that his wife's gravestone had been knocked over, but when we got there, it was fine."

"Who called him, do you know?"

"Hannes said it was from the cemetery office. We thought it was a gardener or a gravedigger."

"Did anybody check that?"

Now he looked directly at her. Was he waking up? "No. I didn't, anyway, and I don't think Hannes did either."

"And afterward?"

"No, not as far as I'm aware."

"But he told all that to the police, right?"

"Yeah, I think so. He told them when they called."

"Called?"

"That's right. We had to take a taxi back to the office, obviously, when my car was stolen."

"So you must have driven past the man who was run down."

"Yes, I realize that now. But all we saw was a group of people standing around something on the pavement. There was an ambulance as well, but we didn't know what was going on. I thought maybe someone had collapsed with a heart attack or something. Lots of old people come to the cemetery, you know, to visit family. I thought it might be one of them."

"Right! So you didn't notice your own car on the side of the road?"

"No, people were standing too close together, and the taxi drove by fast."

"Why didn't the police come and question you in person?"

"Because of COVID, they said. Pretty standard these days, isn't it?"

Rose could practically see Carl rolling his eyes. He'd be losing his shit right now.

"But the department we spoke to was the one responsible for vehicle theft. A couple of officers from homicide came to my place a little while later, and I gave a statement."

"And Theis? Did they visit him too?"

He shrugged. Theis might already have been on his way to Holland by then, he wasn't sure.

Afterward, Rose sat in her car for a minute or two, lips narrowed. How much information was the Investigation Unit actually sitting on— information that Department Q badly needed?

Twenty minutes later, she stood shivering and runny-nosed outside the unassuming premises of DKNL Transport. White, peeling walls and low buildings with felt roofs. Nothing special, apart from the large, newish hall that towered fifteen feet above the rest. Tarmac an inch thick outside the big gates suggested the building was a garage meant for trucks.

The fence that encircled the buildings was clearly marked with the company's name and logo, and a warning sign announced that this was private property—no trespassing. She glanced up at the barbed wire, which, unlike outside a prison, was angled away from the property and toward the surrounding streets. Defense against any "trespassers."

She thought for a moment, then glanced around in all directions to make sure there wasn't a soul to be seen for miles that New Year's Day.

The toolbox in the boot of her car wasn't the kind that could be used to help a poor old aunt put up a shelf, but Assad had always said its contents were the perfect kit for an experienced burglar.

Grabbing her powerful bolt cutters—easily capable of lopping open the padlock on the gate—she went around instead to the rear of the premises, where she cut a neat hole in the wire fence. Rather than break into the office, which numerous enamel signs of a certain age declared was alarmed, she went straight to the garage, took out her lockpick gun, and opened the door.

She waited a moment, but when no alarm sounded, she switched on the fluorescent lights in the ceiling.

22

MALTHE

Friday, January 1, 2021

It was not a visit Malthe had requested. But when he heard the man was a lawyer and had important information about his family, he agreed to take him on as legal counsel so that he could find out more about his brother's situation.

The encounter had turned out rather differently than expected, however, and very much not to Malthe's taste.

The lawyer was an elegantly dressed man, curiously out of place in the visitors' room with its bright, childish colors. Courteous, polite, with pomaded hair, an expensive suit, and an aura of perfume that reminded Malthe of lemons, summer, and sun.

"I appreciate you agreeing to see me, Malthe," he said, gazing so deeply into his eyes that it made Malthe uneasy. "What I'm about to tell you must not go any further, because if it does, your family might end up getting hurt." He smiled warily, but the smile was not disarming.

"You made a mistake in Vestre, but as we understand it, it wasn't solely your fault. We can tell you that the man who interfered and pushed up the price is no longer with us."

Malthe frowned. What did he mean? Had they killed the Jackhammer?

"Of course, we do struggle to understand why you thwarted the second attack on Carl Mørck, but we believe it was because you hadn't fully understood that the job had been given to someone else, so you were still trying to carry it out yourself, is that correct?"

Malthe nodded. Maybe they'd heard about his message to Peter Loudmouth and understood he wanted to finish the job in the remand center.

"Then again, we can't be sure whether that's actually true, can we, Malthe? The facts of the second attack on Mørck speak for themselves, so how do we know we can even trust you? I'm afraid we don't think we can. So I'm here to inform you that we have selected someone else for the task. A big, strong fellow like you. And if you interfere again, it's your family that will pay the price. Do you understand? That's why I've come to see you here today."

Malthe looked down at his hands, which had begun to tremble.

They had killed the Jackhammer. Malthe didn't know how, but it didn't matter anyway, because it meant there were no limits to what they were capable of.

He pictured his little family. His mother working her fingers to the bone to keep everything afloat; his little sister, who'd had to drop out of school to help out a bit—and then there was his brother, who could do nothing but lie in bed and worry about what was going to happen to him. He didn't want the three of them paying for his sins. Were these really the only options? Waiting around for his brother to die or allowing his family to suffer the consequences of the fatal shadow he would cast over them if he didn't come to heel?

He looked at the pomaded man. It would be child's play to snap the lemon-stinking lawyer's head clean off his shoulders; he'd done it before, and he very much wanted to. But Malthe lowered his head, nodded, and said goodbye. He had to think.

Malthe had served enough time that he could instantly identify the various types of inmates skulking around the exercise yard. They were all in there. The con men with the crooked grins, awaiting a vast array of fraud convictions. The overcautious, hanging back because their crimes brought them no prestige. The one who could get hold of anything for you; the skinny, near-transparent junkie; the gray-haired prison aristocrat who could talk to anyone and earn respect. Then, of course, there were the ones awaiting sentences for crimes of varying brutality. There were hideous tattoos everywhere, the purpose of which was to tag the inmates so you knew who you were dealing with. He'd seen more guys in good shape at Vestre, but nobody with such sinewy arms or such massive veins snaking beneath pale skin as the man currently leaning up against the fence, staring at him with a gaze best left unmet.

Most of his fellow inmates were civil, nodding to him and asking cautiously what he was in for, but the guy with the muscular arms soon began to sneer at him for licking the newly arrived policeman's arse. "Pig-lover" was the word he used, and the mood swiftly changed. A couple of the others took up positions by the fence next to the staring prisoner, and one by one they explained to Malthe with customary bluntness that if this was true, he was about to get fucked up. Being the size of a barn door wasn't going to help him. One or two other prisoners protested, asking if they realized he had killed some guys with only a couple of punches, but they just laughed.

Wait and see—Malthe could feel it in the air.

A few minutes passed, then one of the female prison guards arrived, escorting some more inmates from the second floor.

Most of them, including Malthe, nodded respectfully at the last man who entered.

The guy was a human mountain, six foot seven, the type to hold a plank until he tasted blood, then follow up with two hundred straight-leg push-ups. Well-built was an understatement. Even the man with the sinewy arms gave him a resolute nod of respect.

"Well, well, well," said the mountain as he passed Malthe. "So that's what you look like?" He held Malthe's chin and shook it slightly, as though addressing a toddler, and the others all drew back closer to the fence so that if the whole thing exploded, they wouldn't get caught in the blast.

Malthe reached for his hand and shook it. "You must be Little Shit, right? Nice to meet you!"

The mountain seemed a little taken aback—what was he supposed to say to that? Yes or no would both sound wrong. So instead, Malthe got an equally firm handshake in return, and there they stood until both sets of knuckles shone white. Malthe wasn't about to yield a single inch, not to this man. He was the one they'd chosen to kill Carl Mørck, Malthe was sure of that.

They probably weighed about the same, he thought, but the colossus in front of him was roughly five or six inches taller and had a wingspan like an albatross. Not much of a contest, or so it might seem—and the man Malthe had nicknamed Little Shit made exactly that mistake. Like a hydraulic pump, Malthe's handshake shifted up a gear, producing an audible crunch in the giant's hand. The man was sweating, but he decided to squeeze back even harder, which only prompted Malthe to shift up again.

Back home on the farm, Malthe had quickly learned that when pain was accompanied by hard, honest effort, there were almost no limits to what could be achieved. After all, the rusty bolts stuck in the wheels of the tractor simply had to come out, otherwise his dad wouldn't be able to finish sowing the field. The big horse that had served them all Malthe's life simply had to be dragged into the knacker's van. As a teenager, his strength had solved all sorts of problems, and the result was smiles and delight, so he had learned to develop and control that strength to the full.

Once Malthe could see his reflection in the mountain's shiny eyes, he knew the man was finished.

"Okay . . . let's . . . say we've . . . met," said the guy with difficulty, his eyes fixed on the camera above them.

"Yep. Appreciate the welcome," Malthe said, and then he did something that perhaps he shouldn't have done. He gave the mountain's hand one last squeeze, making him gasp and his hand collapse with a few tiny pops.

His face was white as he retreated toward the others, but the hatred in his eyes was black.

"You certainly know how to make lifelong friends," said the prisoner bringing around dinner that evening, and the corrections officer who came to say goodnight repeated the same thing.

"You'd better be careful, pal. You crossed a line today, and you ought to know an arm in plaster hits harder than one that isn't. We're not putting anything on your record today, because we know him. Plus, there might be one or two of us in the guard room who enjoyed seeing him put in his place for once."

"What's his name?" Malthe asked, so that at least he knew what to call his greatest enemy.

"Tom Gravgaard. Calls himself 'Cassius' after Cassius Clay, Muhammad Ali's original name."

"Muhammad Ali? Who was that?"

The officer's lips twisted. "You've never heard of Muhammad Ali?"

"Nope!"

"Well, if you ask me, he was the best heavyweight boxer the world has ever seen. They say our Cassius could have been a star super heavyweight, but a broken hand put the kibosh on his career. The same hand you crushed today, incidentally."

"What's he in for?"

The officer shook his head. "You know we're not allowed to talk about that stuff."

"Fine. Then do you know who gave that lawyer access to me?"

"No, I wasn't on shift. Might have been a request from Correctional Services, though." Then his tone changed. "I can tell you we've been reading all about Mørck's most recent cases on the *Gossip* website, the ones he solved just before he was arrested. Crazy stories. It's hard to imagine him having enough skeletons in the closet to end up here."

He nodded and patted Malthe on the shoulder. "Tomorrow you'll be moved down to the cell next to Carl's, and we'll also arrange for you to visit each other's cells occasionally. Maybe you can play a game or something."

Malthe smiled. And not for the reason the officer thought.

"Oh, and you'll be given yard time together."

"Okay. Just the two of us, then?" It sounded like a major stumbling block was about to be removed. He was the one who'd be given unfettered access to Mørck, not the mountain with the injured hand, so why would the bosses object if Malthe was the one to kill him? Now, at last, there was some hope for his brother.

Malthe returned the officer's smile.

"Nah, I'm thinking the prisoner in isolation at the end of Carl's corridor would probably like to go too. He's afraid of the others, but not you and Carl, and if he goes with you two we don't need to spend the extra time on him."

Malthe shook his head. "Isn't he a pedo?"

"Whether he is or not is none of your business."

"I hate that shit. If he's coming out with us, he'd better climb up onto the roof. Otherwise I'll fucking batter him."

The officer said he would take note of that.

Malthe wasn't the brightest bulb, but it couldn't be a bad thing, surely, the officer suddenly getting all formal.

Malthe sat for a while on his bed after they'd switched off the light. Had he crossed a line? The men behind the pomaded lawyer were bound to find out what had happened between him and the mountain. Had he put his family in danger after all?

He rocked faintly back and forth—it was almost too much for his little brain to cope with, this. Apart from the giant, he wasn't worried about how the inmates in the prison would react to the incident. They had seen him ascend the throne with their own eyes. But outside the prison—how would they react? He'd have to try to speed things up.

And as the yells from the windows slowly fell silent, Malthe figured out a plan that would work out to everybody's benefit.

Everyone except Carl Mørck.

23

EDDIE

Friday, January 1, 2021

The viral infection was unexpectedly bad, and by New Year's Eve all three of them were struggling. Femke had a migraine-like headache, and like Eddie she was coughing and very snotty. Their daughter lay in her small bedroom with a fever, in a sleep that bordered on unconsciousness. She had been like that for nearly twenty-four hours.

How sick had they been, he wondered, the people who had thrown their used tissues into the bin outside the hospital? Eddie wished he knew, because if his little girl's temperature didn't drop soon, they'd have to get help. Otherwise things might get serious.

Eddie was uneasy—for several reasons.

They had killed the Jackhammer. He knew because he'd been checking the email inbox he was secretly accessing at the office of his Danish contact. Even the Danes were starting to get a bit worried.

They had just sent a man to the remand center where Carl Mørck was being kept. Eddie hadn't been told who it was, so clearly his employers were taking matters into their own hands.

Have I already been rendered superfluous? he thought. Had it finally come, the moment he'd long dreaded? Was he next on the hit list?

Not if he had anything to do with it. For a couple of days he had defied COVID, sitting at his computer for hour after hour and writing.

Systematically and chronologically, he described the crimes that had been committed. Nothing was forgotten. Murder, drug dealing, customs fraud, bribery, threats—and that was just for starters. He was going to put together a clear and coherent document to use as insurance against any aggression from his employers, who would certainly be facing lengthy prison terms if their crimes were ever made public. He would deposit it with a lawyer, and if he or his family were attacked, the lawyer would make sure it was passed to the relevant investigative bodies and the prosecutors.

Of course, Eddie hoped it wouldn't come to that.

He hoped that the mere knowledge of the document's existence would be enough of a deterrent, because it listed names and exactly what role each individual had played, as well as how disloyalty toward the organization had very often ended in death.

Eddie was counting on that. If he got enough time to himself, he could finish it and deliver the file to a lawyer within the next couple of days. He gazed with satisfaction at his catalog of names, each of which was accompanied by a list of the crimes they had committed. It felt almost as though he were a prosecutor at one of the historic trials. Like the all-powerful prosecutors who had gathered evidence against war criminals in Nazi Germany, in Japan and Serbia. He even forgot, occasionally, that the document was a double-edged sword—that it could just as well be used against him, if the authorities got their hands on it. Still, surely he had a trump card as a chief witness, as long as he was one hundred percent cooperative and remorseful? Surely he could expect some kind of forgiveness if he served up one of the biggest cases in Dutch history to the police on a silver platter?

He didn't hear the movement behind him until it was too late.

"What are you doing, Eddie?" It was Femke, standing close behind him, with red-rimmed eyes and a bunch of snotty tissues pressed to the tip of her nose.

Eddie leaned toward her, blocking her view of the screen. "A crime novel, I think it's going to be. But you're not allowed to read it, Femke, it's early days yet."

"I think Marika's temperature is rising, Eddie. What are we going to do?"

The mere fact that she used their daughter's name and not "Little One" made him get to his feet.

She was lying very still, but her breathing was rapid and her cheeks a fiery red.

"Her temperature's over one hundred degrees now," Femke said, stroking the little girl's sticky hair.

"Has it risen in the last couple of hours?"

"Yes, I think so."

"We should take some of her clothes off, Femke; it's warm enough in the room. Then we'd better keep a close eye on her for the next few hours."

She nodded a little reluctantly, but then again, she had no idea about Eddie's real problem. How could they contact their own doctor when they were so far away from home? And how could they contact their nearest hospital without handing over Marika's health insurance card?

Eddie knew all too well how easily his enemies would be able to trace them if Marika went into the hospital.

"Why don't we put a damp dishcloth on her forehead? That should cool her down a bit," he said.

"You sit with her, Eddie. I have to go and lie down. Take her temperature every half an hour, I want you to promise me."

He kept writing as quickly as he could, but with every thirty minutes that passed, he was forced to admit that the little girl's temperature had risen by half a degree. When she reached 102 degrees Fahrenheit, he went to wake up Femke.

"I'm driving you to the hospital in Aachen. Get dressed and we can be there in forty-five minutes."

She gazed uncomprehendingly at him, her eyes unfocused.

"What's her temperature?"

"One hundred two!"

"Eddie, why don't we drive her to Maastricht? That's only fifteen minutes."

"Because I heard the hospital in Aachen is better equipped for this than the one here."

"But, Eddie, Aachen is in Germany, it's another country. They won't let us in without showing our COVID certificates, and obviously we can't do that right now."

He waved some bits of paper. They were a few months old, it was true, but not expired.

"We'll use the ones we got when we visited your aunt at the hospice. Come on, we're wasting time!"

Femke was angry and on the verge of tears. The queue at the border was long, and both she and Marika were burning up.

But Eddie got them through by showing his police badge, which he also used at the hospital reception, and after a thirty-minute wait he received his daughter's medication and instructions to keep her hydrated and appropriately supervised.

"Now that the fever is coming down, you can go. But next time I'd recommend driving to Maastricht; it's a really good hospital," the doctor said. It was just as well that Femke had decided to wait in the car. "And of course it's much easier for all concerned, isn't it, given that the child is a Dutch citizen? Since you were here, we had to look at her, but I don't think we'd be able to admit you again." He held out his hand to Eddie, palm up. "Could we see the child's health insurance card? You didn't show it at reception."

"No, we were in too much of a rush to get her onto the ward. Can't I just settle up now?"

The doctor and nurse stared at him, eyes astonished above their masks. "Maybe in Holland, but not here."

Hesitantly he took out Marika's card and gave it to them. Perhaps her information would be traceable with a lot of effort, but there had to be a certain inertia with these kinds of exchanges between two countries, so that would buy them some time. And why would his employers be searching for his child's health insurance card anyway? Even if they did, it would only tell them about where they'd been, not where they were going next. No, it felt safe enough.

Although he didn't feel too good himself, he let Femke sleep and watched over his daughter that night. After a couple of hours, during which her condition got no worse, he pulled his computer onto his lap and got to writing.

For security reasons, he'd either never learned the names of many of his contacts or they'd used cover names. He'd be able to recognize a lot of them, obviously, if he got the chance, but certain contacts he knew by their real names, so of course he put those in.

As he wrote, he underlined the men who had posed a threat to the organization's activities, and especially those who had ended up with nails rammed through their skulls—the ones who had been disloyal or tried to fiddle the accounts.

Finally, he listed the honest officers who had worked closely with him on specific narcotics cases, as well as the ones from homicide who had occasionally got a little too close to the truth.

Wilbert de Groot was the detective who had been leading the investigation for the past couple of years. An immensely careful man, he had taken every precaution he could not to end up like his predecessor, Hans Rinus, the officer who had been looking into the nail gun murders in Schiedam.

Rinus had been naïve, but he was also a diligent and incorruptible detective who had choked on his own vomit after a drinking binge, and next to his name, Eddie made a brief note: *Rinus normally drank very little. Did the organization have a hand in it?* It would be one way of getting rid of an external threat like Hans Rinus.

Finally, he made a list of the criminals who had worked within the system and who for various reasons had eventually been eliminated. Eddie had reported to his employers whenever significant disparities had appeared in the accounts. The quantities of narcotic substances that he passed on to Rasmus Bruhn, who was responsible for distribution in Denmark and Sweden, had certainly not been recorded correctly. It was one thing to skim a little off the weight and the price, but it was quite another to do what Bruhn had apparently done: start recruiting the organization's dealers and middlemen for a rival drug ring in Rotterdam.

Somehow, Bruhn must have gotten word that his employers suspected he was double-crossing them, so overnight he disappeared. Obviously, the organization had been eager to remove anybody who had been involved in his activities.

Bruhn was the first person they wanted to eliminate, but only after they had squeezed some names out of him: the others in the distribution chain. At the time, Eddie hadn't understood how they tracked him down, but it took that devil with the odd-colored eyes only one day before Rasmus was thrashing in his net.

The way they'd killed Bruhn was both cunning and brutal. They tied him up and dragged him back and forth through a drainpipe, and every time he came out, they beat him mercilessly with an iron bar as he begged ever more desperately for his life.

After they'd gotten the names they wanted, they left him to drown in the drainpipe, and yet another weak link in the organization had been removed.

Eddie turned from his laptop to his child's bed and stroked the little girl's forehead. Her fever had come down, and her breathing was slower and deeper.

He sniffed a few times, nodded slightly, and glanced back over what he'd written about Bruhn. They'd made short work of him—they hadn't been able to trust him, and on top of that, he knew too much. Goodbye, Rasmus Bruhn.

But how had they found him so quickly?

Eddie nodded off for a while as dawn slowly began to break above the picturesque rooftops of Valkenburg. His throat was increasingly sore and his nose was running, but he was relieved. Femke had been sleeping heavily since they got back, and Marika was doing much better now. He was looking forward to telling her mother.

He woke abruptly with such a powerful sense of unease that his body quivered. What was it? Was it the fever worsening or something else? He closed his eyes and tried to recall the moment before he woke up. A moment without images, only a thought that grew larger and larger until eventually it overshadowed everything else—but what thought?

Then, instinctively, he bent his head and looked at the screen in his lap, and instantly he began to shake again. The thought he'd been circling was right in front of him. It was the final sentence he'd written before he shut his eyes.

But how had they found him that quickly?

Eddie leaped to his feet so suddenly that the laptop almost slid to the floor. He pulled on his socks and shoes, and, shrugging into his down jacket, he left the apartment and ran down the street. Their SUV, now somewhat advanced in years, was parked a few hundred yards away on a sloping stretch of road, half dusted in the light snow that had fallen during the night. And despite his illness, despite the snow and the cold weather, Eddie rolled onto his side on the tarmac and wriggled close enough to the undercarriage to look beneath it.

It wasn't easy to see much under there, because the whole thing was plastered in dirt, grime, and gungy muck, but then he spotted it, in the middle. It wasn't very big. But it was there.

He had heard about GPS trackers but had never had one used on him, and Eddie was petrified. Now he understood how Rasmus Bruhn had been tracked down so fast, and it dawned on him in the same moment that if he and his family didn't get out right now, they would run out of time altogether.

24

CARL

Saturday, January 2, 2021

Should I start scratching lines into the wall? wondered Carl.

Today marked one week since his arrest, but to him it felt like half a lifetime. Everything that had happened since he left Vendsyssel had made so much sense. Now it was as though his years as a detective had volatilized and slipped away. The sense that he had done his best and done it well was being ground out of him, leaving only the thought that he had failed, had suffered an unforgivable lapse of attention.

He was being treated like a criminal, and after only a week he felt like one. Almost infinitely distant from the hands that might hold him, from the brains that thought like him, from the emotions that had welled up in him in recent years. He heard the sound of doors being locked, of bars slamming shut, of keys rattling and the faint voices of inmates in the prison corridors, going about the dawning routines of the day.

This was his life now.

In the past, Carl had always felt strong. He'd possessed the traditional Vendsyssel stoicism, its steadiness of mind. He'd been the one with the power and sometimes even the glory. But now the scornful voices in his head were jeering that no one out there felt sorry for him and that he shouldn't feel sorry for himself either.

Come on, Carl, he urged himself. He sure as hell didn't deserve to be sitting in this hole with the criminals he'd spent half his life trying to catch.

And now they had their chance to take him down. It might not be as overt as it had been at Vestre, but there were other methods. He would have to watch his every step, that was for sure.

They could come up from behind with a garotte; they wouldn't need much. A shoelace, a length of chain, the wire he saw wrapped around a box in the corridor yesterday, Carl thought to himself. Assaults on fellow inmates usually happened from behind, so if he kept his back to the walls and his head turned slightly to the side, he could make that more difficult.

Then there was the food. A single drop in the salami just before he ate it might do the trick, if the poison was strong enough. Or an "accident." As a detective he had witnessed time and time again how murders could be camouflaged as accidents. This recent business with Sisle Park had consisted of virtually nothing but.

Jesus, Carl, this isn't good, he thought, and almost jumped out of his skin when he heard the key put into the lock.

"Good morning, Carl," said a female officer he knew fairly well from the days when he'd occasionally driven down to the remand center on police business. Klara Kvist, she was called, one of the most senior members of staff.

"All right, Carl. You've got a rather busy morning, so try to get something to eat now, then I'll come and get you in fifteen minutes. Your wife's going to call you. It's a bit of an exception—we wouldn't normally allow that outside of normal telephone hours, but obviously we know what happened to you in Vestre, and your wife wants to hear that you're all right, straight from the horse's mouth. We'll do it at the desk in the guard room. You'll have ten minutes. And later today, after your case-worker has dropped in to say hello, you have another visit scheduled, although I don't know much about that one. Oh, and I wanted to let you know that Malthe, the guy they brought down with you, is going to be transferred to the cell next door. Going forward, the two of you will be given yard time together, and you may also be allowed some time in the same cell." She moved toward the door but stopped with her back still turned, tilting her head as though there was something she'd forgotten to say.

"Thank you, Klara," said Carl, taking a sip of coffee.

She turned around with a wide smile. "It's good to see you again, Carl, but I'm sorry it's under these circumstances. It must be very strange for you. It certainly is for us."

He nodded. "Strange"—was that the word for it?

"We've been reading the articles in *Gossip* on your latest case, and it's pretty amazing. I wanted you to know that's what we think."

He smiled. Suddenly the coffee had a bit more kick.

"Oh, and you should know that the reward, the seven million that's being offered for any information that clears your name and gets you released—it's probably the biggest news in Denmark right about now."

Carl had no idea what she was talking about.

He found out a little more when he was escorted to the telephone, and Mona's voice in short bursts restored to him a little optimism.

After a few assurances that he was fine, that she didn't need to worry about his safety, and that he would pass on her sincerest thanks to Malthe, the news came pouring out of her.

She had been thinking of him a lot, especially on New Year's Eve, and she'd been keeping as busy as the team at Department Q. But while she updated him in veiled terms on their investigation and all the frustrating spokes thrust into their wheels, Carl sensed she was holding back what she really wanted to tell him.

"Hardy is coming to see you today, Carl," she said at last. "We saw him on New Year's Eve, and he's totally on your side."

"What did you say? Hardy's coming? Here?" He was stunned.

Mona told him about Hardy's exoskeleton and the implants in his skull. That he was able to stand at his full height and that his mind was clear. That the operations, the rehab, all of it had surpassed their wildest expectations.

She had to repeat that last part. Carl was overwhelmed. He was so moved he could barely hold the phone, and his nervous system was pulsing in sine waves. For a moment he felt as though he might start hyperventilating or throwing up, but then he grabbed hold of the desk, took a deep breath, and absorbed the extraordinary news.

If it was really true, then everything else instantly mattered less—the charges, the arrest, the assaults, and the precariousness of his position.

Carl had only just gotten a grip on himself, repeating several times that it was incredible, that he was more delighted than he'd ever felt before, when the next bomb came hurtling at his head.

Rose had received a visit from Merete Lynggaard.

It took him a beat, absorbing the echo of her name, to understand.

Many times over the years he had wondered how she was doing after they rescued her from certain death in her kidnapper's pressure chamber, but Carl had never dared to check. Despite his curiosity, he was too afraid that the reality might be brutal.

Merete Lynggaard had been barely a shadow of her former self when she was released. The gulf between the strong, self-assured political figure—the woman who had, perhaps, once aspired to be Denmark's first female prime minister—and the mutilated soul and tormented body that emerged from the pressure chamber was simply too great for Carl to imagine she had survived with her sanity intact.

But Mona told him only good things about her life and then mentioned the enormous reward Lynggaard was offering. She said several people whose lives Carl had touched during his investigations had joined forces with Merete and that several voices in the media were now actively looking for stories that cast him in a positive light.

"Carl, are you there?!" she asked, when he stopped reacting to the barrage of information.

The corrections officer standing beside him managed to grab him just in time before his knees buckled.

After they had said goodbye he sat in his cell for an hour, unable to stem the flow of his tears. So many knots in his stomach were loosening—in true Vendsyssel style, he could scarcely breathe.

In his hometown in the dark north of Jutland, his father had impressed upon him that in life, experiencing genuine pain was all the more reason to hold your head high. Adversity had to be confronted, looked directly in the eyes. If there was nothing you could do to finish it, you either died or were locked in an eternal battle to keep it at bay. Carl had never quite understood where his father was going with these absurd ruminations, but right now his philosophy was difficult to ignore. The adversity was still undeniable, but what he'd just heard had made the battle easier to bear, he had to admit. And when he finally felt the stream of tears ebb away, he dropped his head to his chest and sighed so deeply that the noticeboard on the wall nearest to him quivered.

Unusually, Carl was led into the visitors' room first. With the colorful hot-air balloon at his back, he sat waiting for nearly half an hour before he heard the heavy sound of approaching footsteps.

He stood up, heart pounding. He had felt this way before, each time he'd stood in front of a door he knew might change his life when it was opened. The door leading to the green desks where he'd taken his exams; the door that a girl he'd fallen in love with, although she didn't know it, would soon open; the door to his grandmother's shadow-shrouded death-bed. Decisive doors in his life—and now, another one.

Hardy was a lot taller than he remembered. His features now were very clearly drawn, his arms stronger, his gaze more direct, but his smile was the same as in the old days.

It was an extraordinary sight: Hardy moving straight toward him in his enormous armored suit. Carl had planned out how he was going to welcome him, but his tongue felt glued to the roof of his mouth, striking him dumb.

"Hey there, buddy!" Hardy said, pulling him in for a hug as the mechanical arms whirred. As he did so, Carl tried to reach around Hardy's waist, but all he grabbed was the hard shell around his hips.

He caught Hardy's eye somewhere above his head and returned his smile with trembling lips.

Then Morten came into the room, accompanied by a police officer and a man Carl didn't know but presumed was Hardy's carer. Then in came Klara, the prison guard, bringing a chair from the guard room for Hardy.

It took a minute to get Hardy seated, and only once they were all in their chairs did Carl's vocal cords loosen enough for him to express how glad he was to see Hardy moving almost under his own steam and how grateful they were to be visiting him in this godforsaken place.

They soon got the initial pleasantries over with: Hardy's regret that they were meeting again under such circumstances, Carl's immense gratitude that things had gone so well in Switzerland, his astonishment at seeing Hardy upright after so many years. He nodded to Morten, thanking him for his perseverance and asking him to pass on his best wishes and thanks to Mika as well.

Then, in a barely audible voice, Hardy asked Morten and the carer to wait for him behind the open door of the next room, where the police officer was sitting. He and Carl had some personal matters to discuss.

Carl was startled. Was Hardy expecting him to confide something, for Carl to fall to his knees and confess? Or did he have some unpleasant surprise hidden behind his armor?

"I'm sorry, Carl" was the first thing Hardy said when they were alone. "Come over here and take my hand."

Carl did.

"I have to admit," Hardy continued, "I've thought things about you that should never even have crossed my mind."

Carl shook his head. "Thank you, Hardy, but I understand why you might have doubted me. Anker and I must have seemed very close. Sometimes I even doubt myself—I start wondering whether I might unwittingly have been involved in something illegal. That body in the crate, the suitcase in my attic, the trumped-up evidence against us. Why would anybody do something like that, Hardy?"

Hardy's hand tried to squeeze Carl's at the mention of his name. Then he closed his eyes, his nostrils quivering slightly.

"It's strange, but over the last few months I've been seeing things much more clearly than before. All my senses feel heightened; I don't know why. My hearing is better, my voice is getting stronger. And my sense of smell, that's much sharper now as well. Even just the smell of citrus in here, it practically bowled me over when I stepped into the room. Is that your cologne?"

Carl shook his head, inhaling deeply through his nose, but he registered only the barest trace against the other odors of the prison. Yes, it was there, and yes, it carried a top note of citrus.

"As I said, my senses are heightened, and I intend to make full use of that for as long as it lasts. I've also been thinking more deeply than I have in years, and things have been popping into my head that I must have forgotten long ago. I've been seeing connections where I didn't see them before. Maybe all that pain and rehab I went through in Switzerland strengthened other things as well, including in my brain. I felt it, day by day. You mentioned the dismembered corpse they dug up in a crate under old Georg Madsen's house. A pretty macabre, monstrous thing to find. But what about the anonymous tip-off we received? That the corpse was someone called Pete Boswell, a guy from Jamaica who was connected to the company Kandaloo Workshop? Who gave us that tip? The Dutch found out that Pete Boswell was actually a pen name used by the drug dealer Rasmus Bruhn, but Bruhn was still alive when the body was found. And before that, he got into a scrap with Anker, which was when you got dragged into it. But has anybody properly looked into the company mentioned by the tipster, Kandaloo Workshop? I've seen no sign that it was investigated, which is rather curious, don't you think?"

"I don't know, Hardy. We never discussed that case in Department Q. I mean, I was too close, you know? But it is weird that it wasn't solved long ago, if you ask me. What's your take?"

At that moment the policeman appeared in the doorway. "Let me remind you that you are not allowed to discuss the ongoing case against Mr. Mørck. As you well know."

Hardy raised one arm. "We know that, Officer. We're just chatting about the old days."

Carl eyed the officer for a moment. Was that a wink? Then he retreated back to his seat in the next room, where the others were waiting too.

"Anyway," Hardy said, almost at a whisper, "that's what I've been working on over the past couple of weeks, and that's what I want to talk to you about. The Dutch found out that Rasmus Bruhn, alias Pete Boswell, had a partner, a Haitian man by the name of Gérard Gaillard. According to the commercial register, he was the sole owner of Kandaloo Workshop. The register also says that the company was insolvent for pretty much its entire existence, and after Gaillard's death, it was dissolved by court order."

"Okay. I got the impression that the business imported furniture from the Middle East or something, right?" Carl asked very quietly.

"Not so much as a chair, if you ask me. The company's name was just a couple of lines on his business card, that's all. But the man was obviously doing pretty well for himself, because the deeds to several rather valuable properties were in Gaillard's name. A couple of warehouses in Rotterdam and one in this country. An apartment on Gråbrødretorv and a farm in Albersdorf in Schleswig. All debt-free and collectively worth somewhere in the vicinity of ten million euros on today's market."

"Suspicious!" murmured Carl. After all, somebody must have known. "What happened to the properties? I mean, it resulted in a man's death."

"Well, I haven't finished my investigation yet, but I'll find out."

"Why did you send Morten and your carer out of the room? Surely it doesn't matter if they listen in?" he whispered.

"Glad to see you haven't completely withered away in here, Carl. Why, you ask? Because my carer is new, is the answer."

"And?"

"At first I had someone else assisting me, a French-speaking Swiss man who worked at the clinic, but when I was discharged they gave me this guy. He seems nice enough on the face of it, but he's been asking a lot of questions about me and about what happened all those years ago in Amager."

"I see! Let me guess—he approached the clinic himself, didn't he?"

Hardy tipped his head forward several times.

"And he's a French speaker, of course, but Belgian, not French—am I right?"

The creases on Hardy's face, harrowingly etched by frustration and pain, relaxed. "Thank you, Carl," he said. "Looks like we're partners again!"

They spoke in low voices about anything and everything for another half an hour, then suddenly it was as though all Hardy's batteries died.

But the plan was clear: Hardy would keep investigating who had taken over the properties belonging to the late Gérard Gaillard, and he would do everything he could to uncover the purpose and identity of his Belgian carer. Meanwhile, Gordon would dig further into the Dutch connection, and after that they would reconvene.

Carl then exchanged a few brief words with Morten. He could tell Morten was holding back tears—he had always been a sensitive soul—so Carl patted his arm and tried to reassure him that everything would be fine. "Say hi to Mika for me," he said as they parted.

They left a yawning void in Carl when they departed, even the friendly police officer, but especially Hardy, once he staggered away, receding down the corridor with hard, echoing steps. For a moment before he was returned to his cell, Carl sat still and tried to wrap his head around the whole thing.

He gazed around at the motley-colored room with its gentle decorations, his breath coming in anxious jerks. Then, in a sudden rush, he was struck by the scent of citrus that had had such a powerful effect on Hardy. He inhaled deeply, filling his lungs several times to a bursting point, then exhaled very slowly through his nose. Each time he did so, it was as though the smell grew more concentrated and more readily apparent.

He stopped breathing entirely when he recognized it, holding the air in his lungs until he remembered the first time he had noticed it.

He could picture the man clearly now. Pomaded hair, threatening him in the exercise yard in Vestre Prison. The man who had come and gone like a ghost.

What's going on here? What was he doing at Slagelse? Carl wondered, but he didn't know. It was a deeply disquieting feeling.

"Sooo," said Klara, when she came to escort him back. "Wasn't that a big surprise? It was for us, anyway—I can't believe we saw Hardy Henningsen. We've just been reading about him in *Gossip*. It's marvelous what science can do these days, and it's nice to see him getting so much help from his Danish friends and that French carer. Did you ever think he'd walk again after so many years?"

Carl shook his head. But he'd been hoping for it every single day.

Then he looked directly into her eyes. "Klara, you can help me by giving me some information, if you want to."

She frowned. "Maybe. It depends . . . What do you want to know?"

"There's a faint scent of perfume in here. Kind of sweet and acidic at the same time, very fresh, actually. Like citrus fruit. Can you smell it?"

She smiled at the harmlessness of the question. Then she sniffed the air a few times.

"Oh yeah, maybe. Why? Would you like us to get hold of it for you?"

"Mm, no, I don't think so. I was just wondering who was in here wearing that perfume. Was there anybody in the visitors' room before me today?"

"Visiting? No."

"What about yesterday?"

"Well, yes, there was a lawyer here yesterday. Now that you mention it, it might well be his cologne. Someone you used to know, is it?"

"Maybe. Do you know his name?"

"Carl, you can't ask me straight out like that, as you well know. Unless he's your lawyer, I'm not allowed to tell you."

He nodded. "But can you at least tell me who he talked to?"

She pursed her lips. The regulations were making the cogs in her head spin.

"Oh, all right. If you keep your mouth shut about it, then who cares, I suppose. He spoke to two people, both in his capacity as their legal counsel: first, your friend from Vestre, Malthe, and then a little while later to that overgrown lump from the first floor, Tom Gravgaard. The one they call Cassius. Come to think of it, it was those two who got into a pissing contest in the yard later that same day."

25

EDDIE

Saturday, January 2, 2021

What the hell was I thinking? Eddie's brain was in a whirl as he rushed back up the slope in the Valkenburg dawn, the GPS tracker in his hand. It was a medium-size magnetic device about four inches across, and it had been placed in the middle of the undercarriage, so that he'd had to stretch out his whole body to reach it.

It was a sophisticated model that weighed less than a pound and cost nothing. Eddie clapped a hand to his mouth when he considered how long the battery on one of these could last. Sixty days. *Sixty* days! It could have been sitting there for weeks, but the chances of them neglecting to change the battery after the two months had passed did not strike Eddie as particularly high. His paymasters did not forget things like that.

He hurried past the holiday apartment at the top of the hill and a few hundred yards farther down a side street, where he photographed the tracker and put it under one of the parked vehicles there. "Best Baker in Town" was written on the side of the van, and Eddie hoped the baker would remain so even after his employers found the GPS.

Oh my god, what am I doing? Am I going to come clean to Femke or what? he thought, and stopped short. *Do I have to, if we're still safe in the apartment?*

Then the brutal truth hit home.

It was January 2, and they had fled Rotterdam four days ago. That meant the people who had put the tracker under his car knew the family's route and thus their current location.

Eddie was paralyzed. This explained Rasmus Bruhn's fate. Even though the man had fled, he'd never stood a chance of escaping, and nor did Eddie and his family.

His enemies must be somewhere nearby.

For the second time that morning, Eddie dashed back in the direction of the SUV, and when he was still sixty or seventy feet away, he slowed down and approached with caution.

Was somebody lying in wait? It would be remarkable, actually, if they weren't.

Had they seen him remove the GPS, perhaps already replaced it with another one?

Eddie was desperate to slip back under the vehicle to check, but he didn't dare, not here.

After passing a couple more side streets, he leaned around the corner of the street where he'd parked, and since there was nothing out of the ordinary to be seen, he made a break for the SUV and flung himself into the driver's seat.

Halfway out of town, he pulled over and crawled underneath his car for the second time that morning. The asphalt was ice-cold and hard beneath him, but what did that matter, so long as he made sure they hadn't managed to replace the tracker he'd put under the bakery van?

In the morning light, as the town slowly began to wake, Eddie sat quietly behind the wheel, at his wits' end.

If the tracker had been working—and why wouldn't it?—that meant the organization knew precisely where they were, and they would be keeping the area under observation.

If that was the case, all was lost.

He rocked helplessly back and forth, until at last he made up his mind. For a moment he'd considered simply putting the pedal to the metal and disappearing. Heading out of town, anyplace that wasn't there. That might keep Femke and the little one out of danger.

Eddie gasped at the thought. What the hell was he thinking? Of course they'd still be in danger. The people he had worked for would stop at nothing, and besides, his laptop was still in the room, trumpeting his betrayal from the rooftops.

If, instead, he picked up his loved ones and made a run for it, Femke would not be satisfied with excuses. She would force the truth out of him, and then she'd leave him for sure. No, Femke couldn't find out.

That left him with only two options. He could call his colleagues and turn himself in, but who could he trust? What if there were others besides him who worked for the organization? And would they even get here in time, before it was too late? He doubted it. The other option, of course, was to ascertain whether they had actually been tracked. If he switched his phone off airplane mode and skimmed his text messages, that might tell him if he was still in the organization's good books. But if he did that, he'd have to be quick about it, because otherwise they could trace the phone's GPS. It was like choosing between cholera and the plague.

But that was the option Eddie chose.

Not thirty seconds passed before the messages began filtering in, becoming one drawn-out ping.

Eddie scanned them as fast as he could. Half were from his superiors in Rotterdam, expressing their confusion as to where he'd gotten to. At first their tone was irritated, then increasingly concerned. Well, that was something.

The second half, on the other hand, were more frightening.

Where are you? Check in, said the first. It was almost reassuring, because they clearly didn't know where he was.

Farther down, however, they took a more serious turn.

What are you doing in Valkenburg? What are you doing in Aachen? Why aren't you checking in?

And as more messages pinged in, the tone grew increasingly blunt.

You don't have much time left, we know where you are—And then the final message, which turned Eddie's blood to ice in his veins.

Eddie Jansen, we saw that you removed the tracker and that the car is gone. Come back to the apartment in Valkenburg or you won't see your family alive again.

He hurtled down the streets of the town at full speed. He loved his Femke and little Marika more than himself. If he could exchange his own life for theirs, then so be it.

He parked the car halfway up on the pavement outside the apartment complex, ran up the steps, and let himself in.

There stood Femke in her dressing gown, Marika in her arms, looking at him with a mixture of astonishment and anger.

"Where have you been, Eddie? You can't just take off like that. I was . . ."

Eddie glanced around in all directions. There didn't seem to be anyone else in the apartment.

"Femke, don't ask any questions, just do as I say. Put your clothes on and get ready to leave."

She protested, hurling baffled and indignant questions after him, but Eddie slunk past her without replying, opened his laptop, jammed a memory stick into it, and began to download his document.

"Come on," he shouted at her.

She was glaring at him stubbornly with an obvious antipathy that was hard to stomach. "We're not well, Eddie—what on earth do you want?"

Eddie just shook his head, pulled out the memory stick, and slipped it into the pocket of Femke's kimono. Then, putting his face tenderly to her cheek, his lips close to her ear, he whispered that she should take good care of it and give it to the police in Amsterdam. Nobody else, for God's sake.

Then he turned to the computer and deleted the file. Afterward, when he caught her eye, not a single line of her expression suggested that she understood the gravity of the situation. She was just standing there, warming up for another furious outburst, he could tell.

"If we're not out that door in five minutes, you can say goodbye to me forever, Femke. They're coming for me," he cried.

He stroked Marika's hair as the little girl nestled close to her mother and began to snivel.

"You're scaring Marika. Who's coming for you?" she hissed.

Eddie took a deep breath. He was on the verge of giving her a glimpse of the awful truth when another text message pinged onto his screen.

Holding up a hand to ward her off, he read the message.

It's a good thing you came back, Eddie. We can hear you arguing, because we're right outside your door. Your wife doesn't know anything. Luckily. That means your family is safe, but you aren't.

Then the doorbell rang.

26

CARL

Saturday, January 2, 2021

Yard time was a solo performance with accompaniment, taking place after delivery of the evening meal, plus next day's breakfast and lunch. It was brief, because Carl didn't need fresh air, he said, although that wasn't entirely true—but right now he was more interested in mulling over Hardy's visit.

That morning he had felt so powerless it was suffocating, the walls of his cell growing steeper and starting to tilt in over him. Then he'd heard Mona's voice, which had been light and clear, giving him a sense of closeness. A feeling that the world outside remembered him, that there were forces being brought to bear that would help make sure the situation ended well. It was comforting. And then he'd met with Hardy, who had told him with a long-buried note of calm in his voice that there were circumstances and events yet to be explained, a case that could perhaps be solved. For the first time since his arrest, Carl felt like himself, like he wouldn't put up with anything that didn't serve his interests.

He smiled quietly when the lock in his cell door rattled and Klara Kvist poked her head inside.

"I've got Malthe here, Carl. We thought you might like to chat for a bit before he goes into number 7. Funnily enough—I mean it almost never happens—we're doing a bit of reshuffle. There's someone going into cell 5 across the corridor. It's like musical chairs out here!"

She laughed, then stood aside to make room in the doorway for Malthe, who took up the full width of the floor space in front of Carl's bed.

"Twenty minutes," she said, and locked the door.

Carl stayed sitting down. He gave Malthe a nod. "Why don't you sit on the edge of the table? I hope it holds," he said, laughing good-naturedly, but he observed the confusion on Malthe's face. Would he have preferred to sit on the bed beside him—was that what he expected?

"Thanks for your help in Vestre. I said it already, but it bears repeating. You saved my life, you know that?"

There was no change in the man's expression, and he remained standing.

"I have a young daughter and a wife I love more than anything on Earth. You saved their lives too, in a way. I just wanted to tell you that. Oh, and my wife, Mona, sends her warmest wishes."

Malthe's shoulders dropped a fraction. For a moment it looked almost as though his solid, stoic body had lost its footing on the floor. Then he snapped back into the same posture as before.

"My family means everything to me, you know. And the fact that you're so close to me means Mona feels safe enough to sleep at night. We're both very grateful to you for that, Malthe."

Carl smiled at him cautiously. Did the man really understand the depth of what was going on here? It seemed unlikely, because his expression hadn't changed at all.

"You know what! Everyone I know who cares about me is working to prove my innocence, just as everybody knows you protected me and you're still at my side. So, again: thank you, Malthe."

Carl paused. It was as though his words simply glanced off the man. He might have responded with a single weak nod when Carl mentioned the word "family," but he wasn't sure.

"What about you, Malthe? Do you have family outside these four walls too, people thinking of you?"

For the first time, he averted his eyes from Carl's. For a minute, there was silence between them, and Carl wondered if the big man in front of him might be a little slow. Perhaps the words were coming at him too quickly and from directions he could not predict.

But then he met Carl's gaze again, and in a surprisingly harsh tone of voice, he said, "My little brother is dying, and I can't think about anything else day or night. I think you should know that."

Carl sat in silence for a moment. The close-fitting armor around Malthe dissolved, and instead of his powerful frame, Carl saw only lips that trembled, eyes that were no longer gray, hands that dangled limply.

Why does he think I should know that? wondered Carl. Was he trying to explain his reserve while they had been transported to Slagelse? Was there even a reason? Perhaps the dull-witted impression conveyed by his heavy, pudgy body and general demeanor was in fact correct. Perhaps there were certain things his mind simply couldn't contain.

"I'm sorry to hear that, Malthe. Is there nothing that can be done?" he asked.

Was that a nod?

"What's wrong with your brother? Is it operable?"

"It's his pancreas." The words were toneless, no trace of emotion. "They won't operate on him here in Denmark. In his situation it's too dangerous and too expensive, they say."

Carl got up off the bed. The pancreas—what could be worse?

"So the health service has given up on him, is that it?"

He nodded. "In Denmark they won't treat him anymore. But in Germany they offered to do the surgery."

Carl nodded. "So they'll have to do that, right?"

Malthe took a step closer to Carl. His breath was hot, and a vein throbbed hard at his temple. "It costs money, lots of money, and we don't have it."

"How much money, Malthe?"

Carl might as well have held an arm out toward the man, because he froze midmovement at the question, as though turned to stone.

Then the lock rattled again, and Klara stood in the doorway, sleeves rolled up, apologizing for having to cut their conversation short. One of the officers had started coughing, so they'd sent him home to isolate. That left nobody to fetch Malthe later, since they also had to put the new guy in cell 5.

"One second, Klara, I'm sorry. Malthe was about to tell me something."

Carl held out a hand to the prison guard, but Malthe's face shifted once again. The vulnerability stiffened it, and his eyes narrowed. Then he shook his head.

"Forget it, Carl," he said, with a strange edge to his voice.

Carl nodded. Maybe they could pick it up the next time they met, he thought.

"You had a visitor yesterday, Malthe. Who was it?"

"If I had a visitor yesterday, I don't remember them."

Carl looked at Klara, but she didn't react. She couldn't, of course.

"Okay. My mistake, I suppose. It happens." He smiled at Malthe but received nothing in return.

Afterward he sat back down on the bed. Every word, every inflection, everything that had gone unsaid in his encounter with the heavyset man was analyzed and minutely examined, and all told it left him with a bad feeling.

From that moment on, Carl knew for certain he was still alone in this comfortless place.

27

FEMKE

Sunday, January 3–Monday, January 4, 2021

After a few minutes Femke left the apartment, not the least concerned about the luggage she was leaving behind.

Still sniffling heavily and pale with shock, she tried to think rationally. Never had she imagined a situation like the one she was in now.

I need to grab the bag of Marika's clothes, my purse and keys. Put my coat on, pick up the little girl and leave, she thought mechanically. She had to get out of there.

As she ran down the street, hoping to find the SUV, her mind raced. Who was the man with the different-colored eyes, what had Eddie done, was the lottery win all a lie she'd bought into, and where could she go if the man knew their address in Schiedam?

She stopped at a street corner and looked around, her warm breath like fog in the cold air. *Oh no, where's the car?* she thought frantically. *Isn't it down there, in the middle of that street on a hill?*

Then she heard an engine rev, a vehicle approaching from behind. Instinctively she hugged her child close and shrank back against the wall. She caught a glimpse of the man who had taken her husband, sitting behind the wheel of a black Skoda station wagon.

He didn't see me, he didn't see me! she recited hopefully to herself as she tried to memorize the letters and numbers of the car's red Belgian plates.

Her eyes darted back and forth across the row of parked cars. *Eddie, Eddie, why didn't you tell me where you put it?*

She began to feel the cold now, and Marika was starting to shiver and cough. "Mama's going to find Daddy's car, Marika. Hang on just a minute and we'll be there."

And then there it was, barely visible behind a large truck. Halfway up on the curb, its front wheels turned toward the road.

"There, my darling, there we are." Quick as a flash, she got Marika into the car seat in the back and herself behind the wheel.

Femke considered herself a good driver. Over the years she had learned there was nothing dangerous about traffic, as long as she kept her distance and remained alert. So she released the handbrake and skidded across the lane in a single fluid movement.

They must be pretty far ahead of me by now, she thought, stepping on the accelerator. Other drivers honked at her as she careened down the narrow streets, but Femke didn't care. If she was stopped by the police, she could give them a good reason for speeding, and once they heard why, then . . .

Twice she ran through yellow lights just before they turned red, hearing the screech of brakes from side streets, which told her in no uncertain terms that she should have stopped.

When she was nearly out of town, she caught a glimpse of the black Skoda farther ahead. It was going at a fair lick but seemed to be keeping to the speed limit and generally observing the laws of the road.

"Just one more red light and I'll be right on their tail," she said aloud, narrowly avoiding mowing down a cyclist who couldn't wait for the green light. She glanced into the rearview mirror, and above a laughing Marika she saw the cyclist was unharmed enough to get up unassisted and start bawling threats at her in the middle of the road.

Maybe he'd gotten her license plate, maybe not. She couldn't care less. She was close enough now to the Skoda that she could easily follow it at a distance.

During the next two hours, they crossed the border between Belgium and Holland twice. North from Valkenburg at first, via Maastricht and into Belgium. Then through Antwerp and back into Holland, continuing west toward the province of Zeeland, where she had never been before. After passing through flats that seemed to go on forever, former wetlands that had long since been dammed and cultivated, she found herself reaching the polders. At this point she slowed down, realizing that if she went on much longer, she would be discovered.

"We're going to get Daddy back, Marika," she said uncertainly to the little girl, who had been asleep for the last hundred kilometers. Femke allowed the black car that contained her husband to vanish into the powdery white landscape, where there wasn't so much as a copse of trees for her to hide behind. Out here, somewhere in this godforsaken, all-too-flat, and fertile landscape, her journey ended. And, she feared, it might be the end of the road for her husband too.

She found a room at an affordable hotel in Middelburg. It was a little way outside the town and sufficiently secluded that she could use the time to think and make up her mind.

Give the memory stick to the police in Amsterdam. Whatever you do, for God's sake don't give it to anybody else, Eddie had said. But why not to his colleagues in Rotterdam? She didn't understand. What was even on it?

Utterly exhausted, she put the little girl into her nightie and ordered a small meal from room service, and then at last they both fell asleep.

She woke up the next morning with the memory stick clutched in her hand and her daughter sitting on top of the duvet in high spirits.

After they had eaten breakfast, Femke could wait no longer.

She scooped up Marika and went downstairs to reception.

"Could I please borrow a computer? There's a couple of things I need to check," she asked.

The two friendly receptionists showed her into a small room adjoining the lobby, saying that if she needed to print anything, she could pay at the desk.

Then she put Marika on the floor, inserted the memory stick into the PC, and examined its contents.

Femke was an experienced secretary who frequently had to problem-solve when confronted with her employers' ineptitude around technology and computing, and she had to call on all that ingenuity now. Her husband had saved his document in a newer Word format that was not supported by the hotel's ancient PC. She looked around, peering into the sitting room area, where a well-dressed young gentleman was typing away on his laptop with a cup of steaming coffee by his side.

"Excuse me," she said. "Sorry to disturb you, but the hotel computer only has an old version of Word, and I have a file on this memory stick that's saved in a newer one. I couldn't possibly use your laptop to convert it to an older version, could I?"

He shook his head. He couldn't let a stranger put some random memory stick into his computer. His company simply didn't allow it.

After a short search, she found a used laptop at a store called Lowbudgetpc on Zandstraat in Middelburg, which they assured her was both fully charged and installed with all the software she needed. Then she took Marika to the Albert Heijn around the corner, bought nappies and a few things for herself, and returned to the car.

"Mama just has to quickly look at something, Marika, then we'll find a café where we can change you."

She handed the little girl some leaflets from the supermarket to flip through, inserted the stick into the laptop, opened the document, and began to read.

Five minutes later, she began to cry. Her whole life was crashing down around her ears. She tried to compose herself, but it was impossible, even when Marika began to wail as well, loudly enough that an old woman knocked on the window and asked if everything was all right.

Femke's hands were shaking as she started the car and gripped the steering wheel. Her husband had been party to terrible things. Many of the unfortunate people she had read about in recent years, people killed by a nail to the head, people drowned, shot, or stabbed, were named in the document. Drug trafficking, leaking confidential information, tax evasion and aliases, contact with middlemen and people at the docks who were shipping narcotics into the country—her husband had been aware of all of it; in fact, much of it he'd actually participated in. How could he?

There seemed little doubt now that everything they owned had been bought with the proceeds of Eddie's criminal activities, which meant that her entire life would collapse if she gave this document to the authorities.

Halfway out of town she found a café where she could change Marika. Once they were finally seated at the café table, she with a cup of strong coffee and Marika with milk and a few Dutch doughnuts that sent both her blood sugar and her mood skyrocketing, Femke put her mind to work.

Was she even going to try to fulfill her husband's wish? That was the question. Why should she, frankly, given what a terrible person he was and how badly he had treated her?

What if she simply drove back to Schiedam and went on with her life as though nothing had happened? Told his colleagues he'd walked out of their holiday apartment in Valkenburg and she hadn't heard from him since? Would she be able to keep the cabin and their home and all the money she was sure he'd stashed away somewhere? Judging by what she'd read in that document, she wasn't likely to see him alive again. So why not just let sleeping dogs lie, if there was no benefit to her or Marika?

No. Femke shook her head. No, it would serve no purpose. She would make sure she erased all trace of the memory stick as soon as she possibly could.

She gazed out the window as the quiet town sedately went about its life. They were well outside of tourist season. People strolled past chatting along the slushy streets, shopping carts waited to be filled, cyclists trundled by. A totally normal, insignificant day—wasn't that all she wanted for herself and Marika right now?

Then she noticed the black Skoda station wagon roll past, beyond the bare trees, trailing white exhaust. It was heading toward the town center.

28

ROSE

Saturday, January 2, 2021

Carl's old terraced house in Allerød was virtually unrecognizable. Hardy's hospital bed had been replaced, and although his new one was in its former place, with a hoist of some kind erected above it and controls added to elevate the backrest, the gold bedspread and pair of Empire-inspired nightstands erased all trace of the institutional.

The living room had been painted and the furniture rearranged so that conversations could be held and television watched. Everything felt brighter and much more orderly than before.

"Mika and I are still spending most of our time in the basement," Morten said, "but we sleep on the first floor."

Rose glanced around the living room and the adjoining kitchen. Not much sign of the many years Carl had lived in the house remained, but Mona remarked that personal effects and knickknacks had never really interested him.

"Wasn't Molise Sjögren supposed to come today as well?" Gordon asked.

Assad shook his head. "We agreed to meet another time. But she said she'd had an encouraging talk with Noah Rommel at the PCA, although unfortunately there was nothing new to report. She said the PCA have sent a man to liaise with the Dutch police, but she wasn't told where or why. She'll find out at some point, though."

"So what else have you discovered, Assad?" Mona asked.

"Me?! I've been back to Nørrebro, because I had a couple of things I wanted to discuss with that Niels B Marquis de Bourbon guy, but he'd cleared out. I went into his garage, and there was absolutely nothing left. Nothing on the walls, only a few bits of junk and paper on the floor. Like he'd just up and bolted."

"What about the homeless guys who knew him? Did you speak to them?"

Assad stroked his hedgehoggy chin. "They asked me what the hell . . ." He paused to think for a moment. "What in the ever loving hell I'd said to him, because they'd not seen hide nor hair of him since. And then one of them suggested I needed a boot up the arse."

"A boot? Bet that would have hurt," said Hardy from the sofa.

Assad stared at him uncomprehendingly.

"It's a little concerning to hear that about Niels B," said Hardy, "but I have another worry to add to the pile. Terje Ploug has suddenly been taken off the nail gun case, with no explanation except that his services could be better used elsewhere, now that the PCA has taken over the investigation."

"But, Hardy, you can still sound him out and get his advice, right?" asked Rose.

"Maybe, I'm not sure."

"Because?"

"Because Terje Ploug has just met with the chief constable. I think she's dangling the prospect of being promoted to Jacobsen's job as homicide boss when he retires."

"What difference would that make? It seems like the obvious line of succession," Rose said.

"It makes a difference if Terje starts obstructing Carl's investigation. My bet is he's been muzzled."

"Fuck's sake. Isn't there anybody left in homicide who has Carl's best interests at heart?"

"What about his colleague Bente Hansen? She was always fond of Carl, wasn't she?" Mona asked.

"Yep, I can vouch for that," Hardy said. "But I heard Bente was also hauled in to see the chief. Maybe she'll be the one who gets Marcus's job. Equality, you know! So we'll have to wait and see what she wants and doesn't want."

The mood in the room was flagging. Uphill work, whichever way they looked at it.

"Yeah, that's not great. On the other hand, I did break into DKNL's premises in Vanløse yesterday," said Rose.

Oddly enough, she had set off no alarm in the vast garage, and not because there was nothing valuable inside. Far from it. The van alone, a large, relatively new Iveco with a tail lift, parked in the middle of the space, had to be worth well over half a million crowns.

Rose had peered around the garage under the blinking fluorescent lights. On the face of it, the place had seemed meticulously organized and tidy; certainly she'd seen plenty in her time that were anything but. There were no rusty, discarded old machines in here, no tattered posters of naked girls on the walls, or oil-spattered floors. DKNL had seemed, at first blush, to be a well-run, well-regulated company. Along one wall, running all the way from the floor to the ceiling twenty feet or so above her, had towered a metal shelving system divided into numbered shelves and spaces. Space 27 on shelf 4, for instance, had contained three large moving boxes labeled *Rob de V., Groningen*, and in the space next to it were three more boxes, inscribed with the words *Daniël Wouters, Haarlem*. More than half the spaces had been filled in this way, amounting to maybe more than a hundred boxes in total.

Rose had blown her nose, stuffed the tissue into her pocket, and let her eyes wander across the shelves. When she'd reached a shelf at about chest height, closer to the gate, she'd paused. On this shelf were no boxes, only a series of thin, dated record books.

Rose had stared irresolutely at the books for a moment, then grabbed the most recent one and opened it. Within less than five seconds she'd seen that they contained order numbers and a detailed description of the contents of each box on the shelves, including when it was due to be shipped and to what address. The middle box in space 27 on shelf 4, for example, to Rob de Vries in Groningen, had contained sixty Le Klint lampshades, the third box twenty rolls of fabric-covered cabling. Rose didn't have to be a mathematical genius to realize the contents of the shelves were worth a fortune.

Rose had run her finger down the delivery dates. By this time next week, the vast majority of the boxes would have been loaded up and driven away. Taking out her phone, she'd snapped a few photos of the pages, wiped her runny nose, and strolled over to the van.

She'd shaken the Iveco's doors. Both of the doors to the cab had been locked, so she'd dragged a box over to the running board and peered inside. There had been a sweetish smell, a fug that was presumably coming from a plastic bag of half-rotten bananas tossed onto the passenger seat. On the dashboard were two unopened packs of Prince cigarettes, a bag of Haribo gummies, and something that had appeared to be photocopies of the record books she'd just been looking at. Everything had seemed to indicate that the van had been loaded up and made ready to set off, maybe even a few days ago.

"I think something bad has happened at DKNL Transport," she said, looking around at her listeners. "That van should have been loaded up and driven off before the New Year, if the company wanted to get everything delivered in time."

Gordon's expression was disapproving, but then again, he was a stickler for the rules.

"After that, I broke into the low building next to it, where the offices are, and strangely enough that one wasn't alarmed either." She shrugged. "At any rate, it gave me a chance to go through the two rooms with a fine-tooth comb. There was a small office with a desk and a printer, and another even smaller one next to it filled with archival folders, newer ones and ones dating back a while."

"Jesus, Rose, you know you could be fired for this." Gordon looked scandalized.

"Yeah, but if the Sniffer Dog's department can't be bothered to search it, we have to resort to other means, don't we, Gordon?"

He shook his head slightly, and his face changed color. She generally had that effect on him.

"Anyway, long story short, I found this."

She spread some photographs she'd printed out on A4 paper in front of Hardy, and the others clustered around him.

"I grabbed the most recent ring binders first, then worked backward from there. Mostly, it was just order confirmations and invoices, but there were also a few folders containing correspondence and copies of other documents, going quite a long way back. And I found a couple of things that surprised me." Rose looked around at her colleagues.

"The company's telephone book was lying out on the desk in the office, so I flicked through it. And I saw, among other things, the number of a supermarket delivery service, nemlig.com, the kind lots of us are using these days, so I'm thinking the list must be relatively up-to-date. I also noticed that Hannes Theis was pretty into junk food, because there were some McDonald's wrappers in the bin."

"Nemlig.com—I've used them too," Gordon said.

"So there weren't any desktops or laptops in the office, Rose?" asked Mona.

"No! If there had been, I'd have brought them with me. I wondered about that when I saw the printer, but I imagine Theis has taken the office laptop with him. What really surprised me was that I couldn't find a single import-export company in the list of phone numbers. I searched through the pile of business cards as well—I've got them here—but there weren't any importers or exporters in there either, and anyway, who uses business cards these days?" She placed the stack of worn and obviously long-out-of-date cards next to the photos.

"I did, however, find three names under 'drivers.' Jess Larsen's name we know, and I've already contacted the other two. One of them now works full-time at another company, but the conversation with the other one was more interesting. He was clearly annoyed and complained about his experience with DKNL Transport."

"Interesting how, Rose?" Hardy asked.

"Because he's currently their only long-distance driver, and he was supposed to have set off on December twenty-ninth or thirtieth."

"But he didn't, so the orders couldn't be delivered on time, correct?" Hardy shut his eyes and sat in silence for a moment, as though sorting through the various pieces of the puzzle.

"All right, people! Why don't we have some chai—I think we could all do with that, in this cold weather, couldn't we?" said Morten chipperly, and he began to pour.

"Did someone tell him not to make the deliveries, Rose?" asked Hardy.

Wrinkles gathered along the edge of Rose's upper lip. "Good question, Hardy. That's exactly the nub. Yes, someone did! In point of fact it was our driver, Jess Larsen, no less, who called him and said they had to postpone the whole operation by a fortnight because Theis was in Holland, and only he could fill out the paperwork."

"How weird!" said Assad and Hardy at the same time.

Rose pointed at another photograph. "The next thing that caught my eye was this ring binder with a cardboard cover, one of the oldest in the room. As far as I could see, it covered the years 2000 to 2005. And here on page five . . ."

She pointed to the next photo, and everybody drew forward slightly to make sense of the scrawl.

". . . I just about had a heart attack. Take a look at the signature."

"I can't read his handwriting—what does it say, Rose?" asked Gordon, squinting.

"Gérard Jerome Gaillard. It's right there in goddamn black and white."

By this point, Gordon's nose was practically touching the paper. Perhaps the man should look into getting a pair of glasses?

"Yes, the body in the crate. He bought the office and warehouse in

Vanløse for his Dutch company Kandaloo. The garage, the premises—the whole caboodle. That's a cool one and a half million euros, straight into the pocket of Hannes Theis. So I think we can safely say we've found a connection between Theis and Gaillard, to put it mildly. And then from Gaillard to Rasmus Bruhn and their unsavory dealings since then."

If Hardy had been capable of it, he would have clenched his fists and raised them victoriously into the air, that much was obvious. Instead, he contented himself with simply saying "bloody well done" and "yes" over and over again.

Everybody agreed with him. Assad even gave Rose a cripplingly heavy clap on the shoulder. It was a quantum leap in the right direction.

"That's not all," she said. "Look at this."

She took out the sheet of paper with the third photograph.

"This was at the very front of the most recent binder. Just a pencil note on a piece of paper, nothing special at first glance, but take a closer look once I've read it out."

Turning it toward her, she read aloud.

12-26-20

7:25 a.m., instructions changed.
Contact person here btw. 10 and 11.

HT

"We can assume the initials stand for Hannes Theis, and that was the most recent thing I could find on him. And before you ask who his contact person in Holland is, I couldn't find anything more about that."

"December twenty-sixth. That was the day Carl was arrested and just one day before Theis and his driver went to Vestre Cemetery."

"Hang on, those timings sound like a pretty big coincidence—I think we need to dig deeper into this, Rose," Hardy said, nodding as Morten poured him more chai. He jerked his head back. "Jesus Christ, Morten! That smells a bit strong—what did you put in it?"

"Really? It's just cinnamon and some other spices. I bought it pre-mixed."

Rose sniffed it. "I can't smell anything out of the ordinary. You must have a good nose, Hardy."

"Yeah, I've been noticing that lately," Hardy said with a nod. "Might be a reverse side effect of all this COVID trouble. But tell me, when was the driver supposed to drive to Holland . . . ? And what was his name, anyway?"

"His name is Birger Ottesen. Older guy, but clearly good at his job, because he pretty much knew the orders up till January tenth by heart."

"Birger Ottesen, right. When was he supposed to set off?"

"December twenty-ninth or thirtieth."

"So we're assuming Hannes Theis's note has something to do with why Ottesen's deliveries never left the warehouse?"

"We can't say for sure," Rose replied. "But it's a possibility."

"So why didn't the boss call Ottesen himself to cancel the delivery—surely that's what you'd expect? Why would he get his other driver, Jess Larsen—the one who didn't make international deliveries—to break the news?"

Gordon shrugged, and Assad scratched his beard. They had no answer for that either.

"Honestly, Morten, this chai is very strong, Hardy's right. Are you sure you didn't put any chili in there?" Mona put one hand to her throat and dabbed her eyes with the other.

"No, I didn't." He turned to Mika. "Did you?"

He tried to shake his head. "Um, maybe a little bit," he said at last.

Morten shook his head, and everybody lifted their cups and sniffed.

"Smells lovely and homey. A bit of gunpowder in the spice mix never hurt anybody," Assad said, but he seemed to be the only one who thought so.

Then a couple of deep furrows appeared between his bushy eyebrows. He and Hardy had exchanged a glance. Something wasn't right.

"Tell me, Rose! How long have you had a cold? You weren't sick when we met up on New Year's Eve, were you?"

"I think it started as I was walking home from Mona's that night."

"And you've had a cold ever since? As bad as now?" Hardy asked.

Rose smiled. "No, it's a lot better, thank goodness."

"But you could smell the bananas in the Iveco, even though the doors were closed?" he went on.

Again, Hardy and Assad exchanged a look.

Rose's eyes darted from one to another. The wrinkles in her brow slowly dissolved. Then she clapped a hand to her head. "Holy shit," she said very quietly.

"I think we should get going, shouldn't we, Rose?" Assad had already risen to his feet. "The rest of you can brief us later if you come up with anything, okay?"

29

ASSAD

Saturday, January 2, 2021

On an ordinary Saturday night, when the traffic wasn't very heavy, the journey from Allerød to Vanløse would normally take around ten or twelve minutes, but Rose hurtled along at such a speed that she shaved off at least four minutes, despite the slushy state of the roads. And with each bend, each curve or set of lights, Assad's brown eyes grew bigger and bigger.

"Do you think a minute here or there really matters, Rose?" he asked cautiously.

"Stop it, Assad, this was my mistake, so now we just need to get there—*right now*!"

Assad put his feet up on the dashboard and braced. *I wonder if this'll be any help in a head-on collision?* he thought, the kind of thing he sometimes mused in an elevator: whether, if the cable snapped, jumping into the air at the precise moment the car came crashing down to the basement floor would make him more likely to survive.

As the sweat poured from Assad's scalp and armpits, they jerked to a halt outside the gates of DKNL Transport.

Assad took a deep breath one more time, gazing at the buildings. "What? The gate's open and there are lights on in the forecourt. There's someone here, Rose!"

"Come on!" she said determinedly as Assad wriggled out of his seat belt.

Rose didn't hesitate; she knew what she had to do. Sprinting across the forecourt, when she reached the open gate of the garage she stopped short and signaled to Assad to pull back to the side and prepare for the worst.

Assad swore under his breath. It had been a long time since he'd been armed.

"*Police!*" Rose yelled into the darkness. "Come out with your hands up!"

"What are you going to do if they come out, Rose?" he whispered, but she shushed him. Gun or no gun, Rose was dauntless.

Deafening silence from inside the garage. Where were they, the people who had prepared everything for departure? Assad glanced around. Were they about to be attacked at any moment from the side or from over by the office building?

"Out. Now. Or we're coming in!" Rose yelled even louder.

Assad eased his phone out of his pocket and prepared to dial.

"What the hell are you doing?" she whispered.

"It's really stupid doing this alone, Rose. We need backup. If there are people in there, they're not going to mess around. Remember what happened to Hardy and Anker—and they were actually armed."

But Rose had other plans. She stepped out into the open gateway with her arms outstretched and her hands crossed, as though she was holding a loaded weapon ready to shoot.

Assad was dumbfounded. He had the strong urge to drag her back and get them out of there.

Then there was a clatter from the other side of the garage, and a puff of wind lifted Rose's tousled hair.

"Goddammit, Assad, that's coming from the side door. You go into the garage and I'll run around the outside."

Assad cursed inwardly, squinting into the gloom. A large white van obstructed his view of the back wall, and it was from there he expected the attack might come. So he slipped right, proceeding very warily along the tall shelves of ring binders and all the boxes, as silently as his hard soles and 220-pound frame allowed.

There was not a sound to be heard, apart from Rose's staccato commands from the area by the side door.

"Come out! I'm not going to hurt you as long as you keep your hands in the air," Assad tried, his heart racing. He'd made it through so many ugly situations in his life—surely fate had more in store for him than ending his days on a garage floor in a town whose name he couldn't even pronounce properly?

"The dickhead's gone!" Rose called from the doorway. "He got away through the hole in the fence, the one I made myself—but it was just a kid. I could hear him out there, giggling with one of his little buddies!"

Could you be quiet for just a minute, Rose? thought Assad, preparing to edge around the back of the van.

It was then he was struck by the sickly stench. He knew immediately what it was. Far too many times over the years, he had been confronted with the definitive evidence of rotting flesh.

He stepped out from behind the rear of the vehicle, finding himself in front of a tower of old tires and a worn, grease-stained workbench against the back wall.

Still no sound, apart from his own breathing. It seemed they were alone.

He ran his hand over the table, finding several tools. When he reached a wheel wrench, used to remove hubcaps and wheel nuts, he stopped.

Then he called out to Rose, who at that moment switched on a strip of blinking fluorescent tubes in the ceiling.

And in the sharp light, they both stood by the side door of the van, hesitating for a moment before Assad jammed the flat bar into the gap and levered it.

The unbearable stench of the decay almost knocked Assad off his feet as the door sprang open.

"I wouldn't advise you to blow your nose right now, Rose," he said, but she had already raised her forearm to cover her nostrils.

"What can you see, Assad?" she asked.

"I can see we need to give our colleagues a call."

Rose edged closer.

Inside the van, a figure lay on its side. It had clearly been in there some time.

"Look, I have to report that you were the ones who found the body!" Terje Ploug did not look happy. "Why were you here, and why did you break open the door of the van? You'll have to come up with a good explanation for the boss, or you'll really be for the high jump. He'll be here in a few minutes, so think fast!"

The forensics techs got there a minute before Marcus Jacobsen's vehicle came plowing through the puddles of rainwater.

"We were in Vanløse on another case, and we happened to be driving past," Rose told them without batting an eye.

Jacobsen made no comment when he arrived, but the message had clearly been passed on, because he was so angry he skidded sideways into the forecourt.

They set up the lights and illuminated the corpse. It was not a pretty sight.

The dead man's frightened eyes were wide open, as though his killer were still looming over him. His arms were crossed over his larynx; perhaps he'd thought the attack would land there, but the hammer still lodged deep in his temple told a different story.

"Is that Hannes Theis?" asked Jacobsen, addressing Terje Ploug.

He nodded at the same time as Rose and Assad. "I'm going to assume he was usually the one who set the alarms on site, but obviously that would have been a little difficult in his current condition." He gave a tiny grin, the kind you could smile only after a lifetime on the job.

Jacobsen turned to Assad and Rose. "And of course we have you two. Are you seriously asking me to believe that it's sheer coincidence you're here and that you know what Hannes Theis looks like?"

"His picture is on the intranet, Marcus. The whole force knows his face," Ploug said, coming to their rescue.

Hope he gets someone to upload that photo pretty quickly, before Marcus checks, Assad thought.

30

TORBEN

Sunday, January 3, 2021

It had been years now since Torben Victor's wife had given up on him. At first she had threatened to be unfaithful, if he'd rather be at work instead of at home with her and the kids—although frankly they made themselves scarce the minute he showed up anyway. And since deep down he was almost relieved that he no longer had to service the woman sexually, he merely shrugged and let her do as she pleased. As expected, not long after that she demanded a divorce, but when he told her how cleverly and profitably he'd covered his back financially, the preparations he'd laid for a divorce, she had decided to stay after all.

It was a Sunday, and most of the staff at *Gossip* took weekends off, so there was no better place for a responsible editor to be. The television on the wall was playing the news on an endless loop and the weather outside was dank and cold, so the office at *Gossip* was simply Victor's absolute favorite place on Earth.

Since Thursday's edition of *Gossip* had hit the newsstands, they had had to reprint twice. His imprudent promises of bonuses for staff if circulation exceeded 250,000 hits were now long overdue to be fulfilled. Never before during his tenure at the paper had it had such momentum.

And now here he was, taking stock of the last three days.

In front of him were the three piles he had asked his secretary to print and sort. The first, overflowing pile contained all the emails and texts praising *Gossip* for their excellent coverage of Mørck's case and career. The second, somewhat smaller pile represented the opposite point of view: that *Gossip* was only covering the case to increase its circulation (which was of course absolutely correct), that the pictures they published were nearly always out of context, that the paper was being entirely uncritical of a policeman who had been accused of serious crimes, that the police weren't above the law, and that *Gossip* should also be writing about cases where the police *had* been guilty of misconduct. Finally, there was the third pile: the threats, warning that if they didn't immediately stop what they were doing, they'd be in trouble.

It took Victor barely a minute to sort that last stack of emails into three smaller piles. The ones that came from the usual shit-stirrers, which always went straight into the bin. Then the ones who thought they had information about Mørck's case, casting it in a rather less positive light than *Gossip* did. And, finally, three emails: one from the chief of homicide, Marcus Jacobsen; one from the chief constable; and one from the lawyer representing the state.

Torben Victor simply couldn't help but relish these three. If such prominent people felt compelled to try to stop future issues of *Gossip*, then that meant his publishing strategy was a huge success.

Getting to his feet, Victor walked into the editorial office, where he distributed pile two among a couple of his best researchers' in-trays. It would be their headache, trying to figure out if any of those claims held water and, if so, how much it would cost *Gossip* to use the material. Personally he doubted there was much to them. That was usually the case.

Returning to his office, he fed the three missives from the police directly into the shredder, but Victor wasn't naïve. The police wouldn't simply go away. They'd be back—with drastic demands—if *Gossip* continued its current editorial line despite their warnings. The publishers would be in for various fines and slaps on the wrist and God knew what else, but by that point another issue of the paper would have come out, with a circulation of more than four hundred thousand, so the bigwigs might decide they could afford a lengthy wrangle with the police.

The fact of the matter was that the police didn't have a leg to stand on. Danish law enshrined both freedom of speech and freedom of the press, so unless *Gossip* did something illegal, they were untouchable—and the authorities would have a hard time proving that was the case here.

Victor glanced up at his whiteboard, where the next print edition of *Gossip* and the upcoming online versions were outlined.

He slid his calculator toward him and began to tot up the numbers. Department Q's work on the various high-profile victims of Sisle Park was an absolute gold mine. One of the murder victims had had his hands cut off and had bled to death. Another had been decapitated in an accident staged while out horse riding, and a third had simply been kidnapped and executed with potassium chloride. The source at Department Q hadn't given them all the details yet, but it was already shaping up to be a strong story.

And as the calculator spat out strings of numbers, both *Gossip* and Torben Victor seemed to be growing richer and richer. If he could spin this out for just another three months, his personal bonus would hit ten million kroner. Wonder of wonders, as his wife would have said in happier days.

He heard the distinctive creak of the swing door at reception and footsteps heading toward his office. But he hadn't expected to see Pelle Hyttested barge straight in without knocking.

"What are you doing here, Pelle? Aren't you supposed to be on your way to Nuuk?"

Pelle shrugged. "First I think you should swivel your chair around and take a look at the flat-screen, Torben. The police have announced a press conference that's starting any minute. Then maybe you should listen to me."

What the hell was he playing at? Torben Victor shook his head. It was about time the slimy bastard toed the editorial line—or did they really have to frog-march him onto the plane in order to finally stop hearing about his personal vendetta against Mørck?

But the next three minutes changed everything.

Jacobsen looked unusually prepared and authoritative as he stood outside the Investigation Unit in Sydhavnen, defying the awful weather. At his side were the chief constable and her public relations officer. All in impeccable uniforms, chests emblazoned with as much official bling as they could get away with.

"It has come to our attention that both the case against Carl Mørck and the overarching case regarding the various Sisle Park killings over the last thirty years have been a subject of great interest in the press and that a significant amount of information has been released that has proved inconvenient for us and the investigations."

Jacobsen turned his face directly toward the camera, addressing it very intently, so that nobody watching could be in any doubt that it was he and he alone who was making the decisions.

"In consultation with senior management at the Copenhagen Police, I have therefore decided that tomorrow we will make public all the information about the Sisle Park case and the way it was investigated. We will also—subject to approval from the Police Complaints Authority—release details of the charges against Carl Mørck and give an update on what has happened to him since his arrest.

"It's my sincere belief that this is the best way to give you a clearer picture of how we in senior management handle criminal elements on the force. Let me emphasize that as yet Carl Mørck has not been convicted of anything, so we will have to be patient and await the conclusions of the PCA."

Then he flashed a grin so broad and direct that Victor understood the whole performance was aimed at him and *Gossip*'s sources.

Pelle Hyttested said nothing. Which was probably for the best, since Victor's mood at that particular moment was at rock bottom.

Fucking hell, he thought, over and over again. The streaks of rain before his eyes now seemed almost a mockery. *Gossip* no longer had an exclusive on the Carl Mørck case. It would be covered by everyone from unread local rags to his direct competitors in the gutter press and the vastly overstaffed public service stations. All of which meant that huge numbers of sold copies had just been snatched away from him. *Stolen* away from him, in fact.

"How did you know in advance what Jacobsen was going to announce?" Victor surveyed his reporter with eyes so cold, there was no need to guess what he was thinking. If Pelle Hyttested had a hand in the police's new strategy, he would personally make sure that he ended up in the Frederiksholm Canal—permanently.

"What are you suggesting, Torben?" Hyttested replied, with a face so infuriatingly guileless that Victor wanted to slap it.

"Perhaps I should ask for your source, then, Pelle? Let's say two seconds, shall we, and then you tell me."

"Why don't you just take a look at the screen? I can turn up the volume, if you're going deaf to the facts."

Victor turned and saw a fourth person approaching the microphone. "Sergeant Terje Ploug," read the text at the corner of the screen. An old acquaintance, and one who solved an unusually high number of cases every year.

As scattered snowflakes drifted down between him and the camera, the sergeant explained that the Major Crimes team was currently working on vital, ongoing cases that, in parallel with the cases the chief of homicide had just mentioned, would be investigated using all available resources.

A murder victim had been found in a truck in Vanløse, he explained, a middle-aged man by the name of Hannes Theis, whom they had previously believed to be the passenger in the vehicle used to kill Carl Mørck's court-appointed lawyer. It was now apparent that he had died prior to the incident, and as a result an arrest had been made in the case, but nobody had yet been charged with the murder in Vanløse.

Torben Victor switched off the TV and turned to his reporter.

"Fine, so something is going on in little old Denmark—but what's your point? You didn't actually answer my question."

Victor had seen the crooked smile Pelle Hyttested gave him many times before, and as a general rule it was followed up with information of tremendous use to *Gossip*.

So he listened.

"For the past few days I've been keeping a pretty close watch on the

movements of Department Q, and yesterday their two best detectives—
Rose Knudsen and Carl Mørck's right-hand man, Assad—decided to go a
little off-piste. I followed their car through Copenhagen and to a company
in Vanløse by the name of DKNL Transport.

"As you may have gathered from Terje Ploug's appearance just now,
the company was owned by Hannes Theis, the man who was allegedly a
passenger in the Passat later used to run down Mørck's first lawyer,
Adam Bang. So. Off they went into the dark, Department Q's intrepid
little detectives, absolutely determined to search the place. And what did
they find? Well, you just heard."

Victor nodded.

"When more police arrived, I took a few steps toward the open gate
while they were busy lighting up the forecourt with floodlights and conferring in little groups," Hyttested went on. "The chief of homicide was
talking with the Department Q lot, and frankly he looked a bit pissed off.
At any rate, they were asked to leave the area two minutes after that, and
then they drove away."

"Did they see you?"

"No. I'm well aware of your deal with Mørck's wife, so I was careful.
They don't know I was there."

Victor was listening attentively.

"I took plenty of pictures, if you're interested."

Victor leaned back in his office chair and lit a cigarette. "I am indeed.
But that still doesn't explain how you knew that press release was just
about to drop."

"There was a lot of coming and going, so I thought maybe someone in
the forecourt could give me more information. I tried to get in by showing my press card. They stopped me, of course, but Jacobsen saw me."

"Jesus, Pelle—and he recognized you?"

"He did, yes!"

The smile that still adorned his smug face was no longer endearing
him to Victor. Was he proud of having acted so clumsily?

"Jacobsen looked pretty pleased as he was beckoning me over to the
gate, shouting that he was glad *Gossip* was on the scene and that he

wanted to let me know he'd be addressing us indirectly during a press conference the following day at twelve."

"So you *are* the reason we've lost our scoop!"

"That's not what you think, Torben, surely? He's just doing the smart thing—and now we're going to do the same, yes?"

"There's still time to put you on a plane to Greenland, Pelle. It'll be an extended stay, I can tell you that."

"Ha. You're not sending me to Greenland, Torben. You and I are going to steer the editorial line back in its original direction. Once the police release the details of the Mørck and Sisle Park cases, we'll no longer have an exclusive, so instead we'll have to write about corruption within the force—including about Carl Mørck—and we'll also dig into all the cases where Department Q hounded people to death. Nothing but doom and gloom, doom and gloom. You up for that? Or shall I consider myself fired? Because you're not shipping me off to Greenland, I'll tell you that for a fact."

31

CARL

Sunday, January 3, 2021

At least ten times, Carl had tried to estimate the size of his cell. It reminded him, in fact, of the farmhands' room his parents had let him use throughout his childhood. Had it really been no bigger than this? It couldn't add up to more than eighty-five square feet, but it felt more like seventy-five at the most. The only difference was that on the farm, the door could not be locked, whereas here it always was.

What a stupid bloody situation to be in on a Sabbath morning. Normally he'd be standing in front of the stove at home, engulfed in the smell of bacon frying in the pan, with Mona using the blender behind him. He could almost hear her humming, and Lucia running around on pattering feet.

But his reality was different now. Seventy-five square feet and a lock: that was his whole world, and he could see no prospect of it changing any time soon.

There were individuals out there, thank god, working on his case while the PCA went about its investigation. Maybe they could scare up a few people to speak in his favor. He hoped so.

If only he could get a chance to speak to Rose and Assad at some point, then . . .

Carl broke off his train of thought and sighed. That wasn't going to happen. Continued meetings with his lawyer and perhaps with Mona and Hardy would probably be his only opportunities to sway the course of the battle.

Carl looked around his cell. Nothing whatsoever happened at the remand center. The highlight of his day had been washing most of the red dye out of his hair and gradually coming to look like his boring self. Apart from that, there was nothing to do. Maybe he'd pick up a book in a day or two, but what kind of book would be exciting for a detective who'd already spent decades elbow-deep in crime and depravity? The TV didn't offer much entertainment either. In fact, the contrast on the teeny-tiny screen was so low and the picture so indistinct that it barely mattered if it was on or off. Still, it made him feel somehow as though he wasn't alone in the world. He'd heard similar things from inmates he'd visited over the years. And although the selection of channels in Danish prisons was often minimal, TV was generally an inmate's best friend.

Good Morning Denmark had been on since breakfast, and the repeat wasn't exactly thrilling. Why would he care that a sauté pan was the perfect tool for frying vegetables or that you could find the recipe for this or that on TV 2's website, when he didn't have access to the internet?

Carl read the subtitles, recognizing names who in better days had been clamoring for interviews with him. That was then.

Worst of all were the adverts afterward; he'd always thought so. But in the before times he could simply get up and go for a piss or grab a beer.

He glanced over at the bell, by which a former occupant had added an ironic comment. *Room service,* the man had written in black pen.

Carl eyed the sink. The option was always there, but he still thought he was too good for that. Hardened inmates were happy to piss in sinks, but not him. Not yet.

I'd better order some Nescafé and fill up the fridge a bit more. It's a good thing Mona transferred some money, he thought. They were allowed three thousand kroner in the account. That was something.

Then, in a colorful orgy of menstrual pads that made the woman on the TV immensely happy and relieved, the adverts came to an end, replaced by a group of people who apparently found it incredibly entertaining to do nothing but play on digital slot machines.

It just goes on and on, he thought. All the Sisle Parks in the world couldn't stop that idiocy.

Then a press conference was announced for twelve o'clock—only one minute to go. How many times were members of the government or representatives from the health service going to pop up and lecture Danes on how to behave, or explain what new mutations of that bloody COVID-19 virus would be plaguing the country?

So he was surprised to see his office in Sydhavnen appear onscreen behind a light veil of rain.

Leaning forward, Carl watched uneasily as Marcus Jacobsen and the chief constable stepped forward in full regalia, leaving the public relations officer slightly in the background. Had they ever held a press conference outside the Investigation Unit before? If they had, Carl didn't remember.

A mere ten minutes later, the new situation was painfully clear to him. Thanks to the efforts of Mona and *Gossip*, he had been benefiting from glowing press coverage and plenty of goodwill, but now he had to admit that Jacobsen had gained the upper hand, executing an ambush so complete it was almost sublime.

I need to speak to Mona, he thought, pressing the bell.

Even though he asked very nicely, his request was denied. Some of the staff were off sick, so they didn't have time for this sort of spontaneity, said an officer he hadn't seen before. In any case, inmates' access to the telephone was strictly limited, ten minutes every three days—but of course he knew that.

"Do you think anybody in the guard room saw the press conference outside the Investigation Unit just now?" Carl asked him.

He nodded. "Yep, I think we all did. And we felt the chief of homicide did a great job. All that cloak-and-dagger stuff serves no purpose."

He was friendly and smiling, the halo above his head seemingly almost glued on.

"Anyway, it's time for your first trip to the exercise yard with Malthe Bøgegård. It's cold out, so put on an extra sweater. You'll be with your new neighbor in cell 5, plus that guy from isolation, who asked to be kept away from gen pop. It's been a while since he was outside. We call him Åbenrå, because that's where he's from."

Carl was disappointed that his request was so promptly turned down.

Always remember that patience is the greatest virtue, son, Carl's father had said again and again, and how incredibly fucking wrong Carl thought he was.

He snorted. What good had patience done his dad as he planned the new, bigger barn for forty extra cows that never materialized? Or as the endless football-pool coupons piled up on the radiator in the kitchen, even though he never won? No, Carl was not a patient man, but he had to accept that he was no longer calling the shots, so he kept his mouth shut.

Carl was the first out in the yard. The guard wasn't wrong about the freezing weather. They called it fresh air, but it was agony. Above him was a lattice of bars against a gray bank of clouds. The two dingy tables with worn garden benches along one wall weren't exactly inviting. Apart from that, there was nothing. Red brick all the way around, with a small football goal painted in black on the far wall and a forest of bars at the other end. If this was supposed to help perk him up, he'd have preferred something a bit greener and a bit warmer.

When his fellow prisoners entered, the cameras in the top corner registered them before Carl did.

"Hello," said one of them. A good-looking older man with the elegant, discreet manner of an accountant or a banker.

"Paul Manon, your new neighbor," he said, holding out his hand. "Shrewd habitual criminal, or so they call me."

He smiled warmly, then drew back against the wall.

Malthe came out with his hands buried deep in his pockets. He scowled at the man by the wall as though he'd already rubbed him the wrong way.

"Hi," he said tersely, going to stand beside Carl.

The third man, the one they called Åbenrå, had the classic pedophile look: a withdrawn little man with darting eyes. Carl had seen plenty of the type over the years. Guys like that, somehow you just knew it wasn't a good idea to leave them alone at a daycare. He was neither young nor old, just a body that had already been through far too much.

Åbenrå fumbled in his jacket pocket and took out a pack of cigarettes. "Anybody want one?" he asked hopefully.

Carl nearly gasped. Hell yeah he wanted a cigarette, he thought, nodding as the other two looked away.

The guy's hands shook as he took out his lighter and clicked it. Did he think Carl was about to snatch the whole pack out of his grasp, then smack him in the jaw for good measure? Had that happened to him before? But when Carl said thanks and sucked down the first draw like a drowning man inhaling his final breath of oxygen, the guy's lips parted and a silent sigh of relief made his chest sink.

Oddly, in that moment of bliss, Carl thought of Rose. Would she give him a cigarette in this godforsaken place? he wondered.

"Have another one," said the pale little man, handing him the pack.

Then Malthe stepped forward, and the alleged pedophile tottered back. Evidently, he only needed one look before all his survival instincts kicked in. If his sentence was a long one, thought Carl, he wouldn't make it out of prison.

"I asked them if we can start doing an hour of shared cell time in the afternoons, if that's okay with you," Malthe said.

Carl gazed for a moment at the hulking prisoner. Was that a look of hope on his face? In a way it was almost touching. But probably, as for Carl, any form of distraction made the days pass more quickly for him.

"Are you absolutely sure you can trust him?" The question came from the "shrewd habitual criminal."

Paul Manon fixed his gaze on the triangle between Malthe's eyebrows, where the furrows were deepening. Yet the man seemed fearless as he approached them.

"Trust him? Do you know something about him that I should know? Malthe saved my life—isn't that good enough?" said Carl.

"This guy?! He doesn't know anything, so he'd better just shut his mouth." Malthe turned to the man. "You got that, Manon?" he said, reaching out one arm to seize the man's throat. As he squeezed, Åbenrå gasped and backed toward the door.

"Hey, stop that, Malthe, what are you doing?" cried Carl.

But Malthe's large hand was steady. He turned to Carl. "He says he knows everything, but he doesn't know shit." Then he let go and shoved the man away, leaving him wheezing for breath.

"He was in the cell opposite yours in Vestre, Carl—you didn't see him?"

Carl shook his head.

"I don't know why you came to Slagelse, Manon, but you should be very careful about the gossip you spread."

"Don't turn your back on Malthe, I'm just saying," said the man, coughing.

32

WAYNE

Sunday, January 3, 2021

When Wayne Peters was just four years old, he had discovered the joys of lying—an extraordinary revelation. Everything could be explained away with lies; a yes might in reality be a no, and a maybe was usually the best thing to say if you didn't feel like answering.

Wayne had lied his way through childhood with such aplomb that neither his parents nor his classmates knew who he was or what he was capable of.

I wonder if lying will protect me if I carry out my fantasies? he mused as a teenager. So he experimented, stealing from his parents, killing the neighbor's cat, and attacking a random man on the street. Every single time, he managed to protect himself with more or less plausible cover stories, until at last he came to realize that the world was his oyster.

"I'll be a multimillionaire before I'm thirty," he used to declare, although he had nothing to support how that might happen.

"You've got delusions of grandeur," said his dad, which perhaps wasn't the wisest thing to say to someone who actually did.

So Wayne plotted his revenge, which turned out to be another remorseless but wonderfully practical element of his personality.

His dad died very quickly after Wayne started experimenting with switching out the pills he kept in the bathroom cabinet. It was established at autopsy that too much nitroglycerin wasn't good for a patient with a dodgy heart, and nobody challenged Wayne's assertion that his father had been talking about suicide for a while. His mother was shocked, of course, because she'd never heard him say any such thing, but then again, Wayne had been closer to his father than she had been.

The body was scarcely cold before Wayne, now legally an adult, asked her to sell the house, persuading her that his father's express wish was for Wayne to have half of the proceeds immediately, so that he could get a leg up in life. When she hesitated, he administered his coup de grâce: faked bank accounts clearly showing that she couldn't afford to live there any longer anyway. In the end, his stunned mother decided to accept the bitter reality and gave in.

Within only a couple of weeks, the house had been sold and his mother relocated to a cheap apartment a few miles away.

Wallet now bulging in his back pocket, Wayne drove his father's car to the Red Light District in Amsterdam and persuaded a couple of sex workers that he had their best interests at heart.

Installing them in booths, he made sure the prostitutes did as they were told and handed over to him half of what they earned for their services, and always in cold hard cash.

When a violent war broke out among the pimps a few years later, he took a step back from his operation and turned his attention to the drug trade instead.

If his father had lived, he would have had to eat his hurtful words, because by the time Wayne was thirty, he had more millions than he ever could have dreamed of.

When one of his regular lady friends expressed doubts that he was the man he claimed to be, demanding to see evidence of his money if she was going to believe all the bragging, Wayne lost it.

The girl was never seen again. Although frankly, she'd had good reason to doubt him: If he really had gotten as rich off drugs and prostitution as he said, then why hadn't he been jailed long ago? So from then on, Wayne retreated into anonymity.

It took Wayne a few months to work out a clear picture of a safer and more attractive future. As far as he was concerned, the most important thing was to be so extremely rich that he had unfettered freedom and the financial means to accomplish his goal, which was to achieve absolute, uncompromising control and power over everything around him.

Next, he had to make sure that no one, absolutely no one, could find out who he was and what he was doing. If anybody ever did get in his way, he would wipe them off the face of the earth, just as he had done with the girl and with his father, plus a few others along the way. He would become the invisible, unchallenged power behind every throne.

But you don't get stinking rich without other people to rake in the money for you. Wayne knew that better than anybody, so after a decade his network extended far beyond the borders of his own country. He himself lived modestly in one of the idyllic villages south of Rotterdam, basking in his neighbors' blind faith that he was simply a middle-aged business-man who had taken early retirement and was always generous and oblig-ing toward the young people in the village.

Yes, Wayne Peters was well liked, but he wasn't the neighbor they thought he was. Despite his gentle smile and kind eyes, he had developed into a full-blooded arch-psychopath, entirely without empathy for his victims—or for his helpers, for that matter.

Weak links were made to be broken, that was his motto.

His headquarters, if you could call it that, was in Rotterdam, where ships docked and set sail every day. From Rotterdam, supplies of drugs—primarily cocaine from Colombia, Peru, and Bolivia—were distributed across his network. For years the market had been agitating for heroin from Afghanistan, but Wayne had been extremely hesitant about that particular drug. Heroin was despised in every country and society, whereas cocaine was viewed as an upper-class, less addictive drug. It wasn't cocaine addicts, after all, sprawled in the gutters of Los Angeles, Barcelona, and Vesterbro in Copenhagen. Cocaine was "more sophisti-cated," as were the clientele, who were usually able to pay for their habit without committing crimes for the money. True, a few hundred kilograms of heroin were distributed across his network every year, mainly to the Spanish and Dutch markets but sometimes also to Scandinavia, but that would always be a secondary business.

The kingpins at the top of the drug hierarchy were always the investors, who made the important decisions while also maintaining the greatest distance from their consequences, and since Wayne was the organization's only investor, he was also the person with absolute and final say over what was needed to maintain his position in the market.

Beneath him were the importers, who in many cases were in direct contact with the producers, the impoverished farmers who never made much profit from the industry.

Then there were the middlemen, who took the goods from the importers and arranged transport for distribution: these were the three links exposed to the greatest scrutiny.

Scandinavia in particular was a fantastic market for cocaine. People were wealthy and discreet, and it was becoming more and more commonplace for even ordinary, middle-class individuals to snort it when they were partying or trying to boost performance. Over the years, however, the market had become rather trickier and riskier, especially in Denmark. Anybody caught skimming or—sometimes—being too loose-lipped was punished severely, and several transporters and dealers had to be eliminated.

Like the importers, the middlemen were best off living in obscurity, merely reaping the rewards of their leadership and network. This meant the path from them to the dealers and on to the street-level pushers and end users was well camouflaged and concealed.

In Holland, Wayne Peters had arranged things cleverly at an early stage so that the organization had informants in the police, which helped them thwart plenty of raids and drug busts. When he discovered that these informants could also be made to transport drugs and money, he realized he had the best smoke screen he could possibly have wished for.

From the outset, Wayne had made sure the organization cracked down hard on disloyalty and theft. He had no scruples when it came to murder, but he soon learned that he had to strike a balance: there was public outrage to think of, as well as the lengthy sentences that murders often entailed.

Then again, Wayne had grown to take a certain satisfaction in demonstrating his authority through spectacularly elaborate punishments. And it was just such a punishment he needed now.

A large shipment of drugs and currency, stolen from his organization in 2007, had recently been found in a suitcase hidden in a Danish attic. And it had awakened in him a long-dormant rage. Despite all the punishments he'd devised and the measures he'd taken, neither the shipment nor the person responsible had ever been found, and Wayne had been forced to live with the humiliation of being outwitted by a common thief.

He'd had several possible culprits liquidated at the time, including one of the Danish middlemen, a police inspector by the name of Anker Høyer.

Sometime later, a distributor on the Danish market, Rasmus Bruhn, was revealed to have been involved in the theft. As punishment, Wayne had him drowned in a drainpipe, but only after he had named under torture several other disloyal operators in the chain below him. Unfortunately, one of those was a policeman Wayne Peters now considered a significant risk. His name was Carl Mørck, Høyer's former partner, who was now a suspect in the theft, which the Dutch police—in collaboration with the Danes—had gotten wind of.

When the missing cargo had turned up in this selfsame Mørck's attic, the final traces of doubt were erased from Wayne's mind.

Mørck had to be eliminated, cost what it may. Now that he was in prison in Denmark it was more urgent than ever, before he went blabbing to the police or tried to make some sort of under-the-table deal to reduce his sentence.

So far the man had evidently kept his mouth shut, but the head of the local organization in Denmark had explained in no uncertain terms what a talented, shrewd policeman Mørck was. If there was anybody they should be afraid knew too much about the operation, it was him. No efforts had been spared to eliminate him, but so far they had failed.

So Wayne took it seriously when one of his key people went missing.

Eddie Jansen, that was the man's name, a police officer from Rotterdam who had come to learn a lot more than was good for him. That his disappearance coincided with the spiraling events in Denmark was suspicious.

But why hadn't Jansen had Mørck killed before things got this far? Was he protecting him somehow? They had to find out.

Wayne Peters had always been a cautious man. His official income was the interest earned from successful investments in the stock market over the years, and since he lived very simply, he was confident he wouldn't attract the attention of the tax authorities.

A lot of his transactions were made with cash, piles of it shipped in bulk to the Cayman Islands and hoarded in safe-deposit boxes distributed among the islands' various financial institutions.

Nobody in the organization knew his true identity, and he had spread rumors about a whole array of businesspeople residing in the Dutch Antilles that they were the true string-pullers. It amused him, because who would suspect a pensioner with gray hair and creaky hips of being the head of one of Holland's biggest drug cartels? Lies and deception had always been his preferred methods, the secure foundation on which his organization was built.

So he made sure that all contact between his network in Holland and elsewhere took place on the dark web. If he wanted to see someone in the flesh, he would arrange a meeting at one of the many coffee shops in the towns nearby. He would watch from a distance as his highest-paid employee set to work: the man with the two different-colored eyes, who called himself Cees Pauwels, although his real name was certain to be something else.

Wayne would usually sit in the corner like any other café patron, observing the meeting and the subject Pauwels was recruiting.

He was rarely the one who made the final decision. Recruitment was Pauwels's responsibility, which meant it was also his responsibility to remove anybody who didn't live up to his and his employers' expectations.

Unfortunately, this was the case with Eddie Jansen, and Pauwels had texted five minutes ago to say that the man had now been brought in.

He didn't know yet whether Jansen had been in direct contact with Carl Mørck. Regardless, Jansen wouldn't be in the organization's service much longer.

And Mørck? Well, there were plenty of people gunning for him, so it was only a matter of time before one of them succeeded. Wayne was currently considering more drastic measures than they had previously used, but so what? As long as they worked.

33

MONA / ROSE

Sunday, January 3, 2021

Less than half an hour after Marcus Jacobsen dropped his verbal bombshell outside the Investigation Unit, Mona was striding through the *Gossip* editorial room toward the office of Torben Victor.

Three journalists were seated opposite the editor in chief, Pelle Hyttested unfortunately among them, and although she didn't enter quietly, none of them bothered to raise their head toward her.

"First I want you to summarize what strategy the police are currently pursuing and why," Victor was saying to the female journalist. "In the meantime, I want you two moving full steam ahead with what we've already agreed. Off you go!"

"Bad news, eh, Mona?!" whispered Hyttested with a smug cackle as he sidled past her. So. The damage was done.

Once they were alone, Victor asked Mona to close the door.

"I'm sorry, but I'm afraid our deal is off," he said, shaking his head. "Current circumstances being what they are, we no longer have a story, so that means no agreement either. If you want to complain to someone, complain to the chief of homicide. He's the one who pulled the rug out from under us. He's doing exactly what he thinks is best for him and the Investigation Unit."

"But it's a disaster for Carl." Her voice was shaking.

He threw out his arms. "Yeah, well, I'm gutted too. All those lovely copies we could have sold. But you've got to understand, we have to compensate for the loss by taking another angle."

"And what angle is that?" She had to make sure.

"The one we took to start with. To dig up dirt on corrupt police officers and publish it."

"So you're not going after Carl?"

He shook his head. "Some of Department Q's cases and Carl's cases before that came at a cost to those involved, you know that, don't you?"

"I think you should save those for last, Victor. Because I can tell you right now that Carl has never—and I mean *never*—deliberately harmed anybody."

His smile expressed both courtesy and skepticism. "Well, we'll just have to see where this all goes, Mona. We'll have to see."

• • •

"So you didn't go in all guns blazing?"

Mona sighed. "I'm afraid he's crafty enough to know I was bluffing."

They all sat in silent thought for a moment. If it had been difficult to help Carl before, it was all but impossible now.

Assad scratched the skin under his sideburns. "Do you know the one about the camel who hated green grass and loved hay?" he asked.

What was he playing at? thought Rose. Surely they were past camel stories by now?

Assad persevered. "Yeah, you see, one of the camels got to the trough too late and had to eat the freshly cut grass, which fermented in its stomach and gave it such nasty-smelling gas that the camel driver started beating it. So it nudged its neighbor. 'Can I swap my grass for your hay?'

"The other camel wouldn't.

"'Great,' said the first camel. 'I just had to ask.'

"'Why is it great? Green grass makes you fart, and then the camel driver will get upset and beat you.'

"The first camel replied, 'Yeah, but a few kicks and punches are better than trudging out into the desert with a heavy pack on my back for days on end. If I fart, the camel driver won't want to take me with him.'

"At that, the second camel stopped chewing. Had the other camels heard? it wondered.

"And when the other camels simply kept on chewing, lost in their own thoughts, the two swapped places after all."

Assad got himself a cup of tea and began to pour in sugar directly from the bowl.

"Honestly, Assad, why are you telling us this, what's the moral?" Mona asked.

He sipped the tea, then poured the rest of the sugar bowl into the cup. "Yeah. The second camel didn't get the moral either."

Gordon, polite as ever, held up a finger in the air. "The first camel was lying, wasn't it? Because all the camels were sent into the desert anyway?"

Assad nodded approvingly. "Well done, Gordon. The clever camel ate its fill of the good hay, while the stupid camel that ate grass farted the whole way through the desert hellscape and was beaten so many times that it was never fooled again."

Rose looked dissatisfied. "I'm sorry, I figured that out too, but what the heck does that have to do with *Gossip* and Mona?"

"We're going to make them eat fresh grass."

"Who?"

"*Gossip*, of course. Preferably we'll feed it to that little twerp Pelle Hyttested."

"And what is the grass, Assad?" asked Rose.

"Lies!"

"Jesus, Assad, we've all figured that part out, but what—and why?"

"Give Pelle What's-His-Face a juicy, tempting story about Carl and Department Q that has sweet fu—" He stopped short for a moment, baring his ivory teeth. "Has nothing to do with reality. Then we give the other magazines and newspapers the real story, so they can rip *Gossip* and Hyttested to shreds for bad research. Maybe it'll get him off our backs. What do you say?"

Rose looked pensive. "When are you going to Holland, Gordon?" she asked.

"Tomorrow. The detective there couldn't meet with me any earlier than that."

"Okay, then you'll be the one who gets the honor of making up false information to feed to *Gossip* and Pelle Hyttested, all right?"

He nodded and rubbed his hands.

"Oh, and by the way, we've got an ally in our old friend Terje Ploug!" said Rose, and Assad nodded. "He called me this morning to tell me what the West Copenhagen Police found at DKNL Transport last night. He says that Hannes Theis can't possibly have been a passenger in the car the day Carl's lawyer was run over, because he'd been dead as a doornail for up to twenty-four hours prior. Theis's stomach contents proved that this morning during autopsy. They found the remains of a hamburger in his oral cavity and teeth. We know he made a card purchase from the McDonald's on Jyllingevej in Rødovre at 10:09 a.m. on December twenty-sixth, and the packaging was found at the top of the bin in the office. Combined with the fact that the body had been kept cold in the van, death is estimated with a fair degree of certainty to have occurred the day after Christmas, December twenty-sixth, the day before the collision."

"You took a picture of the note you found in the DKNL Transport file, right?" asked Assad.

Rose nodded and looked it up on her phone.

"Here," she said, pointing.

12-26-20

7:25 a.m., instructions changed.
Contact person here btw. 10 and 11.

HT

"Holy shit!" said Assad. "It's right there in black and white. Theis reads it in the morning, and a few hours later he's dead. Has Ploug seen it?"

Rose nodded. "Of course. Hardy showed him. His thesis is that Theis might have had a meal with his killer. That they went straight into the lorry afterward, where Theis was knocked down with the hammer. There were plenty of tools on the workbench near the back of the van, so it would have been easy to find something to kill him with. Both the West Copenhagen Police and Ploug agree with Hardy on that score."

"Hang on a minute," Gordon exclaimed. A thought had drained the color from his already pale face. "Isn't there a chance the McDonald's packaging in the bin came from his killer?"

Rose shrugged. "Who knows? But forensics only found the fingerprints of the McDonald's worker who handed over the meal, apart from Theis's."

"Gosh, they work fast." He nodded, impressed. "So Theis *wasn't* in the car the next morning," Gordon repeated.

"No, he wasn't, and we can thank the autopsy for that. Without the remnants of Theis's hamburger, we wouldn't have known for sure," Rose said. "Which means we also know that his driver, Jess Larsen, is full of shit. Ploug's already arrested him at his apartment. He'll be charged with the murder of Carl's first lawyer at the preliminary hearing tomorrow morning."

"*If* it was really him driving," interjected Gordon from behind his computer.

"Ploug also told me he'd spoken to the cemetery admin about the alleged call to Hannes Theis, the one where he was supposedly told his wife's gravestone had been knocked over," Rose went on. "As far as they remember, that call never took place. They checked the gravestone, to be on the safe side, and it did look a bit wonky, but nothing crazy."

"I don't understand why your colleagues didn't investigate this immediately after the incident," Mona said. "Why didn't they get a statement from Theis that same day?"

"Ploug is trying to find out who was responsible for that, don't worry." Rose shuffled through her photographs and papers. "Oh, right, I almost forgot—Larsen was stupid enough to keep Theis's work computer lying around his apartment. Ploug's people took that in as well, so we may learn more once they crack it."

Then she found the picture she was searching for. "Here, look at this." She placed the printout in front of them. "There's a lot you could read into it, but the gist seems pretty obvious, even if you don't speak Dutch, don't you think?"

"Does it say anything about why the next shipment wasn't picked up as agreed?" Mona asked, and Assad—after enlisting the help of Google Translate—nodded.

The email had been received on December 23, but there was no reply. Perhaps Ploug's team would find one on Theis's computer?

"I'm excited to see what they get out of Jess Larsen. He must be one hell of a liar, because I didn't suspect a thing after I spoke to him. And I should add that, as far as Ploug can tell, Theis ran an entirely aboveboard import-export business."

"Sure, but he was bribed to look the other way," muttered Gordon from the corner.

"Oh yeah, definitely! I think that's why he was able to buy those buildings from one of the middlemen for a gong," Assad added.

Mona nodded. "A song, Assad, not a gong. That'd be a lot noisier."

Assad frowned. He didn't get it. "Anyway, Hardy told me to say hello for him. He believes that Theis was painted into a corner and wanted out."

"He probably got cold feet," Rose said. "He couldn't know it was Carl they were after. He must have just felt the situation was getting too hot for him, don't you think?"

"I don't get it." Assad shook his head.

"What don't you get, Assad? It's pretty simple."

"I don't get why his feet would be cold if the situation was too hot."

34

MALTHE / CARL

Sunday, January 3, 2021

In one hour, Malthe would be let into Carl Mørck's cell, and they would be alone. The door would be locked. He had gained Mørck's trust, and there would be plenty of time to get close enough to put him down. To get a swift, solid grip around his head and under the chin—then one hard shove to the shoulder as he twisted his head around. A tiny crack, and the man would be lifeless within tenths of a second.

Then Malthe would knock on the door and confess what he'd done. That there had been a disagreement, he'd lost control, that he hadn't known his own strength. He would apologize sincerely, maybe even get his voice to shake a bit. He would have liked to shed a few tears as well, really lay it on thick, but he wasn't good at that. Only the painful thought of his terminally ill brother could bring that sort of emotion to the surface.

Malthe's eyes wandered unfocused across the scratched wall opposite. As long as Mørck hadn't listened to that slimy piece of shit Paul Manon just now. Malthe had had a bad feeling about him back in Vestre too, watching the man slither around like a viper on the hunt for prey. Poking his nose into everything and dispensing advice on all sides. He'd been friends with half the prison, and the rest were irrelevant to him. Just who was Manon? One of those inmates who hid behind his money and his contacts and was eventually bound to be acquitted. He'd sat around in the intake unit for months, waiting for his case to come to trial. Now things had obviously dragged on so long that he'd been transferred to the remand center at Slagelse.

Did Manon know anything about the agreement Malthe had entered with Peter Loudmouth? Had he seen something he shouldn't have?

Malthe took a deep breath, sucking the air so firmly into the depths of his lungs that it hurt. He had to man up. In an hour's time, none of this would matter. He would be immediately transferred into some type of custody, where he would have to wait for the legal system to figure out what to do with someone like him. Whatever it was, he didn't care. His only worry was that the organization would forget all about transferring the half million kroner to his family.

He punched his thighs a few times, fists clenched.

"Wake up, Malthe," he said out loud. "They know I'll talk if they don't give me the money, and somebody'll be for the high jump. First Peter Loudmouth, and if he blabs too, then they'll all wish they'd just paid up."

No, they would pay. Once the job was done.

• • •

"Come in." Mørck kept his voice friendly, as though this was an ordinary day and an ordinary invitation. And although there weren't homemade cakes on the table or coffee in the cups, he'd been to the commissary, which was open twice a week, to buy chocolate biscuits and cold Cokes from the fridge, so that the atmosphere in the cell was almost civilized.

Malthe stared in confusion at the can Carl was holding out to him.

"You don't like Coke?" asked Carl, but the guy only nodded and made to sit down on the bed next to Carl.

"No, you sit on the chair. That way we can look each other in the eyes without having to turn our heads all the time."

"It's too small for my fat arse," said Malthe, again lowering himself toward the bed.

"Then I'll take the chair, although my arse isn't exactly small these days." Carl smiled as he edged around Malthe.

"So, what's up?" asked Carl, picking up a can of Coke.

"What do you mean?"

"What are we going to talk about? You didn't bring playing cards or anything like that in here, did you?"

"Talk about?" Malthe seemed tense, fiddling with his can of Coke.

"I heard from my dad this morning." Carl tried to get him chatting. "He called to tell me my mum wants to visit and that they're thinking of me. Apart from yard time, that's all I've done today."

"Your dad?" A muscle twitched in Malthe's face. Was he surprised?

"Yeah, my parents are still around. Both in their eighties now. Farmwork gives you a strong heart and ruddy cheeks."

Like a child who'd just been told a lie, the big man tilted his head and filled the gulf between them with doubt. "My dad worked a farm as well, but he died when he was fifty. Maybe you're just lucky," he said.

When you'd interviewed thousands of people, you got a sixth sense for when you'd put a foot wrong. A flicker around the mouth, a vigilance in the eyes, perhaps even the nostrils quivering in anger. *Maybe you're just lucky*, Malthe had said. Was there an undertone to his voice? Carl looked him straight in the eyes. From a strictly limited perspective, the man was right—he was. Losing a father that young was inevitably going to inflict a wound on the psyche.

"Yeah, well, my parents are all right, I suppose, but they could have been a better mum and dad to me. I don't want to complain, but I can't say I've ever felt much warmth from them. I get the sense that your relationship with your mum and your siblings is very loving, Malthe, and a lot of people might be envious of that."

The man turned his head a fraction to the side, still trying to hold his gaze as Carl opened the packet of biscuits and handed it to him.

He shook his head and took a few deep breaths before letting his can of Coke drop to the floor. He lunged furiously toward Carl and seized hold of his head, scrabbling to get his hand underneath his chin.

All of Carl's blood vessels dilated in a millisecond. Adrenaline coursed through him. "What the hell!" he croaked, instinctively slamming his elbow into Malthe's rock-hard diaphragm.

But the large man was utterly silent. He was still stubbornly trying to twist Carl's upper body toward him as his right forearm began to crank around Carl's neck. The smell of his sweat was acrid, the hairs on his arm stiff as hogs' bristles.

Carl held his breath, tensing the muscles in his neck, and at the same time he swung his free arm backward, still gripping his can of Coke, and slammed it repeatedly into Malthe's eyes and the bridge of his nose.

Even then, Malthe didn't make a sound, but his grip on Carl's neck loosened for a second, and Carl began to smash the can as hard as he could against the other man's neck and larynx. The reaction was like pouring alcohol onto fire, the vapors condensing and fueling the explosion, which came barely a microsecond later, with unexpected force. Malthe began to fling his massive fists desperately in all directions, wherever there seemed to be an opening on Carl's body and head. He was hurling several blind blows per second, but Carl managed to prop himself halfway upright, one knee on the bed, and rammed the Coke can again and again into Malthe's nose.

Then the man fell backward, blinded by the blood that had spurted into his eyes.

"Aarghhhhhhh!" he howled, as Carl reflexively staggered over to the sink and soaked a cloth in cold water.

"All right, Malthe," he said, pressing the rag to the man's nose and chin with hands that shook. "Hold this tightly and sit still."

Carl looked around the cell. Blood everywhere on the bed, on the wall above it, on Carl's hands, and on one shirtsleeve, from cuff to elbow.

He was shaken. He couldn't believe what had just happened. Although—wasn't this exactly what that smart-arse Manon had warned him about in the yard, barely an hour earlier? If he hadn't been holding that Coke, Malthe would have killed him.

Carl glanced over at the large body. The man was crumpled against the wall like a defenseless animal, his neck bent and his whole face covered by the dripping cloth. Was that his chest moving, as though he were trying to choke back a sob? Was the man crying?

He drew his legs in as Carl knelt down and placed a hand on his thigh. Then he gave the muscle a squeeze.

"Why did you do that, Malthe? Can you tell me?"

Malthe shook his head as the stifled tears shuddered through his rib cage and belly.

"I'm not going to tell the staff," Carl said, his voice calm. "We'll say you tripped and hit your head on the bed frame. I'm smearing blood over it right now—can you feel me doing that?"

Still, Malthe only shook his head. He seemed to be in shock.

"We'll figure this out, Malthe." Carl leaned back. A thin, watery secretion was now dripping from Malthe's nose. He couldn't hide it.

"All right, listen. You just sit there for a minute and collect yourself, and then we'll talk about it."

Carl rose, sat back down on the chair, and observed the man in front of him. This was the same person who had saved his life in Vestre a few days earlier, and now he was trying to take it. What had happened in the meantime, and what had happened before?

"I won't tell my wife either. She can't know what you just tried to do to me. It would crush her if she had to spend the whole time fearing for my life. Do you understand that, Malthe?"

Malthe nodded, and then abruptly, unconstrainedly, he let the tears fall. Like the sky opening in a cloudburst, revealing the power it contained.

Carl shifted over to the bed beside him and put an arm around his shoulders.

And there they sat for quite some time.

The hour in the cell was nearly up, and Carl and Malthe had done what they could to clean up Malthe's bloodied face and neck. Each hammering blow had left bluish indentations and lacerations across the bridge of his nose and his left cheek. If anybody believed their explanation about Malthe tripping and hitting his head, it would be a miracle, because he'd been badly hurt. The hemorrhaging in his eyes was already so severe that the white sclera were almost obscured. And within the past ten minutes, the area around his eyes had swollen so badly and gone such a violent shade of blackish blue that it looked as though he'd just done ten rounds in a heavyweight boxing match.

Several times, as Carl tried in a low voice to comfort Malthe, he had heard something among the sniffles that might have been an apology, but he wasn't sure.

Now he took hold of the man's broad shoulders and shook them slightly. "Tell me why you're crying, Malthe. Are you sorry about what you just did, or are you sorry you couldn't finish the job?"

The sniveling stopped. Malthe turned his head, gazing straight at Carl with eyes like Dracula's.

"Because now my little brother's going to die," he said briefly.

Carl listened. It was as though the words lifted the veil on every secret all at once.

"Okay, I understand. Someone is paying you to kill me, aren't they?"

He dropped his gaze. So it was true, then.

"And you saved me the other day because you didn't want someone else to get the bounty, am I right?"

A nod.

Carl let go of his shoulders and slumped backward into his chair. The sudden clarity was almost physical, and it hurt.

He sucked in oxygen, filling his cheeks with air, held his breath for a moment, then exhaled very slowly into a sigh.

"How much are you getting for it, Malthe?"

"Half a million." Malthe's voice was quiet.

"And you were going to use it for your brother's operation. I understand."

The response was nearly inaudible. "Yes," he whispered.

Carl rocked slightly back and forth. Half a million—that was all his life was worth? No more than that?

"Who's paying you?"

"I don't know. It was Peter Loudmouth in Vestre who approached me."

"The prison guard?" asked Carl, as if he didn't already know how deeply embroiled the man was.

"So what went wrong in Vestre? How come you weren't involved in the attacks on me?"

"That guy they called the Jackhammer stole the job out from under me. So I had to take it back, and I could only do that if you survived."

"You said the guy they *called* the Jackhammer?"

"Yeah, he's dead. When he got out of the hospital they pushed him down the stairs. I don't know if he was already dead, though."

Very slowly, the whole thing became entirely logical.

"And you were discussing this deal with the lawyer who visited you the other day?"

Malthe hung his head. "No," he said, his voice subdued.

"Do you know what his name is?"

"He did say, but I wasn't really listening. I'm sorry. I said he was my defense lawyer because he had information about my brother. But that wasn't why he came. He told me not to carry out the attack after all. He said they'd given the job to that big guy from the first floor, the one they call Cassius. But I crushed his right hand in the yard, so I don't think he's involved anymore. And anyway, he doesn't have this kind of access to you. Each floor has a different schedule."

Carl nodded. Piece by piece, everything was clicking into place. He bit his cheek, wishing he had a cigarette. He had to act. And if he wanted Malthe on his side, he had to act fast.

"I can get the money for your brother, if in return you watch my back. If you look out for me, no matter what happens."

Malthe jerked upright. His face was contorted, expressions shifting in a flash, like an out-of-control traffic light. Mistrust, hope, mistrust, incomprehension, mistrust, resentment, hope again, relief. His emotions were in turmoil. Could what Carl had said really be true?

"I know someone who has promised a reward of seven million kroner to anybody who can provide proof of my innocence. So I'm sure she'd be willing to offer a tenth of that to keep me alive. And if she won't or can't, my wife and I can get the half million, I can promise you that. You just have to tell me where to send it. Do we have a deal, Malthe?"

Carl looked at Malthe's hands. Gradually, the big man straightened his fingers, then they began to tremble. His forearms followed spasmodically, the corners of his mouth twisting downward, and his diaphragm twitching so violently that his whole body juddered. Now he was weeping so openly and uncontrolledly that parallel streaks of blood were painted down his cheeks. All his pent-up cries for help were released in that moment into one profoundly moved smile. And Malthe embraced the man who, one hour earlier, he had been trying to kill, hugging him so warmly and so tightly that he won back Carl's trust.

Only later that day did Carl's reaction come. They had explained to the prison guard who took Malthe back to his own cell that there'd been an accident, but otherwise all was well.

They must have been short-staffed that day, because neither Carl nor Malthe heard any more about it.

But Carl's whole body was shaking. Not because at that very moment he could have been lying cold and dead in a morgue somewhere, but because from now on he was a dead man walking—because the knowledge of the threat weighed heavily on his shoulders. When would the next attack come? And would this one succeed?

It almost made his knees buckle.

35

CEES

Sunday, January 3, 2021

It had been approximately twenty-four hours since Eddie Jansen opened his front door, his face a mask of terror. Perhaps he'd realized his hour had come, because he had made no move to resist. Cees had been able to simply barge in and push him toward the living room, where his whey-faced wife stood in a kimono with her little girl in her arms, clearly not understanding what was going on.

"I'm taking your husband with me. Unless you want me to take the girl too, you'd better start telling me what you know about your husband's activities." He held up a forefinger, underscoring the gravity of the situation by drawing his gun out of the holster in his belt and pressing it to Eddie's temple. "Answer. Now. Or watch what happens to your husband. It's not going to be pretty, for you or the kid."

She and the little girl both began to cry while the wretched policeman begged for their lives but, oddly enough, not for his own. His wife knew nothing, he insisted. She believed the money had come from a lottery win. Eddie tried to turn his face to Cees to emphasize his words, but Cees shoved his head away with the barrel of the gun.

"It doesn't seem very likely that your husband could have kept it a secret for so many years," he said. "He's been useful to us, but he's not very clever, and you surely can't be so stupid that you never suspected a thing?"

At that the wife pulled herself together, rocking the child to calm her—but she couldn't control her anger.

"I've only seen you and your ugly mug with those weird-looking eyes a couple of times in my life, and let me tell you I have no idea what your business was with my husband then or now. He works for the police, so there are certain things I don't need to know or can't know. Now why don't you shut your fucking mouth and leave us alone."

Then she sat down heavily on the corner sofa, cradling the little girl. She didn't look up, and he was surprised there was no distracting screaming or yelling, no entreaties as to what her husband had done. She simply withdrew into the private space of her shock and tried to bring the sobbing child with her.

"Get your laptop, Eddie," said Cees, pointing at the dining room table where it sat.

"I promise we'll be watching you," he said to Femke as he shoved her husband ahead of him. "Go home and stay here, that's my advice. And say goodbye to your husband."

After that, Eddie had been limp as a damp cloth. His face had been white, but he seemed remarkably at peace as he stared at his guard, defenseless. Strapped to a chair, he couldn't lash back anyway.

"Who have you been talking to?" Cees had asked again and again, but the man said nothing. Only when Cees threatened to seize his wife and daughter and make them pay the consequences for his silence did he straighten in his chair.

"Whether you believe it or not, I never"—he was shouting now, saliva hurtling from his mouth—"*never* did anything I wasn't supposed to. I have been completely loyal to this organization. Not getting rid of Mørck has *nothing* to do with whether or not I'm trustworthy. I tried. Again and again." Then he slumped backward, the air going out of him.

Cees watched the man intently. Eddie had explained they had gone into isolation because of COVID. Their visit to the hospital in Aachen corroborated that. And how was Eddie supposed to know they couldn't just go away for a few days without letting anybody know? He'd done nothing wrong. Or had he?

It wasn't the first time Cees had held a suspect in that chair, and it wouldn't be the last, long after Eddie was gone and forgotten, he was sure of that.

He had taken Eddie to his sister's house. The former smallholding was conveniently situated in a remote area among the Zeeland polders, and as yet nobody had shown any signs of wanting to visit him there. His normal private life was restricted to the city center of Liège. Liège was where he had his Belgian family and where he had his official office, managing his funds. He was not a man of grand gestures, and the house out here was under his sister's name. As long as she remained a vegetable at that care home in Zeist, everything was under control.

What are we going to do with you, then, if you're not going to talk, Eddie? he thought, logging into Tor, the browser he used to access the dark web, where all interactions with his employers took place.

It wasn't long before he got the answer he expected.

We're not going to kill a child, so instead I want you to bring in someone who's stealing from us. I suggest the two couriers from Katowice, the ones dealing with western Poland. I've had a report that the market price in the area has risen by 35 percent during COVID, but they haven't passed that on to us. Frighten all of them, the couriers and Eddie Jansen, then kill one of them in front of the others. As usual at the courier level, use a nail gun. That'll get them talking.

Cees turned to Eddie. "We'll be going through your life with a fine-tooth comb over the next couple of days. Let's see what we come up with."

There was no answer from the dazed man, and no resistance when Cees gagged him.

36

GORDON

Monday, January 4, 2021

The train journey from Schiphol in Amsterdam to Rotterdam Central Station took just twenty-five minutes, and Gordon's eyes were glued to the place names and the landscape that rushed by.

At another time of year he would have loved to play tourist, but right now he had a job to do, and a plane he had to catch in a few hours.

After taking the metro to Rådhus Station and finally arriving at the huge, V-shaped, pale-blue police headquarters in Rotterdam, he was therefore frustrated to learn that it was unfortunately not possible to speak to Sergeant Wilbert de Groot that day because he was home sick with COVID.

"Yes, the wife's just been on a course in England, and she brought that lovely little Alpha variant home with her," said the man flatly when Gordon spoke to him on the phone. "I'm really sorry, but we can't talk in person right now. You wanted to know more about Rasmus Bruhn, I know. I discussed him with your colleagues from the Police Complaints Authority in Aarhus a few days ago, so maybe they can fill in the blanks if I forget something."

Gordon thanked him but didn't comment on the latter. As far as he was concerned, the PCA was a nonstarter, and he was irritated. If he was going to settle for a telephone conversation, he might as well have stayed home.

"I hope you and your family aren't feeling too rough," he said, trying to sound sympathetic. "I'd love to see your report on the case, if I may?" he went on, with a hunch that the coughing man probably wouldn't agree.

"Yes, it's a pity I'm not in the office, since you've come all this way, but my reports are digital, and I can't really give you access to them."

"Then perhaps you could try to answer my questions, now that I have you?"

A long pause, then the man cleared his throat. "I can give you fifteen minutes, then I have to go and rest."

Gordon pictured him shuffling around in a dressing gown and slippers. Was this what passed for a staunch nemesis of the drug trade here in Holland?

"All right, let's talk about Rasmus Bruhn. The PCA doesn't generally give much away, but your department collaborates with the police and the prosecutor's office in Denmark through Europol's Joint Investigation Teams, so hopefully you're able to confirm that he was the one in charge of distribution in Denmark?"

"Our search of his residence supported that assumption, yes."

"Good, then that's settled. Were you aware that Bruhn had a hen to pluck with Carl Mørck?"

"A hen to pluck?"

"Yes, sorry about my English, that's what we say in Denmark. We have a theory that Mørck inadvertently made an enemy of Bruhn years ago. Some people might call the disagreement trivial, and most people wouldn't have held a grudge, but clearly Bruhn did."

"Trivial, eh? What happened?"

"Bruhn was drunk and belligerent at a restaurant in Copenhagen where Carl happened to be, and Carl burned his driver's license. Afterward Bruhn threatened him and said he wouldn't forget it."

Gordon waited for a reaction of some kind from the other end, but none came. Was the man even listening?

"We believe that in revenge Bruhn named him as Anker Høyer's associate and accomplice," he went on. "He may also have identified Carl as the person who stole a large shipment with Høyer, but we can't be sure, of course. Does that theory fit with what you know?"

"That Bruhn was trying to get revenge on Carl Mørck? No, we hadn't considered that."

Gordon sighed, as though he hadn't already figured that out. "But then why did you tell the Danish police to take a closer look at Carl?"

De Groot was silent for a few seconds before he answered. "It was you, your colleagues with the Copenhagen Police, who gave us his name several years before. When you dug up a crate containing the body of Gérard Gaillard."

"And you're aware that Gaillard was identified by an anonymous tipster at the time as Pete Boswell, i.e., the pseudonym Bruhn used as a journalist, and that it was several years before Bruhn was killed?" asked Gordon.

"Of course."

"Funny thing to do, don't you think? To kill a man and leave coins in the box with your fingerprints very plainly on them?"

"You're a detective, aren't you?"

Gordon tilted his head. It was nice to be described as such—it didn't happen often. "Yes, I am."

"So you know, then, that killers often like to brag about what they've done by leaving a signature?"

"Yes, thank you, I'm aware, we've just solved a case exactly like that, but I find it hard to imagine you really believe someone of Carl Mørck's caliber could be that stupid."

There was laughter at the other end. Gordon didn't like it.

"We don't think Mørck is stupid. Surely that's exactly our problem right now—that he isn't?"

It sounded almost as though he'd already passed judgment on Carl. Not a good sign. Gordon looked around the room, where Wilbert de Groot's heavy-lidded colleagues were doing their best to round up the dregs of society. More than a decade had been spent on this particular case. When the hell was one of them going to jump up and shout, "I've got it!"?

"Tell me, de Groot. Which Danish officer gave you the original tip-off about Carl Mørck? It's really important for me to know."

"Who? The Copenhagen Police just give us copies of reports about any cases that might intersect with ours. And vice versa."

"Right, but who was coordinating that in Copenhagen?"

"Come on, this was ten years ago. Anyway, I think more or less all of your colleagues at the station have done it at some point."

"If I give you names, do you think you might remember?"

"You can give it a shot."

"What about Terje Ploug?"

"Yes, he's a valued colleague. He's probably the one who's had the most to do with that case over the years."

"Leif Lassen from narcotics, aka the Sniffer Dog. Does that name ring any bells?"

"I mean, yeah, of course. He was involved in Carl's arrest, for one thing."

"And Marcus Jacobsen, our chief of homicide."

"Look, it was my predecessor, Hans Rinus, who was coordinating back then. In those days we were divided up into God knows how many districts. I only deal with what's going on right now."

"Right now, you say? Are you familiar with the name Hannes Theis, then?"

"Theis! Yes, he owns the import-export business DKNL Transport. We're very familiar with that company; we've been keeping an eye on it for a number of years. Not least because Gérard Gaillard used to use it many years ago, and also because we know that Gaillard and Bruhn worked pretty closely together back then."

"Theis—did you suspect he was involved in transporting drugs?"

"Suspect? We don't have any direct evidence of that, no."

"So if he wasn't involved, then why do you think he might have been found murdered in his own transport van on Saturday night two days ago?"

There was total silence on the other end.

"Did you catch what I just said?" asked Gordon.

"You know what, that information hadn't reached me yet. It's been a day or two since I checked my emails." Then more silence on the line.

I won't say anything, thought Gordon. The next move had to be de Groot's.

"Hey, why don't you grab a cup of coffee?" de Groot said after a pause. "I'll come down to the station. It'll only take me twenty minutes; I live just around the corner."

"Here? But you're sick!"

"Yeah, but I'll wear a mask. It'll be fine. We can social distance."

"It's a shambles down here, Rose," Gordon said into his phone on the way back to the airport. "Wilbert de Groot was kind of an oddball, once he finally arrived at the station. I think he fell asleep at the wheel when he was working that case. But I did get something out of him, mostly because I patted him on the head and commiserated about him getting COVID. Not that he looked particularly ill—far from it. People always seem to get the virus when they fancy a day off. Or ten."

"Anything that might help Carl's case?" she asked.

"He switched on his computer and let me look over his shoulder. Like I have a PhD in Dutch or something. But we did go through the material from the search of Bruhn's apartment in 2014, where various names, including Anker's, were mentioned. At the time, Rinus concluded that the only reason Bruhn's killers didn't go to the trouble of removing the computer from the apartment was because it only referred to people who had already been eliminated. De Groot's own investigation, however, has revealed indications that parts of Bruhn's material *had* been deleted, so it was probably edited by his murderers."

"There was nothing about Carl?"

"Not on the computer, no. But Bruhn had a noticeboard, and on a little yellow Post-it note, there was a whole list of other names. Including Hannes Theis's, the driver Jess Larsen's, and, unfortunately, Carl's."

"Was that all they got?"

"From Bruhn's residence, yes. But I also saw material from searches at the homes of members of rival drug gangs, which de Groot carried out himself after taking over the investigation. He found notes about Bruhn's partnership with Gaillard in the early 2000s, and the body in the crate in Amager was identified as Gaillard. That was news to me, but of course Hardy did tell us. I also saw correspondence between Marcus Jacobsen and Hans Rinus that remarked how close Carl was with Anker Høyer. Just insinuations, nothing more. And when I told de Groot that the Danish press and radio were either calling for Carl's head or to have him immediately exonerated, he laughed and said he thought Carl and the case in general had been vastly overexposed in the media. They would never allow it in Holland."

"What did he say about Theis's death?"

"He hadn't heard about it, but he was surprised to learn the murder weapon was a hammer. Oh, and they've been keeping his business under observation for a while now."

"But they've never caught them in the act?"

"I haven't told you the strangest part yet, Rose. The man in charge of the investigation into DKNL Transport was a detective by the name of Eddie Jansen. Matter of fact, he had his fingers all over this whole sprawling case. And shortly before the New Year, without a word of explanation, he apparently vanished off the face of the earth. No known address where he might be staying, no mobile phones—and to top it all off, he took his wife and daughter with him."

37

CARL

Monday, January 4, 2021

Twenty-four hours had passed since Malthe's attack. And although Carl had promised himself after his arrest that he would never, ever give up hope, paranoia was slowly but surely creeping up on him.

The amount of contact he had with Mona wasn't ideal, to put it mildly, and although his lawyer, Molise Sjögren, had announced she would be visiting later that day, he felt both abandoned and dejected. Every second of his waking state he was reminded of his hopeless situation. The noises of the prison were hard to ignore, as much as he didn't want to hear them. The clatter of cooking utensils, carts trundling down to the workshop, and yells and raucous conversation while the others showered. When he woke up from a nap, he found himself with his hands pressed to his ears.

"Stop it, Carl," he admonished himself. "It's too soon. You've been in here hardly any time at all, and you could be in here ten times as long before this even goes to court, let alone if you're convicted."

Murder, fraud, drug offenses, misuse of office, lying—those were just a few of the accusations they could heap on him. And why? Because he was stuck in here, unable to defend himself by conducting a solid investigation or producing any counterevidence. It felt like having his hands tied behind his back while the executioner raised a sword above his neck, despite the powerful people working on his behalf outside the prison.

The question was, were those people powerful enough to combat the ones trying to bring him down? Klara Kvist had explained that in the outside world, public opinion was swinging between sympathy and antipathy like an increasingly wild pendulum. That rag *Gossip* had done a complete 180 and was now suddenly on the attack. Old, grainy black-and-white photos of a sinister-looking Carl Mørck on the job had, overnight, replaced the significantly more flattering color shots of him smiling.

"It's hard to keep up with what the press are doing," Klara had said, "but they just want to sell copies. Us ordinary folk take the whole thing with a giant pinch of salt, don't you worry."

Carl wasn't so sure.

During yard time, his fellow prisoners were still yelling out their windows that he was a fucking pig, and although the prison guards were busily trying to keep a lid on things, it started all over again as soon as they looked the other way or took a coffee break.

This was how paranoia was fed. Not by the gloomy, fog-drenched nights and echoing footsteps of hoary old crime novels, but by the mere fact that broad daylight very obviously made him an easier target.

All morning he'd been considering whether to offer his assistance at the workshop, where inmates assembled small plastic pump parts for a local soap factory in exchange for pennies. It would be a distraction, but he didn't dare leave himself so unprotected. If he was going to work, he'd have to sit and tinker in his cell. That too was part of the stranglehold paranoia had on him: the prison staff didn't have the capacity to supervise him all the time when he was out of his cell, he knew that. And although the inmates who accepted the offer of work tended to be the most well-adjusted ones, it was still unclear what his enemies had up their sleeves. If the threat didn't come from Cassius, the man-mountain, and if it didn't come from Malthe, then the next attack would be launched from a direction he could not yet foresee. But how could he foresee it if he knew nothing about the other inmates at the remand center?

Would it be wise, he wondered, to discuss it with that Paul Manon fellow the next time they were in the yard together? At first glance the man appeared to have a sixth sense and an extensive knowledge of the goings-on behind the prison walls, so maybe he could point out the warning signs. Carl was full of doubts—maybe he was blind.

It had apparently been decided that he and Malthe would spend another hour in the cell together that afternoon. Klara explained that they had patched up Malthe at the hospital. A couple of stitches on his forehead and across the bridge of his nose and a quick dab of yellow iodine to his other wounds, which, combined with the blackish-blue bruising around his eyes, lent him a dramatic, carnivalesque look.

"You got into a scuffle," she said. "Malthe admitted to me he was the one who started it. He also told me he got pretty violent and that afterward you helped him anyway, without judging him."

Klara took a step closer. "You were kind to him, and that shook him." She put a hand on his shoulder. "You did the right thing, Carl. I can tell he's deeply affected by your faith in him. So as far as I'm concerned, this matter won't be going any further. I promise."

Carl thanked her, but afterward he was racked by doubt. Was Malthe really the only person in here he could trust? Could he even trust Malthe? Where would the next attack come from? Swiftly he ran through the day's routines in his mind.

He was woken at seven thirty by the prison staff, and they rarely came near him. Then there was the necessary visit to the toilet after breakfast, complete with a variety of written instructions. After a few trips to the toilet block, Carl knew the most important ones by heart: *Please close the door after pooing.* Or the reminder to throw used toilet paper only into the toilet bowl, and not onto the floor or in the bucket. That was how you knew you weren't in your own home. Later in the day, there was yard time, and as long as he was escorted from the cell and into the yard, as long as his only companions in the ugly yard were that wretched little pedophile, Malthe, and gray-haired Paul Manon, as long as the walls were solid and he was constantly looking over his shoulder, he wasn't worried about that.

Then there was the food, brought in from Jyderup Prison. During his career as a detective he had encountered numerous ways of administering a lethal dose of poison via food without affecting its flavor. The botulinum toxin, the active ingredient in Botox, was easy to concentrate into fatal quantities and had no obviously discernible taste. He had seen several such deaths caused by poisoned sausages, and it wasn't pleasant. In fact, there was no shortage of toxins capable of bringing about a horrible, choking demise. Then there was parathion and similar insecticides, which caused cardiac arrest and, with a little persistence, could often be found in the musty corners of old garages and outbuildings.

But who actually cooked the food at Jyderup Prison, and was it even possible to target him specifically? Carl didn't know. But if there was even one person in the whole food chain who could use an extra half a million, that might seal Carl's fate, and the same was presumably true if he ordered his food from the kebab place in town.

Carl sat staring at the floor between his parted feet. What other lurking dangers were there? A physical attack in the corridor when he was being escorted to the toilet or the visitors' room or to the various hearings or briefings in the video room? Could he be gunned down in the corridor? Shot through the window on the toilet just before he sat down? Was that even possible? The yard was directly behind it, wasn't it?

Shot? Carl looked up at the window above him and froze. Time and time again, he had stood in his cell in such a way that both his head and chest would be visible through the crosshairs of a rifle.

He got up and dragged the chair over to the window, climbed onto it, and peered out. Where would a sniper be positioned? A short distance beyond the prison walls rose a canopy of bare branches on stunted trees, which looked scarcely capable of supporting the weight of a human being. But in the gap between them, a little farther off, looming tall and menacing, was the fire station tower, used for drying hoses. From there it would be possible to get a shot at him the minute he got up from the bed.

Carl jumped off the chair and sat back on the bed, his eyes still fixed on the window.

Maybe he could ask for permission to swap cells with Paul Manon, he thought, considering the idea.

For a moment he felt relieved, but then his anxiety started all over again. Was it even possible to swap cells? On reflection, he doubted that would be allowed. And would it do any good anyway, being moved a few feet farther away? And what if somebody doused him in flammable liquid and set it alight? Such a thing was most likely possible, through the window or the slot in his cell door.

I have to stay alert. Sleep lightly, approach the cell door in a crouch so I don't make myself a target. Speak to the prison staff about the possibility of boarding up the window or having the glass tinted so I'm not visible from the outside.

At that he began to breathe a little deeper. If only he could regain some sort of control, it would be harder for his adversaries to strike.

But the paranoia was still there.

"Got it, Carl. I'll tell Merete Lynggaard to transfer half a million to Malthe Bøgegård's family and to make sure his brother gets the treatment in Germany," his lawyer was saying. "Anyway, when you're returned to your cell, tune into the TV 2 news, because Jacobsen has called another press conference. We have to keep an extremely close eye on how the media is presenting your story, and we'll do our best to suppress the worst of it, but at the same time we need to accept that we can't control or clamp down on everything, or even close."

She eyed Carl with a vague look that suggested the case had taken up more of her bandwidth than she'd originally anticipated.

"After Jacobsen went public with all aspects of the Sisle Park business, the public was of course impressed by your work and Department Q's, but at the same time it fueled the idea that you've been allowed a bit too much latitude for a few too many years." Molise shrugged. "And the scummier elements of the media have also been insinuating that because of that you've developed your own moral code."

Carl nodded. Perhaps he had.

"As your legal counsel, it's my job to combat anything that might cast you in a negative light, but right now the pendulum is swinging so wildly it's a bit difficult to keep up."

"Then let it swing, Molise," said Carl. "But tell me, why haven't I seen anything of Assad, Gordon, or Rose? Hardy was here, so surely they can visit too."

Her worried, lopsided smile couldn't conceal the acidity in her words. "I've spoken to Hardy, and he says the police have now given clear instructions that they don't want him visiting Slagelse Remand Center, and the same goes for your colleagues in Department Q. Unfortunately, they've included Mona in that as well, since she works for the Copenhagen Police and is therefore in a position to find out a little too much detail about the investigation against you. The point of all this is not to obstruct the PCA's ongoing investigation, they say. So the police are taking a firm line on visits and letters: from now on, you'll have to settle for visits from me and what I can tell you. They can't deny us that, after all."

"I don't understand. That means I won't get to see Lucia until after I've been tried. And that could take months." He shook his head, trying to keep his voice under control. "They can't do that to a small child." He hesitated a moment as the full weight of it dawned on him. "Or to me, for that matter!"

"I'm afraid they can, Carl. But only for eight weeks. You're an old hand, Carl, surely you must have known this was coming?"

Carl nodded, but he was still shaken. They had sabotaged his ability to communicate with his colleagues and Mona about his case, effectively blowing up all his bridges so thoroughly that he might as well be awaiting his fate in a dark cave. And again, there was Lucia. How was he supposed to maintain contact with her?

Carl tried to collect himself.

"Listen, Molise," he said, to keep the shock at arm's length. "I don't know why, but I've just remembered that I was threatened in Vestre by a man wearing a citrus-scented cologne—isn't that weird?"

Molise cocked her head and narrowed her eyes a little. It was certainly a rather abrupt transition from the serious discussion they'd just been having, but she didn't comment on it.

"A man reeking of perfume in a prison isn't an everyday occurrence, that's why I noticed."

Molise nodded. "Yes, I've never met anybody like that at Vestre."

"No, exactly. And then the other day, I smelled it again. Here, in this room."

"Here?!"

"Yeah. A lawyer had come in to speak to a couple of the inmates, and it was the same smell—do you follow me?"

She nodded. He had gotten through. "Have you ever noticed any of the inmates wearing a perfume like that?"

Carl grinned. "Bit too fancy, I reckon. Ice Blue Aqua Velva and Old Spice, sure, but people probably don't wear those anymore."

Molise smiled. "By the way, I wanted to let you know that Gordon is currently in Holland. We're all very excited to hear what he has to say when he gets back."

Carl nodded. "Okay, I'm assuming he's gone to speak to Wilbert de Groot, is that right?"

She nodded. And after that, there wasn't much left to say.

The old guard was once again arrayed outside the Investigation Unit in Sydhavnen, their faces earnest and their expertise emblazoned on their shoulders, as microphones were held out toward them.

The sound was terrible on Carl's tiny flat-screen, so he sat with his nose pressed almost against the display as he tried to decipher what they were saying.

"Department Q deserves tremendous credit for their tireless efforts," Jacobsen was saying. "Without these efficient and talented officers, Sisle Park would no doubt have had even more blood on her hands. Of course, thankfully, everybody at the Investigation Unit is working hard to ensure the safety of the Danish people."

He had deftly transferred the credit for the Park case to the Investigation Unit more generally—but what else did Carl expect? He felt like
throwing up, particularly when Jacobsen referred in the very same
breath to the links the media had published that morning, giving the
public in-depth access to both that case and the ongoing proceedings
against Carl Mørck.

They couldn't go into all the details of the Mørck case, of course, said
Jacobsen, but the charges were serious and the case had now been handed
over to the Police Complaints Authority. Journalists were welcome to approach the PCA, naturally, but it was doubtful they would provide additional information.

Carl switched off the TV, promising himself that the very first chance
he got, he'd start screaming from the rooftops how badly he'd been
treated.

A rather unpleasant and oddly immature thing for an adult and a veteran detective to be thinking, really.

38

EDDIE

Monday, January 4, 2021

In and of itself, the room was hardly terrifying. If Eddie was going to compare it to anything, it would be his grandmother's apartment in Groningen. Armchairs too large for the room but enjoyable to sit in. Faded floral curtains, a thick dark cloth on the coffee table, plenty of knickknacks on the sideboard and windowsills.

What frightened him was that he was handcuffed, and that the handcuffs were tied to a heavy rope attached to the wooden floorboards.

The man with the different-colored eyes had apologized for his roughness and threats, but Eddie had been brought here so that the organization could establish his loyalty. He had beaten Eddie with his fists in between the questions, letting him slump back into his seat from the pain and consider what he was going to say.

The problem for Eddie was that no matter what he said, his captor didn't believe him.

They'd been going back and forth like this for hours, switching between threats and a smattering of conciliatory conversation.

"It's funny, really, but I suppose I never introduced myself, did I?" said the man with the peculiar eyes, and carried on without waiting for an answer. "You're sitting in a house my family has owned for many years, one that now belongs to my sister. It's very remote, so you can forget about somebody walking by or anybody hearing if you start to call for help." He smiled. "Not that I think you would, Eddie. By the way, my name is Pauwels, and my first name is Cees, after an uncle in Zandvliet, and when I'm finished with you, I'll go home to my daughters and my wife south of the border. It's all very simple, really."

I don't want to know this, Eddie thought, his mind churning. The less he knew, the greater the chance the man would eventually release him, or at least he hoped so. But hope was all it was, because he knew his own organization's modus operandi all too well. A suspect had never been given the benefit of the doubt, and this approach had led directly to the deaths of at least fifty people who had fallen under suspicion.

Eddie nodded. "It's a nice house. Did you come here as a child?" he tried.

The man ignored him. "I want to know if you've kept a record of your contacts and the jobs you've carried out for us."

Eddie tried to gather his thoughts. How much did the man already know?

"A record, you say? Well, yes and no. I put together an overview, which is in one of my hanging folders in the office in Rotterdam. The file is labeled 2003, but nobody but me could decipher its contents, I assure you."

"An overview? And what exactly possessed you to do such a thing, Eddie?"

Answer him as calmly as you can, Eddie, he thought, but the hairs on his arms were prickling.

"I'm a systematic person; you have to be, in my line of work, as you know. You've sent me quite a lot of jobs, and I've often found it useful to come up with a list of tasks, contacts, and addresses before I set to work."

Cees Pauwels shook his head. "Not good enough, Eddie! I think you kept a record of our interactions so you'd have dirt on us if things ever went sideways—isn't that right, Eddie?"

"No, I did it because—"

The man threw another punch at Eddie, this time hitting him in the throat.

"We'll find common ground, you'll see," he said, nodding toward two men who were ushered into the room at that moment by the driver who had picked them up. Eddie wasn't sure—had he seen the driver before?

The two men were smiling, a little chubby and with bad skin, as was often the case with middle-aged guys who didn't put much effort into their appearance.

"Sit down," Pauwels said to the two men, signaling to the driver to leave the room. "We have some questions for you about your recent accounts. Take no notice of the man over there—we're just showing him how we reward people we can rely on, so he behaves himself in future, isn't that right, Eddie?"

Eddie tried to smile—was that the wrong move?

The two men stole a glance at each other. At first it hadn't seemed like they had anything to hide, but in that moment Eddie knew otherwise. A slight twitch of one man's eyebrow revealed that he knew exactly what Pauwels was referring to.

"We're pleased with your work," Pauwels began, and both men nodded. "As you've been told already, you were brought here to have your bonuses paid out."

It was odd he was being made to witness this, but Eddie breathed a sigh of relief. The atmosphere in the room grew warmer.

But then he spotted the outline of a figure at the back of the room. A man was standing stock-still in the gloom, watching them.

The blood froze to ice in Eddie's veins. The man's presence boded nothing good. Eddie tried to listen to what his captor was saying to the men, who seemed to have Polish accents, but he couldn't concentrate. Had the figure taken a step forward?

My time has come, he thought, his eyes still glued to the figure. *These two are about to be taught a lesson—Jesus Christ, they've been brought here to see me executed.*

"There's just one thing I don't understand about your accounts, but maybe you can help me," he heard Pauwels say to the two men.

The figure was far enough into the room now that Eddie could make out a medium-size object in his hand.

"Why haven't you been keeping in step with the market price in your area?"

One of the Polish men frowned. "We have," he said, but then the figure stepped out fully into the light behind them. Ruddy-cheeked and freckled, he looked quite harmless, but that was a fatal misjudgment.

Handling the combustion nail gun as though it weighed nothing at all, in one swift motion he raised it to the speaking man's temple and fired.

The *clunk* sounded almost innocent compared to the result: the man who had just been executed barely had time to widen his eyes before he collapsed forward and thudded to the floor like an animal.

The second Polish man recoiled in his chair, but he'd scarcely let out a gasp before the executioner put the nail gun to his temple and held it still.

Eddie's arms were shaking so hard the handcuffs rattled. He stared rigidly at the man who only seconds ago had been alive, the urge to vomit welling up. His face felt cold as ice, his diaphragm pumping like a piston to keep up with his hyperventilating breathing.

"Sit still, both of you," said Cees Pauwels.

Eddie tried to tamp down his despair, squeezing his eyes closed, but a treacherous sob was already forcing its way up. It was unbearable to think about what must inevitably happen next.

"You've been stealing from the organization in Poland, and you won't be doing that anymore, understood?"

The man tried to nod.

"You're lucky you were on the right side, my friend. But next time it'll be your turn, if you don't pass on the increase in the market price, is that clear? Now. Tell me how much the price of cocaine has risen in your district in the last ten months, and don't try to be smart with me, okay?"

He nodded more visibly this time.

"Well, come on. How much has it gone up?" The man with the nail gun nudged his temple slightly with the side of the tool, so he didn't hesitate.

"I don't know exactly," he said in a trembling voice. "But at least forty percent, I think."

Cees Pauwels nodded. He almost cracked a smile.

"That's better," he said, and turned to Eddie.

"You and I have a lot to discuss, now that you understand the gravity of the situation. Don't we, Eddie?"

Eddie tried to reply, but the words got stuck in his throat.

"Well. That's given you something to think about—which was the point." Pauwels turned to the Polish man. "You, you're going to help get your friend out of here. You go with Gustaaf, the driver who drove you here. He'll show you where to dig. There are tools behind the shed. And after that you can leave. Got the message?"

The man said that he had, and the sweat pouring from his face made it abundantly clear he wasn't lying.

"And you, Eddie. We'll give you a bite to eat and drink, then we'll talk again tomorrow. By then I hope you'll have a clearer head, and you can tell me everything. You've just witnessed that as long as you're honest with me, you'll be allowed to leave."

Eddie didn't move. He barely dared to breathe as they dragged the corpse out of the room, footsteps fading behind them.

39

PLOUG

Monday, January 4, 2021

Jess Larsen wore a rather hangdog look as Sergeant Terje Ploug maneuvered him out of the waiting room on the ground floor of the Investigation Unit.

"What's going on?" asked Larsen as he was led into the sterile room the police used for preliminary interrogations, where his lawyer sat waiting.

Hangdog, yes, but not exactly shaken, and Ploug had often seen that with men like him. For various reasons, life had not equipped them with the normal responses of the human psyche.

It was now Ploug's job to break through his armor and squeeze out whatever the man hadn't already told him and the court.

Ploug pointed to a chair and asked him to sit next to the heavily perfumed lawyer who had assisted him during the preliminary hearing.

"The judge has instructed that you remain here until we've interviewed you," said Ploug. "And once we're satisfied, you'll be transferred to Vestre Prison."

"He said remand would last four weeks, didn't he?"

The lawyer and Ploug both nodded.

"Four weeks at present. But we'll see."

"Yeah, well, I haven't done anything wrong. My car was nicked outside Vestre Cemetery, then it was used to kill that lawyer, that's what happened. So what am I doing here?"

Ploug sighed. Contrary to popular belief, the callous, stupid ones weren't actually the easiest to interrogate.

"Hannes Theis was with you in the car. He was the reason you were driving to the cemetery. Have I understood that correctly?"

Larsen ran his index finger a couple of times under the tip of his nose. "Yep. As I've explained to the police, repeatedly."

"Indeed," said Ploug, turning a page of his report. "You have. Bringing Theis must have been a bit of an effort, no?"

"An effort?"

Ploug tapped his watch. "You see this? It's so smart it's also got a stopwatch. Look!" He pressed a button on the side and a small hand at the top began to move. "I'll give you exactly one minute to change your story, Jess, and if you don't, I'll make sure your bullshit comes back to bite you in the arse so hard you'll be begging to tell us everything." He was trying to get the measure of this lawyer, who was slowly beginning to frown.

"Your lawyer will tell you that if you stick to this story about driving Hannes Theis to Vestre Cemetery, it's so far from the truth, it could cost you months extra in prison if we disprove it."

Jess shook his head. "How? I haven't done shit!" He nodded to the lawyer. "They heard it all in court. I'm innocent."

"You pled not guilty, Jess, but that's not the same thing as actually being innocent, don't forget. But fine, Jess. If you're telling the truth, then perhaps you can explain to me how it's possible you were driving Theis to the cemetery on the day in question when Theis had in fact been dead for twenty-four hours."

The lawyer shifted slightly in his chair; that was his only reaction.

"Dead! No, he wasn't." Larsen allowed himself a little snort, as though the notion was flat-out ridiculous.

"I'd just like to point out that Jess Larsen is in custody on suspicion of being involved in the collision with Adam Bang and nothing else," the lawyer said reprovingly, but Ploug ignored him.

"You're telling me Theis wasn't dead? Bollocks! What I've got in my hand right now is the report from Hannes Theis's autopsy, and on the very first page it establishes a time of death. We know with total certainty that his skull was cracked by a hammer on December twenty-sixth. The prosecutor said so this morning, actually, but maybe you weren't listening." Ploug tapped the report. "It's our contention that you knocked down Carl Mørck's lawyer, Adam Bang, on the morning of December twenty-seventh, and that at no point since then have you told us the truth about what happened that day. Hannes Theis couldn't have been with you, because he was already dead in a van in the DKNL garage, which means you had no reason to be anywhere near the cemetery except to kill Mørck's lawyer. Were you trying to send a message to Mørck about what might happen to him?"

Larsen's eyes were darting back and forth in his head. Was he surprised they had established time of death so precisely?

"I heard what they said at the preliminary hearing, then I ignored the rest of it. It was bullshit from beginning to end."

"Really? You and your lawyer were doing a lot of whispering, and he was taking plenty of notes."

"Lawyers always do that." He looked at the man beside him. "Aren't you supposed to be doing something in exchange for the rip-off rates you're presumably charging?"

The lawyer nodded and picked up his briefcase. "I think we should call a halt to the interview at this point, Mr. Ploug. My client and I need some time to clear up what's going on here."

"Sure, just one moment! I'm sorry, but I have to repeat the question: Was the murder of Adam Bang a message to Carl Mørck about what might happen to him?"

The lawyer held out a restraining hand. He and his client needed a minute to confer, he said, before they decided how to proceed.

Only ten minutes passed before Ploug was called back in to hear

Larsen's answer to his question, but he got nothing. And from then on Larsen kept his mouth clamped shut so hard not even a crowbar would have opened it. The lines of communication with Jess Larsen were definitively cut.

Clearly, Larsen had a will of iron, or perhaps his lawyer was more powerful than he should have been.

Ploug certainly wasn't happy. There was no telling whether Larsen's silence might be permanent—after all, he couldn't be forced to testify against himself. That could mean months without progress. Ploug had, unfortunately, seen it before.

Here was a man who in all likelihood was a murderer, and probably the only person who could reveal the motive behind why that poor law-yer with two young kids had to die. A senseless killing, it seemed, yet there was surely a purpose behind it. There had to be. Then there was the murder of Hannes Theis. How likely was it that the murders of Adam Bang and Hannes Theis had been committed by the same person? Had that investigation also come to a standstill?

Terje Ploug was not without ambition, and he liked to think that when Marcus Jacobsen stepped down he would be the next in line for chief of homicide.

The chief constable had made it clear to both him and Bente Hansen that if and when she was asked to suggest a new head of Major Crimes to the chief superintendent, it would be one of them. Contrary to general convention, she saw no reason why there shouldn't be a certain continuity in the department, so who else would she choose?

Terje and Bente had, in fact, tremendous mutual respect for each other. She was even-tempered, honest, immensely reliable as a detective; plus she was single, practically married to the job. On top of that she was a woman—which would be a first for a chief of homicide—so she had a lot going for her.

Ploug possessed none of her charm, nor did he have unlimited time at his disposal, if he wanted to respect his wife and their teenage kids. And if, on top of that, he was mired in two unsolved and very recent murder investigations, he knew which one of them he'd choose.

"Fuck right off" was an expression his son had picked up over the last year, much to his mother and Terje's chagrin, but frankly it was the only phrase that popped into his head as he sat contemplating the mess he was in.

Fuck right off. Jess Larsen wasn't wriggling out of it that easily.

In the room assigned to Ploug's team, Knud sat hunched over the computer they had seized from Jess Larsen's home. If anybody could retrieve information out of digital hiding places, it was him.

But if there weren't any fish in the sea, you wouldn't catch anything, as Knud always said, and right now he was swearing under his breath that the mesh in this net was too wide.

Terje left him in peace. In a few minutes he would be receiving a visit from the notorious Merete Lynggaard, whom he'd already met with three or four times since Carl's arrest.

She arrived so elegantly dressed that even Knud glanced up. After she and Terje had met for the first time just over a week ago, Terje had gone digging through the archives trying to recall the poor woman Department Q had freed after six years in a pressure chamber. In those days she had been skin and bone, a grimy walking skeleton whose skin hung loosely off her bones, covered in wounds and eczema. Now, fifteen years later, she looked twenty years younger than the day she'd been liberated. Sometimes life smiled on those who survived with their inner strength intact.

"So, Terje. Our messenger is in position, and he's made contact, but Carl doesn't realize it yet."

The sergeant nodded. "So what is the latest on Carl?"

"According to Paul Manon, there's something fishy about that Malthe Bøgegård. Malthe came out of a visit to Carl's cell so bashed up that they admitted him to the hospital. As far as I'm aware, he needed stitches for a number of lacerations on his face, which were apparently the result of tripping and banging his head on Carl's bed—but who believes that? So Manon may be onto something, but Carl still appears to trust Malthe."

"And you're keeping an eye on the area around the prison, you said?"

"Yes. There are certain areas around the back of the premises that very definitely do not seem safe. But that's Category 3 prisons for you. We don't expect significant trouble from the inmates or anybody from the outside. I have, however, put one of my best people on the job down there. His name is Kenneth, a former professional soldier, and he's keeping a sharp eye on an area of wilderness directly behind the prison as well as on the neighboring building, a disused fire station with an old fire tower that offers a clear view over the cell windows, including Carl's."

Terje nodded. "Great, well, that all sounds reassuring. I'm afraid I'm at a bit of a standstill with Jess Larsen. He's clammed up like an oyster. On his lawyer's advice, I think."

"Do you know the lawyer?"

"No. At the preliminary hearing they announced his name as Christian Mandrup. I checked him out, and he's the type of lawyer who makes his money as a business consultant, but evidently he's retained his license as a defense lawyer. That alone is a bit odd, if you ask me. He's a fancy, well-dressed guy with an expensive haircut and an exclusive cologne that smells like spring and citrus."

"I see! Any skeletons in the closet that you know of?" Merete asked.

"None. Pure as the snows of Kilimanjaro."

Sitting at a clone of Hannes Theis's computer, Knud began to mutter increasingly loudly, typing away like a madman.

"I've got something here," he said at last. "He was certainly one weird dude, Hannes Theis." Ploug rolled his office chair over to the desk, and Merete went to stand behind him.

"His emails looked pretty suspicious to me from the start, because there's nothing but incoming personal messages. Birthday invitations, messages from family members and school friends. All superficial and not very significant, really."

Knud pointed at one of the invitations. "This one, for example, is from a niece in Uelzen, which is a little way down into Lower Saxony in Germany. 'Invitation' is the subject line, but they forgot to say for what. And it's the same thing again and again. Invitations from a friend or a family member, mentioning a city and a date but not the occasion."

"What do we think of that?" asked Terje. "Could be notifying him of times and locations to hand over a shipment? They transport it from Holland to Germany, then they load the shipment into a different DKNL vehicle and take it to Denmark?"

Knud thought it over. "Hmm, yeah, why not? We're assuming the shipments originate in Holland, so I was thinking maybe they deliver furniture, lamps, and other inventory from Denmark to the relevant location in Holland, then they load up the drugs. In limited quantities, of course, which could easily be hidden on a big transport vehicle during the return journey. But it's conceivable they unload and reload in Germany to make the whole process harder to trace."

"Limited quantities of drugs. But hidden in what, do you think?" Ploug asked.

"Could be returned goods, maybe? A chair with a broken leg, a box of broken pendant lamps, but what do I know? Can't you check the DKNL warehouse to see if they have any damaged furniture lying around somewhere?"

"But Theis probably wasn't doing the driving," Merete objected.

Knud pointed to the bottom of the invitation. "I reckon these invitations refer to two different drivers. One who drove from Denmark to Germany, and another who started in Holland and also drove to Germany."

"BirgerO/xx," it simply read.

40

MONA / CARL

Tuesday, January 5, 2021

At twelve o'clock on Tuesday, January 5, 2021, the prime minister appeared on television and shut down the country. The new strain of COVID-19, called the British variant, was described as highly contagious, and citizens were once more required to adhere to the health authority's recommendations: wear a mask, avoid all unnecessary contact with others—and especially with vulnerable populations—and stay home as much as possible.

Fifteen minutes later, the city streets were packed with cars driving away from workplaces. Essential items were picked up at the supermarket along the way, and virtually all schoolchildren and kids in daycare were collected as well.

Lucia was delighted to be home, because she loved her mother and enjoyed bouncing around the huge apartment, but Mona was less enthused. Who knew how long the lockdown would last this time?

"Mama needs to make a phone call," she told her daughter as she dialed Merete Lynggaard's number.

"Don't worry, Mona," Lynggaard said. "I spoke to Paul Manon last night and he's going to tell Carl today that the five hundred thousand for Malthe Bøgegård's brother is being transferred to the hospital in Germany. He'll also let him know that Ploug is mapping out DKNL's transport network and that Gordon has been to Holland and learned that they don't have much on either Carl or DKNL Transport—and that one of their key investigators, Eddie Jansen, has disappeared into thin air."

"I don't know what that last part means, but next time please ask Manon to tell Carl that this lockdown will send the media into overdrive, so they'll be deprioritizing the Sisle Park case, maybe putting it on the back burner for a while. That means less coverage and less support from the commenters who were backing him up."

Lynggaard promised to pass that on. Her team was already analyzing the potential threats to Carl at Slagelse. Mona wasn't to worry.

But worry she did.

• • •

Carl saw the new lockdown announced on TV and shook his head. Here in prison, the virus wasn't such a problem. A mask or two here and there, of course, but since he wasn't allowed visits from anybody but his lawyer anyway, it didn't really affect him personally. As long as the inmates had no contact with the outside world, COVID was unlikely to make much headway.

Today's yard time, then, was a carbon copy of yesterday's. Malthe, Paul Manon, and the pedophile from cell 10 exchanged greetings, then they started passing around the cigarettes. Carl was delighted to be mixing the fresh air with nicotine. He'd never enjoyed a cigarette so much in his life. Before he even got the first one lit, he sucked the air so avidly into his lungs that they expanded to their full capacity, ready for the first intense drag of smoke. Fifteen seconds of delicious dizziness, then he exhaled, sending all his frustrations and general disgust with life skyward. Bliss.

Only then did he turn to his fellow prisoners.

"So, looks like another lockdown. Going to be tough on a lot of people," said the man in cell 10, known as Åbenrå. "Personally I'm not that bothered, because my little company went out of business when I got arrested, but what about you lot?"

Paul Manon laughed. "I'm on a permanent contract, so it doesn't affect me. And I get two-thirds of my salary while I'm still on remand. My wife's on a permanent contract too. I'm more worried about whether she'll be able to get hold of decent food for herself and our daughter."

But Malthe was silent, shifting very close to Carl. In the gray light he looked like he'd been in a car accident, his face was so covered in abrasions and stitches. And although that chapter was now closed, his expression was glum.

"Just a minute, Malthe," said Manon from the corner. "I need a word with Carl first. Would you mind coming over here a second, Carl?"

"It's not up to you who he speaks to first, you little shit," hissed Malthe, fists clenching, but Carl stopped him.

"We've got time, Malthe, just take it easy." Noting the urgent look on Manon's face, he turned his back on Malthe.

He was led over into the corner, where Manon stood close enough to him that Carl could just about make out what he was whispering.

"Don't say anything about this here. It's best if only you and I know about it. This might surprise you, but Merete Lynggaard is an old acquaintance of mine, going back to her days in politics."

Carl took a half step backward.

"Just play it cool, all right? She and I fell out of touch for some years, but she's just had me transferred here. Don't ask me how, because I don't know, but the reason is so that I can look out for you and your . . . 'welfare,' shall we call it?"

Carl sucked down another breath, deep into his alveoli. He had to do something to help him digest that information.

"You can tell Malthe over there that half a million has been transferred into the hospital's account." Manon paused for a moment. "Politeness trumps curiosity, so I won't ask why, but if you have a spare half million left over, then I'm sure I could find a bank account with my name on it." He brayed four times, eyes half closed.

"From now on, I'm your postman. Since you're not allowed visits or unopened letters—which also delays them—all future correspondence in and out of the prison for the next eight weeks can take place via me. Is that okay with you?"

Carl coughed a plume of smoke into his face, half obscuring it. He was astonished, but his relief that he didn't have to be censored and isolated was so strong that for a moment it rendered him speechless.

"What are you doing whispering over there, Carl?" Malthe yelled. "Don't believe the bullshit he's feeding you."

Carl held up his arm. "Just a sec, Malthe. I'll be right there." He felt the urge to hug the small, dapper man in front of him but restrained himself. "Thank you. I'll come back to you in a minute, Manon. You have no idea how much this means to me. And to him."

Manon smiled, then lit his own cigarette.

"Malthe," said Carl, striding across the yard toward him. "As it turns out, Manon and I have some mutual friends, so he was just giving me a much-needed breath of air from the outside world."

Malthe stood nodding, like a wounded animal in distress. "What about the money for my family? I can't think about anything else. I talked to my little brother yesterday. Do you know what he said to me?"

"No, what did he say, Malthe?" Had the brother already been told that the money was being transferred for his treatment? But then why did Malthe look so sad?

"He said . . ." The young man had to collect himself for a moment, swallowing several times so that his emotions wouldn't get the better of him. But his lips quivered as he pulled himself together.

"He said goodbye, Carl. That's what he did. Not like he usually does, much more serious. I could hear he was giving up."

Carl looked deep into his eyes. Was he trying to say his brother wanted to commit suicide? That would be terrible, when help was so close at hand.

"Are you afraid he's going to hurt himself?"

Malthe shook his head, tears in his eyes. "He would never do that to our mother, I know that. But he's completely lost his will to live, and I know how dangerous that is for somebody as sick as he is."

Carl put his hands on Malthe's shoulders and drew him in. "You can't give up now, any of you, all right? The money has been transferred to him, Malthe, it happened earlier today. Half a million kroner, like we agreed. He'll get his treatment."

More than once Carl had seen a person killed by a shot to the head, and the truly eerie thing about it was the way the body instantly collapsed, like a piece of dropped cloth. So it was a shock when the same thing happened to Malthe. Though he was still fully conscious, all his muscles went slack within a millisecond, and the big man crumpled and sank to his knees.

Summoning all his strength, he raised his face to Carl's and held his gaze, looking at him in a way nobody had ever done before. There he remained, dumbstruck, until Carl and puny little Åbenrå hoisted him upright and helped him over to the rotting bench.

"Is that true, Carl?" Malthe asked in a thin voice.

Carl nodded. "It's Tuesday, and strictly speaking, you won't have access to the phones until Thursday, but why don't you ask the guards if you can make a quick two-minute call, just this once, tonight at eight fifteen, after the second floor have finished theirs. Say it's life or death. I bet they'll let you stand at the desk in the guard room."

A smile broadened across Malthe's lips. Like a child finally granted his most heartfelt wish after years of pestering, he wore an expression that could be read only as unconditional happiness. He said nothing, merely sat shaking his head as though he could scarcely understand it.

A key rattled in the lock, and the two guards on duty hurried into the yard.

"What's going on here?" One of them placed himself between Malthe and the others, while the second officer asked Malthe if he'd been assaulted. Even when he shook his head, they weren't convinced.

"You just collapsed—were you stabbed?"

"Take it easy, friends," said Paul Manon in the corner. "Don't you know what tears of joy look like? If you take him with you and let him call home for just two minutes, everything will fall into place."

They were certainly taking him with them, so that at least they could check he was okay.

Carl looked over at Manon, who nodded gratefully to him as he approached.

"You saw with your own eyes how he took it, so you can pass that on," said Carl. "You don't think I have anything more to fear from Malthe, do you?"

Manon shrugged. "There were rumors going around in Vestre he'd been hired to kill you while you were in there."

"That's true. Malthe admitted everything. He needed the money Lynggaard's just given him."

Carl thought for a moment. "Malthe had a visit from a lawyer who told him he was off the job. I assume he's in direct contact with the people trying to kill me, because the same man threatened me in Vestre. I don't know his name, because the staff won't tell me and Malthe isn't sure it was even mentioned, but I'm sure it's the same guy, because we both noticed a strong scent of citrusy cologne. Quite a good-looking man, about five foot eleven, with dark pomaded hair. Could you ask our contacts on the outside if they can identify him? I think he might be a key player in all this."

The smaller man nodded. "By the way, nobody ever told me why they're trying to bump you off. What the hell did you do?"

Carl took one last pull and stubbed out the cigarette. "I haven't done anything, but clearly someone doesn't believe that."

"Hmm. Well, I can tell you one thing . . ." Manon pointed skyward, toward the open air. "Somebody out there is watching over your safety. I don't know how, I was just told to pass that on."

"Okay, good to know, thanks!"

"Also, someone called Gordon has come back from a trip to Holland. He didn't find out much, but the detectives over there are more interested in the fact that one of their lead investigators in Rotterdam has gone missing. Eddie Jansen, I think his name is. Do you know him?"

Carl shook his head.

"Oh yeah, one more thing. They've arrested the guy who was driving the car that killed your first lawyer, apparently. Somebody by the name of Ploug is running the investigation, and he's in touch with Merete as well as someone else she knows—I believe his name is Hardy."

41

FEMKE / CEES / EDDIE

Tuesday, January 5, 2021

For twenty minutes, Femke drove around the narrow streets without the faintest idea of what she would do if she saw the black Skoda suddenly parked in front of her.

Would she ruin everything if she made herself known to the man? And did she really want to run the risk, with her daughter in the car seat?

Femke was torn.

She had already realized that the chances of her maintaining her current financial standing were slim, whatever happened next. If she abandoned her husband to his fate, and if that fate was death, then she would have to figure out how on earth Eddie had hidden their fortune from the authorities for so long. Had he really been canny enough that neither the tax authorities nor the local councils in Rotterdam or Schiedam were aware of their assets? She had no doubt that he must have raked in considerable sums of money over the years and that he had earned it through criminal activity that would very probably put him behind bars for the rest of his life.

Femke hated him for the things he had done, that much was certain, and there was no way she would ever take him back after reading the file he'd given her.

But what if she rescued him after all, wherever he was? Could he arrange for them to keep everything, then disappear out of her life and get out of Holland? Was that a scenario she could even live with?

Or couldn't she?

She had decided back at the café not to turn her husband in, which meant not handing over the memory stick to the authorities either. Because when it came down to it, how could she feel safe from the people her husband had gotten on the wrong side of? Surely this memory stick was her only protection, if Eddie died and she was next in line to be shot?

She found the Skoda parked on the outskirts of town, outside a shop selling car parts, and she had no idea what to do next. *Maybe I should just keep following him?* she thought, when the man came out of the shop. For a moment he stood still, then he patted his pockets and stared into the plastic bag he was carrying before he went inside again.

Should I just run him down when he comes back out? she thought.

She had once killed a deer on a country road, and apart from a bump and some considerable damage to the car, it hadn't been particularly dramatic. Would it be different with a human being? A terrible human being, mind you.

She glanced around. There wasn't anybody on the street, so it was possible. What were the chances there were cameras everywhere in this remote little town? Certainly she couldn't see any.

And while the man was gone, she tried to weigh the pros and cons of his death.

For one thing, it now seemed unlikely she would ever find her husband. She had already lost sight of Eddie's abductor once, and the polders were enormous.

Femke turned to Marika, who was murmuring drowsily in the back seat. She'd gotten so big in the last few months and was starting to understand more and more. How could Femke justify knocking down and killing another person while Marika was in the back?

No, she couldn't. So then what? The man with the different-colored eyes wasn't going to let Eddie go, she was sure of that. Given everything that Eddie had witnessed, everything he'd been a party to, he had to be a constant threat to his employers. Why else would they have gone to such lengths to track them down?

On the other hand, they might decide that she too could become a threat to them, even though they'd let her go. They'd taken her husband and the father of her child—could they assume she would simply live with that?

But then what did that scenario look like afterward? Could she also disappear to another country—like Eddie, assuming he got out of this alive—with a small child?

Her train of thought was rudely interrupted, because the man was now emerging from the business with a container in his hand. Evidently in a hurry, he was already well on his way by the time Femke even got the engine started.

Once again, she was tailing his car. The white plume of smoke from the exhaust pipe was visible from a distance, and this time there were also a few other cars on the road, so she could fall back while still keeping a close eye on the Skoda.

She seemed to be closer to her target than before, because he turned off just before a copse of trees, where she'd lost sight of him the first time, and kept going. The exhaust was easy to spot in the cold weather, and when she could no longer see it, she drove forward cautiously.

Roughly five hundred yards farther on, she saw the Skoda parked outside a small farm.

Thick smoke was rising from the chimney, indicating that the house had been in use for some time. Perhaps her husband was inside.

She stopped the car near a bend in the road, so that it couldn't be seen from the house; switched on the CD player; and left Marika sitting in the back with some children's songs playing and some fruit on the seat beside her.

"Mama will be back once the songs are over, Marika," she said, trying to ignore her sulky face and sad eyes. "That's not very long, is it, sweetheart?"

Then she went around to the boot and picked up the jack, weighing it in her hand. If she was careful, she might be able to get close enough to her husband's abductor to smack him over the head with it. She was certainly going to try.

The fields were still sprinkled with snow, so Femke left a delicate trail she could easily follow back at a run if she had to.

One wing of the farm came into sight, presumably a former stable block that had since been fitted with modern windows and doors.

She slowed down for a moment, listening for signs the man was holding more people inside the house besides—she hoped—her husband.

She turned her head instinctively to the west, where the wind was blowing in from. She had caught something out of the corner of her eye that stood out from the rest of the landscape. A patch of dark earth, a stark contrast to the snow.

Then she froze, turning to ice.

Was this really happening? She was already too late?

She stared at the freshly filled-in grave and knew in her heart that she could stop looking for her husband.

Then she set off running back to the car and drove back toward the town. There she would buy a prepaid card and call the police.

For a moment Femke wept, until the little one started crying too.

The man with the two different eyes had killed her husband, the father of her unwitting little girl—it was too horrible. Just a week ago they'd been so happy, so blithely unaware of what was about to happen. And now!

Right there, she stopped crying. What kind of delusional nonsense was that? Eddie was the one to blame! He had brought this on himself, she couldn't forget that.

And whatever else happened, she couldn't let his killer do the same to her.

No, she would call the police and tell them where to find the murderer. They would ask who she was and where she was calling from, but she wouldn't tell them that. And then she'd throw the prepaid card far away and drive on home.

• • •

A few hundred yards outside of town, Cees Pauwels noticed the car tailing him. For several years he'd been regularly crawling under Eddie Jansen's SUV to change the battery in the GPS tracker, so when the car came into view around a bend a little way back, he recognized it immediately. As he headed into the open expanses of the polders, the SUV still steaming ahead like a tiny dot in his rearview mirror, he knew it was the cavalry on its way to Eddie's rescue.

Stupid of you, little Femke, he thought. Now he'd have to get rid of husband, wife, and child to fully cover his tracks.

He was low on antifreeze, so he only occasionally accelerated with the clutch down, making the white exhaust more visible and allowing Femke behind him to follow it.

I'll drive all the way up to the farmyard and park. Then I'll get out and keep watch on the last stretch of road. That way she won't sneak up on me if she has a weapon. She is married to a police officer, after all, so there's a good chance he owns a gun she knows how to use, he thought, pulling in close to the wall.

He parked as near as he could to the house and waited until he could hear the vehicle approaching the property, moving at a crawl. It stopped while it was still at a distance.

She had pulled over somewhere behind the trees, he realized, which would make it easy to creep up on her.

What happened next he didn't know, but by the time he'd rounded the copse she was already running full pelt back to her car.

He considered taking chase, but until he'd topped up the antifreeze in his car he wasn't going anywhere. The engine would simply overheat.

He watched the car drive away, wondering at her courage. How remarkably audacious of her. He knew where she lived, after all, barely a few hours' drive from here.

That was one option. The other was to keep Eddie alive for now, because he still hadn't squeezed everything out of him, and then negotiate with Femke for his life.

• • •

Try as he might, Eddie couldn't forget the dreadful sight of the Polish man's wide eyes as the nail bored through his skull and killed him.

He had been alone for a couple of hours while Cees Pauwels did something in town, and Eddie had used the time diligently, pulling and tugging at his bonds like a madman. He had to get out of there. For the last forty-five minutes he'd been bleeding profusely from his right wrist where the rope had cut into his flesh, but his left hand was doing better. It seemed to get a little looser with every passing half an hour, and now it felt almost as though he could get one arm free.

Then he heard Pauwels's car pull into the yard outside the house. For a moment, Eddie froze. Couldn't he have waited just a little longer, just fifteen more minutes, just half an hour? Eddie jerked frantically at the rope around his left arm, until the hand turned black and blue and the blood began to trickle from that wrist as well.

Why isn't he coming in? he thought, his brain in a frenzy, and then the last loop of rope fell from his wrist.

Eddie was desperate. He couldn't let his captor see him this close to escaping—he had to finish the job or the punishment would be immediate; he knew that instinctively. And as the seconds ticked by, he wrestled with the knot on his right hand.

Come on, come on! The words beat a rhythm in his brain as the car door opened and slammed, and moments later he heard the door open on the porch.

Finally, in the seconds while his captor hung up his coat and kicked off his boots, Eddie got a good grip on the knot with his fingernails and wriggled it loose.

"I can't untie my legs," he gasped, and reached with all his might to one side, groping for the nail gun that lay on the table.

He had just worked the fingers of his left hand onto the handle and pulled it an inch or two out from underneath the box of nails on top of it when Pauwels appeared in the doorway and saw what was going on.

A second later Eddie had grabbed the nail gun and pointed it at his captor, who was lunging toward him.

But when he pulled the trigger nothing happened, and the blow Pauwels gave him was so hard and so unexpected that Eddie's head ricocheted back against the chair.

"Idiot," Pauwels sneered as he tore the nail gun out of his hand. He took a step back, surveying Eddie's bloodied wrists and the ropes that lay on the floor. "It's a good thing I came back when I did. Ten more minutes and you'd have been gone. And I'd have had to head back out into that shitty weather and haul you back in. How far did you think you'd get?"

He brandished the nail gun. "And this thing only works when it's pressed directly against the object you want the nail to go through. It doesn't send nails flying through the air. That would be dangerous."

Then he hit Eddie one more time, now with the side of the nail gun, and Eddie saw stars.

When he opened his eyes, he had the taste of blood in his mouth and an urgent need to vomit and found himself staring straight up into Cees Pauwels's icy stare.

"That was a close call. Can't risk that again," he said, seizing Eddie's arm in a viselike grip and forcing the palm flat onto the armrest. Then he rammed the nail gun hard into the back of Eddie's hand and shot a nail through it.

Eddie screamed, realizing too late that his other arm was also being dragged down to the armrest and the hand pierced by a nail.

"Go ahead, scream. Wail all you want, Eddie, but you're not getting away again. Our Lord and Savior was nailed to the cross, and now you two are sharing the same fate. My apologies."

Eddie's whole body was trembling with pain and fear. "I haven't done anything. Why are you treating me like this?"

"Orders from above. Your actions have been inappropriate and hard to understand, and our instincts are telling us you pose a major security risk. We can't have that. So now we're cleaning up, getting rid of anything that might jeopardize us. It will be a temporary setback for the organization, of course, but we'll soon be back on our feet. Once the weeds have been pulled up."

Eddie shook his head, agonized and helpless. "Weeds! But I haven't done anything, I'm telling you. I have a wife and a young daughter to take care of, and that's all that really matters to me. So why would I threaten you? You've looked after me so well for so many years, and it's benefited me and my family. So why would I?"

Pauwels's eyes narrowed. "Ah yes. Speaking of your wife, she knows too much. She was here just moments ago, in fact, running around out-side. Which means I have to leave you now, Eddie. I've got to refill the antifreeze in my car, and then we'll see if I can't track her down. At least I know you won't be going anywhere in the meantime, that's for sure."

Then he patted Eddie on the backs of both hands and walked out of the room.

42

MONA / ASSAD

Tuesday, January 5, 2021

To hell with this lockdown, Mona thought. The pantry at the back of the kitchen was still well stocked with tinned vegetables, rice, pasta, oatmeal, and other dried goods from the last lockdown, but unlike last time, she now had to do everything alone, and Lucia was a year older and a more demanding child.

How was she supposed to help Carl like this? It seemed impossible. She couldn't visit him, couldn't call him, the PCA were still tight-lipped, and worst of all the lockdown meant she couldn't easily meet up with his colleagues from Department Q.

She called Rose.

"What are we going to do now?" asked Mona.

"Gordon and I are working as hard as we can. The way things are now, nobody at the Investigation Unit is keeping us under observation. They're far too busy with their own cases."

"And Assad?"

"Well, that's not such good news. His son, Afif, has been having some emotional problems, outbursts of rage, and Marwa can't control him anymore. So he's dealing with a burly, angry twenty-one-year-old, and meanwhile the two daughters are bickering constantly, which makes the boy overreact and his temper flares. So Assad's been using this opportunity to work from home a lot, although I know he's trying to track down where Niels B Marquis de Bourbon has gotten to."

"Okay, well, we're all doing the best we can to get through this, I know that. And although I do feel very alone right now, Merete Lynggaard has fixed it so that we can send messages in and out to Carl via a go-between also imprisoned in Slagelse."

"I know, I spoke to Merete as well. I can tell you, if Merete hasn't already, that Carl has informed Malthe Bøgegård that the money has been transferred to his brother, and he broke down when he heard the news. So you don't need to worry about that. Merete, Ploug, and also Hardy, to a degree, are working on the case as well, keeping Department Q continuously updated so that hopefully we can get answers to all our questions. Oh, and by the way, I think you should take a look at the *Gossip* website. I hope you'll find it amusing. I can explain everything."

Mona slid her iPad out of its holster and brought up the online newspaper.

"Are you seeing it yet?" asked Rose.

Mona read the headline, which left her speechless. In gigantic red type against a yellow background, it read:

"MØRCK TO DIVORCE"

with the subheading:

"POLICE INSPECTOR HIDING MILLIONS IN FOREIGN BANK"

"I don't know how hilarious I really find it, Rose, now that we're actually doing it, but at least I was prepared. How many people read this paper, do you think?"

"A few hundred thousand, if not more. The top bit of 'fake news' was sent in by Gordon under his own name, so the editors at the paper have no reason to doubt its veracity, since all the other information he's given them has been accurate. The other one, however, he sent in using a false name, but evidently *Gossip* wants all the angles it can get. Why don't you read a bit further down? There's another bit of fake news Gordon's planted."

Mona scrolled past a couple of articles about strong winds on the Great Belt Bridge and about a news anchor who'd been fired, and then there it was.

"CARL MØRCK, DISGRACED HEAD OF DEPARTMENT Q, PREPARES CONFESSION"

"You don't need to read the rest of it, it's total nonsense from beginning to end." Rose laughed. "*Gossip* fell for it hook, line, and sinker. They didn't even try to fact-check the stories, because if they had, you'd no doubt have heard from them. Thank god you and the editor in chief aren't on good terms at the moment—they probably assumed you'd deny it anyway. And now Merete tells me that Torben Victor has been hauled in to see *Gossip*'s owners in Stockholm. It wouldn't surprise me if before long they start looking for a new editor in chief, especially because we've had several other papers call in to check if it's true. We're dying laughing over here."

"So Assad was right, feeding them lies might stop *Gossip*'s smear campaign."

"Well, we'll see, but I'd put money on it," Rose said. "And Pelle Hyttested, the one who actually wrote those pieces, he'll find himself in some hot water too."

Mona sighed. "I wonder what Carl will say about all this."

"Oh, he's ready for it. Don't you worry."

• • •

When Assad stepped through the door of his apartment, carrying four full bags of shopping, he sensed the atmosphere inside was close to a boiling point.

The four of them were sitting at the bare table in the kitchen. Silent as the grave, with eyes that darted past one another.

"What's going on, Marwa?" he asked his wife in Arabic.

She looked up wearily. "Afif's been shouting and shouting all morning, and the girls are going nuts with all the noise, so they've been fighting. Nella and Ronia and I just agreed not to say anything, and then he stopped."

Assad put down the bags and laid a hand on Afif's, who simply jerked it away. The boy wasn't well.

The yelling had begun on New Year's Eve, when Afif had gone down to the garages with some of the other immigrant boys. Assad and Marwa had heard a gigantic bang in the apartment, the sound of a firework going off, and two minutes later Afif had come upstairs with blood pouring out of his ear, sobbing and later screaming in pain.

At A&E they were told one eardrum had been punctured and that he was completely deaf in that ear. Assad had nodded and said Afif had always been hard of hearing. They had long been afraid the silent boy might be struggling intellectually, but only in recent years had they come to understand what his real problem was.

"There's help available for deaf-mutism," they'd been told. There was a bit of a wait time, admittedly, but they were assured it would be worth it.

Yet the screaming had continued, and Afif seemed inconsolable. Perhaps, helpless as he was, he was trying to communicate, but they didn't understand what he might be saying, except of course that he was in pain. It had been five days now.

"I'll take him out for a drive, Marwa," he said. "Give you a bit of peace and quiet."

The most recent tip he'd been given about Niels B had come from his homeless friends on Baggesensgade, after they'd calmed down a bit.

Niels had, as it happened, mentioned several places he liked, and only yesterday Assad had visited the small village of Gurre near Helsingør, where he had inquired in vain whether anybody knew the aforementioned Niels B. He had even gone up to Gurre Castle, which he discovered to his surprise was only a ruin and hence not a fit residence for a nobleman, even one whose bar was as low as Niels's. He had then tried his luck at Gurrehus, a fifteenth-century manor house, but nobody had seen a man of his description.

Assad knew perfectly well it was a long shot and that the chances of finding the man were extremely slim, if he was even alive; but he was going to give it one more go. Niels B's mates from Baggesensgade had mentioned him talking about how he wanted to get back to "the butter hollow."

"It just means he wanted to go back to somewhere nice," the leader of the group had explained to him, but since Assad hadn't heard that Danish phrase before, he looked it up.

Sure enough, he found that "butter hollow," in addition to the pat of butter traditionally dolloped on top of rice pudding, also meant a place that was peaceful and enjoyable to be. And it seemed fair to assume that Niels B was looking for just such a place. Somewhere he could live in peace and quiet without fear of something happening to him.

Earlier that day, when Assad had googled the word, it turned out that not very far away from where he'd been the day before, there was a park called Smørhullet: "Butter Hollow." It was a long strip of green along the edge of Helsingør, the town where Kronborg Castle was located.

So now he was driving up there, with Afif whimpering at his side.

As he usually did to calm him, he put Afif's hand on his throat and sang a few of the songs Marwa used when Afif was at his worst. A young man who had spent his whole childhood with that murderous bastard Ghaalib, the monster who'd abducted him, understimulated him, and isolated him, would never be normal, Assad and his family knew that, but they were doing their best. He was their son, after all.

Something deep inside the boy reacted to Assad's singing. So Assad turned up the volume to eleven, singing so heartily that Afif began to sway with the beat, maintaining contact with Assad's throat all by himself.

Probably for the best he can't hear properly, thought Assad, because it sounded worse than a pack of howling dogs.

As they neared the road into Helsingør, he began singing "Frère Jacques" in Arabic, which had been Afif's favorite song a few years ago.

"Abbi Jakob, Abbi Jakob. Aantanaim? Aantanaim? Haltasma alsaato? Haltasma alsaato?"

And just as he was finishing the verse, Afif let go of Assad's neck, leaned back, and burst into song, bellowing the tune with all his might, louder and louder. "Ding, dang, dong! Ding, dang, dong!"

Assad nearly veered into the cycle lane, and although there were cars beeping behind him, he pulled into a turning lane and switched off the engine.

He was dumbfounded. It was the first time he had ever heard Afif be so articulate, and not only that—those were the right notes in the right order. Suddenly it was as though a closed world had opened up before them both, to Assad's boundless joy and ecstasy. "Ding, dang, dong!" went Afif, over and over. Assad grabbed Afif's hand and tapped it against the seat to the rhythm, and Afif laughed between the words as he went on and on, like a machine brought to life after years of rust and inactivity.

Ding, dang, dong!

Assad began to sing along in his calcified voice, and after they'd sung it a few times, Assad started again from the beginning. *Abbi Jakob, Abbi Jakob.*

Afif's face lit up. He seemed delighted by the connection the little canon gave him.

After a couple of verses he stopped abruptly, looking at his father with tears in his eyes in a way he had never done before. As though he'd just understood his own breakthrough, sensed his own possibilities.

Assad climbed over to his seat, put his arms around him, and hugged him close. He was so looking forward to going home and telling the others about it. And as he sat quietly, holding his son, a tiny whisper emerged from Afif. At first Assad couldn't understand it, but then the words came to him—because words they were.

"Abbi Jakob, Abbi Jakob."

Although Assad had thought at first they ought to drive straight home and share the news, he noticed at that very moment the road that ran alongside the park he was looking for, leading off to the right.

"We'll just have a little look in the park," he said to Afif, and stopped a few hundred yards down the road, where a blue sign half covered by branches announced that the track up into the park began.

"Come on, buddy, we're going on an adventure," he said. "We're looking for a man called Niels. He might be in here." He took Afif's hand and led him out of the car.

Afif pointed at a phone tower that came into view on the left after a hundred paces. He laughed and rocked again from side to side as they trudged on up the path and past a sign put up by the council. "Kong Peders Park, south of Kongevejen," it read. Assad would do his best to remember that name forever.

When the park opened up before them, a long strip powdered with white frost, Afif let go of his hand and stretched, waving his arms like a bird and chanting, "Abbi Jakob, Abbi Jakob, ding, dang, dong."

Assad hadn't been this happy for years, not since the girls were little. To see his boy so free, so effervescent with joy, was an indescribable feeling.

"Can't you keep him calm?" said one of the older women walking hesitantly past. "He's dangerous," the other added.

Assad smiled. If they only knew who was dangerous and who wasn't.

And he ran after Afif across the smooth gravel, shouting, "Ding, dang, dong" along with him.

The mission was to search for Niels B, but right now that didn't matter. He just wanted this moment to last forever.

Afif spotted a playground with a couple of exercise machines a bit farther away, and out of sheer zest for life he flung himself toward them, yelling, "Ding, dang, dong."

After he'd tried the first couple of machines, he stopped in front of

Assad for a moment and said, very articulately and calmly, "Dad," in Danish, before he immediately ran back and had a go on all the others.

The word echoed through Assad's brain. He couldn't wrap his mind around it. Was this the dam finally breaking? Was the boy about to let out a flood of words he'd been storing up? Was there a future for Afif? Right now Assad thought there might be, although he scarcely dared to formulate the words. Afif had said "Dad."

Only then did he realize they were not alone. Glancing to one side, toward an enclosed area thirty yards away where a covered fire pit was emitting a plume of smoke, he saw a group of dark-skinned people holding court. He waved at them, but they didn't wave back.

"I'll just go and have a chat with those people over there, Afif. Stay here, I'll be back in a minute."

Maybe it was a large family, because there were three or four underage kids, two men and two women, and also an older woman who might be the kids' grandmother.

"Hello," said Assad, noticing a couple of them jump as he did so. "Do you mind if I ask you something?"

"We're allowed to be here," said one of the men.

Assad came closer. One of the men had a convulsive grip on the knife he was using to cut meat.

"Of course you are, it's a public place. Who says you aren't?"

"There's a lot of people who aren't fond of the likes of us . . . or you."

"Sure, but they don't get to order us around. What are you doing? Looks nice, but isn't it a bit cold, cooking out here?"

"When we all get together—me and my brother-in-law, the wife and her mum and sister, and the kids—we can't fit in the kitchen, so we come out here and just put on some extra layers."

Assad nodded, glancing over his shoulder. Afif had let go of the playground equipment and was on his way into the enclosed area.

"This is my son," Assad said. "Are you here often?"

"Every day since New Year's. Over the Christmas holiday we were in Pakistan," said the guy.

"I'm looking for this man. Have you seen him?" Assad pulled out the old photograph of Niels B and held it up to the group.

The men shook their heads, but one of the women looked quizzically at them.

"I know, it's a really old photo. He looks a bit different these days," said Assad, registering that Afif had moved closer to the fire pit and was nodding at everybody. He stared at the photo for a second, then went over to the kids, who were rocking on a wooden disk mounted on some heavy-duty springs.

"Are you sure? Isn't that him?" the woman asked. The men leaned in toward the photo, scrutinizing it for a moment.

"Maybe," said one.

They explained that they thought they might have seen him once or twice, because a man who looked a bit like the photo had also been cooking food in the park. If it was him, then he was also the one who'd been piling up loads of firewood next to it. He'd been chased off by the same young men who had also threatened them, but since the family was a bigger group, they weren't as scared.

Assad held his breath for a moment. "Why did they chase him off?"

"They called him a pig and said he was dirty and smelled like shit. Told him to fuck off out of their park."

"When did they do that?" asked Assad.

They exchanged glances. "The day before yesterday," said the woman who had recognized him.

Assad looked over at Afif, gently rocking the children while he stood with his back to the fire. Every time he pushed the wooden disk down, he said, "Ding, dang," and when it bounced back up, he said, "Dong!"

All was peaceful. His son seemed emotionally settled; somehow, something important had fallen into place.

"Do you know where he's living?" Assad asked.

They all shrugged. He'd just vanished, and they had only ever seen him near the fire pit.

"Did he say anything to you?"

"Nah. When we came into the area with the fire pit we said hi to him, of course, but he just nodded."

"Was he scared of you?"

"Maybe," said the woman, with a tiny giggle. "But I guess there's quite a lot of us."

At that moment Afif stopped chanting. For a moment he stood in total silence, then he yelled so loudly he startled the children.

"*There*, Dad!"

Everybody by the fire pit turned to see the boy pointing into the thicket beyond the enclosure—and he was right.

There, almost entirely hidden by the stark bushes, stood Niels B Marquis de Bourbon, mouth open and eyes wide with fear.

Then he took to his heels.

43

FEMKE / CEES

Tuesday, January 5, 2021

Femke had to visit three different mobile-phone shops before she found a prepaid SIM, and time was passing.

Marika was howling at the top of her lungs in the back seat. She wanted to go home. She wanted her dad. She didn't want to sit in the car anymore, and she was hungry.

Your dad, thought Femke. *You'll never see him again, my darling.* She glimpsed her little girl's face in the rearview mirror, so delicate and pretty and oblivious to the awful reality of the situation her father had landed them in. In a way, though, the sight of the freshly dug grave had been a relief. She no longer had to worry about coming to her husband's rescue, when doing so could have torpedoed her life. Now all she had to think about was herself and Marika—and stopping the man with the different-colored eyes. Moving on.

"I have information about a murder and the man who committed it," she began, when she got through to the officer on duty at the police station in Breda.

"Where are you calling from? I can't—"

"The victim is buried a hundred yards from the house where the murderer lives. You can see the grave in the field next to the gravel track," she continued stubbornly.

"Could you please state your name and where you're calling from? I can hear a child crying in the background. Are you in danger?"

"I believe the victim may be one Eddie Jansen, a detective with the Rotterdam police. You can confirm his name and identity by calling the homicide unit there."

The officer repeated his question, but Femke ignored him.

"The killer lives just outside of Middelburg, in the polders." She gave him the GPS coordinates. "And you'd better hurry, because the man is extremely mobile."

Then she hung up the phone, took out the SIM card, and snapped it in half.

She breathed a deep sigh of relief. So. That was that. Now time to get back to Schiedam. Psychologically she was at the end of her rope, but physically she was feeling much better. A bit of a sore throat, sure, but the coughing had stopped, and it seemed like Marika also had the worst of the virus behind her.

"Mama knows you're hungry and tired, sweetheart. We'll drive north for half an hour, then we'll find somewhere, all right?"

As Marika's dissatisfaction grew in strength, her face turning beet red, Femke cracked the window open, and she tossed the two halves of the SIM card out the window, a few hundred yards apart.

The most logical and shortest route would be to drive toward Goes and then head north along the N256, but Femke didn't feel comfortable doing that. Surely that would be the road the killer would take, if he was also going north? So she opted for a detour via Bergen op Zoom. That would also make a suitable pit stop, give her a chance to cheer up Marika.

A rest, a quick sandwich, and something to drink, then they'd drive home. There were papers to be read, files to be examined, the contents of the safe to be removed.

• • •

Cees threw a quick glance into the living room, where Eddie Jansen was writhing in his chair. The blood that had pooled under the armrests had begun to congeal on one side, while the other was still a steady trickle. If he was back within twenty-four hours, Eddie would probably still be alive, and Cees could finish wrangling the truth out of the man before he died.

He set off north as the sun slipped below the horizon, confident that before the day was out he would have dealt with Femke and Marika Jansen.

He would use a knife. In a high-rise block like theirs, brute violence echoed all too clearly through the concrete walls. A silenced pistol wouldn't do the job either. It had to look like a robbery gone wrong, and if you were going to shoot someone in that scenario, the shot would be loud, which again wouldn't do. After all, what ordinary burglar used a silencer? Nobody.

On his way up to the connecting spit of land near Breezand, he noticed police cars racing southward, sirens blaring, which was not something commonly seen in the area, but then again, Middelburg was no longer a tiny backwater. There was a lot going on these days.

After sixty miles he reached Schiedam and Louis Raemaekersstraat. It was late evening, and the vast majority of residents had come home from work. He drove slowly up and down the nearby parking areas, but Eddie Jansen's SUV was nowhere to be seen.

She hasn't driven the same route, he thought, gazing up at the family's pitch-black windows. Maybe she had stopped along the way. She did have a child in the car, after all. He knew all about that.

Patiently waiting, he leaned back in his seat and texted his employers.

Can soon give a positive report re Eddie Jansen and his family.

He signed off with his initials and let his eyes slip out of focus. He found that the best way to relax during a surveillance job.

A few minutes later, a response arrived.

You're cleaning house, that's good! That just leaves Carl Mørck. The ultimate solution to that problem is already being finalized.

Cees Pauwels nodded. Once the Jansen family were dead and his report was delivered to what he hoped would be his employers' satisfaction, a package would arrive at his residence in Antwerp. Last time it had been one hundred thousand euros in fifty-euro notes. Would it be roughly the same this time? he wondered.

He sensed a beam of light sweep over the parked cars, only just ducking down in time as it reached his.

Femke had definitely looked better than she did now, carrying a drowsy little girl out of the vehicle. Cees straightened up immediately.

I'll do it down here in the carpark, he thought, getting out of the car.

He could hear her chattering away to the kid. She took the bags out of the back of the car, pausing for a moment, because the girl was in a mood. The mother sighed.

Cees crept closer behind the nearest row of parked cars, drawing out his knife. First the mother, then the kid. One swift slit to the throat. Not a sound.

He edged between two cars, now only a few feet away. Even if Femke saw him, there was no escape.

Suddenly, blue lights began to flash against the concrete walls of the carpark, and Femke pointed them out. "Look, Marika, a police car," she said, but the kid didn't care.

Cees did. He ducked.

The lights concentrated rapidly as the white patrol car rolled toward her, and for a moment she was blinded by the beams.

Then the passenger-side door opened, and a woman in civilian clothes got out and went over to Femke, the uniformed driver following. Femke seemed to recognize them, giving them a smile that stiffened even as it crossed her face, but the female officer's expression was unmistakable. This was no courtesy call. Not by a long shot.

Cees was only a few feet away when the woman hugged Femke. He crouched down between the cars, trying not to be seen.

He had only a partial view of the scene that was unfolding. The woman said something to Femke, who looked like she was about to collapse with her daughter in her arms, and then there was a moment's silence. The woman added something else as she eased Femke's daughter out of her grasp.

Then Femke began to cry.

44

ASSAD

Tuesday, January 5, 2021

For a brief moment they heard the man crashing through the dark, dense undergrowth, and then there was silence.

Afif pointed to a gap and a narrow path speckled with a thin layer of frost, which led toward a residential road. He signaled eagerly for Assad to follow, but Assad was momentarily rooted to the spot. Was the young man beckoning him on truly the same boy who had been whimpering in their dining room just hours earlier?

What had happened to him?

But Assad followed the boy's gesture, and the ruins of a house soon appeared in the dusk, the building long since collapsed and fallen in. An empty doorway stood forlorn and alone in the freestanding wall, bidding them welcome amid the tangled bushes. A little beyond it stood the remains of a longer wall, once the side of the building, where two more doorways kept the whole thing together. Primitive tags and plenty of colorful graffiti indicated that the place had been extensively used by trespassers.

Assad scanned for clues that might tell him if this was where Niels B had been living, but there was no sign he had relieved himself or slept there. He turned to his son, but Afif was already moving on.

The few times they'd been in the forest with Afif since bringing him to Denmark, the boy had been very afraid of dense foliage, where the tops of the trees loomed far above his head. He was used to a colorless life in arid desert villages, so all that vegetation overwhelmed him. But not right now, it seemed.

"Come!" he shouted, inarticulately but intelligibly.

Assad stiffened. So he knew that word as well.

"Come, Dad! Come! Come!"

Pushing the branches aside, Assad sprang forward toward other areas of the building, these much better preserved. Afif was pointing at some yellow-brick walls that marked out what had once, not so many years ago, been a magnificent villa. At the back of the house was a gorgeous wrought iron spiral staircase that led up to a terrace cut into the gable roof.

The villa was situated on high ground, facing the road, and was partially illuminated by lamps at street level. Assad had noticed it briefly as they drove past. Bare, empty windows and wide, crumbling brick steps that led up to the front door. A crying shame for such an idyllic neighborhood that a beautiful house like this had fallen into such disrepair.

They went down some steps toward a door where they could enter the building unhindered, emerging into what was evidently the basement, although it was above street level. And despite the fact that the only light inside was cast by the streetlamps through the gaping windows, it was enough for them to get their bearings.

Assad looked around for an interior staircase linking the basement to the ground floor, but there wasn't one.

Here too the local youths had been busy, smashing everything and plastering the walls of the many rooms with their infantile drawings, marking territory that had never been theirs and never would be.

At that moment both Afif and Assad felt a faint tremor from the story above them, sending microscopic dust and plaster sifting down over them.

Got you now, thought Assad, taking the exterior staircase in a few bounds and grabbing the handle of the front door without hesitation.

The door was locked. He rattled the brass handle.

"Niels," he called. "It's me, Assad. I'm outside. Can you let me in, please? I'm not going to hurt you."

If it had been possible, he would have gone around the back of the building and climbed in through one of the empty windows, but the only access to the main level was via this door.

"Come on, Niels, I only want to ask a couple of questions," he went
on, but the faint creak of crumbling floorboards on the other side of the
door was the only sign the man was inside.

"Shall I call the police, or are you going to let me in, Niels? This isn't
your house, is it?"

No answer.

"Last chance before I kick the door down."

He signaled Afif, standing behind him, to step aside so he could take
a run-up. But before Assad knew what was happening, Afif had lunged
forward and slammed his heel full force just beneath the door handle.

It didn't budge so much as an inch, and Afif toppled backward toward
the iron railing. Whether in pain or shock, he howled so loudly that it
echoed across the whole neighborhood.

And then, very slowly, the door handle was turned from the inside,
and the door opened the merest crack.

All three of them were sitting on the floor in a dark, windowless room
with grimy walls, strewn with rubble and broken glass. A pretty
wretched place to live for a man who bore the title of marquis, thought
Assad, but the plastic bags from Netto were full of food, and the carpet
on the floor was thick, no doubt more than warm enough to protect him
from the ground frost at night. The furniture from the garage in Nørrebro
was piled higgledy-piggledy in the corner, and all the loose odds and
ends were packed into moving boxes stacked along the end wall.

"I screwed a metal plate into the door so it couldn't be kicked in," he
said consolingly to Afif, who was still clutching his aching hip.

Niels B turned to Assad. "I know exactly what you're going to ask
me," he said.

"And I know what you're going to say in reply," Assad countered. "I want to know why you did a bunk from Nørrebro, and you're going to say it's because you felt threatened."

Niels B nodded.

"But *what* did you see, Niels, that scared you so badly?"

Niels was silent for a moment, thinking.

"My grandma and granddad lived just across from this house, when they were alive. And when my mother and I visited, I used to play around the back, in the park they called Butter Hollow. In those days this villa was the grandest on the street, I always thought, and I dreamed that one day it would be mine. I came by again a few years ago, when my mother's funeral was held in town, and I saw how dilapidated it was."

"You thought it might be a good place to hide, I understand. But hide from what, Your Excellency?"

Niels B smiled at the title. "You remember I told you that after I was released I found Paslode nails in my bed, and I was so scared I left the apartment in Slagelse?"

"Yes. That was probably a good idea."

He nodded. "Did I also tell you that I noticed a smell in the apartment?"

"No, I don't remember that."

"The air was heavy with perfume, something citrus-scented."

"Okay, and what's the significance of that?"

"A few days ago I was in Netto on the corner of Nørrebrogade, and while I was standing in the queue for the till, I smelled it again."

"It could have been a coincidence."

"Yeah, I thought so too. It could have been from the cleaning products aisle or the fruit and veg, but when I came out onto the street I saw a man chatting to one of the locals. He was very nicely dressed, not someone who usually walks down that street. At least, I'd never seen him before. But the way he was talking to the other guy told me they didn't know each other. He'd just stopped a random passerby, or so I thought. I huddled up to the wall when he walked by me, kept my back to him, and there was that smell again."

"You think he was looking for you?"

"I know he was, because I ran in the other direction, toward the man he'd just spoken to, and he told me he'd been asking for someone by the name of Niels B Sørensen."

"You're sure?!"

"Yes I'm bloody sure. I ordered a haulage van right then and there, and half an hour later we loaded up my stuff and the boxes from the garage and drove up here."

"Do you have any idea who he was?"

"I'd never seen him before, and I certainly don't fancy ever seeing him again."

"He spoke Danish?"

"Yes, fluently. Like somebody who grew up near Copenhagen."

"We'll put a stop to him, Niels. I promise."

"And what about the people who sent him?"

Assad paused, taking his time. Furrows that weren't there before had branched across the man's forehead. Was this something he'd been brooding over for a while? Was he inviting Assad to question him more closely?

"Now that you mention it, Niels, I'd like to know a little bit more about all that. Maybe you can help me."

The furrows neither deepened nor smoothed out. He was ready.

"Those two mechanics you were hanging out with at the workshop in Sorø. Did they ever tell you anything about the drug-related stuff? I think it would be a big help for both of us if you could remember."

Niels B was silent, gazing at him for a long time before he took a deep breath and answered.

"If you want me to talk to you about all that, there's something you have to promise me first!"

45

WAYNE / CEES

Tuesday, January 5, 2021

That afternoon, Wayne Peters had had a small gaggle of local children around to visit. Word of sugary aromas wafting from the house had spread rapidly: the old man had baked his famous buns and mazarin cakes. In spite of the weather, he had thrown open the veranda door and carried the various treats out to the garden tables for the occasion, so that the children could help themselves to pastries and the fresh juice he'd set out in vast quantities.

Putting on events like these afforded him a certain status. Parents greeted him with the same veneration as though he were a beloved member of the family. Any time weeds popped up in the front garden, he could be sure somebody would soon be around with a hoe. A person like Wayne Peters was one of life's rarities, and such individuals had to be cherished, treated with warmth and respect.

Wayne loved the mask he wore, because behind the irreproachable façade he could do as he pleased. In the last two weeks especially, he'd had to dig deeper than ever before into his capacity for ruthlessness.

Within the last twenty-four hours alone, information had emerged from his employees via the dark web that had carved ever-deeper furrows into Wayne's already furrowed brow.

There wasn't much good news right now—to put it mildly.

They were closing in on Carl Mørck so efficiently that for a while it pushed all the other news into the background.

Yet according to reports, it seemed cracks were beginning to appear in both the Dutch and Danish sectors, and those would have to be patched up pretty damn quick.

He didn't know the latest on Cees's interrogation of Eddie Jansen, so he didn't yet have a clear sense of who could be trusted and who could not. Wayne had texted Cees a few times in the last hour with no reply, and he was not best pleased. When Wayne reached out, his staff were expected to respond immediately, day or night. Eddie Jansen was going to die, Cees had told him so yesterday—but was the job done yet?

The head of the local organization in Denmark had reported that the Mørck situation was starting to veer out of control. Wayne's Danish consigliere, the lawyer Christian Mandrup, had identified several more people now investigating Mørck's role in the case: it wasn't just the Police Complaints Authority anymore. Even Mørck's former unit, Department Q, seemed to be operating at full throttle. Like a tanker, its inertia made it virtually unstoppable. Someone from the department had gone to see that detective in Rotterdam, Wilbert de Groot, and regardless of what information they'd exchanged, it was probably time for de Groot to be retired—in a wooden box six feet under.

It had been decided that another former suspect in the Sorø killings, Niels B Sørensen, resident of Nørrebro, would also have to be sacrificed. Previously they'd contented themselves with a warning, and he'd stayed under the radar ever since. But now they'd discovered he'd been talking to another detective from Department Q, and Wayne began to worry he might know more than he ought to about the old days, when Rasmus Bruhn was still alive.

And now this Niels B was missing.

Then, as if that wasn't enough—what with all the other red warning lights going off—one of the top homicide detectives in Copenhagen had apparently launched an investigation into the murder of Hannes Theis. And although Mandrup had done his best to prevent it, Theis's driver, Jess Larsen, had been taken into custody.

Wayne hated mess. It infuriated him, actually, but his greatest strength had always been his ability to rein in his paranoia and keep things in perspective. When he considered the various people currently jeopardizing his business in Denmark, their main objective seemed to be protecting Carl Mørck. But what if they discovered that he didn't deserve their loyalty? That he'd been arrested for good reason? If it was proven that he *had* committed a crime, had taken Anker Høyer's stolen money, cocaine, and heroin for himself, all while playing a double game as a celebrated, gifted detective? Would Cees Pauwels, Christian Mandrup, and his other employees in Denmark be able to spread information that would stop Mørck's supporters from wanting to help him?

No, it seemed unlikely. The solution to all of it, the one thing that would thwart these unpredictable attacks on Wayne's organization, was very simple: Mørck had to die. After all, if the key person was taken out of the equation, surely there'd be nothing left to investigate? He'd received the same advice from the head of his organization in Denmark.

Wayne Peters knew perfectly well what he would do if the net began to close too tightly around him and his people. If that happened, he'd have to make sure a certain percentage of his middlemen were liquidated. The occasional purge was good for an organization like his—the only question was when to give the signal and who should be on the list.

He settled down at his laptop, lit a cigarillo, and messaged Cees Pauwels for the third time that evening.

Check in, he typed, then sat back and waited.

• • •

Cees was still crouched between two cars as the officers helped Femke Jansen with her bags and escorted her and her daughter up to the apartment. He'd half risen to his feet when he saw them emerge onto the external walkway on the seventh floor and go into the apartment. The lights came on in the front room, and he could see them moving around inside.

By now the temperature had dropped so low that his teeth had begun to chatter, so he returned to his car and moved it farther away in the carpark, where he could keep the engine running and the heating on undisturbed.

What the hell was that all about, he wondered, and what had happened since Femke went sprinting off from the house in the polders? She'd had time to do almost anything. She might have called the authorities and alerted them to search the property, but if so, what had they found? Had Eddie Jansen already passed away? That might have been why she'd broken down just now. Even though he hadn't managed to get an explanation out of Eddie as to why he'd gone AWOL or what threat he might now pose, it would certainly be preferable if he wasn't found alive. Yet as long as Cees didn't know the full facts, he couldn't report back to his employers, even if said employers were pushing him for information.

Cees leaned back in his seat and switched on the stereo. Listening to Herbert von Karajan's *Adagio* album usually helped him think. The opening of Karajan's slow interpretation of Gustav Mahler's "Adagietto" immediately lowered his heart rate and allowed him to breathe a little more freely, which was crucial when he was under so much extra pressure.

Chances were, his hiding place among the polders had been compromised. And although he knew he'd not left anything in the house that could be traced back to him, there was no doubt about who owned it. The deed was in his sister's name, and he couldn't be sure that one of her friends or carers wouldn't let slip that her brother used the house from time to time. Cees thought it unlikely, though—who would even know? Nobody ever visited her at the care home, including him. So he ignored that possibility for now.

There was, of course, a chance that they'd found Eddie alive, and that was potentially much more damaging. Cees had given Eddie a name to use for him, but not the one that appeared on his birth certificate or by his doorbell in Antwerp, so it would be a dead end if the police tried to trace it. Nor would his trademark mismatched irises be an issue, because that was only a gimmick that could be reversed in seconds, if he wanted.

A flick of the wrist, and the brown contact lens in his right eye could be replaced with a clear one. Even his faint Dutch accent was put-on.

Turning up the heat a little, he drew the blanket on the passenger seat over his legs. This might turn out to be a long night. What if the police stayed in the apartment? What if Femke had already said too much? It might be time to take extreme measures. He'd killed police before, although it had been quite a few years ago now, but if that was what was required, then . . .

He cast another glance up at the external corridor, which ran from the lift and past all the apartments on the seventh floor. If he was going to make a clean getaway after clearing the apartment, he'd have to be sure nobody came up via the lift or the fire escape. Nobody had come along in the last thirty minutes, it was true—but who knew how long that would last? Someone coming off an evening shift, someone who'd been out drinking a little too much. They might suddenly be face-to-face with him, and the result would be more victims than he'd like.

No, he had to wait until the coast was clear. That would also give him time to pressure her into telling him everything she knew before he killed her.

Cees still had a hunch Eddie and his family had gone into hiding because Eddie had been planning his exit from the organization. As far as Cees could tell, the man had stashed away at least ten million euros, apparently laying the groundwork for a life far away from Rotterdam and Holland.

The gist was presumably that Eddie had started to fear for his life, that he'd been planning to cease work for the organization and send in an anonymous tip about all the people he knew were involved, making sure they were arrested. He must have known his name would eventually surface during the investigation, and he would have taken that into account. If high-ranking Nazis could make themselves permanently vanish in Argentina or Bolivia, then so could Eddie Jansen.

If Eddie was indeed alive and in the custody of the authorities, he'd have to shelve the getaway plan for now. But what would he do instead?

Would he admit his involvement or not? It was enough to make Cees's head ache.

Every fifteen minutes, Cees glanced up at the large window at the front of the Jansens' apartment. Why the police weren't already long gone he didn't understand. Were they interrogating her straightaway, creating a vacuum to suck everything out of her before lawyers began to intervene?

He looked at the clock. By now he'd ignored multiple messages from his employers, who were demanding an update. Hopefully, they would assume that his phone had run out of battery, but he knew that tactic wouldn't work much longer. The very second the police left Femke and her daughter alone in the apartment, he would hurry upstairs, find out what had happened to Eddie and what the police had wanted with Femke, and then he'd draw a hard line under the whole thing.

His mind was made up.

46

FEMKE

Tuesday, January 5, 2021

Eddie was dead. That was what her former colleagues from the police station in Rotterdam had told her when they showed up at the carpark. As though she hadn't been expecting it already—she'd seen that fresh grave in the field, after all.

Yet it was a different man, they said, buried in the grave the anonymous voice had described to the local police. That man had been killed with a nail gun, and several items of clothing and objects in his pockets suggested he was Polish.

Then came the shock. Her husband was dead, yes. Their colleagues had found him in a chair when they searched the house. He must have died only moments before they arrived, because his body was still warm when they found him.

That was more or less the same time I was there. The awful reality dawned on Femke, and her legs gave way beneath her. If it hadn't been for her friend Siri, she would have dropped her daughter.

They stood there for a moment to let Femke recover, and Siri gathered Marika into her arms so that she wouldn't wake up and be scared.

Then the two officers led her up to the apartment.

———————

The Middelburg police had found Eddie after an anonymous call, and they were still working to find out who had phoned them. Sadly, it seemed likely that if they'd gotten there even just an hour earlier they would have arrived in time, but that hadn't been what happened. It was very frustrating.

Siri put Marika to bed in her room, and Femke looked around the apartment. How could she possibly stay here, where every little detail reminded her of Eddie? The sofa they'd saved up for many years ago. The silver ashtray Eddie was so proud of having won at school, and which he'd never used. Photos of the three of them, painfully bright and smiling, reminded her of the dreams they'd had, great and small, and the moments that now, at last, were no more than memories. For a split second, Eddie's eyes bored into her out of an otherwise innocuous photograph of him in uniform, suddenly accusatory.

The thought again crossed her mind: *Perhaps I could have saved him.*

"How are you doing, Femke?" asked Boris, her old boss.

She shrugged as though she didn't know, but then she burst into tears, raising her eyes to the emptiness that abruptly filled the living room.

"Do you want to know more?" he asked, taking her hand.

She nodded, although she wasn't sure it was a good idea.

Boris explained to her the information he'd been given by the police on the scene. The house in the middle of the polders, how Eddie had been nailed to the armrests of his chair with a nail gun. That he'd probably bled to death quite quickly, because one of the nails had gone through his wrist, perforating the radial artery.

Picturing it, she felt faint. Shock, dismay, grief, nausea—her mouth fell open as she gasped for breath. The thought of her husband bleeding to death, and the terrible reason why, had knocked the wind out of her.

Boris comforted her as best he could, but Femke could see in his eyes that there'd be questions to answer. She knew what those were, but also that she had to head them off before she gave everything away.

After fifteen minutes, by the time Siri had come back in and given a thumbs-up to show that Marika was sound asleep, she was ready to tell a story of her own.

"All three of us got COVID, so we rented an apartment in Valkenburg where we could isolate in peace," she began. "Our daughter had it worse than Eddie and I did, so we had to go to the hospital in Aachen, where we'd heard we would get better treatment."

They nodded, taking notes.

"When we got back to Valkenburg, Eddie told me in confidence that someone was threatening him, trying to make him back off on some case he was working for narcotics." She swallowed once or twice, to emphasize how difficult this was for her to talk about. "He seemed genuinely scared. I'd never seen him like that before."

"When did they come and take him?" asked the woman, gently taking Femke's hand.

Femke bowed her head, hiding her face in her free hand. "Eddie went out to get some fresh air and think it all over, and I didn't hear from him after that. Oh god, now we know why!"

"Why didn't you report this to the police, Femke?" asked the man.

"Well, I wanted to, but I couldn't be sure why he hadn't come back." She stopped and looked up at them. What else was she supposed to say? It was stupid of her not to have foreseen the question.

Come on, Femke, get it together, she thought, glancing swiftly toward their guest bedroom, where Eddie's mother had often stayed when she was in the area. Inside, at the back of the wardrobe, was Eddie's digital safe, the key to all his secrets. What else could be in there but lists of banks and account numbers, maybe even keys to deposit boxes or bundles of banknotes and other valuables? There, in the darkness, her future beckoned, and she felt sure she could work out the combination pretty quickly. Six digits, that was all. Eddie had been a man of habit, so the combination was bound to be something to do with the mother he had always idolized. Perhaps her birth date—possibly back to front? Maybe.

"Femke, are you with us?" Siri was gently shaking her hand. "If you can't do this right now, we can always come back tomorrow. We understand how incredibly hard this must be for you."

Femke turned to her. "Yes, sorry, Siri, I was miles away. When Eddie told me about the threats, I asked him if he'd told his colleagues in Rotterdam, but he shrugged and said there was no need to worry, that he didn't want to involve anybody else until he'd tracked down the people threatening him."

"Did he say specifically what he was planning to do?"

"No, but that was Eddie. When it came to his work, he was very reticent."

At this point her male ex-colleague became very direct. Unpleasantly so.

"You had COVID and you were isolating in an apartment, you and your daughter. Did you really think he'd just go off on his own to investigate for several days without telling you, Femke? He didn't even take the car, did he? Come on. Tell the truth. Why didn't you report him missing to the police?"

She pressed her fist to her lips. "Oh god, it's so embarrassing I can hardly bring myself to say it."

"Come on, Femke, it's all right," said Siri, patting her arm.

"We'd also gone there to try to fix our marriage, but it wasn't working. We fought from morning till night. In the end I told him to just get out, because he was making Marika cry. So he did."

There was silence in the room. Femke felt a wave of relief: at long last, she'd come up with a plausible explanation.

"I see. You thought he'd taken you at your word, and you didn't connect it with the threats he'd been talking about—have I understood that correctly?" Boris asked.

She sighed deeply. They'd bought it.

"Yes. Then, after a couple of days, once Marika and I were feeling better, I drove home."

Boris nodded very slowly. "And you have no idea who was threatening him? No names, no connections?"

"I'm sorry, but I don't know."

After another hour of questioning, they asked if there was anything they could do for her. Anybody they could call. Did she want a referral to a crisis counselor?

When she politely declined, they left.

Femke was relieved. The way the night had turned out, it seemed like she was in the clear. Nobody knew it was her who'd made the anonymous phone call. Nobody knew how devoted a man Eddie had actually been. And nobody realized that as soon as they had gone, she would go trawling through Eddie's things and that somewhere, probably in the safe, there would be some sort of key to the fortune she hoped existed, and which she had no intention of sharing with anybody.

47

FEMKE

Wednesday, January 6, 2021

Holding Marika in her arms, Femke had dozed off on the bed in her room. The girl had cried a little and asked for her dad, and Femke had switched off the light and pulled her in close, so that her daughter wouldn't see how shaken she was. She could picture her husband in all-too-clear flashes, nailed to a chair, his body slowly draining of blood. Those images wouldn't let her go.

But was it her fault things had ended this way? Had she expected more of her husband and of life than he'd been able to offer her? Was that why he'd felt pressured to do all these dreadful things? Was it for her sake?

Worst of all, could she have saved her husband, if she'd gone straight into the house in the polders? Could she have found something to bring down Eddie's captor? A blow to the back of the head with a spade, perhaps? A kitchen knife to the back?

It was impossible not to think that everything might have been different. That perhaps Eddie's bleeding might have been stanched if she'd been there to tie a tourniquet and bring him to the nearest hospital.

They could have insisted it was an accident at work, then driven straight home afterward. Allowed the passing days to heal his injuries and forced decisions that were firm and durable to the surface.

Then Eddie would have been able to gather their resources—maybe there were already bank accounts, homes, and lives waiting for them.

Femke gazed dejectedly into the gloom. It was all just wishful thinking. Eddie was dead, and his kidnapper was on the loose somewhere. What would he do next? Would he track her down, and if so, why?

He could do it, she was sure of that, because he knew their address. He'd been there several times.

Only then did she realize the possible consequences—he'd almost certainly tortured Eddie in that horrible place. They'd only told her about the nails shot through his wrists, but what other gruesome things had been done to him? Had the bastard managed to loosen Eddie's tongue? Did he already know where Eddie had stashed away his secrets?

Femke maneuvered herself gingerly to one side, letting Marika slide down onto the duvet, still asleep. Then she took the memory stick out of her handbag and put it into the laptop, which was in her little hobby room along with her sewing supplies and the books she couldn't bring herself to part with. Next to the laptop was a photograph in a dark frame: Marika clutched tight in Eddie's arms, taken at the harbor in Hoorn. She had loved that photograph. But that was before. Now she turned it face down on the desk.

She clicked on the memory stick icon, and Eddie's files appeared. At first glance it didn't look like anything special, but it contained a statement more than thirty pages long, a statement that could destroy a lot of people's lives—including her own. Then she made a decision that was easy, attaching the file to an email and immediately sending it to herself.

"Marika 2020," she called the file in the email, then she deleted the contents of the memory stick. To be on the safe side, she copied onto it a folder of photos taken over the last six months. "Marika 2020," she called the folder on the memory stick, then she put it on the shelf alongside their photo albums.

Right. Now the wardrobe, she said to herself.

It stood at the end of the bed in the guest room. A Gregorian monstrosity inherited from Eddie's aunt, but with enough compartments to hold an entire wardrobe for a woman of a certain standing. That was partly why they'd used this bedroom for his mother when she visited, while she was still alive.

Eddie had loved that room. Whether for sentimental reasons or because he found the bed comfortable for reading or thinking, she never discovered. Now that she thought about it, she realized she didn't know much about her husband at all.

Inside, behind a few shoeboxes at the bottom of it, was the safe, bolted to the floor and to the wall behind it, through the back of the wardrobe. Not the sort of thing you could simply grab and run away with.

Femke began systematically entering six-digit combinations. Eddie's mother's date of birth, front to back, then back to front, then the same for his dad's, his aunt's, Marika's, hers, and Eddie's. Then she repeated the procedure with other special dates, like the anniversary of their engagement, their wedding, his first day on the force, and various official holidays, but still no luck. She realized that Eddie, for once in his life, had come up with something a bit more creative than his feeble imagination could usually muster.

She got to her feet and went to look around the different rooms. Where were the numbers hiding? Was it possible he'd written them down, concealed a note somewhere? In drawers, books, between CDs or records?

What did you love so much you would never forget it, Eddie? she asked herself. What passion really meant something to him? What was the source of his best memories and most powerful experiences?

Femke sat down. Maybe she should concentrate on something that was her husband's and only her husband's. The trophies he'd inherited from his dad. Stupid prizes that reminded him his dad had once been an elite swimmer. Doing the hundred-meter medley in a mere fifty-seven seconds had been a big deal in Utrecht in those days. Or there was that fancy silver cup for the hundred-meter crawl, won just after the Second World War.

She checked the dates and wrote them down. All these new numbers— it seemed endless, and sadly hopeless too.

If *she* couldn't open the safe, then who could? And who would do it if they weren't interested in what lay inside?

Femke sank back, exhausted, into the large armchair in the front room as her tired eyes swept one last time across the walls before she went to go and lie down next to Marika and surrendered to some well-deserved and much-needed sleep.

If she found the treasure trove, she would move out of this apartment she had called home for a decade. Right now it looked uglier than ever. In fact, nothing she saw appealed to her.

Over the past week or so, she had put her old self imperceptibly behind her. She could never go back to what had previously defined who and what she was. Get rid of it, everything—husband, day-to-day routine, home, city, country—until only she and Marika were left, and then she would discover who and what she had become.

She smiled at the thought, looking up at a few of Eddie's most hideous monstrosities: the faces of famous rock musicians, cutouts made of old vinyl LPs. Brought proudly home from a flea market in Leiden, they had been arrayed much against her will along the top of the living room wall, where the flat-screen was also mounted.

Her drifting gaze froze when she reached the vinyl portrait of Eddie's greatest hero, Jimi Hendrix. Wild-haired and wispy-bearded, he looked at her from empty eye sockets, and she began to nod.

Hendrix! . . . If it wasn't something to do with him, she'd have to start from scratch tomorrow.

She got up, went over to Eddie's shelf of records and CDs—alphabetical order, of course—took out all of Hendrix's LPs, and examined them one by one. Then she slid out the Hendrix CDs, the bootlegs and special editions, but there didn't seem to be any digits in there that were obviously the combination to a safe.

"That leaves the books," she said softly, going back into her sewing room, where Eddie's reference books and biographies were ranged on the shelf above her own small collection. She flicked through all of Eddie's purchases related to the rock musician before collapsing into her sewing chair, since there was nothing to hold on to. She stared up at the shelf, knowing deep down that something was wrong—something she had overlooked.

Then she remembered that not all the books had been properly aligned: one had been poking out an inch or so.

She dropped her gaze two shelves down. There were her books on the art of sewing, neatly arranged in rows. Anybody wanting to mimic Dior, Balmain, Yves Saint Laurent, or one of the other major haute couture designers had only to pick one out and leaf through. And it was one of these books that had been pulled out about an inch.

She glanced over at the little workbench. On it lay the book she'd used last, which should have been put back next to the one poking out.

So where's the missing Jimi Hendrix book, then? she wondered. Logically, it would be the one Eddie had been reading last, and where would he have taken it if not the guest room? Maybe he hadn't even been reading it—maybe he'd just wanted to keep the combination near the safe. Or so she hoped.

She jumped to her feet, switched on all the lights, and returned to stand in the guest bedroom for the second time that night, now scanning it with altogether more vigilant eyes. *Could it be?* she thought, stepping over to the bed and lifting the pillow. And lo and behold, there it was: *Two Riders Were Approaching: The Life & Death of Jimi Hendrix*, written by Mick Wall.

Femke sat down on the edge of the bed, opened it with her heart in her mouth, and flicked through quickly, in case Eddie had underlined something or tucked a slip of paper inside. When, frustratingly, she realized he hadn't, she started again, and this time she got no further than the copyright page across from the table of contents. There her eyes fell on the ISBN, and above that an even longer string of digits that she assumed was the publisher's own identification code.

"1 3 5 7 9 10 8 6 4 2," it read. All the numbers from one to ten, but in a different order. *Sounds like Eddie*, she thought, because the numbers were easy to remember. But which six digits had he used? Six was all she needed, she knew that. The 10 could be excluded, unless Eddie had simply used the 1 a second time. Another possibility was that he'd skipped the 10 and gone straight to the 8.

She memorized both combinations, making a mental note, then returned to the safe.

Her forefinger was as shaky as the rest of her body as she punched in the first combination of six numbers, and when that didn't work, she began again with the second possibility, skipping the 10.

She pressed the button, and there was an intoxicating click.

The safe door opened.

It wasn't an impressive sight, and she was palpably disappointed. Apart from a single wooden box, the safe was empty. She'd been expecting to see banknotes, documents, deeds, stock portfolios—but perhaps all that could be contained in the unassuming-looking box? Sucking the air in between her teeth, she took hold of the lid. Would the contents of this box be the key to the rest of her life?

As she stared down into it, she felt disappointment settle like porridge in her throat. Then she picked up the gun inside the box and weighed it in her hand. Why did Eddie keep a loaded gun lying around in their home? Were the contents of the box his final way out of the morass he'd been increasingly embroiled in for so many years? Would he have killed himself and left her and their daughter to deal with the humiliation and the fall from grace?

Femke wept. Tears poured down her face. But this was no wave of grief at last over her husband's death, no—it was the grief of realizing the lie, of losing the future he had sworn to give them, but which the gun told her would never come.

Where's the money, Eddie? Where is everything you owe me?

She stumbled back into the living room and tossed the gun onto the sofa, knowing she would have to get rid of it.

Then she was overwhelmed by exhaustion, legs buckling underneath her, and without switching off the light in the front room she crept into the bedroom, where Marika only half turned, still in dreams. Femke slumped down beside her and closed her eyes.

———————

Three noises in rapid succession. The first was only a soft snap, like a twig breaking in the wind, but it woke her. On the seventh floor of a high-rise block, nearly all sounds are inorganic. Metal against metal, the dull *thunk* of concrete, the judder of windows being slammed—but this sound was different.

Instinctively she half rose in bed, listening. She glanced at Marika, lying with mouth open and head tilted back, then turned her eyes to the living room, which was still illuminated. Then came the second sound, more or less a repeat of the first, but louder and more recognizable, and perhaps she also heard the crunch of glass.

In two bounds she had closed the bedroom door behind her and was standing in the living room. It had been only a few seconds since she woke, but her mind was already clear when there was a third sound, a bang, and the door broke open. Even so, she wasn't prepared for how quickly the man burst into the room.

He was still holding the crowbar, and he pointed it threateningly at her as his eyes darted around the room.

Femke froze. This was the man who had killed her husband. The man with the eyes.

"You've been busy," he said, gesturing toward the floor, where Eddie's records lay spread out in front of the bookcase along with the CDs and the contents of various drawers.

"Stay where you are!" he commanded, when she took a tiny step toward the sofa and the gun. So he had seen it, then.

At that moment Femke knew with total certainty what was about to happen, and if he hadn't been holding the crowbar so close to her, she would have screamed in fear. Not merely because the man with the dual-colored eyes was going to kill her, but because her daughter was in equal danger. Femke had no doubt that was what he was planning, just as soon as he'd got the information he'd come for.

"You were at the house on the polders earlier. I saw you," he said.

Femke went completely rigid. The skin of her face went taut, and she began to feel very cold, as though the winter-dark windows had been thrown wide open.

Then he had seen her. And now he'd driven all the way up here to ensure her silence.

"It was you who called the police, I know that. Do you have any idea how much damage you've done—particularly to yourself?"

Femke held her breath for a moment, trying to gather her strength. Where could she turn for help? Where were her escape routes now?

She looked him straight in the eyes, trying to understand how a human being could be so loathsome, and now for sheer disgust she didn't bother to hold back.

"I know you can't go back there now, you murderer! You killed my husband, I know you did, and you also killed that poor man in the grave in the field."

He lowered the crowbar to his hip. A faint twitch at the corners of his mouth betrayed him. He didn't know.

"Who says Eddie's dead? Your friends in the police who were here earlier?"

It was unendurable. Had Eddie died because this man had fled when he heard the sirens? Would he have tried to keep him alive otherwise?

Shaken by the thought, Femke turned to the bedroom. Tiny whimpers from inside told her Marika was waking up.

She spun back around to face the man. "You're not going to touch her," she hissed, and opened the bedroom door, where Marika sat bolt upright in the double bed, her eyes very wide.

"There, there, sweetheart. You just lie back down, Mama will be in very soon." She stroked her hair and whispered into her ear that everything was fine, that tomorrow she could have an ice cream, even though it was winter and too cold, really.

The little girl sighed and lay back down on her side. By the time Femke faced her executioner once more, her eyes filled with tears, Marika was sound asleep.

He was holding Eddie's gun and aiming it directly at her.

"If you shoot, you'll wake the whole building. You won't even make

it to the street before they'll all have eyes on you," she said. Every muscle fiber was trembling, but her voice was cold as ice. "I didn't find anything useful, although I looked," she went on, pointing at the mess she'd
left on the floor. "So I don't have anything to give you. But I can keep
looking while you watch. If I find what you're looking for, you can take
it with you. You'll never hear from me again."

He smiled crookedly, apparently unmoved. He was the one in control,
and he knew it. The apartment was small, there was only one exit, and
she would never make it out of there with her daughter.

He sidled around her to the bedroom door, nudged it open, and backed
toward the double bed. Very gently, as though he'd done it many times
before, he gathered the sleeping child into his arms.

Femke was horrified and confused. "You've got children of your own,"
she said, thinking out loud. "I can tell."

He nodded slightly. "But don't misunderstand. That won't stop me
from throwing her off the balcony if you don't tell me what Eddie was
up to and where he kept his documents. My employers don't like to take
risks. Do you understand me?"

Femke understood him better than he knew. The file on Eddie's memory stick had told her very clearly what he and his so-called employers
were capable of.

"I understand I might have something you're looking for. If you think
it's here, then help me find it."

He frowned. Perhaps he'd lowered the gun a fraction too.

Then she heard the noise. Was that the lift at the end of the corridor,
the door slamming closed?

Now she could hear footsteps too, which came to a stop outside her
apartment. A moment passed during which she gazed in terror at Marika
and the man holding her tightly.

"Anybody in there? Femke, Eddie? Are you guys all right?" someone
called from outside.

The man in front of her waved the gun, signaling her to go and make
the visitor leave. Then he put the barrel to the sleeping girl's forehead.

She obeyed without hesitation, recognizing the figure outside as her neighbor, Job, a young man who worked as a bartender in the city and often came home late.

He stared from the broken glass in the front door and the damaged wooden frame to her, frowning, as Femke put her finger to her lips.

"Eddie's already called the police, Job. The thieves didn't manage to get inside. We don't know who they were, but it doesn't close properly now."

He shook his head wearily, giving her a baffled stare as she soundlessly mouthed the word "police."

"Well, how frustrating," he said, shrugging. "I've heard this sort of thing has been happening more and more often in this neighborhood. Anyway, sleep well, Femke, and say hi to Eddie for me." Then he let himself into the next-door apartment and shut the door.

Femke closed her own door as best she could, then went back into the main room, where the man stood waiting, clearly more than ready to attack.

"He's gone home," she said, sure that Job hadn't grasped the severity of the situation or her terror. Should she have made it clearer, or would that have put him in danger too?

She tried to seem unflustered, but she was petrified. "Well, what do you say? Are you going to help me search? I don't know what you're looking for."

He backed toward the sofa and laid the child down carefully.

"You're so full of shit, you stupid bitch. It's obvious!" He took a few steps toward her, then struck her hard across the face with the butt of the gun. "You think I don't know what you just did?"

Femke raised her hand to her throbbing jaw. There was a squealing in her ear and tears sprang to her eyes, but she was still shaking her head. *He didn't suspect a thing*, said her eyes.

Then he went back toward her sleeping child. "Come on, Femke. I'll give you ten seconds to tell me everything you know. Otherwise she's going over the railing."

Femke looked at her daughter, so unsuspecting and defenseless. It was the worst moment of her life. And at last she realized the game was lost.

"Let go of the girl and put down the gun. Then I'll give you what you're looking for. But you'll leave Marika alone, all right?"

For a second he hesitated, considering the implications. Then he held the gun outstretched, removed the magazine and emptied the chamber, and placed the gun and the ammunition in different corners of the living room.

"There's a file," she said, beckoning him to follow her into the sewing room. She pointed at her laptop. "I sent an email to myself with a file attached. I haven't read it, but I know Eddie confessed everything. He told me so before you took him."

She saw the man noticing the photo frame, which lay face down. He turned it over and surveyed Eddie and their daughter smiling into the camera. Then he nodded to her and put it back without turning it over.

Femke's brow furrowed for a moment, but she gave him the password and helped him to open the email.

When he saw the size of the attached file, he nodded contentedly. He forwarded it immediately to another email address, then deleted the email and the file and removed them from the sent folder.

He turned to her. "That was stupid of you, Femke," he said, before he leaped to his feet and grabbed hold of her, maneuvering his forearm to close around her throat.

She struggled furiously, trying to scratch his face and arms.

He's too strong. This is it. She knew it, even as she fought to stay conscious.

Then there was a loud banging on the door and the sound of a nearby police siren approaching at full speed.

He glanced at the screen, then let her go.

In a few seconds he was in the hall. She heard the sound of a scuffle and yells as she tried to stay on her feet, gasping.

Then there was silence.

Femke staggered to the front door, where she found her neighbor stretched out on the floor of the external walkway. Bloodied but alive.

The man with the peculiar eyes was gone.

48

MOLISE / PLOUG

Wednesday, January 6, 2021

By early Wednesday morning, news of Assad's exploits in Helsingør had spread to everybody working on the case. He had located Niels B Marquis de Bourbon in a tumbledown house in Helsingør, living in a pretty bad state, and the man was frightened. After fleeing his apartment near Slagelse in a blind panic because of the ominous nails he'd found in his bed and the striking scent of citrus cologne he'd noticed there, he'd discovered that a man who smelled exactly the same had been asking after him near where he was staying in Copenhagen. It was these misgivings, the sense that he might be in danger, that made him bolt.

The first person to read Assad's text was Molise Sjögren. Once her husband began to move and stretch at around 5:25, she was usually woken out of dreams, and while he warbled in the shower she checked her latest texts and emails. Assad's message made her sit up in bed with a jerk.

After Carl had mentioned his encounter with a man who wore a similar fragrance, she'd made a few half-hearted attempts to find out what the lawyer's name was, but when it turned out to be trickier than anticipated, she moved on to other tasks.

Now all her alarm bells were ringing.

Her husband stepped out of the bathroom in the nude, dropping heavy hints that he'd be in the mood for some morning fun, but she ignored the suggestions and texted Carl's story to the same group chat Assad had also messaged.

Then she spent the next few minutes with her eyes glued to the screen.

• • •

Terje Ploug was an extremely slow riser that day—as he was every day. To put it bluntly, he wasn't exactly leaping out of bed anymore, thrilled to be on the job. Ever since the Investigation Unit had moved to Sydhavnen, a big chunk of the old team had been transferred to other units and locations, lowering the average age by what felt like decades. His new colleagues ran or cycled to work in their training gear, loudly smug about their state of health in a manner that Ploug could interpret only as mocking of the older officers—officers like Ploug himself, who in another age had kept himself fighting fit on a strict regime of cigarettes and hard liquor. Terje was sometimes so tired in the mornings that he couldn't even bring himself to cough, and on those occasions he knew the rest of the day was going to be uphill work. More than a few of his older colleagues felt the same way.

He flopped onto his side and tried to mash his head into the pillow, hoping the lively sounds of his youthful brood didn't wake him completely. But then that stupid bloody smartphone started beeping on his bedside table. Fuck whoever invented that shit.

Reluctantly, he reached out and picked it up. Realizing it wasn't even seven o'clock yet, he fumbled for his glasses and opened the email from Molise Sjögren.

He read it through twice before excitement washed through him, fueled still further a second or two later when he read Assad's email, which had arrived an hour before.

"Holy shit," he said out loud, and began to chuckle. Wasn't that pretty much what he'd always thought of that pomaded lawyer Christian

Mandrup? A snake in the grass—no, a viper of the worst kind, slithering about all over the place.

One hour later he was in Sydhavnen. He looked like a new man.

"Please could you call Christian Mandrup, the lawyer?" he asked Lis, in the secretarial office. "Tell him we intend to bring Jess Larsen into the Investigation Unit for another interrogation and that obviously we expect his lawyer to be present as well. Suggest twelve o'clock."

Ploug kept an eye on Lis as she tried to ingratiate herself with Mandrup.

"He says no," she whispered, covering the mouthpiece with her hand. "He says he's too busy."

Ploug nodded to himself. No shit the man was busy, what with everything he had going on at the moment, but this wasn't going to fly. If he thought he could track down Niels B before anybody else, he was in for a rude awakening. Assad had taken him back to his own house, and there he was going to stay until things had calmed down.

He took the receiver out of Lis's hand. "This is Terje Ploug, Mr. Mandrup. I'm very sorry, but new evidence has come to light against Jess Larsen, and we need to question him about it as soon as possible. If you can't make it at twelve, we'll have to find another solution. How about twelve thirty?"

He found the chief of homicide in Bente Hansen's office. Hansen's team had just cleared up a fatal stabbing in Amager, and the suspect had been charged, so she seemed mightily pleased. It wasn't every day that Marcus Jacobsen remembered to give his staff personal pats on the back.

"Hey there, sorry to barge in like this in the middle of the standing ovation," said Ploug, not really meaning it. Then he turned to Jacobsen.

"In half an hour I'll be blindsiding a lawyer with charges against himself. He has no idea he's in the crosshairs or that I'm using an interview

with one of his clients to ambush him," he said. "I think I'd like someone
to sit in, make sure all the i's are dotted and the t's crossed. If it's all right
with you, I'd suggest Rose Knudsen, since she's also involved in the Theis
murder case?"

Marcus Jacobsen looked at him as though he'd just been tackled and
deliberately kicked in the knee.

"That case has nothing to do with Rose Knudsen or Department Q,
Terje," he said coldly. "You're ambushing the lawyer, you said? How?"

"I've invited along a guest he doesn't want to see."

"During the interview with his client?"

"No, afterward."

Jacobsen grunted. He obviously wasn't keen to get bogged down in
all of that. "Who's the lawyer?" he said.

"Name's Christian Mandrup. He made threats against Carl while he
was in Vestre, threats of such a serious nature that we can say with certainty he must be an underling working for the people trying to kill Carl."

"Christian Mandrup? That's funny—he's just come onto my radar
too," said Bente Hansen. "Maybe you knew this already, but he helped
to transfer ownership of the DKNL Transport premises to Hannes Theis."

Ploug thought for a moment but said he didn't.

She looked skeptical but shook it off.

"I see! Well, it was many years ago, and a bit of a complicated deal.
I had to take my time over it as well. Back then, those buildings were
the property of one Gérard Gaillard, and they were placed in a holding
company by the name of Kandaloo Workshop, of which Gaillard was
the sole owner. This is the same man whose corpse later showed up dismembered in a crate in Amager. It was mentioned at Carl's preliminary
hearing."

"The transfer of Gaillard's premises, well I'll be damned! Talk about
the mystery deepening."

It always sent a shiver through him when complex cases turned out to
be connected. "It's remarkable how many threads there are linking
Christian Mandrup with this case," he said, a slightly faraway look in
his eyes.

Hansen turned to Jacobsen. "Maybe *I* could do this with Terje," she said. "I'd rather like to meet this Mandrup fellow."

Jess Larsen was looking somewhat the worse for wear after his night in a cell. His police record only mentioned a few previous traffic offenses, and that was all. Maybe he just couldn't stand being locked up.

Too bad, thought Ploug. As the years went by, he'd probably get used to prison. If he still insisted on keeping his mouth shut.

"Your lawyer isn't here yet?" he asked, as he and Bente Hansen squeezed themselves behind the table in the tiny interview room on the ground floor of the Investigation Unit.

Jess Larsen stared at Ploug blurry-eyed. Evidently the idiot had decided to maintain his silence.

"I'm Sergeant Bente Hansen," she said, nodding at Larsen. "I'll be observing during the interview."

He didn't even bother to turn his head, and the derisive curl at the corners of his mouth spoke volumes.

"What the hell are you playing at, dragging me out here at such short notice?" Christian Mandrup was practically spluttering as he burst into the room.

Ploug was already nodding to himself. Mandrup had clearly opted for an extra splash of cologne this morning, because the smell of citrus was already stealing up the walls.

"You haven't said anything, have you, Jess?" his lawyer asked him, and received a heavy-lidded blink as a no.

"I believe we've already established that Mr. Larsen doesn't wish to comment on anything, have we not?" Mandrup said. "So what new evidence are you rabbiting on about?"

"Well, it could be forensic evidence, for instance," answered Ploug. "But sure, if we're not going to have a conversation, I guess we might as well send him back to Vestre. What do you say to that, Jess?"

The driver merely shrugged. He didn't give a shit.

"Fine. I'll ask the nice policeman who drove you here to take you back. And you, Mr. Mandrup, can we induce you to stay behind for a minute or two after this scumbag has been taken away?"

It was clearly not a question open to discussion. Mandrup started grumbling again about how busy he was and how they were playing him for a fool.

"Well, actually, we do have something that I think will interest you, but first I have to compliment you on the scent you've brought into the room. It's almost as though spring has arrived. Do you recognize it, Bente?"

She raised her eyebrows in surprise. "Um, no. Men's colognes aren't exactly my area of expertise. What's it called?"

The lawyer gave her a long stare. "Funny topic of conversation, but if you must know, it's called Terre d'Hermès," he said.

Ploug thanked him, complimented him once again on his good taste, then rose and left the two of them alone for thirty seconds before he came back and shut the door behind him.

"You've been busy lately, Mandrup, as we're well aware. But before we get to that, perhaps you could tell me if you know who the executor of Hannes Theis's estate is?"

Mandrup smiled crookedly. Perhaps he'd been expecting the question. "Well, it's no secret, when you ask it that way. But yes, I am. I worked in a legal capacity for Hannes Theis and DKNL Transport for a number of years."

"Ahh, thank you. That clears that up. But does it seem professionally appropriate to you to be representing the man charged with murdering your deceased client?"

"The whole situation is quite unusual, wouldn't you say? No, I don't see it being a problem. Larsen was Theis's only permanent employee at the company, and he was present many times when I was visiting there. Besides, surely it's my job to ensure as best I can that the murder of my late client isn't pinned on an innocent man."

"So you do believe Jess Larsen is innocent?"

"Naturally, yes. And I shall continue to do so until you find definitive proof to the contrary." He permitted himself a smile.

"You've got a lot of irons in the fire. And you certainly seem to get around," Ploug went on. "Carl Mørck sends his best wishes, by the way. And he was wondering what brand makes your very elegant cologne."

The lawyer's eyes grew suspicious beneath his eyebrows. Was that watchfulness or surprise?

"I don't know anything about Carl Mørck."

"So you didn't speak to him during yard time at Vestre Prison?"

Mandrup's head jerked backward, and for a microsecond he sat there open-mouthed. Then he ran his tongue across his lips and mobilized a twitch around his mouth that was presumably supposed to indicate forbearance.

"I'll be honest with you, Detective, you've been badly misinformed. I—"

"And you didn't speak to two inmates at Slagelse Remand Center the other day, a Malthe Bøgegård and a mountain of a man by the name of Tom Gravgaard? It's easy enough to check the official record down there."

Mandrup smiled broadly. "I'd imagine you have already, but I can't see what that has to do with Carl Mørck or anything else. I spoke to them in my capacity as legal counsel, obviously."

"Whose? Not Malthe Bøgegård's, surely?"

"Right, I think that's enough! You know I'm a busy man, I need to be going. We can talk about this later, if it's really that important to you. As long as this has nothing to do with the charges against Jess Larsen, you'll have to wait."

"Okay, fair enough." Ploug gave Hansen a nod, who returned it. "But before you go, there's just one more thing I'd like to check with you."

He got up and opened the door leading to the hall.

"You can come in now, Niels," he said.

He turned to see Mandrup's reaction as the man stepped into the room. And sure enough, there appeared to be what statisticians called significant evidence that the lawyer was flustered, while Hansen watched the proceedings with a frown and a baffled expression.

"Over the past few days, Mr. Mandrup here has been searching high and low for this man. May I introduce Niels B Marquis de Bourbon?"

"What's this nonsense now?" Mandrup tried to seem indignant and annoyed, yet his voice shook. Only a fraction, but enough. He'd been caught napping.

"Do you recognize Mr. Mandrup, Niels?"

Niels straightened his back, although his eyes avoided the lawyer. "Yes, he's been looking for me all over Copenhagen. I recognize his perfume from Baggesensgade in Nørrebro as well as my apartment in Slagelse, just after I was released by the police. If you like, I can get hold of the man he questioned about me and my whereabouts for you."

"Christian," said Ploug, dropping all pretense of respect. "Why was it so important for you to find Niels here? What do you want with him? Were you going to threaten him, the way you threatened Malthe Bøgegård and Carl Mørck?"

"You're way out on a limb here, Sergeant." The lawyer turned to Bente Hansen. "Can't you put a stop to this farce, whoever you are?"

Ploug met Hansen's gaze. Almost imperceptibly, she shook her head at him. "You need to tell me where you're going with this, Terje. I'm not sure I'm following," she said.

"Certainly! Mr. Mandrup, why don't you tell me who hired you to do all these things? Because right now you seem suspiciously entangled in Carl Mørck's situation and whatever is pulling the strings behind these charges. You're always popping up where you have no business being. What exactly were you discussing with Malthe Bøgegård, for example? Isn't it true that you told him point-blank he was no longer going to be the one to kill Carl Mørck and that Tom Gravgaard had been chosen instead?"

"You must be out of your mind. I was there to advise those two inmates in connection with their cases."

"That's what you say, sure, but Bøgegård told Carl Mørck a different story."

"What is all this about Carl Mørck? I've read about him in the news, of course, but I don't know the man, and I have absolutely nothing to do with him."

"We could detain you and bring both Carl Mørck and Malthe Bøgegård in here to confront you about what happened."

Mandrup snorted. "Two hopeless criminals who'd do anything to curry favor with the police? Don't make me laugh. And *detain* me? You can't do that, you idiot."

Hansen sighed. It was clear she was trying to tell Ploug that this was going nowhere.

Ploug turned to Niels B, who had been standing mutely by the door. "What do you say, Niels?"

"I don't know anything," he said, eyes lowered. "But when those two mechanics in Sorø were killed, he was definitely there at some point. And that perfume he wears, it's the same one I could smell in my apartment." Then he raised his eyes and looked at the lawyer. "Why were you looking for me in Nørrebro the other day? What do you want with me?"

Mandrup gathered up his papers from the desk, slid them into his briefcase, and got to his feet.

"I know you're only trying to do your job here, and that you're stressed and overworked. But I'd recommend you apply for some leave, Sergeant Ploug, before you end up having a total meltdown."

He nodded politely to Bente Hansen and shared a condescending sneer between Ploug and Niels B, who stepped aside to let him out.

Ten minutes after Niels B had been packed off back to Assad's apartment in a taxi, Ploug and Hansen were sitting opposite each other, both with their own version of what had just occurred.

Chewing her top lip, she told him bluntly she thought it was a pretty lousy attempt to bluff someone into a confession and that she'd have to search long and hard for a good reason not to report what had just happened to Jacobsen, word for word.

Ploug, sitting opposite, appealed to her. Couldn't she see how entangled the man was in his own web? How many encounters had been arranged and how many coincidences there were with Carl's situation—coincidences that surely couldn't be accidental? Shouldn't they be talking about what to do next to chop that viper into tiny pieces?

Hansen stood up. "I assume you wanted me to sit in as some kind of backup for your claims and accusations, Terje. You're normally so professional and levelheaded, so of course I was happy to observe, but I don't even recognize you right now. You're obviously desperate to throw Carl a lifeline, but you've just dumped them all in the sea. Mandrup had good explanations for all the accusations you laid at his door, so I'm pretty sure it'll be a miracle if he wants to talk to you again."

Then she patted him on the shoulder and left the room.

49

KENNETH

Sunday, January 3–Wednesday, January 6, 2021

Helmand Province had been Kenneth's personal hell, the desert dust his nightmare. A heap of junk by a roadside. A wrong turn in the dark. A wrong turn by day, because the bombs were a constant threat, of course, while his eyes were glued to binoculars. Once in Iraq and twice in Afghanistan, which was more than enough. Luck wasn't a friend he could count on.

After he got home he'd sat in his little house in Roskilde and tried to deaden his senses, to forget. To just move on. He had killed: a direct hit right to the windpipe of a very young boy. For Kenneth, the mark of a Taliban fighter was a bit of down on chin and cheek. And no, he hadn't told anybody, not even Mia. He never breathed a word until Merete Lynggaard came to see him.

She had read about him saving a young woman, Mia, from a fire, and that his vigilance had—quite by chance—been a tremendous help during one of Mørck's cases, a few years after Merete's.

She had also learned that although he did struggle from mild PTSD, he executed the various duties of his role as a security consultant for a Danish-owned global tech company to their full satisfaction.

Which was why, when Merete expanded her late husband's business into Scandinavia, Kenneth had been headhunted. He'd proven particularly useful in hostage situations because he was sharp, did not shy away from risky jobs, and got them all—except one—successfully wrapped up.

"We both owe Carl Mørck and his team at Department Q a huge debt of thanks," she said to him much later, when news of Carl's arrest first hit the headlines.

"I have good contacts in the police and at Vestre Prison, so let's do our best to protect him while he's in custody. He's now been transferred to Slagelse Remand Center, which is a good but also fairly open prison. A bit too open for my liking, given the security concerns around an officer as high-profile as Carl Mørck."

Kenneth nodded. His wife, Mia, wouldn't be alive today if it hadn't been for him and for Carl. Sweet, beautiful Mia, who still took his breath away, he was so in love. Kenneth was in.

"Okay, what do you want me to do?" he asked.

"Go down to Slagelse and observe who's coming in and out of the center and scan the area around the buildings thoroughly. We can't allow an outside attack on Carl's cell."

He checked in at charming Hotel Lillevang, ten minutes' walk from the prison. He booked a whole month in advance, explaining that he was writing a dissertation and needed peace and quiet to finish it.

On the fourth day he was out the door at six a.m., as usual, strolling up the track behind the prison and into the undergrowth, where he sat for an hour or two in the frozen thicket or on a tree stump behind a bush. From there he could see one side of the prison, as well as the tall fence over which some of the inmates' friends had thrown money and cigarettes, hoping they would end up in the right hands during yard time. Recently, however, the net over the yard had been reinforced, so traffic of that kind was largely eliminated.

Then Kenneth walked a hundred yards back down the path, where he inspected the patch of ground, easily accessible and overgrown, that offered a clear view of the back of the prison and the cell windows. Someone with a digger or a loader would have no trouble driving down the path and through the fence, and then they'd be very close to Carl's cell, which was located more or less in the middle, the window a couple of yards above the ground.

Kenneth didn't like it.

Then, finally, there was the disused fire station just around the corner from the prison. His eyes wandered across the now empty garages and all the doors, then up toward the roof of the tower, which loomed high above the terrain. The prison would be worryingly exposed from up there, and memories of ambushes in Afghanistan—where a brief flash of light from higher ground might mean death or loss of limb—put him on high alert when he realized how vulnerable the prison would be from that angle. Somebody leaning out of a high window in the tower or from the one at the very top that directly overlooked the prison would have a pretty clear line of sight into Carl's cell, and there were various types of weapons that would pose a serious threat to anybody inside.

He swung the strap of his rucksack over one shoulder and cautiously approached the door that led directly into the tower. It was still locked, thankfully. When he peered through the pane of glass in the garage door nearest to it, he saw there was also an access point from the garage block, a passage that led past a bathroom and into the tower itself. It was clear he had to go in and secure it.

There were several options. At first he'd thought the easiest thing might be to force open one of the garage doors with a crowbar or a small jack, enough to crawl underneath. Another, less good option was to climb onto the roof of the garage block from the back, rest one foot on the solid-looking lamp above the door immediately under the bottom window in the tower, break open the window, and crawl in through that.

He walked past the door of the tower and down a short passageway to another low building that adjoined the tower block. He'd observed it from the other side as well and knew it offered access to a flight of basement stairs, where yet another locked door led into the tower. Here, however, at the rear of the building, there was a different door—also locked—and when he put his face close to the glass, he could see that to his left there was an open doorway directly into the tower. He could smash the pane, of course, but the sound might be heard by someone farther down the path, and he didn't want that. The simplest and most discreet option was to lever open this rear door so that he could enter and secure the tower and the building.

The first task would be to plant a bug inside the tower itself, and since several of the company's transmitters were capable of broadcasting a signal one kilometer, he had plenty to choose among. Next he would position a few of his miniature cameras on the roof of the low building directly opposite the tower; plus he also had to cover the fronts of the buildings from the overgrown wooden-plank fence that bordered the area.

I'd better do it tonight, when I'm least likely to be disturbed, he thought. During the day the area around the front was used as a carpark, so the constant activity and open access to the road that ran past the prison a little farther down might easily mean he was noticed.

He reported back to Merete Lynggaard and asked her to get hold of the surveillance gear and a lockpick gun, and then he considered what weapon would be best to use. A pistol would be useful, of course, but also a little problematic given that they were on Danish soil, Merete said, so they made a joint decision to give him a couple of Tasers, which although also illegal weren't in the same category as guns. On top of that they'd pack the usual equipment: knife, rope, pepper spray, and handcuffs. He decided to omit telling her about his own backup weapon. That way, at least, she didn't have to take responsibility for it.

She replied quickly, saying the package would soon be ready for him, with enough gear for him to monitor the track behind the prison as well as two or three patches of undergrowth.

"Make sure the prison staff don't spot what you're doing when you're setting it all up, Kenneth," Merete said. "They might jump to the conclusion that you're a bad guy, because they're used to keeping their eyes peeled and thinking the worst of people. Find a café nearby, sit down with your laptops, and act like you're diligently typing away on one while you're monitoring the sounds and images on the other."

"And what if they get suspicious anyway?"

"Then you get the hell out of there, Kenneth. If need be, we can re-place you with someone else."

50

CARL

Wednesday, January 6, 2021

When Tove Mørck arrived at Slagelse Remand Center and her bag was scanned, she was asked to deposit a cozy knitted jumper, a few kilograms of biscuits, and a pound of half-frozen shrimp into the box, because they wouldn't let her bring them into the visitors' room and give them to her son, Carl Mørck.

She told this to Carl, outraged, in an undiluted Vendsyssel squawk that did little to conjure up a sense of homesickness.

After she'd been venting for a couple of minutes, Carl could tell that the officer standing at the door was starting to feel sorry for him.

"How come they allowed you to visit, Mum?" he asked. It was better than asking her why she'd come.

"Why shouldn't I be allowed to visit my son? Do you have any idea how many times you have to change trains when you're going from Hjørringvej in Brønderslev to the prison here in Slagelse—and in *this* weather?"

She was about to give him a list, but Carl cut her off just in time. "I'm sorry you have to visit me under these circumstances, Mum. It might have been best if you hadn't come."

"Oh, you've always been an ungrateful little fellow, Carl," she said, quivering with indignation. "You ought to have done what your father always said, you should have done your agricultural training and taken over the farm while you still could."

"Yeah, but—"

"But no, you absolutely had to go to *Copenhagen*, if you please, and look how that turned out. What sort of room is this, anyway, all those crayon drawings on the wall, and is that the back of an elephant?"

Carl thought of the decorations in his childhood home, which mostly consisted of knickknacks on small triangular shelves and carved wooden mangle boards. There had been only a single painting on the many walls, and when the string snapped, it wasn't put back up.

"It's for the children, so being here isn't quite so rough on them."

"You're surely not telling me you drag little Lucia down here, are you?"

"No, actually, I'm effectively prohibited from receiving visitors, so I'm afraid it's not allowed. That's why I don't understand how you got permission."

"Well. I called up the police and I gave them a piece of my mind. What would I have to talk about that they don't want me telling you? I don't know anything. You never tell me anything, do you?"

"They might think you've been reading the papers or going online, maybe watching a bit of television."

"Oh, for goodness' sake. They said so too, but I told them, I said Lord knows I don't have time for that, not with the farm and when my husband is sick."

"Dad's sick?"

For a moment her gruffness fell away. Were those tears in her eyes?

"Dad's worn to a frazzle, that's what he is. And are we getting any outside help, you may ask? No, I can tell you that for starters, we're not getting *any*. It was just the same with your older brother when they killed all his mink. What was he supposed to do? There was no help to be had from that awful prime minister, was there, eh?"

"But can't Bent help out on the farm, then?"

"Who do you think is doing it, while I'm down here visiting his stupid little brother, who's got himself banged up in prison?" By now her tears were beginning to fall.

"But he's no good at farmwork, Carl. It was such a blow when they gassed his mink, he's just not up to it anymore. What sort of family is this, eh?"

Carl took her hand. "I'm sorry, Mum. Can't you sell up?"

She reared up at the insensitive question, head quivering. "I came here to tell you, among other things, that your childhood home is mortgaged to the hilt. All we've been doing is working to pay it back, and if we lose that too, neither we nor Bent will have anything to fall on. Do you understand?"

"I'm so sorry to hear that." He thought for a moment. "Mona and I have been saving up. I think we have six hundred thousand, if that helps you?"

For a moment she softened, and for the first time in years, she placed her hand on his cheek. The officer behind them was about to tell them touching was forbidden but thought better of it.

It was obvious now that his mother had grown old, but this was the first moment Carl had seen it. Her eyes were sunk deeper in their sockets, her lips drearily thin. But her hand was as warm as when he was little. He still had his parents; he had to be grateful for that. But would he still have them when he got out?

His mother sighed. "It's kind of you, Carl, but it's not enough. We're hoping Bent will be properly compensated at some point for the mink and the farm, because if that happens we'll be all right. We're also hoping that when you get out, you'll come down and say hello, maybe lend us a hand."

Was that why she had come? Not to tear a strip off him or heap his head with blame. She had come to reach out a hand.

He glanced up at the officer, who gave him a brief nod, then looked away.

"I'll do that, Mum," he said, pulling her in close. "You've spoken to Mona, have you?"

She nodded. "She's a good girl, Carl, and she really misses you."

Then she probably knew more about the case than she was letting on.

"Give Dad my love, and tell him I'll be there, okay?"

"Yes, because you're innocent, aren't you?"

There it was, after all.

"Of course, what do you think?"

"If you'd said anything else I'd have taken the biscuits back to my niece. I'm staying at hers tonight. Now the prison staff can have them instead, and I hope they'll take extra good care of you."

He was still puzzling it through in his mind as he stepped out into the yard, where the snow was beginning to fall. How sick was his father? *Worn to a frazzle*, his mother had said, but what did that mean?

He gave Malthe and Paul Manon a nod. Each stood in his separate corner, glaring at the other.

Skinny little Manon walked over. This was the highlight of the day for all of them, because the rest of it was spent under the white-walled regime of the prison, and time in front of the TV was dull as the sound of a grandfather clock. *Tick tock*, it said. And the passing seconds brought them nothing. *Tick tock, time is marching on, and you'll never get it back.*

Manon smiled, pulling his jacket closer around him. "News from the home front," he said. "You should be listening to this too, Malthe." He nodded over at the big man, who stuck his hands into the pockets of his windbreaker and took a few steps toward them.

"Are you okay, Malthe?" asked Carl.

He shook his head. "My sister says my little brother is very sick, and they don't know if they can find someone to transport him to the hospital in Germany. Something about insurance."

Carl frowned. "Is it just a question of throwing more money at it?"

"Maybe. My mum and sister are trying. But even if they do find someone, he might die on the way there."

He was shaking slightly. They weren't tears, exactly—it seemed more like the aftershock of tears that would no longer come. It was clear Malthe was grieving from the depths of his childlike soul.

"We could ask my contact for help," Manon suggested tentatively. "She's the one who paid for your brother's treatment. She has resources, I know she does. Should I?"

Malthe raised his head to look at him. It was as though he couldn't quite believe someone like Manon wanted to help.

"I'll need an address, of course, for your brother and for the hospital."

Malthe nodded. Then he took the last couple of steps toward Manon and wrapped his heavy arms around him. In that moment it was the only thing he could offer in exchange. "Thank you," he said, and held him tightly.

"What's going on out there? Everything all right?" asked one of the corrections officers as he brought out a pale-looking Åbenrå from cell 10 and saw the two men in a close embrace.

Malthe let go. "Thanks," he said again.

Manon waited until the officer went back inside. Then he spoke, his voice low. "You've got a man outside keeping the prison under surveillance, Carl. You know him from the old days, Merete says."

"Okay, that sounds reassuring. Who is he?"

"His name is Kenneth. Professional soldier and current employee of Merete Lynggaard's security firm, so he should be more than competent."

Carl smiled. "Mia and Kenneth, I remember them like it was yesterday," he said quietly, almost to himself. "Yes, he's a good man. That's good."

"He's set up small cameras everywhere so he can monitor activity around the back of the prison. Oh, and I'm supposed to say hello from Hardy. He's sorry he's been a bit quiet in the last couple of days, but he's had an offer he can't refuse. So, after much consideration, he's decided to say thank you for the use of your house in Allerød over the years, but now he's moving out. It's already underway."

Damn, thought Carl, picturing Hardy walking stiffly in his massive suit. Was a move really the best idea for him and for Morten?

"Please tell him I'm happy for him, and I hope very much I'll get the opportunity to visit, but right now it seems like that might not be for some time."

Manon nodded. "But I've saved the biggest news for last, I think.

They've identified the man who threatened you in Vestre, the one who spoke to Malthe and that lumbering hulk on the second floor. He's a lawyer by the name of Christian Mandrup. It was his perfume that gave him away, mainly. Men should be careful not to get too vain."

"Who tracked him down?"

"It was a joint effort, including yours, but mostly it was your colleague Assad and a detective called Terje Ploug."

Good old Assad, of course he'd had a hand in it. Same for the ever-industrious Ploug.

"Are they charging him with anything?" he asked.

Manon shrugged. "Might do, down the line. For now, he's a free man."

Carl squatted down, folding his hands between his legs. Would this turn of events shift the focus of the case away from him, or would it intensify it? That was the question. Right now he'd give anything for just a few hours outside these walls, time for himself and his colleagues to come up with a strategy for the investigation ahead.

51

WAYNE / CHRISTIAN
Wednesday, January 6, 2021

On the whole the day had started off quite peacefully. Wayne Peters had decided that the latest shipment of Colombian cocaine was best kept in storage until he had a clear sense of his organization's current status. Wayne's belief was that crime only paid as long as everything was running smoothly, and if it wasn't, then he hunkered down until the coast was clear. Minimizing unwanted attention, that was the ticket: it was crucial to plug the leaks.

Just past noon, a message from Cees Pauwels finally arrived, and its contents were brief and precise.

He announced that Eddie Jansen was dead and that he had the wife—who knew nothing—under control. He had plugged the leak, and not a moment too soon, as was apparent from the highly compromising file Eddie had been working on, also attached to the email to Wayne. For the time being, Cees would have to scale back his work for the organization, until he'd found a good alternative to the house in the polders where he'd previously been operating.

It took Wayne twenty minutes to read through the thirty-page attachment. If its contents had ever seen the light of day, it could have razed the network to the ground.

Some of Jansen's speculations on the last page in particular sent Wayne's blood pressure skyrocketing.

After years working for the organization, Jansen had apparently begun to wonder whether there really was a network of powerful men at the top, or in reality only one—which would make the organization more vulnerable.

How the hell did he reach that conclusion? Wayne cursed. He leaned slightly to one side, reaching for a bottle of Campari, which he usually resorted to only when his hip was acting up.

Two sips and he was feeling no better.

He read the final sentence over and over. *More vulnerable*, Jansen had written.

Where did a scummy little cockroach like Jansen get the balls to even think something like that? And who else had read it? Jansen's wife, maybe. And Cees Pauwels, of course.

Neither of them would survive that bit of presumptuousness.

Wayne took another couple of sips, throttling his spontaneous burst of rage. Then he replied to Cees Pauwels, saying he was grateful for a job well done, especially for so conclusively tying up the loose end with Jansen's wife. His bonus would be ready for him the next day. He added, however, that before Cees went to ground, he had one more urgent task to perform: neutralizing Detective Wilbert de Groot. If he could make it look like a car accident, that would be ideal.

Then Wayne made himself a pot of herbal tea, settled down with another cigarillo, and wrote to his Danish contact that he was pleased the news from Denmark was so precise and had arrived so quickly. He confirmed that he had also judged Christian Mandrup to be a security liability, on par with Jess Larsen and Carl Mørck, despite his past usefulness. Only once all three had been pacified in one way or another could they sleep soundly at night.

He would leave it up to the Danish contact exactly how to accomplish that, but if Mandrup was willing to be immediately transferred to Colombia, they could find a use for him over there. If not, well, then he'd like Mandrup's activities to be stopped. Ideally a little spectacularly, if he could put it like that.

As for Larsen, it had already been agreed that they would transfer him a large sum of money in exchange for his continued silence, until eventually the police would be forced to drop the case against him.

Carl Mørck, on the other hand, had to die. He might strike a deal with the prosecution at any moment. The mere fact that the Danish authorities believed he'd colluded with Høyer to steal the shipment back in 2007 was reason enough to have him removed.

Finally, Wayne informed his contact that a couple of Dutch experts had been recruited to carry out the latter task, which the Danes were evidently finding more difficult than usual. The experts were already in place.

• • •

The first thing Christian Mandrup did when he got home from his bolt-from-the-blue meeting at the Investigation Unit with Terje Ploug and Niels B was to take a shower, scrubbing hysterically to remove all trace of the cologne. It had been his wife's favorite. When she left him, it had never occurred to him to switch to something else. Fuck's *sake*.

Over the years he'd made a good living off the organization. It had paid for his children's studies abroad, kept him in clothes befitting his standing, bought him expensive homes and exclusive cars. So far he'd stayed more or less on the right side of the law. Sure, he'd occasionally played messenger when there were threats to be delivered, and he did have knowledge of a network that was shipping contraband back and forth between countries. But nobody could prove he was actually aware of the drug trafficking, murders, and tax evasion. It was true he often found himself in close proximity to violence, but that was all part and parcel of being a lawyer.

He received the first text a little later that day.

You will shut your practice down immediately, it began. *There will be tickets to Amsterdam in your dropbox, departing approximately 10:00 p.m.,* *and from there you will travel to Bogotá tomorrow morning. There is a job waiting for you as a coordinator in our office there. Your base salary will be $160,000 a month, with additional remuneration for good results. The contract is ready for you at your destination.*

All your emails must be copied to us, and laptops and iPads must be in your hand luggage. Once you reach your destination, make a list of what you want forwarded and which of your possessions we can sell. You have several hours before you need to be at the airport. You don't want to know the alternative option. Delete this text immediately. Safe travels.

Christian was shaken. *You don't want to know the alternative option.* As though he couldn't figure it out. And what about after he touched down in the godforsaken city of Bogotá, especially during a pandemic? Surely it would be much easier for them to make him disappear down there?

He read the message again a couple of times, unable to make up his mind. If he didn't obey, he would have to cut ties with the organization and seek the protection of the police, because nobody was off-limits once they were suspected of disloyalty. A nail through the skull—that was one potential consequence. He shuddered at the thought, and although he knew plenty about the structure of the organization and its methods, he had no idea who might give the order or who might carry it out.

If I go to the police, I'll be jailed. Is that what I want?

He thought about it for a while, then replied to the text to say that of course he understood why they were asking this of him, since the police were now looking at him more closely, but that the authorities didn't actually have anything on him and that he'd be able to fend them off, so perhaps they should just bide their time?

Barely an hour later the shadows were in his front hall, watching his eyes dart as he begged for his life, a noose around his neck.

52

PELLE

Wednesday, January 6, 2021

For the last twenty-four hours, Pelle Hyttested had been a bubbling cauldron of wrath and frustration. *Gossip*, under his name, had published a series of articles that, in hindsight, were a load of embarrassing bollocks, nothing but hoaxes and prevarications. The feeling that everybody in the industry was laughing at him only added insult to the injury of being taken for a ride—a privilege he usually reserved for himself.

The consequences had been swift. Torben Victor had been called to Stockholm and summarily fired, and Pelle was sought out at home and hauled in for a conversation at the editorial offices. Several of his colleagues had attended, and all had had notes in front of them.

It wasn't just about setting an example, said the acting editor in chief, an incompetent bungler who couldn't tell the difference between a real scoop and a fluff piece about the royal family. Did he really think he could run the office, especially now that so much of it had been hacked away? There was no way they could keep up with the exploding circulation figures they'd been accustomed to lately.

"We've been instructed to ask you to hand in your laptop and access card immediately. Gather your things from your desk and leave the building. Those of us around this table have been piecing together your history of fake news and realized that you've caused irreparable damage to the magazine." The editor in chief pointed at his colleagues' notepads.

"Over the last five years, your colleagues have noted thirty other instances where you fabricated stories, and we fully intend to look for more. The latest piece you wrote has been, as you know, widely discussed in the media. We believe the Press Council is going to clamp down hard on us for this."

Pelle was seething. As if he was the only person at the paper who occasionally made a bit more out of a story than it really merited.

"You'll be hearing from the company lawyer, Pelle, regarding how we intend to proceed."

"You can't do shit," he blurted furiously. "What's done is done, so just stop fucking whining about it." He turned to his colleagues. "And as for the rest of you, sitting there like sacred cows, you're a bunch of idiots."

"Yes, yes, Pelle, we're familiar with your rhetoric. These days it bounces right off us. We believe, actually, that we could get a pretty considerable compensation claim in court, probably more than you're able to pay," the bungler continued.

Afterward, as Pelle gathered up his things, he vowed silently that both they and that arsehole at Department Q who'd fed him false information would come to regret this.

He was, therefore, holding on for dear life to a shabby brown notebook that contained information neither his bosses, his colleagues, nor the public knew about. A notebook he had been saving for just such an occasion as this, when he had to start scouting for new employment.

The public, he knew, would be slavering to read the kind of dirt he'd been hoarding in this notebook. Salacious revelations concerning the deepest darkest secrets of the royal family and the slimiest fraudsters in the world of finance. Lengthy summaries of infidelities committed by famous people and their partners, meticulously detailed. There were notes on insurance fraud among the 1 percent and lists of undiscovered lies told by prominent politicians, as well as the damage they had inflicted on Denmark over the decades. He even had stories about the less charming sides of well-known actors and about authors plagiarizing other people's work.

All in all, there was enough explosive material in that notebook to send every news website, tabloid, and magazine in Denmark stampeding right into his arms.

Or so he thought, anyway.

He was brushing the snow off himself, having reached the front office of *Gossip*'s nastiest competitor, *The Weekly*. He expected to see the usual frantic hive of activity in the large editorial space, where journalists were usually pounding away at their keyboards day and night.

Only they weren't. Nobody was at their desk. Instead, they were all clustered around the largest flat-screen TV on the wall.

Pelle stared up at it, and for a moment his jaw dropped. If anything was breaking news, this was it—in fact, what was happening at the Congress offices in Washington right now was in a league of its own.

Vast numbers of Trump supporters were storming the steps of the Capitol like rampaging bison, and the reporter sounded both frightened and incredulous. The riots had apparently been sparked by a speech given by the outgoing president, Donald Trump, who was refusing to accept the results of the election, and around two o'clock local time the pressure cooker had exploded. TV 2 News, as well as probably every other TV station in the world, had gone into overdrive.

Pelle went to stand behind some journalists, who watched in silence as the proud Capitol building was raided. Never would anyone have thought such a thing could happen in America, and all illusions of law and order in God's own country were smashed to smithereens in a single second.

Pelle glanced around the editorial office as the feeling that he was in the wrong place at the wrong time slowly began to come over him. He looked over at the corner, where the editor in chief was yelling at the senior reporters while the senior reporters were yelling at everybody else. It was chaos. Astonishment and wild confusion.

He stuffed the notebook back into his bag.

When the time was right, he would show them all what the people really wanted.

53

PLOUG

Thursday, January 7, 2021

It was Christian Mandrup's cleaning lady who found him. Twenty-eight minutes after she had made a shaky-voiced phone call to the dispatcher at the Copenhagen Police, attempting a coherent explanation, Terje Ploug was standing by her side, trying to calm her down.

"You arrived at nine o'clock and found him like this?" He pointed at Mandrup, who was still dangling from a rope in the hall.

She nodded, trying not to look at the corpse. Ploug understood. It wasn't a pretty sight: the noose around Mandrup's neck; his wide, terrified eyes; the blue tongue protruding out of his mouth.

"And there was no one else in the house?"

"No, nobody ever comes here. He got divorced a few years ago, and I've still never seen his kids, even though I've been cleaning for him for seven years."

Suddenly it seemed to occur to her that this chapter of her life was over. Her voice wobbled and broke as she tried to compose herself enough to tell the crime scene techs what she'd touched.

When that was done, they could send her home.

Terje swore inwardly. He'd just been rudely deprived of his chief witness—why the hell hadn't he made sure he had grounds to detain him the day before? He wondered if Bente Hansen was regretting just a little that she'd been such a stickler for procedure, now that things had turned out the way they had.

It was a tech who cut Christian Mandrup down, and the coroner confirmed with an ironic smile that he had died by hanging, although that was obvious to anyone with eyes. He noted that the rope had been pulled up between the banisters of the stairs above, suffocating him relatively slowly. Perhaps somebody had suggested making it a spectacle.

"I can say for sure that Mandrup died here, and he definitely thrashed about a bit," said the senior crime scene tech, pointing at some marks underneath the body and to the shoe that had been kicked toward the hall mirror. "We can assume there were at least two of them. He wasn't hanging very far off the floor, so one man could have hauled him a few feet up while the other lifted him, I reckon. He wasn't a very heavy man, I think it's safe to say."

"Fingerprints or footprints? Traces of DNA?" Terje asked. "There must have been something, given the terrible weather yesterday. There's still snow in the front garden."

A shake of the head. "Not apart from the deceased's, and it's snowed again outside, so if there were any prints, they'll be gone now. We think the killers were pros. As you can see, his hands were bound behind him with two zip ties, to make sure he didn't twist free during the hanging. We're working on the assumption that they wore plastic overshoes and gloves, and probably masks and coveralls."

"How did they get in? Any ideas?"

"My personal opinion is that they were lying in wait and watched him unlock the door before they attacked him."

"You two look into that," Terje said to his detectives, who were standing beside him. "Knock on all the houses along the whole street and ask them if they saw anything suspicious." He turned to the coroner. "When was time of death, roughly?"

He shrugged. "Well, it's winter, but indoors it's relatively warm, so there's a small margin of error if we're going off body temperature. We could go back and forth for hours, but for now let's cautiously say between seven and nine p.m. last night, plus or minus a couple of hours. Rigor mortis has fully set in, I can tell you that."

Terje nodded and turned back to his two detectives. "Concentrate on the hours between six and ten last night. Any activity in the area, and specifically around Mandrup's house, anything at all. Check if the neighbors have cameras that cover the areas beyond their own perimeters and ask about traffic on the road."

They nodded, and Terje was left feeling as though he was standing on one leg at a dead end.

His phone rang. It was Gordon from Department Q.

"I hear you're investigating the death of that lawyer, Christian Mandrup, so I'll make this brief. I'm calling because I've just been told that Wilbert de Groot, the detective who was investigating the nail gun murders and the drug trade in the Rotterdam area, was killed in a car accident late last night."

For a moment Terje felt as though he'd been punched in the gut, and it took him a beat to shake it off.

"Ploug, are you there?" asked Gordon.

"Yes, yes! Jesus Christ, what happened?"

"De Groot was on his way home when a lorry came hurtling straight through a T-junction and smashed into his Mazda. It didn't stop until de Groot's car was crushed against a tree on the opposite side of the road. He was dead by the time the ambulance arrived. It was probably instant, actually."

Ploug's head drooped. "And the driver was gone, and the lorry was stolen, I assume."

"Exactly! So what now? They're starting to thin out the ranks."

Ploug asked Gordon to hang on for a moment while he tried to collect himself, retreating slowly toward Mandrup's front door so that the techs could continue their work undisturbed.

"Make sure you get his laptops, desktops, phone, and any tablets down to my office as soon as you've checked them for trace evidence!" he called to them.

Then he put his phone to his ear. "I'm back, Gordon. Yeah. What now? Good question."

"Rose and I agree that there are probably several people in serious danger right now, not just Carl. We're thinking of Jess Larsen and that crooked prison guard, the one they call Peter Loudmouth. Has anyone got eyes on them?"

Peter Joensen, alias Peter Loudmouth, did not live quite as modestly as one might expect of a prison official, even one at a higher pay grade.

He had one of those old terraced homes that had originally been built to house two or three families working at the Carlsberg brewery. Not especially grand, sure, but they still went for somewhere in the region of ten million kroner these days, and he was the only person living at the address, situated at a convenient distance from Vestre Prison. According to the land registry, he had owned it for nearly four years and had put down a considerable sum of cash, so Terje could only assume he'd inherited the money or had a significant income beyond his state salary.

The analysis of the last two hundred conversations on Christian Mandrup's phone had come in about an hour ago, none of them unexpected, given his profession, but at least ten of them had been made to Peter Loudmouth Joensen's mobile, so that was somewhere to start.

Peter Loudmouth had been on sick leave since the attack in prison, but by all appearances he looked to be in rude health.

He didn't seem especially happy about Ploug's visit, perhaps because he'd been interrupted watching a handball match on television that hundreds of thousands of other people in the country were watching too—it was on at full volume in the living room—or maybe because Terje suddenly showing up and flashing his ID had unnerved him.

Frankly, Terje was just relieved to see the prison guard alive and that he got willingly into his car when Terje told him Mandrup had been found hanged in his villa and that it wasn't suicide.

This time Ploug didn't ask Jacobsen's permission to bring Rose in to observe the interview, and in contrast to Ploug's understated manner, she went straight for the jugular.

"We might be your only friends right now, you do realize that? Because we're the ones trying to keep you alive," she said. "As far as I'm concerned, you can go to hell—literally, actually, because we know you were the direct reason why Carl Mørck came *this* close to losing his life on your watch in Vestre." She held out her fingertips almost touching, to show what a close call it had been.

He shook his head and said in a muted voice that he didn't know what she was talking about.

"Your cash cow, Christian Mandrup, has been murdered. And it wasn't pretty." She illustrated by putting an imaginary noose around her neck and yanking at it, hard. Peter Loudmouth gave a visible shudder.

"We have strong evidence that you and he have been having regular conversations ever since Mørck was admitted to Vestre. And right now, at this very moment, our financial crimes department is poring over your tax returns and your spending habits. So you might as well confess. I know you don't want us to bang you up in Vestre with your former colleagues and all the inmates you've pissed off over the years, but if we can promise you that if you come clean we'll have you transferred to a secure prison—so that you'll actually survive the next five or six years—then what do you say?"

Her eyes flashed at him. They did not invite hesitation.

Finally, Ploug swooped in with the coup de grâce. "Of course, the other question is whether you can even hope for a sentence that short. It depends on how we interpret your roles. Perhaps, for now, we should say that you aided Christian Mandrup with a variety of undertakings at the prison, but you yourself were not an active participant?"

The guard nodded eagerly.

"Then you need to tell us who else was on the lawyer's payroll."

"Fine." The answer was immediate, the tone remarkably obliging.

"Are you aware of any danger to one of the prisoners on remand, Jess Larsen, for whom Mandrup was acting as legal counsel?"

"No, I don't believe so. I'd know about it."

Rose and Ploug exchanged a nod. Hopefully, that was one less thing to worry about.

54

KENNETH / ASSAD

Thursday, January 7, 2021

The surveillance equipment had been in position for more than twenty-four hours now, and Kenneth started day two by buying another pastry at Sejers Konditori at half past six, then immediately getting into his car in the carpark opposite and settling his laptop onto his lap.

The interlacing surveillance images were reasonably sharp even in the darkness of January, while the sounds from the bug in the tower hummed with all the traffic going to and fro in the area in front of the fire station.

For several hours he sat and watched people filing past the entrance to the old fire station, children running down the track, and tramps lurching into the bushes behind the prison to take a piss. When one o'clock approached, the plan was to drive to Restaurant Superbowl and grab a Wiener schnitzel or some barbecued pork, then nap for a couple of hours with the laptop in front of him.

The difficulty wasn't staying focused on the task, it was constantly being ready to leap up, adrenaline pumping, willing to put his life on the line. That was the skill of a professional soldier.

Kenneth knew he might have no more than seconds once alarm bells started blaring. And, unfortunately, that Thursday he had only just inserted a fork into his schnitzel when he glanced up at the screen and immediately felt uneasy. A man in a dark coat had started pacing the area, seemingly aimless. His tread was light, and there was no indication he was carrying a heavy weapon. Yet Kenneth had the distinct sense the man did not belong. It was only when the man put the flat of his hand up to one ear that Kenneth knew for sure he had to intercept him. Pronto.

Abandoning the Wiener schnitzel, he swung the Volvo into the car-park near the prison barely three minutes later.

By then the man was gone.

• • •

Ever since Afif had started talking during their trip to Helsingør, there had been some drastic changes in their home life.

Ronia, usually so combative, so reluctant to speak Danish, would sit with Afif for hours, endlessly repeating words and sentences like a teacher and showing a level of patience the rest of them couldn't live up to. What had happened to Afif no one could explain—it was as though some psychological blockage had evaporated, and suddenly he heard every single word that was said.

"I bet he was never stupid at all, or deaf or mute," suggested their elder daughter, Nella.

Marwa was beside herself with happiness. What had happened to her son during the drive with Assad had brought the family together, and Assad would now be able to go to work without worrying about what was happening at home.

He had brought Niels B back to stay the night. Ronia complained, of course, about having to share a room with her big sister, but apart from that, Niels B was an easy houseguest, and Marwa was, as ever, a warm hostess, welcoming him with open arms and putting him at ease.

After Niels B's apparently unsuccessful stunt with Terje and that lawyer, Assad had helped relocate him to a new, safer place than he'd had in Helsingør. No one knew better than Assad what stealthy paths a person might take if they really wanted to disappear.

———————

When he called the Investigation Unit, Rose and Ploug were interrogating Peter Loudmouth while Gordon was gathering all the available information on Wilbert de Groot's death.

"The Dutch are saying it was deliberate," said Gordon. "And considering the execution of Christian Mandrup last night, we should be taking extra care of Carl."

Assad nodded. He was in complete agreement. "I read a report this morning that weapons were stolen during the night from the Antvorskov Barracks near Slagelse. The types of weapon stolen and the way the theft was carried out are worrying me a bit—it's not even two miles from the remand center, after all. I think I'll drop by on my way in, see if Kenneth needs a quick pat on the shoulder."

Then he unrolled his prayer rug, thanked Allah many times over for bringing his son back as though newborn, and gently reminded Allah that there was a man in prison who was in need of his almighty protection.

He parked the car close to the remand center in Slagelse just before two in the afternoon, bringing fresh energy to the languid calm that had prevailed, in stark contrast to the oppressive atmosphere behind the prison walls.

How he wished he could spend just ten minutes with Carl. Get a sense of him and of his state of mind, of how he was holding up under his current circumstances. It had been almost two weeks since they'd last spoken, their longest period of silence in fourteen years. Only his separation from Marwa and the girls during those nightmarish years they'd been held captive in Iraq had felt worse than this.

Then he got a call from an unknown number.

"It's Kenneth! They just told me you were on your way. Where are you now?"

"I'm in the carpark by the prison—where are you?"

Kenneth laughed loudly, so loudly it could be heard both through the phone and right behind him.

Assad hadn't seen him since the message-in-a-bottle case eleven years earlier. Annoyingly, the man hadn't changed a bit, except perhaps for a little extra weight and somewhat larger muscles.

"I saw a man on the surveillance feed talking and holding a hand to his temple, like he was wearing an earpiece. Just over there, near the start of that track behind the prison. But he's vanished now, and it's giving me the heebie-jeebies."

Assad stared at him. What were heebie-jeebies? Was it some sort of disease?

"What do you think's about to happen?" he asked.

Kenneth pointed at the thicket beyond some bushes and then at the fire station tower.

"If I was going to fire into Carl's cell, I'd do it from one of those two locations," he said.

Assad agreed. "Where did you put your monitor?"

"It's in the car." He passed Assad a headset. "It's fully charged. Try saying something to me, I'll answer."

Assad gave a thumbs-up once they'd tested the device. Now they could communicate.

"If you watch the monitor in the car, you can keep me updated," Assad said, feeling for the first time in a while like he was on home ground. Now, perhaps, he could do something to help Carl, and despite the cold and the slush after yesterday's snowfall, it felt good to be in action. Very different from spending all day sitting in the little flat with his wife and three kids, and a far cry from those endless days at a screen in the office.

They tried to plan out what they each might do if the worst should happen.

Neither he nor Kenneth had a firearm, so they could only stop an attack by neutralizing the aggressor with a knife, tear gas, or a stun gun.

"Here," said Kenneth, giving him a pistol-shaped object.

Assad weighed the Taser in his hand. It couldn't weigh more than half a pound, easily slid into a pocket.

"It shoots two barbed probes at the victim, right?" asked Assad.

"Correct, but it's only really effective within five or six yards."

"Not sure I find that very comforting," said Assad. "I think we can assume the attacker will be significantly better armed."

"Definitely! But if it looks like something serious is about to go down, I'll call the police on the emergency line and tell the local officers at the station to get out here quick and to expect armed resistance."

He saved the emergency number into Assad's phone, and then they wished each other luck.

Aside from the cold and damp, and despite the potential danger, Assad felt in his element doing fieldwork, as countless marks on his body testified. His left wrist and thumb were still scarred and darkened, courtesy of the electric shock and severe burns he'd incurred in Øland. His body bore evidence of numerous gunshots, stab wounds, and whippings. He'd endured smoke asphyxiation and a minor stroke, which even after all these years still manifested as a slight droop of his facial muscles. He had undergone brutal torture, and in certain situations he still experienced vestiges of PTSD. He had killed people and watched comrades and friends suffer the same fate. After all that, his shock of hair was now more gray than black, and the curls on top were growing increasingly thin. Yet despite it all, here and now, he felt clearheaded and strong.

Hugging his windbreaker more closely around him, he stomped on the half-frozen ground, trying to get the blood circulating in his feet; then he sat down on a log and kept a hawkeyed watch on the rear of the prison and the track that ran along the back of it.

There were scattered shouts coming from the cells, but he couldn't catch more than a word or two. "Mørck" was one, "dead" was another. It was tempting to yell back, tell them to shut their fucking ugly mouths, but Assad kept his silence.

After an hour, he finally heard a sound from Kenneth.

"I can see a car turning in to the area outside the fire station," said

Kenneth's voice in Assad's earpiece. And a minute later: "It's coming back out again—it's driven into the carpark—right behind my location."

Assad stood up, trying to peer through the bare bushes toward the fire station in case the car had dropped somebody off, but there was no one.

Then he felt vibrations in his pocket—a phone call.

A little confused, he fumbled for the phone, dropping his headset into the sludgy grass as he drew it out.

He'd thought it was Kenneth, but it was Marwa.

What now? he thought, putting the phone to his ear. There was laughter in the background.

"Hey, Zaid," she said, her voice bright. "Can you hear them in the background?"

Assad was relieved to hear her tone. "Yes," he said, adjusting the headset back into place. "What are you doing?"

"Oh, Zaid, Afif's singing 'Abbi Jakob' again, just like you told me." She paused for a moment, and when she spoke again, she could barely contain her emotion. "He knows all the words in Arabic," she said, her voice trembling, "and he's singing them over and over. We've been singing with him for the last half an hour. Ohhh, I'm just so happy, Zaid, that's all I wanted to say." And she hung up, already heading back to the others.

Assad stared into the gray gloom collecting in the undergrowth. It was hard to wrap his head around everything at once.

He lifted his chin and sucked the damp air deep into his lungs, bringing him back to reality.

"How are things at your end, Kenneth?" he asked.

There was a hiss, and he repeated the question. They were obviously still connected, but why wasn't Kenneth answering?

He trod cautiously over the withered branches on the ground, out onto the track and to the very end, where he could just make out the carpark and Kenneth's vehicle at the edge of it.

He appeared to be sitting quietly behind the wheel, his face bent over the computer in his lap.

Assad crossed the road and went up to the car. He hissed Kenneth's name once or twice through the headset, but still no reply.

Even from a distance he felt a prickle of unease, so he slunk farther back between the ranks of vehicles until he could approach Kenneth's from behind unseen.

Thirty feet from the car he realized the passenger-side door was ajar and that there were footprints in the slush outside it. He glanced around. Was somebody watching him? Somebody who knew he was taking part in the surveillance operation?

All Assad's instincts were now on high alert. *Where will they come from? Who are they? Take out that stun gun and switch it on*—which he did. Then he called the emergency line and informed the local police, just as Kenneth had instructed.

Like an animal creeping up on its prey, Assad neared the car step by step. Close up he could see that Kenneth's head was limp, his chin resting on his chest.

Assad threw open the door and flung himself into the passenger seat. He seized Kenneth's arm and shook it. When he didn't react, he felt for a pulse in his neck. Assad held his breath until he felt the vein throb, very weakly. Then he dialed the emergency line once more. "Send an ambulance to the carpark by the fire station," he instructed curtly.

He looked around. Circled the car, then peered through the windshield at Kenneth's slack body. It was only then he noticed the hole and the shattered glass on the dashboard.

Assad opened the driver's-side door and put his head inside. The shot had struck Kenneth just below the neck, and there was blood on his jacket, but judging by the bruising, it had missed the artery.

For a second he considered driving him to the hospital himself—the key was already in the ignition.

Should I drive, or . . . ? he wondered, but then a sound from Kenneth's laptop made him freeze.

The alarm in the tower had been activated, and he could hear what sounded like footsteps. Gently tilting Kenneth's head a fraction to one side, he scanned all the camera angles on the monitor in Kenneth's lap.

There appeared to be nothing out of the ordinary, so Assad set off at a smooth run toward the garage doors. He had just reached the area outside when there was a faint pop, and the slush and tarmac at his feet was torn up.

Any rational, unarmed man instantly retreated when shots were fired at him, so Assad flung himself against the door closest to the fire tower. The angle of the shots told him the person was firing from the tower itself.

Silenced gun or not, that fucker isn't getting out of here, he thought, praying the Slagelse police would turn up any minute.

"Hey, you up there," he shouted. "What are you going to do now? You didn't think there'd be more than one person on watch, did you, you bastard?"

The answer was immediate.

The shot tore open the leg of his trousers and sent him instinctively diving sideways as he realized the bullet had nicked his calf muscle. He flung himself away from the garage doors and toward the one in the tower itself, which had been broken open. By the time the next shot came, he was already inside.

So there were at least two. One opposite, maybe on the roof of the low buildings across the entry road, then another farther up the tower. He pulled up his trouser leg. His calf was bleeding, but the wound was superficial.

Focusing all his senses, Assad was standing very still when a sudden noise—as though someone was hammering something farther up the tower—made him jump. After a moment's more banging and clinking, he realized the uppermost window of the tower had been smashed.

I'm too late, he realized with a jolt. If the guy was up there with a rocket launcher, like an NLAW missile, for example, which could blow everything to smithereens with immense precision, Carl was a dead man. Assad had witnessed several times on video what that dreadful weapon could do. Just as he was about to dash up the steps, he heard a muffled crash from above, then barely a second later an earsplitting explosion that blasted all the windows out of the tower and engulfed the prison building opposite in a whirl of smoke, fire, and broken masonry. Car alarms sliced through the air with a howl from carparks everywhere in the vicinity, mingling with screams from the prison.

Now Assad heard someone bounding down the stairs toward him, and he immediately backed past the door to the toilet and into the garage itself, so he wouldn't be gunned down by the person fleeing. Then, activating the Taser, he held it out toward the doorway leading into the tower, pulsing with shock and rage.

As the dust sifted down outside the garage doors, he finally caught the sound of approaching sirens in the distance.

Through the panes in the garage doors, he glimpsed a shadow standing up on the roof of the building opposite and leaping down on the other side. Assad took a step back against the rear wall of the garage, positioning himself behind a row of steel tables. From this area of the garage there was no direct exit, so the man in the tower was unlikely to pursue him in there—he'd probably run straight through the tower door, across the forecourt, and on around the back of the buildings, past the prison.

He heard the tower door being thrown open, and after a second or two he cautiously followed the stranger.

Through a haze of dust, he could just make out the man sprinting around the buildings opposite the garage as he tore off his military jacket and dropped it onto the wet tarmac.

Already a crowd was gathering in the carpark and outside the main building of the prison. Some came from inside, others from the nearby houses, and at long last police cars were pulling up and officers were jumping out of them.

Assad stuffed the Taser into his pocket and followed, just in time to catch a glimpse of the man slipping into the throng outside the prison.

He recognized a couple of the veteran guards, who were standing some distance away as though paralyzed, watching the shambles and the fire engines bulldozing through the fence to get closer to the fire.

More and more people arrived, until a semicircle of curious, sensation-hungry local citizens blocked Assad's view.

Where had the man gone? Had he run over toward the carpark? Kenneth had said a car had pulled up behind his just before Assad lost contact with him.

He jostled through the crowd, yelling profanities in every language he knew as he tried to get people to move.

An ambulance was parked next to Kenneth's car, and a huddle of people stood around him on the gurney, working on his limp body.

Glancing at the vehicle, Assad noticed a gray Mercedes trying to leave the carpark. He decided to run toward it, and when it emerged from the mass of people, he caught a brief glimpse of the man in the passenger seat. He held up his middle finger. Then the car accelerated and was gone.

55

CARL

Thursday, January 7, 2021

Carl and Malthe were back in Carl's cell, and Malthe was almost happy. They'd had yard time earlier with Paul Manon and Åbenrå from cell 10, and Manon had told Malthe his brother, Hansi, was now on his way to the German border, accompanied by a doctor in a specially equipped ambulance. His pulse had been weak in the morning, but the prospect of the journey had invigorated the patient's mood and heart function, and once again Malthe flung his arms around Manon and Carl. Even the little pedophile got a hug.

Carl was sending all kinds of good thoughts Merete Lynggaard's way. His time inside had taught him many things about himself and the law-breakers he'd devoted his life to tracking down and catching. And he had realized that although as a detective he had dealt in misfortune and untimely death, he had also been the cause of much joy, which was now being returned to him. The soldier, Kenneth, was watching over him outside, and so were Mona and his family and Merete Lynggaard. His friends in Department Q were standing by him, and he had Malthe and Manon as allies inside. So although Carl was still gripped by a sense of injustice and felt depressed by the bleakness of the prospect ahead of him, life still had its bright spots.

"Do you think they'll make it to the hospital in time?" asked Malthe, beside him on the bed, as Carl handed him a Coke.

"They're doing everything they can, Malthe, and the doctors are waiting for him at the hospital."

Carl looked up at the sky through the bars on the window. Another gray and chilly day. It must have been around half past two, so it wouldn't be long before Mona picked Lucia up from nursery. Maybe in half an hour they'd be in the kitchen, mashing bananas for the cake they often took to nursery on Fridays? He smiled at the thought. Banana cake!

Malthe raised his head. "Did you hear that?" he asked.

Carl had noticed too. A couple of dull pops coming from the fire station, sounds that didn't quite fit. He was about to ask if the building was being torn down, perhaps, but . . .

There was less than a second between the initial drone and the enormous, deafening explosion, which made everything go black—until the flames began to lick.

Carl tried to catch his breath. An inferno of destruction seemed to have appeared around him. Everything not bolted down in his cell had been hurled against the door, and Carl realized he was lying on top of the cupboard underneath the sink, which had broken in two. Beside him, Malthe lay gasping underneath the bed, which was now tilted up against the wall. All the clothes on his right side had been ripped off him, and blood was dripping from deep gashes on both arms and legs.

But he was alive.

Carl tried to haul himself upright, doing his best to free himself from the massive chunks of rubble that had gone thudding into his body, almost certainly breaking several of his ribs. His slippers were gone, and some shards of glass from the television screen were deeply embedded in his left calf and foot. Through the cacophony of high-pitched whining inside his own head he could hear them both hacking and coughing. The air was a thick swirling cloud of masonry dust and plaster from the walls and ceiling, forcing him to squint, because the particles were almost blinding. Then he stretched out a hand to Malthe and gave his arm a powerful squeeze. Malthe reacted with a startled jerk, turning his head with difficulty.

The ceiling creaked ominously above them. Huge slabs of masonry were crashing down from the floors above them, gathering into a mountain outside the large hole that had been blown in the outer wall of the cell.

Everything organic was in flames. The window frame, the desk, the chair, the shelves above the desk, all of it was on fire, and the smoke was growing black and dense and mingling with the dust, making each and every breath an assault on the throat and lungs.

"We have to get out of here, Malthe, it's not safe," Carl shouted with difficulty, hauling himself up into something like a sitting position. The pain in his ribs and lower legs, which were covered in rubble, was so intense he gasped for breath to keep from passing out. Coughing violently, he shoved with his left arm as hard as he could to remove the sediment and red bricks that had showered down on him and Malthe.

"Come on, help me, Malthe," he rasped. "Did you break something?"

Malthe nodded. "My left arm, and there's something wrong with my knee, I think . . ."

Now they could hear screaming from outside. The ceiling nearest the hole in the wall was starting to give way—it was only a matter of seconds before it collapsed. Tensing every muscle in his upper body, Carl tore himself free. In that moment the pain was secondary. Twisting around, he scrabbled through the debris to reach Malthe's body, although his fingers and the palms of his hands began to bleed.

"Are you ready, Malthe?" he cried, dragging him loose.

Malthe was pale as a corpse but said nothing. Both of them glanced down at his left knee, where the flesh was exposed all the way to the bone.

Carl got to his feet, hooked Malthe under the arms, and heaved until tears drew streaks in the dust on the poor man's cheeks.

Every step toward the opening meant balancing on broken brick and snapped wood, and the ceiling was still groaning menacingly above them.

"I'm sorry," Malthe moaned. In that situation it seemed out of place, but Carl understood him. The balance of power between them had long since tipped, and Carl was putting his life on the line for Malthe's sake.

The final stretch by the opening itself was blocked by a rampart of enormous chunks of brickwork. Carl stared down at the icy, chaotic ground and his bare, bloodied feet as he dragged Malthe over it.

Only once they were on the other side did he realize the scale of the explosion. At that same moment the screams of pain from Tom Gravgaard's cell reached heartbreaking intensity. And then, within a second, there was total silence. The brickwork above Gravgaard's cell was beginning to crack threateningly, and—equally horrifying—the cell next to Carl's was now engulfed in explosive blue and orange flames.

"Paul," yelled Carl several times, but there was no answer.

Carl swayed on his feet. Guilt rushed in like a wave—it was because of him that this terrible thing had happened; he knew that. The attack hadn't been quite accurate. A little too far to the right, a little too high. Either way, it was he who should have been killed in this godforsaken place, not anybody else.

Then he felt a tremor from the building. He tugged Malthe away from the wall with the last of his strength, sitting him down on the slippery grass near the fence.

Carl looked back just in time to see the central building crack in two, and all the cells above Carl's and Paul Manon's fall to the ground with an infernal crash.

There were yells of shock from the main building and the road and frantic cries for help from the other cells.

The pressure in his ears had finally equalized, and now he could hear the swiveling sirens in the distance.

Carl looked around. He was outside. True, the fence around the prison was still largely intact, so if he was going to make a run for it, he'd have to duck down and try to find a hole to crawl through.

He turned to Malthe.

"I have to get out of here before they get to me, Malthe, and before they hurt more innocent people. Maybe I can figure out what the hell is going on."

Malthe nodded. He was clutching his knee with his right hand while his left hung limp at his side. The cuts on his face had almost been stanched already by the dust, and the bleeding from his tree-trunk thighs and calves was no longer as heavy. He was going to make it.

On the other side of the trees, near the fire station, a petrol motor was started, and a second later, there was the rasping sound of wood being cut. In less than thirty seconds the tree toppled to the ground, revealing the forecourt and the garage. Men began cutting the tree into pieces, and bystanders hurried up to help push the chunks of wood and foliage aside, clearing a path from the forecourt to the prison fence.

"They're going to bring the fire engines in that way, Malthe, so they'll probably cut the fence just there, to get closer to the fire," he said, pointing at the stretch of fence nearest to the flames.

Gingerly taking hold of the shards of glass still embedded in his calf and foot, Carl pulled them out. The lacerations in his calf were deep and bleeding, but his foot felt reasonably all right.

"I have to ask you something, Malthe." He pointed at his shoes. "Can I have those, please? I won't get very far in this weather without something on my feet."

Malthe nodded and told Carl to be careful when he took them off—with good reason, as it turned out. Nearly all the toes on Malthe's right foot were blackish blue, the ball of the foot was bloody, and there was a deep, bleeding gash along the inside of the left one.

Carl removed them carefully, looking him in the eyes.

"Thank you, Malthe," he said, wiping the blood off the insides of the shoes before he put them on his feet. They were too big, thank god, because Carl knew there was a good chance several of his toes were broken.

"We're alive, Malthe, that's what matters, all right?"

Malthe shrugged and pointed at cell 5, still burning, where Paul Manon must surely have lost his life moments earlier.

"Now how am I supposed to find out how my brother's doing?" he asked, and began to sob.

"We'll find a solution, Malthe, I'm sure of that. There's no reason you can't be in direct communication with the people helping you."

Malthe's eyes were doubtful as the fire engines came screeching into the area outside the disused station, and the horrified faces of prison guards appeared behind the treetops.

"You'll be hearing from me, Malthe, I promise. Look after yourself," Carl said, then left him.

He retreated to one side as the first truck nosed its way cautiously into the gap in the trees. Then the driver sped up, heading straight toward the fence, and rammed into it. Thank god Malthe was at a safe distance when the fence gave way and crashed to the ground.

Once the fire engine was through, it backed up a bit so that the fire-fighters could bring the hoses through the gap in the fence. As massive jets of water beat against the destruction and the fire, Carl limped out onto the forecourt, hidden by the torrent, while the prison staff stood on the other side and called up to the cells that they were doing their best to make sure all inmates were let out into the corridor.

Carl stared straight across the large carpark, then noticed a military jacket a little to his left, apparently thrown down onto the asphalt. He slunk back behind the prison guards, who stood there stunned by the extent of the damage, grabbed the jacket, and put it on in a single movement.

Ahead of him, in the carpark, people were gathered around an ambulance and a gurney, where someone was being given first aid.

He approached cautiously, dodging a couple of uniformed officers running toward the prison, then made a beeline for the paramedics by the gurney.

"I know you've got enough on your plate already—".

He was about to ask for gauze to bandage his lower leg when he spotted the very last person he had expected to see in that place.

The man was standing at the edge of the carpark, back turned, facing a gray car as it sped away.

A man with a silhouette that seemed chiseled from granite and thoroughly distinctive curly graying hair.

It could be none other than Assad.

Carl watched him as he ran back across to the carpark and straight toward the ambulance. Assad was almost upon them when he swerved and got into a dark blue Volvo Carl hadn't seen before.

Amid the shrieks and yells of the crowd around him, Carl hobbled past the next row toward the car Assad had just gotten into.

His friend and colleague had just started the engine when Carl appeared in front of the bonnet and gave him a nod through the rain-streaked windshield, which had been punctured by a bullet.

Assad's dark eyebrows flew up in sheer disbelief, but after a second or two he recovered and waved Carl over to the passenger side, throwing open the door to let him tumble in.

"Where the hell have you been?" said Carl brusquely. They stared at each other for a moment before they broke into a short burst of hysterical laughter that immediately made Carl grimace.

Assad reached his hand to Carl's and gave it an emphatic squeeze. They smiled, tears rolling down their cheeks, but neither said another word until they were out of the mayhem in the carpark and away from the hordes of people wandering toward the prison.

"You've got quite a lot of deep cuts on your face that are bleeding, you know that, right?"

Carl nodded, dabbing his face with the sleeve of the military jacket. It was nothing compared to the agony he felt when he breathed.

"I don't get it, Carl. You're alive and you got out, it's just incredible. You have to tell me everything while we drive. Did you notice a gray Mercedes leaving the carpark just now? The hit men are in it."

Carl looked at Assad's hands, which were gripping the wheel so tightly his knuckles were white. There was dried blood on the seat between his legs.

"So many people died because I couldn't stop them, Carl," he said, clearly emotional.

"It's not your fault, Assad. I don't want to hear that." He laid a hand on Assad's arm. "Whose car is this, and what's that all about?" He pointed at the bullet hole, then at the congealed blood on the edge of the driver's seat.

Assad hesitated for a moment, getting a grip on himself. "It's

Kenneth's. It was him you saw on the gurney just now. My own car was blocked in, so I took his instead. Earlier, when I found him, I noticed the key was in the ignition."

"Do you know if he's alive?"

Assad shook his head. "The shot went through the windshield and hit him just here, under the neck. It looked bad." He pointed out on himself where it had penetrated. "It's a good thing this isn't ordinary glass or we wouldn't have been able to see through the crazing."

Carl tried not to look at the hole in the glass. Yet another weight for him to carry on his shoulders. It was hard to think about.

He coughed and clutched his ribs. His right calf was throbbing painfully, and one of the lacerations from the pieces of glass had reopened. So much blood spilled, everywhere, on his account.

Carl kept his eyes fixed ahead and a little out of focus. The oncoming lane was packed. Unmarked vehicles, cars from the Emergency Management Agency, and motorcycle units were heading toward the column of smoke rising into the sky.

"I'm bleeding on the seat as well, Assad," he said, fumbling in the glove compartment for something he could use to soak it up.

At the very back, among the instruction manuals and half-empty bags of sweets, he found a white cloth. As he drew it out, something heavy fell to the floor with a clunk. A gun.

Carl looked at Assad with a frown, and Assad threw a brief glance at it before turning back to the road.

"Must be Kenneth's. I haven't seen it before," he said. "I had no idea it was in there. He said the only weapons we had were stun guns." Assad patted his trouser pocket to show where he was keeping it. "I pray to Allah that Kenneth survives that bullet, because it didn't look good, Carl. If it hadn't been for him, you and I wouldn't be sitting here together right now, you need to know that."

"You've got a phone, right?" asked Carl, trying not to cough.

He nodded and pointed at the dashboard. It was Bluetooth-activated.

"Assad, can you call Merete Lynggaard so that she can keep us updated on Kenneth's situation? I'd also like to speak to her."

Assad shook his head. "Before long you'll be the most wanted man in Denmark, Carl. They'll find out you got out of that cell alive, so you can't speak to anyone. They'll be monitoring all the traffic on your closest friends' phones. They might even be tapped. Mine too, we can safely assume."

Carl nodded. *The most wanted man in the country.* Unfortunately, that was probably all too accurate.

As they went around a bend on their way out of town, the gray Mercedes came into view only a few hundred yards ahead of them. It was driving south at a leisurely pace, so the men inside probably didn't suspect anyone was following them.

Assad made a call, and someone picked up a few seconds later.

"Terje Ploug," said a dry, weary voice.

Carl nodded. Assad had phoned Ploug—that made sense. He hoped to God he wouldn't cough.

"Assad here. You've heard about the attack?"

"You can say that again. I was watching a news report about the scene at the US Capitol building yesterday when suddenly it just cut off. Now they're showing pictures of the remand center in flames. What the hell happened, Assad? They're saying Carl's cell was targeted. But have they found him, is he alive, do you know yet?"

"I don't know the details, no. But listen, I've just left Slagelse, and I'm in pursuit of the hit men's car."

He gave Ploug the Mercedes's registration number and the GPS coordinates. "We're heading south and we're unarmed, so we're in dire need of backup."

"'We'? Who's 'we'?"

Assad rolled his eyes at the slip of the tongue.

"Please just make sure there are blockades set up farther south. Don't forget about the side roads, we don't want them getting away. And stay in touch."

There was a dial tone. Ploug had already set to work.

"Unarmed, Assad?" Carl coughed, bending down to pick up the

wooden butt of the gun. "Look, a nine-millimeter Neuhausen. Not exactly what I'd call unarmed."

Assad looked at it again. "Is it loaded?"

Carl turned it over and took out the magazine. Then he checked to make sure there was also a cartridge in the chamber.

"Certainly is."

"Okay, well, I couldn't know that, could I?"

Wonky logic. Typical Assad.

Carl weighed it in his hand. A nice, solid thing, roughly two pounds, and about as accurate as a handgun could possibly be. Of course a professional soldier would want a first-class weapon like this as backup, just in case things went south.

56

FEMKE / CEES

Thursday, January 7, 2021

After the assault, both Femke and her neighbor had been questioned about the person who had broken into her apartment and attacked them. She didn't say much when they asked her if she knew why the burglar had been so violent. Did they have anything particularly valuable lying around, and could it have been connected to her husband's death? No, she didn't know anything; she was in shock, which was the truth. As for all the other stuff, she was determined not to let them know about Eddie's criminal activities or the profits he'd made off the back of them. That must forever remain a secret.

Her description matched the neighbor's. The man was tall and strong and looked like a regular Dutchman. Later that night police returned and checked a few areas that Femke thought the man might have touched. After they had gotten some fingerprints, they left her alone.

The previous day, Femke had tried to brush off the near-fatal attack by spending hours ransacking the apartment for anything that might aid her in her pursuit of the treasure trove she hoped Eddie had stashed away somewhere. Anything that might offer a clue was examined before being, frustratingly, cast aside.

She had dropped Marika off at nursery earlier that morning as though nothing had happened, apart from the virus that had knocked them out for a few days. And when she picked her up a few hours later, Marika was as blithe and energetic as Femke was mentally drained.

"Was that man stupid?" asked Marika out of nowhere, as they were eating fruit in the kitchen.

Femke was appalled. What could the girl remember—had she even been awake?

While she racked her brain for an answer, Marika was already busy with her toy. A moment later she turned to her mother and held out a little wooden boat.

"Go sail," she said.

Femke tilted her head back. "Sailing," she said.

How many boats had Eddie gone through over the years? From their first rowboat to a slightly larger one, and later the fiberglass sailboat, which had also been sold. Then one she'd never actually been able to identify, which in recent years Eddie had boarded only when it had been pulled ashore. He liked it best when Marika was with him. She loved to sit on the deck and gaze out at the harbor. Was that what Marika was thinking?

Femke nodded to herself. Of course, there was the summer cabin too! She'd have to drive up and search it top to bottom. Eddie had always loved it up there. Maybe that was where he'd hoarded his gold.

Femke looked at her watch. It was roughly ninety miles from Schiedam to the seaside cabin, so it would take at least two hours. That gave her five hours to search before it got dark.

The streets of Bergen aan Zee were almost deserted in the cold, and when Femke and Marika reached the house around midday, the windowpanes were covered in crystals of ice. The door was sticking on its frozen hinges.

Yet inside the house, a faint warmth lingered. Femke was surprised. Had Eddie gone down in December and turned up the radiators? If so, he hadn't told her.

Oh, Eddie, she thought. A trace of him was still stirring, then. The thought of him nailed to a chair, dying in the polders, returned to her. Like a curse.

She shook it off and looked around. The cabin was quite a lot bigger than the apartment in Schiedam, but it hadn't always been that way. She was ashamed to think now how they'd built on more than five hundred square feet and added a new entrance leading from the dunes ever since Eddie had come into money. Two extra bedrooms, a living room twice the size of the old one, an office for Eddie and a hobby room for Femke, and then last autumn a big play area for Marika.

It was that door that Marika spotted, and in she trotted on her little legs and began to play, still wearing her outdoor clothes. Femke smiled. That would give her peace and quiet for long enough to go through the house.

She started with Eddie's room, where there were no signs he'd been leading a double life. She persisted, checking room after room, but luck remained obstinately not on her side. Eddie's secrets were locked up inside a dead brain in a morgue somewhere in Rotterdam.

• • •

It had been several days since Cees Pauwels was last able to enjoy being fussed over by his family in Liège. His daughters had clung to him from the moment he set foot through the door, and his wife, Lilian, greeted him with the warmest hug anyone could wish for.

They had coddled and looked after him all afternoon, and now, this morning, everybody had come in to shower him with hugs and kisses before Lilian drove the girls to school and went to work.

"We'll be home at four. Remember to leave a note if you have another job in Holland," she had said with an ironic smile, waving goodbye.

The words had gotten under his skin. *Another job in Holland*, she had said.

It was a job he hadn't finished. *The leak has been plugged*, he'd told his employers, but nobody knew better than him that there was only one method of definitely stopping a leak like that. Femke Jansen was alive, and she knew far too much about what he looked like. More specifically still, she knew he had killed her husband and tried to do the same to her and her daughter. She had already proven once what she was capable of, and it was only sheer good luck he hadn't been caught red-handed by the police in that torture chamber on the polders. She'd also had direct contact with the police in Rotterdam; he'd seen it with his own eyes.

What she knew or didn't know about her husband's activities didn't matter anymore, because there was only one solution: to claim her life. But he had now called her apartment in Schiedam several times from his phones with Dutch SIM cards, receiving no response.

Cees was thinking. *Fled already, Femke? Perhaps you found what you were looking for?*

For many years, disloyalty and incompetence in the organization he worked for had been punishable by death. If his employers checked up on him and found that Femke Jansen was still a potential security risk, the hammer would fall hard and fast. He had played executioner many times himself, but he wasn't the only one. He'd seen that demonstrated very clearly when Gustaaf Mulder killed the Pole before his very eyes.

He had to find her, fast, and deal with the problem. Whatever the cost.

Cees put his hands behind his head and lay in bed for a long time, forcing himself to review the events of the past few days.

After he'd been lying there for an hour, he reached a point in the chain of events that should have attracted his attention sooner.

In the apartment in Schiedam, Femke had led him into the sewing room, where she'd given him the password to her laptop. She had frowned just before she did it, and he'd thought it was her reluctance to help him, but right now he wasn't so sure. Cees closed his eyes and took a few mental steps back. Something had been on the table next to the laptop, something that had caught his attention. Pieces of paper, maybe? What was it?

Then it popped into his head. No, it was the photo frame being turned over. The photo of Eddie with the little girl in his arms. Why had it been face down? Didn't she want to look at it? Was that why she had frowned when he didn't put it back in the same position? Maybe the sight of it made her uncomfortable.

If it was grief that had made her lay it flat, then surely she would have expressed that some other way than frowning?

That hadn't been grief on her face, more a sort of disgust at the sight of her husband, who had been holding their daughter in his arms. But why?

Cees nodded to himself—he was almost certain now. That woman knew what her husband had done, and she could no longer stand the sight of him. Femke, although she denied it, had read Eddie's document, and that made her far more dangerous than he had reported to his employers.

Then another thing occurred to Cees. In the photograph, Eddie had been standing on a jetty.

Cees got out of bed, showered, and dressed, then went into the kitchen and left a note on the table with a brief explanation for Lilian and the kids, saying that unfortunately he'd been called back into work, but he'd be home soon, and then he'd be taking a long holiday.

Years ago, Cees had bought Eddie and Femke's summer cabin in Bergen aan Zee at auction. That was how the whole thing had begun. Using the cabin as his trump card, he had negotiated with Eddie, luring him into the fold. That was nearly eighteen years ago now, and Cees hadn't been up there since, so he thought perhaps he could be reasonably sure Femke was unaware he even knew about it. Certainly it was a theory to be tested. Because if she wasn't in Schiedam but hadn't left the country, why not there?

It was less than two hundred miles from Liège to Bergen aan Zee. A four-hour drive at the most, despite the slippery conditions on the road.

57

CARL

Thursday, January 7, 2021

They must have heard the helicopter at the same time, because the gray Mercedes, which was now three or four hundred yards ahead of them, sped up markedly.

"They know they've been spotted, Assad—drive." Carl peered forward at the next exit. "I think they're going to leave the motorway."

Assad nodded and picked up his phone, which had started ringing. It was Ploug, so he put a finger to his lips. Nobody could know who his passenger was.

"We've got a military helicopter following you. I can see on my screen here everything captured on its camera," Ploug explained. "There's an exit coming up—do you think they'll take it?"

Assad confirmed his agreement with a grunt.

"What vehicle are you driving, Assad?"

"I'm in a dark blue Volvo. You can't miss it, I'm right on their heels."

"Stay on the line, so I can communicate with you and we can keep the helicopter crew in the loop. Okay, I can see your car a little way behind, Assad. I think you'll have to step on it if you don't want to lose sight of them."

Assad didn't need to be told twice. He trod the pedal to the floor, forcing them both back into their seats. As he hurtled up the exit ramp, Carl had to hold his breath.

"Now left," Ploug yelled at the last moment, just before Assad sped into a T-junction on two wheels.

"Terje, can you tell me what happened to Carl during the attack?" asked Assad a moment later.

"They're searching, but it looks like he probably survived the attack and made a run for it. Another prisoner who was in his cell at the time of the assault has been taken to hospital, but he isn't speaking. Might be shock."

Carl suppressed a cough and gave a thumbs-up. All was going according to plan.

"And Kenneth, the soldier who was shot in the neck?"

"I don't know, they haven't mentioned that. But I'm sat here by the TV, channel surfing, and already the big story is what's become of Carl."

"Well, I hope he's not badly injured," said Assad, grinning lopsidedly at Carl.

"I'm afraid I'm not sure we can assume that, Assad. They're saying the attack cost the lives of at least three inmates. The other guy in his cell was probably just incredibly lucky. Anyway, listen, we've set up a road-block a few miles ahead, so the helicopter is going to pull back now. We want the Mercedes to think we've lost sight of them. Keep a safe distance. We need to know if they take another route."

Assad confirmed, then muted his Bluetooth.

"We need to get those bastards, Assad, okay?" said Carl. He was genuinely distraught. Three men had been killed, and no doubt many more were injured. Carl tried to wrap his head around it. What kind of hideous operation was behind this? Cynical people who were keeping a nice, safe distance from the attack, for whom blood and trauma were no more than words. He nodded to himself. That was so often the way. But whatever crimes the prisoners at Slagelse had allegedly committed, this was utterly disproportionate and undeserved. Carl could hardly bring himself to think of their loved ones, the people who now had to live with the consequences of somebody trying to kill him.

Carl clenched his teeth. Even if it cost him everything, he would never stop until those responsible were caught.

He turned to Assad, who had his nose almost pressed to the windshield. Several patches of road ahead of them glistened as though they hadn't been salted. This was going to be touch and go.

"This is proper fucking countryside, Assad. Not a soul in sight. What do we do if they take a side road or something?" asked Carl.

Assad pointed at the gun. "If we can, we'll put a bullet right between their eyes. Then—"

Assad stopped abruptly, peering ahead. The gray car had been far ahead of them for a while, but it was now no longer visible.

"Did you see where it turned off?" asked Assad, slowing down. On one side there were open fields, and on the other a line of trees and then more fields.

"No!" Carl had thought there might be a side road, but the problem was there *were* no side roads.

"They're waiting for us, Carl, I can feel it," Assad said. "They're lying in wait a bit farther up."

Carl nodded. The men in the gray Mercedes probably had enough firepower to blow up an armored vehicle, and neither he nor Assad wanted to meet the same fate as those poor souls in Slagelse.

"I don't think it's wise to drive any farther, Carl," said Assad, pulling over by the line of trees. "If you get out on your side and I follow, do you think they'll see us?"

Carl slid out, crept a few steps, and lay down on the ground. He squinted ahead of him in the dim light. There was no movement along the stretch of road.

Assad edged over to the trees, following Carl, and threw himself to the ground beside him, four or five yards from the car.

"You or me?" he asked.

Carl clenched the gun. Of course it would be him who crawled toward the strangers. Wasn't he the reason, after all, that the two of them were sprawled out here in this icy no-man's-land?

A soft hum and a whistle sped through the air above them, and then the Volvo was hit right in the middle of the cabin, setting off such a powerful explosion that the vehicle was lifted several feet into the air, slamming back down onto the roadway in a ball of flames and devastation.

They lay face-to-face, looking into each other's eyes.

Assad pointed at his phone. "Are you okay, Assad?" came a voice. It was Ploug. "I saw the explosion on the news. Idiots sent up a drone to interfere with the chase."

"Good thing we got out, or we'd have been killed instantly," said Carl, pressing a hand to his broken ribs.

"They probably think we were," said Assad with a nod. "They'll just drive off now if we don't stop them."

Carl barely heard the last part, because he had gotten laboriously to his feet and was hobbling toward the fields on the other side of the trees. If they saw him, they'd gun him down then and there, but he had to take the chance or they'd disappear forever.

Now the characteristic roar of the chopper's blades was back. Carl turned to watch it streak across the fields from the east, while other sounds at his back told him Assad was following—about as subtly as a pack of gorillas charging through the jungle. If the men hadn't heard them by now, they were deafer than his ex-mother-in-law.

He shushed Assad and was signaling him to stop when several rattling volleys made them both duck.

Carl looked up to see a military observation helicopter, which swerved and beat a retreat. It was the chopper the hit men had been shooting at—and hit—and Carl seized the advantage of the confusion to take the last fifty yards at a bounding run, heading toward the shooter.

It was the muzzle flare from the machine gun that gave away his position in the undergrowth, and Carl fired several shots in that direction before he flung himself back on the ground. It hurt like hell.

From where he lay, sixty feet back, he could see one whole side of the gray Mercedes, tilted toward the bushes. He took a steady aim and shot out both tires, bringing the car down onto its rims with a bump.

Then he lay still and waited. The man who had just been firing at the helicopter hadn't made another sound. But where was the other man?

Then he heard the crunch of withered leaves behind him. Assad, belly-crawling in his direction.

"Did you see the shadow?" he whispered.

"The shadow?"

"Yeah. I think I saw him heading into the trees by the side of the road."

"You're sure?"

"You hit the other one. I can see his arm lolling out into the field."

Carl rolled, giving himself a view of the field. Sure enough, an arm was sticking out of the tree line, and it wasn't moving.

"Assad, can you hear me?" Ploug was asking faintly from the mobile phone, but Assad didn't reply. He was crawling across the trees toward the road.

"Come on, Carl. I can see him over there, running across the open field on the other side of the road."

The stranger was already about three hundred yards across the frozen furrows, sprinting on the balls of his feet, knees pumping, heading straight for a group of small farms that were scattered across the countryside some distance ahead.

Carl crossed the road, took aim, and fired, but the man was too far away.

Then he heard the faint sound of the television channel's drone, which swung over the trees and hovered in the air above him.

"Don't let them see your face," Assad cried behind him.

But it was too late.

"Jesus Christ!" they both heard Ploug yelling down the phone. "You lied to me, Assad. That's Carl fucking Mørck, wearing a military jacket and shooting at the guy running away. The whole of Denmark is watching the news right now."

58

FEMKE

Thursday, January 7, 2021

After a few hours spent combing meticulously through the straggling house, Femke took Marika's hand and walked them both outside to get some fresh air. The sea was defiant and unapproachable, so they tramped up to the top of a dune and counted seagulls while Marika imitated their sporadic screeches.

Femke was happy and sad all at once. Without Eddie to pay for it, this was probably the last year they could call the cabin theirs. Maintenance, insurance, heat, and electricity had never been her responsibilities, and the truth was she had no idea how much it cost to keep this little slice of paradise running, although she thought she could guess.

Now, gazing out over the town, she knew a precious era in her life had passed, and it wouldn't come again.

Yet they were alive. And even if she didn't find Eddie's vein of gold, she and Marika had each other, which was what mattered. She called to Marika, challenging her to a race back to the rear of the house, and Marika flailed her arms and legs and shrieked like the gulls, while Femke made sure to stay just level with her all the way.

The cabin looked so inviting, its windows glowing brightly at her like cats' eyes. Marika clapped her hand against the woodwork, laughing over her victory, but Femke stopped short. Somehow the back of the house didn't look like she remembered. Eddie's usually unfailing sense of symmetry appeared to have let him down, she thought, as she counted the vertical planks between the windows.

"Come on, Mama," Marika called.

Femke was baffled. She stepped up to the two windows and peered into Eddie's study. Eddie had positioned them in such a way that he could see over the water while he worked. Behind one window was his desk, beside a cabinet against the wall, and through the other she could see along the wall with the bookshelves and on into the dining room.

She shook her head to herself. She had never been good with floor plans and measurements; that had been Eddie's department. Making the whole thing come together in a way that worked.

She looked again at his desk, feeling a lump swell in her throat. Without him everything had grown so empty.

They went in through the back door and Femke locked it, because Marika was a little too fond of the seemingly infinite dunes. Then they sat down in the kitchen so that Marika could fill her belly, still firing off one gull-like shriek after another.

I wonder how much I could get for this cabin? thought Femke, hoping fervently it wasn't mortgaged. Then she got up and went into Eddie's study, pulling a few files off the bookcase in the hopes she might find documentation about the house, and any outstanding loans he might have borrowed against it.

That, at least, Eddie seemed to have organized well, because after examining a few documents, she breathed a sigh of relief. The cabin wasn't mortgaged. The last installments had been made more than ten years ago, and the extensions had been paid for in cash.

Femke replaced the files onto the shelf, and again it seemed to her as though the wall were slightly off-kilter. She got up and went into the dining room, then turned and stared back into the study. It really was a peculiar feeling: no matter which way she turned, it looked wrong.

Again, she slid a file off Eddie's bookshelf. *Extensions*, it read on the spine. She spread out the floor plans on Eddie's desk and studied them for a moment before letting out a tiny, astonished grunt.

In the drawings, the windows in Eddie's study and the adjacent guest rooms were precisely the same distance apart, but in reality they weren't! She had counted the planks between them, and in the drawings the wall didn't slant diagonally toward the guest space that led off from the dining room. It was just plain odd.

While Marika made gull cries and played with blocks, Femke went to stand in the guest room. She had never paid much heed to it before, but the whole room was distinctly asymmetrical: the distance between the walls at the dining room end was greater than at the back of the house.

She knocked on the wall. First on the wooden paneling in the guest room, then in the study. And when she compared the sound to the other newly constructed walls in Eddie's room, there was a clear difference. The other walls resounded dully, but this particular one sounded far more solid, as though there was metal in the wall.

Femke held her breath. It was well done—she'd certainly never noticed before, but now she felt sure. The space between the study and the guest room had been constructed to create a double wall with a cavity in between.

But why on a slant? She went back into the guest room and stared at the paneling. Femke had protested when Eddie first suggested lining the wall with something he had called acoustic panels, because she didn't think it fit with the style of the cabin. But Eddie had insisted, explaining that it would soundproof the study, where he often worked late into the night.

They'd argued a bit, because as Femke pointed out, they never actually had any guests. But by the time they returned the following summer, Eddie had gotten someone in to install it anyway, and it had looked better than she'd expected.

Now, standing in front of the paneling, she examined it to see if there was a way to open it somehow. There were no cracks or hinges, as far as she could see, and pulling at the individual slats of wood had no effect. She pressed each one, hoping there would be some mechanism that clicked the door open, like with newer kitchen cupboards. No result.

Femke took a step back, staring at each slat top to bottom until, at floor level, she discovered a small gray mark, one meter from the dining room door. Like a print left by a dirty shoe.

"Come on!" she said, giving it a kick. The jolt that ran through her when the hidden door sprang open was a peculiar blend of relief and fright. Now, at last, she had opened Eddie's secret treasure chest, but what if it turned out to be empty?

She poked her head cautiously into the cramped space, noticing the faint scent of oil, and after a moment's fumbling she found a light switch.

The narrow shelves on the opposite wall made her gasp. Square foot after square foot of bundled banknotes, all arrayed on the shelves. Title deeds and share certificates everywhere. No account books, no keys to subterranean safety-deposit boxes. It was all here, and Femke couldn't believe it. How had Eddie dared to leave a fortune like this lying here? What if the house had burned down?

She peered around the wedge-shaped room. Was the whole thing fire-proof? Were the walls lined with thick sheets of asbestos? Were they secured with steel plates on the outside, just beneath the plasterboard? She knocked on the walls again, with the same recognition that these walls were extremely solid. She could even close the door from the inside, she realized, pulling the handle shut. It made a faint click.

Extraordinary how well thought-out it was. She looked down at the skirting board, where the locking mechanism was. Then she depressed the little pedal, and the door swung open again just as easily. She sniffed—it smelled a bit like the kind of oil sprayed on recalcitrant nuts and bolts, and the faint glistening of the mechanism suggested the same. Eddie had taken good care of this room.

Femke ran a hand over one of the shelves of banknotes. Tentatively she picked up one of the bundles of fifties, sweeping her thumb over the end as though it was a deck of cards. At least a hundred notes, she thought—in this bundle alone there must be five thousand euros.

She could scarcely breathe as it dawned on her how gilded her future suddenly looked.

Then she clasped her hands, thinking again of Eddie. She wished now that they could have enjoyed this new future together.

She stepped out of the room, switched off the light, and clicked the door shut, flush with the rest of the paneling.

What do I do now? What the hell do I do? she thought, laughing. She couldn't bring that much cash out of the country, but perhaps Eddie hadn't planned to. She could drive to other EU countries without being checked at the border, but where would she go?

Femke smiled broadly. *Not a bad problem to have*, she thought, picturing warmer climes and an altogether less problem-ridden life.

Her eyes fell on the floor plan on the desk in Eddie's study.

"Better get rid of that," she said to herself, and went into the room and began to fold it up.

She was practically brimming with self-satisfaction and pride. To think that she had solved the mystery.

Then, instinctively, she glanced up at the window and found herself staring straight into the face of the man who had killed her husband. He was so close to the pane that he brushed it with the tip of his nose. Both his eyes were blue now, the look in them hard and stabbing.

Femke almost went into shock.

Did I lock the back door? The question flashed through her mind. Could he break a window and get in? Who would hear them if she called for help?

He tapped on the glass, smiling crookedly, then raised his other arm. Through the glass, she saw the barrel of a gun pointed directly at her face.

You're going to die, he mouthed, then he stuck a hand in his pocket and showed her what a silencer looked like.

As he screwed it on, Femke dashed into the kitchen. For a millisecond she considered unlocking the front door and making a break for it with Marika, but she knew deep down that wouldn't help. She was trapped.

"Come on, love," she said firmly to her daughter, dragging her away from her toys.

Marika was about to start screaming, but Femke scooped her up and held her close. "You can have ten ice creams every single day for the rest of the year, Marika, if you don't make a sound until I tell you to."

The girl smiled, thank god—she would take that deal. Then Femke heard the tinkle of shattered glass at the other end of the house, where the windows were biggest, and a faint cold draft skittered across the floor.

Her heart was racing. She kicked the locking mechanism of the hidden door and rushed into the narrow room, switched on the light, and put Marika on the floor, shushing her.

"Mama's going to stop talking now too," she whispered, pulling the door closed.

The pulse in her throat was thudding harder and harder, sweat beading from every pore. She wiped her palm and took Marika's hand.

The little girl was staring all around her, bemused by the sight of all this paper. She reached out an arm to the bottom shelf and tugged on a small wooden box.

NO! Femke's brain screamed, and the second before the box hit the floor, she caught it. She shook her head and put her finger to her lips, signaling once again that her daughter needed to be quiet.

Marika smiled. She had understood.

"Marika, where are you?" They heard a man's voice, faint and ingratiating, from somewhere outside. "It's Dada, I'm home. Where are you hiding? Why don't you come and say hello to Dada?"

Femke shook her head emphatically at Marika, who seemed about to respond. She looked surprised and happy—maybe this was part of the game?

"It's not Dada," Femke whispered very quietly. "It's the stupid man again."

Marika gasped, and her expression shifted from mischievous to terrified, her whole face changing. Femke stroked her cheek gently—she could see Marika's lips beginning to quiver.

"Remember all the ice creams," she whispered into her ear.

"Mariiiiikaaa, where are you? Are you playing hide-and-seek with Mama? Is it fun?"

Then it sounded as though he'd started shooting at the kitchen cupboards. Hushed shots and splintering wood, shattering china.

Bastard! she thought, mobilizing all the resistance she could. *What can I use to defend us—is there anything in here?*

But there was no room on the shelves for tools or weapons. Eddie had never foreseen that his safe, secret world would become a fortress impossible to escape alive unarmed.

Now they heard his footsteps more clearly still. "Mariiiikaaa," he cried again and again. "Dada's got a present for you."

Femke shuddered. That gift was death, she was sure of it. She looked at the little girl's face and felt close to tears when she glanced down into the box Marika was tearing open on the floor.

A half-empty pack of cigarettes and a lighter. So this was where Eddie had hidden them. Sometimes she had smelled it when he'd been smoking on the terrace. Despite what they'd agreed when she told him she was pregnant. She had reproached him, but he'd denied it. If she searched the edge of the dunes, she'd probably find the cigarette butts to prove it.

And now here was proof. Femke bent down to pick up the cigarettes and lighter, revealing at the bottom of the small box a blue spray can. *WD-40*, it read. Presumably what he'd used to ease the lock.

Femke shook the can. It sounded quite full.

Muffled shots were coming from the study, aimed at the cabinet, she thought. It sickened her to think that he wasn't even bothering to check if they were inside before he fired.

"What's that, Mama?" whispered Marika, but Femke waved away the noises; they were nothing.

Now there were faint steps, as though the man were pacing right outside their wall.

Femke held her breath and stroked the little girl's neck. *Is he figuring it out?* she wondered, clutching the lighter more tightly.

Unexpectedly, he shot at the wall they were hiding behind. The clang was loud and metallic, and Marika jumped and let out her gull-like shriek at the top of her lungs, tears welling up in her eyes. She clung to Femke's leg, as the man outside shouted that he knew where they were hiding, that he'd find a way to get to them eventually.

He fired another couple of bullets at the armored wall, and Marika screamed. There was no point trying to stop her.

Letting go of Marika's neck, she bent down to the wooden box and picked up the lubricant. Spraying it against the wall, she found that it was still pressurized and that it reeked of various different things—including solvent.

"I found the treasure. There are millions in here, I think. Plenty for the both of us," she shouted at the wall.

Then she grabbed a couple of bundles and tossed them on the floor next to the locking mechanism.

"Don't shoot, first just look at what I've got for you," she shouted again.

She was more terrified than ever, because the man outside was silent as the grave. Was he simply waiting to make short work of both of them?

"Marika, I want you to go over there and stay there, okay?" She pointed at the far end of the pointed room.

Marika shook her head. She didn't want to let go of Femke's leg, but Femke composed herself and smiled brightly, as though the whole thing were still a game.

At long last she let go and crawled away, huddling in the corner.

Femke closed her eyes, running through the events of the next few seconds. It all had to happen in one smooth movement.

She touched the floor pedal lightly with her foot, and there was a click. At the same moment she pushed the door open a fraction and kicked all the notes into the room.

During the split second in which the man was processing the unexpected sight, bending down toward the notes, she shoved open the door, flicked the lighter, and sprayed the oil at the man through the tiny flame, which made the liquid explode into a burst of fire. His hair caught light, and he screamed in pain. But Femke didn't stop, guiding the flame toward the hand holding the gun.

He flung himself back onto the floor, his clothes burning, prone and paralyzed with agony, firing half blindly toward what he thought was his attacker's blond hair.

Femke leaped aside and edged around to the other side of the man, still aiming her improvised flamethrower at him. He dropped the gun and tried to shield his face, but it was too late.

Femke didn't think, she just acted. Snatching the gun up off the floor, she pointed it at the man writhing at her feet.

Should I just let him suffer until he passes out, or . . .

Suddenly she heard Marika moving in the room behind her.

"Stop, Marika, don't come out here. There's a fire, sweetheart."

And at the very moment she heard the girl pause, she shot her husband's executioner twice in the heart.

59

HARDY / ASSAD

Thursday, January 7, 2021

Hardy was beside himself. The garden alone—never mind the gorgeous house—was enough to take his breath away. An oasis of nooks and crannies amid deep foliage, even in the gray and icy dark of winter, it was a delight for the eyes, the evergreen bushes and wizened perennials whistling decoratively in the wind.

She had come to him after reading about his tireless struggle to regain control of his limbs. And her old feelings had been awoken when he spoke passionately about the people who had helped him get his life back.

Hardy and Minna had divorced ten years earlier. It was he, in fact, who had asked her to embrace possibilities he couldn't be a part of; he had set her free, but now she told him her freedom had always been a gift she felt she never should have accepted.

She had remarried, yes, and lived a privileged life as the wife of a kind and somewhat older man who had left her upon his death a villa big enough for her and Hardy's son and his family on the second floor. Yet the house felt too large, too lonely.

They had met up, at her urging, barely a week ago, and the minute she saw the tall, sinewy man stand upright in his suit of his own free will, beaming with gratitude at the sight of her again, she realized what her new reality might look like, that she had found the puzzle piece that might make everything fall into place.

Hardy, standing in the garden room, felt profoundly grateful and overwhelmed. The part of the house where he and his Belgian carer were going to stay was already being furnished. He was touched almost to the point of bafflement by how well Minna seemed to understand his special requirements, that there would be strangers coming to the house to help him with the things he couldn't yet manage himself.

Here he could see Minna, the two grandchildren, and their parents every day. Their son, Mads, was a doctor, like his wife, and since Bispebjerg Hospital was only ten minutes away, even in the wheelchair he felt safe if something were to happen.

What could be more ideal?

But Hardy wasn't entirely happy, and the rest of the house knew it. The thorn in Hardy's side was the situation with Carl.

"Hardy, get in here," came a voice from the living room.

He smiled. It had been years since he'd been bossed around by Minna.

Out of consideration for him, the living room had been cleared of all superfluous furniture, and the thick rugs had been removed. A TV set had been arranged in the corner, featuring a wide armchair roomy enough for both Hardy and his suit. Beside it, on the sofa, Minna and his carer sat in front of the big TV, their faces grave. As always, Hardy focused first on the yellow "breaking news" banner at the bottom before looking up at the rest of the screen.

"Unknown perpetrators attack remand center in Slagelse with anti-tank missile," read the news ticker.

Hardy stood rooted to the spot, reading on: "Death toll feared high, including imprisoned detective Carl Mørck, accused of murder, drug trafficking, and fraud."

Hardy took a step back and would have stumbled if his carer hadn't leaped up.

"Carl is feared dead?" If that was true, they had all failed him, and Hardy had failed him most of all. For three days he'd scarcely given a thought to Carl and his case—he'd mostly been thinking of the new possibilities in his life.

"*Êtes-vous okay?*" his carer asked him.

Hardy shook his head and allowed himself to be helped into the chair.

"That can't be right, Minna," he said, fumbling for his mobile phone.

It took Terje Ploug thirty seconds to pick up. "I'm looking at the screen right now, communicating with the police helicopter and Assad on another line. Assad is in pursuit of the hit men's vehicle. You can listen in, but I can't talk to all of you at once, okay?"

Hardy tried to piece together the fragments of conversation into a coherent whole, but it wasn't easy. Assad was currently in pursuit of the suspects, but he didn't know what had happened to Carl, he said. At the same time, Hardy—who knew the remand center very well—could see from the news how serious the attack had been. The damage was enormous.

He listened, heart in mouth, until Terje announced the military helicopter was pulling back, and then communication between Ploug and Assad cut out. It was unbearable.

"Look!" Minna exclaimed. She was pointing at the screen, and everything Hardy had been picturing during the conversation between Terje and Assad became reality.

The TV station had sent up a drone, broadcasting live footage of a shoot-out that seemed very intense. Then the drone glided over some trees, and the man aiming at one of the attackers glanced up.

Hardy stopped breathing. It was Carl, dressed in a military jacket, streaks of blood across his face.

For a moment Hardy was so relieved he could have wept.

"It's Carl! It's fucking Carl! CARL MØRCK!" bellowed the news anchor excitedly as the drone swept past, chasing the fleeing man. Then it ground to a halt and turned back to Carl, as though the pilot had suddenly realized who he'd captured. Then, abruptly, the connection dropped.

"He's been recognized. They'll catch him again, Hardy," Minna said from the sofa. "Where can he go, if he can even get out of there?"

Hardy wiped his face and tried to calm his jittery nerves. Waving off his carer, he got up and staggered back into the garden room. If he spoke very quietly, they wouldn't hear him in the living room.

For a moment he considered the situation, then he dialed a preprogrammed number.

"I've been waiting for you to call, Hardy," said Merete Lynggaard at the other end. "And yes, I'm watching everything. Thank god Carl is alive. Thank god."

"Merete, listen, if you're able to pick him up, he can stay here with me. Nobody knows I'm at Minna's. Only you and Department Q."

"I'll do my best. I've already dispatched a couple of vehicles in that direction. Ploug gave me the approximate coordinates from the military helicopter."

"Fantastic, but hurry. And, Merete, I've got a problem. It's my carer. I suspect he might be a plant, so if you do manage to get Carl here, we'll have to get rid of him first."

She laughed. Perhaps she hadn't understood the seriousness of what he'd said. He could hardly bear to think what might happen if the man contacted the people trying to kill Carl.

"Yes, sorry about that, Hardy. You're right. He *is* a plant. He's one of mine—a damn good bodyguard. I told him to look after you for as long as necessary."

Hardy frowned.

"I know. I'm sorry, but I didn't think you'd agree to let me help; that's why I didn't say anything. But Mika and Morten both know."

Hardy was dumbstruck.

• • •

"We've got to get out of here, Carl," yelled Assad. "You can't hit him at that distance anyway."

Carl looked up at the drone sweeping on after the running man, then saw it stop and turn back, at which point the man in the field paused and shot it down. He also fired a shot in Carl's direction, although he was clearly out of range, before disappearing out of sight beyond the distant hedge.

Carl's cover was blown. No doubt it wouldn't be long before other news teams appeared. TV 2 had mobile units everywhere.

"How exactly are you planning to accomplish that, Assad? In their Mercedes? I punctured both tires on the right-hand side."

Assad didn't reply. He ran through the trees and across to the body of the man Carl had shot. The freckled man lay face down in the dirt. It seemed unlikely he'd been killed instantly, given the amount of blood his heart had pumped out of him.

"The bullet hit him right there." Assad pushed him onto his back and pointed at the entry wound just below the ear, then at where it had exited on the other side, taking one of the arteries in his neck with it.

Assad shook his head. "This isn't the guy who gave me the middle finger, Carl. So now I know what the other one looks like, the one who actually fired the missile at the prison. This guy is the one who shot at me from the roof opposite the fire station garages."

Assad bent down and rummaged through the corpse's pockets.

"They were planning to take a charter flight from Roskilde Airport to Billund, then travel onward from there," he said. "Look!"

He showed Carl the booking and held up the man's passport.

Gustaaf Mulder, his name was.

Dutch, thought Carl. *What else did I expect?*

"Come on, Carl, we've got to get that car started."

Years ago, Carl and Assad had chased a suspect on punctured tires for nearly five miles. It destroyed the wheel rims, and it wasn't exactly enjoyable, but they were out of options.

Opening the boot of the gray car, they found a spare tire underneath an impressive arsenal of weapons, most of which had thankfully not been used. While Assad changed the punctured front tire, Carl fished out a black spray can with the encouraging words "Puncture Repair" emblazoned on it. Shaking the can, he eyed the plastic tube that hung down the side. It appeared unused and ready to pump sealant foam into the rear tire.

Assad was kneeling, and as he pulled the jack away from the car, he pointed up at the sky.

"I know the man upstairs, Carl. We'll be fine. A bit of humility and a few prayers never hurt. How's the back tire doing?"

"I think it's doing just peachy, Assad."

They leaped into the car, which was crammed almost to bursting. Their pursuers had evidently been busy.

On the passenger seat lay an iPad with a map of their position, while the back seat was a jumble of tools and electronics. A couple of lockpick guns, listening devices and spy cameras, typical hard-core burglary equipment, plus a satellite phone and even a defibrillator. As for the rest, Carl didn't know what half of it was. Certainly nothing he'd learned about at police training college, a lifetime ago.

"Terje's calling back. You pick up, Carl. I need to focus on driving."

Carl nodded. He hoped Assad would do exactly that, because the whole car was rattling and bumping after their makeshift patch-up job.

"Are you there, Assad?" came Terje's voice.

"No, it's me, Terje. It's good to hear your voice."

There was a moment's silence on the line. "You too, Carl," he said at last. "Thank god you're okay. But listen, I'm pretty sure Assad's phone will be tapped by the police, so we'll have to make it quick. ML has sent reinforcements. Stay on the main road. Help will come to you."

A mile or two farther on, a clapped-out-looking Toyota flashed its lights at them, and the driver pulled out a little way into the road so that his meaning would be unmistakable.

"Quickly," he yelled. "Empty the car and push it into the verge."

Carl took a plastic bag out of the glove box and shoveled in all the papers and small electronics inside the interior, while Assad cleared out the boot.

"If we've left anything that needs closer examination, the police will find it," Carl said, as they tipped the car into the roadside ditch.

It was soon apparent that their driver was more than good at his job.

In addition to his undeniable skill at the wheel, he made excellent use of a pair of small monitors on the dashboard, which showed both their location and the safest onward route.

The engine snarling under the bonnet was definitely not one produced on a Toyota assembly line.

The man drove warily, telling them to lean all the way back into the seat whenever they were passed by flashing blue lights. The moment he judged there was no immediate danger in the offing, he put the pickup into overdrive.

"Right, that's you," said the man fifteen minutes later, pointing at a second car waiting by a verge.

The rest of the journey was uneventful, and within no more than an hour they were pulling into the driveway of an attractive villa only ten minutes' drive north of central Copenhagen.

60

HARDY / CARL

Thursday, January 7, 2021

The frozen, grainy image of an armed Carl Mørck wearing a military jacket in a dimly lit field had whipped the media into a frenzy, and the Danish public was flooded with a steady stream of theories and opinions.

Was the attack on the prison a cynical rescue operation, a ploy to allow Mørck to escape? some were asking. Others argued that being caught shooting at someone in a field didn't exactly speak in his favor. Where had he even gotten a gun, and how had he made it so far from the remand center in such a short span of time? Somebody must have known what was about to happen at Slagelse.

Hardy was practically out of his mind. How in the hell could journalists be so irresponsible and unfeeling?

By now all the news channels had interrupted their regular programming, and everybody had their own hot take.

"Is Carl Mørck running out of his nine lives?" asked one of the military experts analyzing the shocking firepower used at such close range on the prison cells.

"Did Mørck have help escaping the city?" the reporter on the scene for *News* asked rhetorically, while footage from the drone was broadcast in an infinite loop in the corner of the screen.

Another channel brought up historical examples of violent attacks on foreign, mostly South American prisons. A third was trying for the hundredth time to summarize what the whole Mørck case was actually about.

The truth was nobody knew anything, except that this drama could be raked over and examined endlessly until Carl Mørck was caught.

"Mørck can't escape the tremendous efforts we're making to apprehend him," said one high-ranking police officer, explaining that no trains or flights were coming in or out, while bridgeheads and the surrounding roads were being closely monitored.

"We have full control over the road network in South and West Zealand, and we are working intensively to analyze where Mørck might have gone. If anybody has any suspicions he might have broken into an empty house or, more seriously, taken hostages in a private home, please contact the police. All tips will be investigated."

Hardy snorted. It was the usual bullshit they always started spouting in situations like this. In Zealand alone, there were thousands of homes, and even more people who'd be more than happy to lead the police up the garden path, so how could they possibly hope to investigate every single tip-off?

Hardy looked out the window. The closest neighbor was a comfortable distance away, and the evergreens around the house shielded it from curious stares. It would be hard to find a better place for Carl to hide.

"I need to ask you to stay out of this, Minna," he said. "When Carl gets here, we'll take him straight to my part of the house. Then you'll be able to claim later that you didn't realize he was staying at this address."

Minna eyed him indulgently. "I appreciate that, but we all want to support Carl, Hardy. It's not even a question."

• • •

When Assad and Carl arrived at last, they found a warm welcome. Carl was genuinely touched by the faith Minna and Hardy showed in him, but he didn't look good. Clutching his ribs with his right hand, he was in agony. He was coughing hollowly, and the lacerations on his face and leg were weeping.

"We have two doctors in the house, just upstairs," Minna said. "Why don't I—"

Carl shook his head. He didn't want Minna and Hardy's son involved in this.

"Three or four men have died because of me since this afternoon. I've killed a man, the first time in my whole life. One of Merete's people who was trying to help me has been badly injured, if he's even still alive. So if any part of me needs treatment, it's this." He coughed, rapping his temple.

Assad had been sitting in his chair without a word, but now he interrupted his friend. "The only people to blame here are the ones responsible for this madness." He turned to Minna. "Carl would like to release a statement online, which hopefully will be shown on TV. Do you have a laptop we can borrow? We'll send it to Rose and the Investigation Unit, so your IP address won't be compromised."

"Of course," she said, and went away to fetch it.

Carl looked pale, readying himself onscreen to make a statement. They had communicated the plan to Rose via Merete Lynggaard, and then Carl began his first-ever Zoom appearance.

"I suppose I should say good evening?" he began, coughing. "My name is Carl Mørck, and I am a detective with Department Q at the Copenhagen Investigation Unit, currently suspended from duty. I have been accused of a number of crimes I have not committed. At the link below, you will be able to read the charges brought against me by the prosecution under section 41f, paragraph 21, of the Administration of Justice Act. I wish you happy reading—it's pure fiction.

"Today I survived a devastating, heinous attack on the building where I was being held on remand. I have been informed that several people also held at the center have died. I'm deeply saddened to hear this, because whatever their crimes, there were good people there, people I greatly valued."

He swallowed, clutching his side. "I have been forced to go into hiding in order to present my side of the story. I am the victim of a miscarriage of justice, and I am under constant attack, although I don't know who my attackers are or why they're doing this. Within the last eleven days I have survived four murder attempts, and I must express my grave disappointment at how little the police have done to protect me."

He felt a cough welling up in the depths of his lungs. He didn't want to think about how much it was going to hurt, but then the coughing fit swept over him in an explosion of mucus and masonry dust.

It took him a moment to recover, then he turned back to the camera and apologized. For the next twenty minutes, he told his story. And by the time he was finished, the opening of his statement was already being broadcast on television screens across the nation.

61

FEMKE

Thursday, January 7–Monday, January 11, 2021

For roughly ten minutes she let Marika shriek and cry inside the little room while she rolled Cees Pauwels's body into a rug and dragged it into the bathroom.

Everything inside Femke was screaming that this was wrong, but she had no choice. She had killed someone, and even though it was self-defense, she knew the smell of oil and burned flesh would haunt her for the rest of her life.

Hands trembling, she drank several glasses of water, admonishing herself that she only had a few minutes to wallow in shock. Soon she would let Marika out, and by then she had to be the mother she had always been. She would drive her into town and buy her the promised ice cream, then some suitcases, and after that she would play with her until the little girl was tired, giving her time to do what had to be done.

It was late evening by the time Marika finally released her grip on the day and nodded off on the sofa in the living room.

It took Femke an hour to stuff the eight suitcases with bundles of notes and share certificates and carry them out to the large SUV. She had no idea how much money was in there, but it had to be at least fifteen million euros.

While Marika slept heavily, she drove south through the darkness to the flat in Schiedam, where she picked up Marika's toys, some clothes for them both, their passports, and a couple of photo albums.

As she stood in the external corridor and pulled the damaged door shut behind her, she sighed a final farewell to everything that had defined her life with Eddie. For a moment she didn't know who she was.

"It *will* be fine," she commanded herself, returning to the carpark and to Marika, who was still fast asleep.

Her plan now was to drive to Luxembourg and deposit a third of the money into various bank accounts, stay there until Monday, then floor it all the way through Germany into Switzerland.

There she'd make a couple of visits to banks in Bern and a couple more in Zurich, depositing the remaining notes. Somebody somewhere might voice surprise at the sheer volume of them, but Femke's simple story about fleeing a violent Russian husband would ensure their sympathy, or so she hoped.

And she was right.

Using one of her brand-new credit cards, she booked two one-way first-class tickets to Rio de Janeiro with Swiss Air. And when at last she stood at Zurich Airport, holding Marika by the hand, she turned briefly to the camera at security and smiled widely, bidding goodbye to her former life.

62

MARCUS

Friday, January 8, 2021

Never in his life had Chief of Homicide Marcus Jacobsen felt so decisively outmaneuvered.

For a moment he swore to himself, then he turned off the screen and went into the front office, where Lis was standing with some colleagues, gazing at a tiny flat-screen on her desk. It had been playing the same clip of Carl Mørck incessantly since that morning.

The looks they shot him told him precisely where their sympathies lay. Mørck's blanched face had been splashed across every news channel in existence for hours, and Marcus hated it.

"Could you call in the team leaders, please, Lis? My office, ten minutes."

Lis didn't reply, but she did what he asked.

Bente Hansen was the first person to show up. "Good Lord, Marcus, this whole thing feels like being in a bad movie," she said.

He tried to smile, but inwardly he was boiling with resentment and ire. Somebody or something close to him had made this possible for Carl Mørck, and no stone could be left unturned.

"Yes, it's really quite unfortunate. Particularly because the general feeling seems to be that no one gives a flying fuck whether Carl is guilty or not. They're making the whole force look like a bunch of arseholes."

Hansen wasn't easily flustered, but she seemed more than usually perturbed by the situation.

"We need to try to put ourselves in Carl's shoes, Marcus. What else could he do, given everything that's happened to him?"

Marcus was surprised to find her so sympathetic, but then again, she wasn't the one Carl had been ripping into.

"I mean, why are you being so hard on Carl, Marcus?" she continued. "After all, he's—"

Marcus cut her off, quivering with rancor. "After all he's what? I can't think of anyone on Earth who has disappointed me more than Carl; surely you can understand that."

"Okay, but he—"

"I took him under my wing, allowed him to set up Department Q at a time when he didn't exactly have a lot of cheerleaders here. There is nobody I trusted more than Carl, and that was stupid of me. I've known about the Dutch investigation and their suspicions about Carl for several years now, and I've always defended him. But since we found that suitcase in his attic, a lot has come to light that suggests he might not be as innocent as we supposed. Given how much evidence is pointing to Carl, is it really so strange that I feel like he's let me down, Bente? He's broken something in me, you see. He's not getting *my* sympathy."

He hesitated for a moment, then fixed her with a piercing look. "I remember clearly how devastated *you* were when Anker Høyer turned out to be a criminal scumbag of the worst kind, Bente."

Marcus tried to keep his voice calm. "It was your turn to be disappointed then. But you learned the hard way that you can't have a romance with guys like Anker, and that's a bit like how I feel about Carl today, all right?"

Bente Hansen was staring clean through him. He'd obviously hit a bull's-eye. Good. Maybe she'd fall into line.

The door creaked, and the other team leaders began to shuffle into Marcus's office. For a couple of the newbies, it was the first time they'd been summoned to a joint meeting there. During COVID they'd gotten used to meetings of the Major Crimes division taking place in the cafeteria.

Last in was Terje Ploug. Full house.

"I believe we've all seen that drivel from Carl Mørck on TV, is that correct?"

There was a general mumble of assent.

"None of you—" As he looked around the group, he noticed a face missing after all and pressed the intercom to speak to his secretary. "Lis, can you get Rose Knudsen up here, please!"

He turned back to the group and went on. "None of you have been involved in Carl Mørck's case, but please let me know if I'm mistaken." Nobody reacted.

"This is a Police Complaints Authority case, and obviously we've respected that, but an hour ago I was informed that their lead detective, Noah Rommel, passed away early this morning."

A murmur rippled through the office, and then there was utter silence. "You can't be serious!" someone shouted. Terje Ploug looked flabbergasted, shaking his head.

They began to pepper him with questions about the cause of death, and Marcus could understand why. That case had a bit too much going on at the moment.

"No, it has nothing to do with Mørck's case, thank god. Noah has been ill for a long time, but nobody outside his family realized how aggressive his cancer was. His loss has come as a shock to most of his colleagues, and we can assume their investigation will now be delayed. Noah's right-hand man, Senior Detective Laust Smedegaard, will be appointed as his temporary replacement, and at some point over the next few days we'll be getting an update from him."

Marcus's gaze swept across the room. Only the old-timers seemed genuinely saddened.

"Yes, it's a real tragedy. Noah was a relatively young man; it must be very difficult for his family." He nodded to himself. Where the bloody hell had Rose gotten to?

"And now for the other reason I called this meeting. Carl Mørck has just been given a free hand to act as he pleases. His objective seems to be to compromise the police because of the way he believes he's been treated. This is mainly directed at me personally, of course, and I'll just have to live with that, but I won't have him whipping up public opinion against his former colleagues and trying to garner all the sympathy for himself."

Marcus glanced over at the door, where Rose Knudsen was finally walking in and looking around.

He gave her a nod. "Rose, I've just informed your colleagues that Noah Rommel has passed away."

She nodded, but otherwise her face was expressionless.

"Perhaps you already knew that, Rose?"

She nodded again.

"This video of Carl, the one now in the possession of various television channels. It came from an IP address traced back to our division. But perhaps you knew that too?"

She nodded again.

"And you're nodding because you're the one who sent it, aren't you?"

The coward shook her head.

"Shall I bring Gordon up here too?" he asked.

She shrugged.

"You have nothing to say on the matter?"

She pushed herself away from the wall. "I've just had some evidence delivered. I didn't ask where it came from or who it's for. But I know it was gathered from the getaway vehicle used by the men who launched the attack on Slagelse Remand Center."

"Evidence? What sort of evidence, if I may ask?" said Marcus.

"We have the passport belonging to one of the perpetrators, a Dutch passport. There are also receipts for a charter flight out of Roskilde Airport to Billund, guns of various calibers, several electronic devices including surveillance cameras and transmitters, a satellite phone. Bit of everything. All with plenty of interesting fingerprints, I'm sure. Anything we could use, Marcus, or shall I send it straight to the PCA in Aarhus first?"

Marcus needed a moment to take it all in. This was crazy—and there was a spreading unease in the room. There wasn't a single team leader who wouldn't give their eyeteeth to get their hands on that material.

"Maybe it could lead us to the people behind this, Marcus?" said Terje Ploug.

"Maybe." Then his expression changed. His eyebrows relaxed, and he tried to look genial, so that people wouldn't instinctively duck his next question. "Does anybody in here know where Mørck is staying now?"

Nobody answered, but several people shrugged.

He turned to one of his next-in-command. "How about you, Terje?" The insinuation was so obvious that Ploug's head jerked, which to Marcus meant he definitely knew something. "You've been involved in several cases peripheral to Carl's lately, so perhaps that's given you an insight into the overall situation that the rest of us don't have. The investigation into the death of Christian Mandrup, for example—how is that going? Forensics say it would have taken two men to hang him. Were they the same two responsible for the attack on Slagelse? Hm, I can see you don't know, and how could you? But it's possible that forensics might find some DNA or something else that might link the two cases."

Ploug stopped him short. "I don't know what you're insinuating, Marcus, but I can tell you I have no idea where Carl is right now."

"I hear what you're saying, Terje," he said, turning to the others. "Anybody else in the room have any suggestions as to Carl Mørck's current whereabouts? We've been trying to contact Assad, but oddly he's not at home or at the station. We know he was in Slagelse in pursuit of the hit men and that his car was blown up. We know that one hit man was killed, that both the second man and Assad are missing, and that funnily enough, Carl showed up right around the same time and has now also disappeared. Was Carl set free? Did Assad help him escape? Or is he a hostage who needs our help? His phone is switched off, as is Hardy Henningsen's, whose location we also do not know. We've alerted hospitals, hotels, and various other accommodation options. Mørck seems to have vanished off the face of the earth."

"Could he be at his previous office at the old station building?" someone suggested. "Does he have family in Zealand? Didn't he say something about his parents being from Jutland? Maybe he's already there; it's possible, even in that time frame," someone else piped up.

For the next few minutes they batted suggestions to and fro as to Carl's possible whereabouts, but Marcus dismissed them every time.

"It's unfortunate," he said. "We'll have to see what the next twenty-four hours bring and what damage Mørck might cause in the meantime. Nobody but me is allowed to speak to the press, and for the time being my lips are tightly sealed."

He turned to Rose. "I'm sorry about this, but while you've been here, I've issued instructions that your desktop and laptop—and Assad's and Gordon's—be taken for closer examination. We'll be checking who you've been communicating with. Department Q is now shut down in its entirety, so both you and Gordon can go home as soon as you've handed over the evidence you mentioned to me."

Rose said nothing, but if looks could kill, her boss would have been dead on the spot. Several volumes of *Karnov's Legislation and Statutes* thudded to the carpet as she slammed the door behind her.

Marcus looked at each of his team leaders in turn. "Who should I ask to examine the material that has been brought in?"

Several hands went up.

"No, not you, Terje. Hansen's offering too. I can't think of anybody better suited to the task, can you?"

Nobody, of course, could possibly object.

63

ROSE / MERETE

Friday, January 8, 2021

"**They'll be coming** for the evidence any minute, Gordon. Marcus just sent us home, so we've got to get a move on. Did you tap the satellite phone's data and transfer it all to Merete?" asked Rose.

Gordon's laptop was open in front of him, Carl's frozen face onscreen, appealing to the Danish public to believe in his innocence.

"Yep. And since we received the material, I've deleted any trace of communication between you and me and Merete, Hardy, Mona, Assad, and Kenneth. They might be able to reconstruct it, but it'll take time. What about your laptop?"

"I took it home yesterday. It's at my neighbor's house."

"And your desktop?"

"Haven't used it. Yours?"

Gordon smiled. "Only archival material, no communication files."

"Copies of Gustaaf Mulder's passport and photos of all the items?"

"Also sent to Merete, plus I've got an extra copy of the passport." Gordon patted his zipper. Nobody would look there, even if they did decide to search them.

"Did you contact Roskilde Airport?"

"Yeah. No sign of any Dutchman—yesterday or today."

"So we have a killer on the loose and we have no idea who he is. Why are we assuming he's also Dutch?" asked Rose.

"Are we? I'm not assuming anything."

"I can hear them—they're coming. Are you ready, Gordon?"

Bente Hansen was her usual smiling self. "I really am sorry about this, Rose and Gordon. Marcus hasn't gone about this the right way at all. I don't know what's up with him, but he's changed a lot since Carl's arrest." She nodded to a couple of her team members, who were standing beside her. "You take the electronics to forensics. I'll be there in a minute." She moved closer to the desk, where the gun and other paraphernalia from the attackers' car were spread out to give an overview.

"When did this all come in?" she asked.

"It arrived this morning. Gordon received a call to say a taxi was waiting outside with some bags for him," Rose said.

"Do you have the bags?"

Gordon pointed at them. Ordinary nylon gym bags, the type you could get anywhere.

"And it's all here?" asked Hansen.

Gordon nodded. "Yes, everything brought in the taxi. The first thing I did was to note down the taxi's number, and once I'd unpacked the bags I made a list of the items inside. I was wearing gloves, of course, in case you were wondering."

Bente Hansen smiled broadly. "Nobody would ever wonder about you sticking to procedure, Gordon." She drew a pair of plastic gloves from her inside pocket and packed everything back into the bags. "Enjoy your days off, you two. No more getting up early and heading out into the cold."

She left them alone, and for thirty seconds they stood stock-still without a word.

"Did you really get the taxi's registration number, Gordon?" said Rose, breaking the silence. "She can trace that."

"Don't worry. I asked him where he got the packages, and he said he was given them by somebody who flagged him down on the street."

"You're saying he drove two bags and no passengers? They're not allowed to do that."

"No, but the person gave him some long story about how it was important evidence that needed to be delivered to the police, so he wasn't suspicious. Plus I'm sure he got a decent tip. Might have made his day, actually. Not easy being a taxi driver nowadays."

"They might still trace it back to Assad."

"I don't think so, because he wasn't the one who dropped the bags off. It was Hardy's carer, and he flagged down the taxi a long way from Minna's house. Hansen's team won't glean much from checking it out. Anyway, it's Bente, so how bad can it be? Anyway, what now?"

Rose smiled. "What now indeed. Now we quietly sneak off on our own. I'll go home and make some beef hash and await further instructions from Merete. How about you?"

Rose could tell he was angling for an invitation for beef hash and whatever might be served for dessert, but those days were long gone for Rose. She had other fish to fry.

• • •

For a makeshift office, Merete Lynggaard's command center in the flat on Ahlmanns Allé in Hellerup was pretty lavishly kitted out and staffed. Apart from Kenneth, all her employees had been brought on site. Two whose sole job it was to dig into the past, two who were data experts, and two who had been keeping tabs on the movements and activities of Jess Larsen, Niels B Marquis de Bourbon, Peter "Loudmouth" Joensen, "the Sniffer Dog" Leif Lassen, and the late Christian Mandrup and Hannes Theis. There was also a member of staff responsible for communication with the now deceased Paul Manon as well as Hardy Henningsen's carer and another who sorted out weapons, materials, and transfers of money, including to Malthe Bøgegård; then, of course, there was Merete Lynggaard herself, who was in daily contact with Terje Ploug, Hardy, Mona, Rose, and—until the attack—Kenneth, who was now undergoing emergency treatment at the Rigshospital. His windpipe and esophagus had both been perforated, and it was unclear whether he would ever regain normal function, assuming he survived at all.

"The satellite phone data is our first priority," she instructed the techs. "We need to check every number, going as far back as we can. I think it's safe to assume it won't be easy, but it might be a way to reach the person or people who ordered the attack on Slagelse."

"Seems like it's been in use for more than five years," said one of the techs. "But we'll check the most recent data first, of course."

Merete gave him a thumbs-up.

"We can tell from the stamps in his passport that the owner traveled a lot. That might be why he had a satellite phone, because you can use it pretty much anywhere. We should concentrate on communication just prior to the attack as well as in the hour following. Hopefully we'll get some sort of answer." She turned to another couple of employees. "Here's his passport photo. Pretty decent-looking guy, really. Very fair hair, ruddy cheeks. Bastards like that shouldn't be allowed freckles." She grinned and held up the printouts of Gordon's copies. "The man's name is Gustaaf Mulder, and if the passport is genuine, then we also have his date and place of birth, plus a lot of stamps that show activity in Europe and South America. Anyway, have at it, gentlemen. If we can use this information to find his partner, the one who got away from Carl and Assad, then we'll have struck gold."

They nodded. "We've spoken to the drone operator who was flying it in pursuit of the hit man running across the field. It got too close to him, and he shot it down. Guy vanished without a trace."

A couple of the heavier firearms lay on a table by themselves: those particular items had not been handed over to Bente Hansen. Every weapon of that caliber had its own history. Who had produced them and when? How had they come into the attackers' possession? One of the historians was dealing with those questions.

They laid out Gordon's photographs of the other items from the get-away car on Merete's desk. There were close-ups of serial numbers, wider shots of shapes and designs. All told, plenty of information to process and trace. Maybe they could track down the seller or the buyer of just one of the objects—it was certainly worth a try.

"Hmmm." Merete's eyes wandered pensively over the images. "I'm getting the general impression that this whole thing has been bumped up a league. I'm sure there are local foot soldiers involved, but this tells me there's an international organization at work here, and a particularly ruthless and nasty one at that. It's not our job to solve the case; we'll have to leave that to the police. Our job is to find and stop the people behind all this from hurting Carl, and I'm talking about the ones at the very top, the ones giving the orders. The satellite phone is our best bet, I reckon, but let's also try scouring the internet to see if any of the parties involved have been communicating with contacts abroad, particularly in Holland, and see where that leads. There was a missing policeman from Rotterdam that Gordon mentioned. Might be worth finding his online footprint?"

Then Merete paused, thanked them, and turned to Rose, who had just walked through the door.

"Nicely done, Rose. Were you followed, do you think?"

"Part of the way, maybe."

"What about Gordon?"

"I think he went straight to bed. He didn't get much sleep last night."

"And Carl?"

"He and Assad are still pretty shaken up. There was another blow this morning when one more of the prisoners injured in the attack was reported dead. It's been tough for Carl and Hardy to stay indoors, he says."

Merete was similarly upset by the news. This was her screwup too. Worst of all, her go-between Paul Manon had been killed.

"Right, well. We're all waiting for answers from that satellite phone. We know one of the attackers was at one end of the line, but who was at the other? You lot and Hansen's team are both digging into the data, so we're hoping one of you will be successful."

Merete held up crossed fingers.

Rose returned the gesture. "Jacobsen called us in for a meeting today, and I have a hunch he knows more about our activities than we realize."

"I've been thinking the same thing. He went to see Kenneth yester-day, but the poor lad's still in a coma, so he didn't learn much."

Rose was quiet, glancing around the room. Nine dedicated, talented people who would fight in Carl's corner till the very end.

If only he could see it.

64

GORDON

Friday, January 8, 2021

It was a sudden impulse that made Gordon pull over just before Vigerslev Allé. If he drove straight to Vesterbro, he knew he'd be in for an exceptionally tedious evening. Pizza from Istedgade, streaming some show on TV—what was the point? He wasn't even hungry. And he sensed too that if he stopped pushing now, the still-fresh memory of Sisle Park's torture would come flooding back. He'd worked hard all night, been a faithful helper to Rose and ultimately to Carl. Was he really going to stop this close to the finish line, while he still had energy left?

Gordon's eyes wandered across the railway bridge and leftward along Vigerslev Allé, where Vestre Prison was situated a little farther down.

He leaned back his head and thought. There were two people behind those walls who had made life difficult for Carl Mørck. One was the prison guard Peter "Loudmouth" Joensen, a lackey in the service of the people trying to kill Carl. The other was Jess Larsen, Hannes Theis's driver, now charged with the vehicular homicide of Carl's first lawyer, Adam Bang, and suspected of his employer's murder. Peter Loudmouth had been cooperative but not stupid enough to reveal who had bribed him, and now he was banged up in his former place of work. Larsen, on the other hand, had been utterly obstructive since Mandrup had advised him to remain silent. Larsen and Loudmouth both needed outside help if they didn't want to end up in an even bigger mess than they already were. Bribery, conspiracy to attempted homicide, not to mention outright murder. But what could he do to get Loudmouth and Larsen talking?

Gordon looked at his watch, took a deep breath, and called Molise Sjögren.

She listened to him patiently. Declared that she would be happy to help him if she could, but since she hadn't been appointed as legal counsel for either man, she had no access to them.

"Who could give you access?" he asked naïvely. "Jess Larsen doesn't have a lawyer anymore, although I'm not sure if he's even aware of that."

"I could find out if he has a new one, I think. It's not entirely the done thing, but just hang on ten minutes, could you?"

Ten minutes? He smiled, gazing at the traffic shunting down Enghavevej. This was more exciting than slumping in front of the TV with his feet on the coffee table.

It was an hour before she called back, waking Gordon with a start and jerking his head up off the wheel.

"I've spoken to Terje Ploug, Gordon. He's on his way to Vestre now. He had a meeting with Larsen set up already, and I'm pretty sure you can sit in."

Jess Larsen didn't seem especially thrilled to see Ploug, who had been continuing to pester him, but the sight of Gordon's bleary eyes almost prompted a laugh.

"You don't need to say anything, Jess," Ploug began. "You've refused a new lawyer to replace Christian Mandrup, is that correct?"

No reaction from the man, and Ploug sighed loudly.

"Well, maybe you'll loosen up a bit once you hear what this guy has to tell you." He nodded at Gordon.

He seems pretty down-to-earth. I should probably try to be a bit chummy, thought Gordon, attempting a smile he couldn't quite pull off. "Hey there, Jess. My name's Gordon Taylor, and I'm a detective with Department Q, working for Carl Mørck."

The man flinched slightly.

"I know I look like death warmed up, but that's because I've been working night and day to find out who's at the bottom of all this. To find the people you and Carl must be terrified of. They're a pretty hard lot. Might explode with rage at any moment and kill everybody they no longer trust or need."

He was laying it on a bit thick, perhaps, but at least the guy was making eye contact.

"Christian Mandrup thought he could walk on water, thought he was on a level playing field with them, but he was wrong there. He was a loyal soldier and he set a lot of things in motion that did tremendous damage to a lot of people. But Mandrup couldn't walk on water. He couldn't even stand on the floor when they strung him up with a noose around his neck and watched him die a slow, ugly death."

Gordon paused for effect. What the hell was wrong with this guy—he hadn't so much as batted an eye. Did he already know? Perhaps it was time to twist the thumbscrews.

"You're not safe in here, you know that, Jess? Look around you! How many of your fellow prisoners do you think would shank you to death on the spot in exchange for a fortune deposited into their family's account? Carl came very close to being murdered in here twice, and another two times at the remand center in Slagelse. Did you hear about that? It was attacked with an anti-tank missile."

Still no reaction. "You must have done. All of Denmark heard about that. And now, a day later, four inmates are in coffins because of it. They don't show mercy, the people who ordered the attack. You know that, don't you?"

This time Jess seemed curious to hear more. The rapid swallowing and blinking were always a dead giveaway.

"I'll level with you, Jess. Nobody on my side of the law knows what you've done, so they've just gone ahead and charged you. But I actually think you might be innocent. You might be clamming up simply because you're too scared to say anything, and maybe you know too much about the crimes on other people's consciences."

Gordon leaned forward, placing his hands on Jess's, but the man obviously wasn't happy, so he drew them back.

"I'm going to tell you how you can get out of this pickle, Jess. We just need to minimize your culpability, okay? You can't be convicted for silence, of course. But for not saying who asked you to drive that company car to the carpark behind Vestre Prison the day Adam Bang was killed—for that, maybe. And maybe also for keeping quiet about who killed Hannes Theis with a hammer and how they made you look like the guilty one. All of that will cost you, obviously, if you don't help us take down the real culprits."

Gordon leaned back and slid a hand into the waistband of his trousers. The photocopy was a little crumpled when he held it out in front of Jess Larsen, but Gustaaf Mulder's face was clear enough.

Jess's expression didn't change, but his pupils constricted, as though he was being dazzled.

"Was this the man who killed Hannes Theis? The one who ran down Adam Bang? Do you recognize him?" asked Gordon coldly.

Larsen's eyes darted briefly to one side, but when he looked back at Gordon his expression was the same as before.

Then Gordon reached again for the man's hands. "Look me in the eyes. I genuinely believe the charges against you are false."

Larsen dropped his gaze to the floor. His mind was clearly racing.

Gordon turned to Ploug. "I get what you were saying now, Terje. Jess here is a tough nut to crack, but why would he rather risk his life behind bars instead of helping us? I'll tell you. It's because he's convinced that the minute he opens his mouth, he's lost his chance of any help from us. Isn't that right, Jess? But I promise we'll look after you if you answer our questions, and that it will help you when this comes to trial."

Jess lifted his head and looked straight into Gordon's eyes. "I didn't do what they're accusing me of," he said curtly.

Terje jerked forward in his chair. "Thank you for talking, Jess. Now we'll have to see about getting you out of here. I'll arrange it tomorrow, okay?"

Larsen nodded and then again fell silent.

65

ROSE

Friday, January 8, 2021

Rose felt pretty comfortable with Merete's team. Partly because it contained quite a few good-looking men and partly because the dynamic in the room was infectious, and she forgot her weariness.

She sat listening as the four techs and data experts going through the satellite phone data cursed and swore. The Iridium 9575 Extreme was not a brand-new phone, apparently, but it seemed to be a make and model the techs respected, because it was the system that had the best coverage in the world, linking to sixty-six satellites, and because this model in particular had so many options.

But within mere seconds they realized that although the phone had GPS, they couldn't trace where it had called from because the owners hadn't activated that function. Still, they were able to establish after a few minutes that the phone wasn't rented, and they also found the original operator, which had an American number. It was possible, in theory, to get a lot of information out of these operators about which satellites had been used and how, including who had bought the phone. But that sort of thing took time, and Merete's four experts weren't willing to wait.

"Listen," said one of them, addressing the room. "The phone was set up to only store the call history on the prepaid card, but we should be able to use the card's data to trace old conversations, assuming they weren't deleted along the way. We're hoping the attackers didn't have time during those last hours on the day in question to delete any conversations between them and the people who ordered the hit. So we're working on that. There were also prints on it, and Gordon made sure we got good photos. So we're wondering if it makes sense to check whether there are any good matches on the register in Denmark, despite our assumption that both men were Dutch?"

Pretty much everybody thought it was a good idea. What harm could it do?

The guys turned to Rose. "Can you handle that? Since you're with the police," asked one of them.

Rose nodded. Should be trivial for Terje Ploug.

"What about the hit man who escaped from Slagelse? What do you reckon, Merete, should we be worried about him?" asked one of the men.

"I think he's most likely gone to ground, wherever it is he comes from. Assad has given us quite a precise description of the man, because he saw his face close up in the getaway car. And according to Assad, like Gustaaf Mulder, he's a good-looking guy. Pronounced dimples in both cheeks; blue eyes with dark circles underneath; thick, well-groomed hair; and a narrow, almost invisible mustache. Seeing him run across the field, Assad estimated he was closer to six foot three than six foot. So you can keep an eye out in case he shows up around here."

"Who knows that we're working on the case?" asked one of the experts.

"Only the people in this room, as well as Hardy and Ploug."

"Still, shouldn't we assume we might end up being targeted as well?" the man went on.

"Well, then just don't tell anybody, all right?" She smiled and took out her mobile again. *It's Terje Ploug,* she mouthed noiselessly.

A couple of minutes passed, and afterward she clapped her hands to get their attention.

"Ploug just told me Gordon Taylor has got Larsen talking. Ploug is working to have him transferred out of Vestre Prison, because that's the deal, if Larsen spills everything he knows about the crimes he's been accused of."

There was a spontaneous burst of applause from the two techs who had been digging into Jess Larsen's case. Rose was proud of her partner, of course, but also surprised. Hadn't Gordon driven home after Jacobsen dismissed them?

"They'll be taking extra good care of Jess Larsen, Ploug will see to that, so you can take a break from working on him," continued Lynggaard. "Any news on the others?"

They nodded. "We're currently looking into how the head of narcotics, Leif Lassen—the one they call the Sniffer Dog—was able to find twelve million kroner for a luxury villa in Snekkersten. There's probably a legitimate explanation, but we're checking."

"Some of us have also gathered evidence that Peter 'Loudmouth' Joensen has received significant sums of money over the past couple of years, well above his salary as a corrections officer. We believe the bribes can be traced back to high-ranking members of the organization."

Merete smiled. "That sounds promising. Tie up the loose ends and send what you've got to Ploug."

Sometimes, when the brain was overloaded with information, it stopped bothering to sort it and instead chucked everything into a grab bag of loose fragments that, with any luck, reorganized themselves into new configurations and occasionally produced a great leap forward. It was just such a moment Rose was waiting for, because as things stood, she had entirely lost track of all the various intersecting strands of Carl's case.

The talk about the organization, however, had the effect of organizing her thoughts somewhat, focusing her attention on who might want to make sure Carl didn't get the chance to see his case through to the end alive.

The fundamental thing was that Rose believed in Carl's innocence. She had often found herself annoyed by his occasionally excessive sense of honor, and besides, the man was so uninterested in material goods that he sometimes turned his socks all the way around his foot if the hole in his heel was starting to bother him. It was simply too much of a stretch to imagine that he would abandon his ideals for a life of crime and ill-gotten gains.

Carl's weakness in this case was that he'd realized too late it might do him real damage. But why—surely that was odd? He was one of the most brilliant case-breakers she had ever met, capable of thinking both abstractly and rationally. So why was he so out of his depth now? Rose knew, of course, that there were huge gaps in his memory around the time when Hardy and Anker had been gunned down in Amager. But was it like a childhood language, lost when the child moves to another country? How could they nudge him back into the headspace where his lost memories lay dormant?

It was here that the jumble in her brain kicked in, an automatic process that dislodged a thought that had never occurred to her before.

What if the explanation for his defective memory was that there was nothing there to remember? That his trauma—on top of the shame he felt for not protecting Anker and Hardy—came from trying to force a memory to resurface when it had never actually been there in the first place?

Rose's jaw dropped. If Carl had been genuinely convinced Anker was his best, most loyal friend, even though in reality he was to blame for all the terrible things that had happened to him, then there was no gap. Perhaps it had simply never occurred to him.

Vaguely, Rose sensed that the activity around her had increased and that the voices were growing louder, but she was still following her train of thought.

She and Hardy had always believed Anker was the bad guy, the driving force. But what if there'd been someone else as well, even then? Another friend who in reality was Carl's worst enemy? If so, who could it be?

And did this "friend" think Carl knew more than was good for him?

66

CARL

Friday, January 8, 2021

Carl was on edge. It felt like being back in prison, although this cell was much larger and significantly more comfortable. He knew, of course, that if his broken ribs and lacerations didn't heal, then he wouldn't last very long outside, at least not when the police were searching for him so assiduously. But when had something like that ever stopped him before?

He gazed longingly out into the gray winter. It was probably the first time in his life he'd ever felt lured by such dreary weather. Outside was freedom.

"I know what you're thinking, Carl. Drop it," said Assad, although he too was looking like a caged predator.

"Well, perhaps I've got something that will cheer you up a bit," said Hardy, stomping heavily into the room and placing a photograph on the table.

"*Ya walad*, you're kidding me!" Assad's eyes were glued to the image.

Hardy grinned. "Yup. Bright-eyed and bushy-tailed. That was when Marcus was an inspector, and we were his puppies. See, that's Bente, the youngest of us. She was quite a stunner."

Carl nodded. Nobody had been able to resist her, it was true. But he'd been more drawn to Anker, with his wide grin. Always the charmer. How strange it was to think of all that had happened since.

"Mostly I think of Lars Bjørn," said Assad.

Both Carl and Hardy nodded. It had been a terrible blow for Assad when he died.

"I don't know those two," Assad went on, "but look at you, the Three Musketeers. You were so skinny, I barely recognize you."

"And that's coming from *you*, Assad!" Hardy laughed. "But we were a good team, and we stuck together as a team, while other people ended up elsewhere. Man, those were good times. And you, Carl, you were the glue who kept us together."

"Nothing's changed, then," Assad said, looking at Carl. He was fidgeting in his chair—it looked like he had something up his sleeve. "Now it's my turn to show you something," he said.

While he went into the hall, Carl chewed over his words. Right now he didn't feel like he was holding much of anything together. The question was whether he ever would again.

"Look," said Assad, coming back into the front room. He held out a small, faded, tattered book to Carl. *Haiti: A Travel Diary*, read the cover.

Carl sniffed at it. Smelled like machine oil.

"Take a look at the author's name," said Assad.

Carl flipped to the title page.

"Pete Boswell!" He turned to the back of the book, where there was a picture of the author: a very young Rasmus Bruhn.

"Well, look at that! So he became a travel writer," Hardy said.

"Yeah. And check out where the bookmark is," said Assad, as Hardy leafed through.

"Holy shit." Carl stared at the image. Two smiling, raffishly dressed young men standing shoulder to shoulder, posing on an exotic shopping street. *Pete and Gérard*, read the caption.

"Okay, so that's probably how it started for Rasmus Bruhn," said Hardy quietly. "A young, wild, overconfident young man who thought he was immortal, who wanted to experience the world, write about it. Maybe do a bit of smuggling, like everybody else."

"Bruhn found a kindred spirit in Haiti, then Gaillard traveled with him back to Denmark, where he lived. They started smuggling drugs, then they were hooked." Carl shook his head. It had begun so innocently and ended in murder and death. Gérard dismembered and stuffed into a crate, identified by an anonymous tipster as "Pete Boswell." A warning to Rasmus Bruhn, the "real" Pete Boswell.

"Where on earth did you dig that up, Assad?" asked Hardy.

Assad glanced toward the kitchen. Was he smelling coffee too? "I got it from Niels B. He'd got it from Nick, one of the mechanics in Sorø. He used to shoot up and get high with the two of them in the workshop sometimes. He slept on their sofa and witnessed a lot of shit. He told the story very vividly."

Assad tried to imitate his refined way of speaking but gave up, chuckling, after the first sentence.

"The second mechanic, Jake, had a second cousin by the name of Rasmus Bruhn," he said, nodding in acknowledgment when Carl's and Hardy's jaws began to drop.

"Yep, you heard that right. Jake and Nick used their garage as a transit point in Bruhn's drug trade. Everything was hunky-dory until one day they were ordered to a nearby rest stop to pick up a new shipment. And then Niels B got all serious when he told me the next part.

"'They found the courier dead as a doornail in the car, and the dope and all the drugs were gone,' he told me. 'Bruhn was livid, of course, and accused the two of them and me of having stolen the shipment.'

"'Were you anywhere in the vicinity, Niels?' I asked him.

"'No I fucking wasn't. Bruhn was just petrified the organization would blame him for the theft. So he lied to the boss in Copenhagen and said the delivery was just delayed, while he tried to track down the missing shipment. The atmosphere was pretty hysterical.'

"And this is where I could tell the story was about to get interesting."

"I've got to interrupt you there, Assad. The two mechanics, were they the ones who shot us?" Hardy asked.

Assad nodded silently.

Hardy gripped Carl's chair to support himself. Both of their faces were very dark. "But why? What happened? Give us the short version!"

"Short?! I'll try. Christian Mandrup had ordered them to come in for a meeting with the boss, which was due to take place at a specified time in the shed in Amager at Jake's uncle's place, Georg Madsen's. He was their nearest contact person. The meeting was supposedly about Bruhn's strange behavior."

Hardy sighed. That goddamn perfume-drenched lawyer again.

"By the time they arrived they were high as kites, trying to psych themselves up for it, and Nick had pinched a gun from Rasmus without his knowing. Not to put too fine a point on it, they were shitting themselves about that meeting."

"Is that when they found Jake's uncle with a nail in his skull?" asked Carl.

"Yeah, it completely—" Assad rolled the next word around in his mouth. Clearly it wasn't one he used a lot. "It completely freaked them out. They had no idea what to do, so they just waited for the boss, whom they'd never met."

"And then we came along!" Hardy sighed.

"Exactly! You showed up outside in your white coveralls, and they knew they were fucked."

"They hid in the little kitchen, didn't they?" Hardy asked.

Assad nodded. "They saw Anker go up and give the neighbor a reassuring pat on the arm while you two went into the house."

"Which one of them shot us when we were inside?" asked Carl.

"According to Niels B, it was Nick who jumped out and mowed you down, amped up on speed."

"Then they took off!" Carl put his arms behind his neck and took a few deep breaths. He would never, ever forget those seconds.

"So it was two fucking junkies who ruined my life," said Hardy.

Carl reached for his hand, which was on the backrest.

"But they got what was coming to them," said Assad. "Although Bruhn asked them to help find the missing shipment, they got more and more unmanageable. So Bruhn gave them up, and a couple of months later they both ended up with a nail through the skull. Niels B was briefly a suspect in the murders, but he was released shortly afterward. That was what saved him."

"I'm not sure I can take much more of this right now," said Hardy. He sat down in his chair with a thud and stared into space for thirty seconds, before his brows knitted and he gazed questioningly at Assad. "All right, spit it out, if there's anything left to tell."

Assad cleared his throat. Was he thirsty? The smell of coffee was getting harder to ignore.

"Well, Gordon checked the archives for me yesterday, and he found a report about a dead Dutchman discovered at a rest stop near Sorø on December twenty-ninth, 2006. No sign of foul play, just the wrong dose of a very powerful heart medication."

"Unbelievable. So Niels B has been sitting on that story for fourteen years! But how the hell did you winkle it out of him, Assad?" asked Carl.

"Very simple. I promised not to tell anybody until after he was already in the wind."

"No, you didn't?!" Hardy exclaimed.

"Well, otherwise he wouldn't have said a word, what was I supposed to do? I helped him to erase all trace of himself. So now, the marquis"— he smiled crookedly at the word—"has probably found himself a suitable abandoned castle in France."

"Thanks, Assad." Hardy sighed. His mechanical arms tapped his knees. "Well, we've got one side of the story at last. Guess it was about time. And if we believe it's credible, we'll have to start thinking about how we and Anker fit into it."

Carl nodded, but he had a creeping, sickening feeling. What the hell were they looking at here?

"I remember Anker moving out of his and Elisabeth's place around Christmas 2006. After that he stayed in our guest room, and he wasn't really himself. Bit of a ticking time bomb, I thought." Hardy shook his head a little awkwardly. "One night he came home after some punch-up or other, and his clothes were all smeared with blood . . ."

He broke off, smiling at Minna as she carried in a tray of coffee and cups.

"I think you're misremembering, Hardy," she said, beginning to pour. "I assume you're talking about when Anker borrowed our guest bedroom. But he did that on several occasions, actually, the last time shortly before he died. As I recall, that night with the bloody clothes was a little earlier—right after the summer break in 2005, I think. I clearly remember him going outside and burning his clothes in a metal drum in the garden. The flames nearly touched the leaves of the fruit trees. But I agree with what you said about Christmas the following year. He seemed restless, almost paranoid. And soon after that he moved into a hotel."

Carl eyed Assad as he shoveled sugar into his cup. Anker had done the same thing sometimes too.

"Yeah, Anker moved around a bit," said Carl, "but I've just remembered something that fits with the timeline of the theft. Anker came to me sometime around New Year 2007 and asked me to keep hold of the suitcase. He wanted a fresh start for the New Year, said he was going to find a place of his own. I hadn't thought about it before in relation to the shooting, but it was only a few days after the theft."

Hardy contemplated this. "I think Anker knew the shipment of drugs could be stolen that night, and at that rest stop."

Assad scratched at his stubble. You could almost see the light bulb materializing above his head.

"What are you thinking, Assad?" said Carl.

"Well, is it possible that Anker somehow 'helped' the Dutch courier in the car by giving him this 'wrong dose' and causing cardiac arrest?" he suggested, drawing air quotes with his fingers.

"It's a terrible thing to think, but it's possible, yes." Hardy nodded. "If it's true, then I wonder whether Anker gave Georg Madsen's neighbor something similar the day we were shot? He very conveniently died the same day, which is why there are no interviews with him recorded in the archives. But we could probably find out if he and the motorist had the same cause of death."

Hardy was looking as eager as a bloodhound picking up a scent.

"Do you think something happened that morning that Anker didn't want us two to find out?"

"Yes and no, I don't know," said Carl. "I mean, we've previously considered that the shooting—and particularly Anker's shooting—might have been arranged in advance. In which case I think we can assume Anker wasn't behind it."

"If Niels B's story is correct, then the mechanics were instructed to show up at a particular time," said Hardy. He glanced beseechingly at his carer, who stepped forward and helped him with the coffee.

"Yes, that's right. But bringing a gun was their idea," interjected Assad.

"I can't stop thinking that we were the intended victims," said Carl. "But who set it up?"

"I reckon it was Rasmus Bruhn," replied Assad.

"I'm not so sure about that, Assad," said Hardy as his lips were wiped. "Rasmus Bruhn is dead, and it was the discovery of the stolen drugs two weeks ago that triggered the attacks on Carl."

"I'd say that Anker's behavior, that morning especially, suggests he did know something in advance," said Carl. "We have to assume he was in it up to his neck."

"Of course. But going back to the body in the crate in Amager, is it too far-fetched to imagine that Anker planted his own fingerprints?" asked Hardy. "Then again, perhaps it suggests that whoever planted the evidence might be someone close to both of us. Maybe even someone who's still active. It's not a very pleasant thought."

For a minute or two they were all quiet. Then Carl broke the silence.

"I'm not sure Anker was Machiavellian enough for that. But you've reminded me of an offhand comment he made to me once. He said: *You already know who, Carl!* I just can't remember the context." He absorbed the expectant looks on the other men's faces.

"Then, when Slagelse was bombed, there it was again. First, the feeling that it was because of me all these terrible things were happening, destroying so many other people's lives. Then the sense I could have prevented it, if only I could grab hold of something that deep down I should have known. It's been on my mind for days, but I haven't been able to say it out loud to myself.

"Because I definitely don't like it!"

67

BENTE / ASSAD

Friday, January 8, 2021

Bente Hansen's team was among the most experienced in the Investigation Unit, which meant the cases they were assigned tended to be the more complicated ones. Only Department Q solved more crimes than Bente's team, and her people worked so independently these days that Bente had to issue only general directives, which suited her just fine.

"Any legible data on the satellite phone?" she asked.

"We haven't gotten around to that yet, because we're still trying to trace who bought the various pieces of equipment in the Mercedes. But to be honest I doubt there's a whole lot of data to retrieve, because we think the satellite phone was used solely for criminal purposes, so it was set to only store data on the SIM card. Since it's a prepaid card, we also believe the owner switched it out a lot and that they regularly deleted the call history."

"I'd like to take a quick look at it," she said, "then we can carry on with the other effects tomorrow. We must be able to get something off a couple of them, surely."

She pointed at the two detectives at the back of the room. "It's your turn to do the weekend shift, right?"

They nodded.

"Then I'll say goodnight. I'll stay behind for a while."

After her people had gone, she locked the door and sat down by the tables covered in the items from the car. She picked up Gustaaf Mulder's bloodstained passport and opened it, glanced at the photograph, and shook her head. *Idiot*, she thought.

She scanned the various objects on the tables before examining the satellite phone and the booking for their charter plane. The information on it was minimal, only the departure time, destination, and price. Nothing about who the passengers were or which bank account or credit card had been used to pay for the tickets. *Smart. They paid cash*, she thought. The tickets themselves must have been in the possession of the man who escaped, since they'd not been found on the body or in the gray Mercedes, which had ended up in a ditch a few miles away.

A traffic unit had also found a blue Volvo blasted to pieces, registered to the Kenneth Fisher who was currently in the Trauma Center at the Rigshospital. Logically, this suggested Mørck had stolen it during his escape from the public carpark near to Slagelse Remand Center.

And just where was Carl? Was he still near where he'd left the Mercedes? He must be somewhere indoors, she knew that at least, if he was sitting in a living room and transmitting videos.

Then there was Kenneth Fisher, whom Bente vaguely remembered as a soldier from one of Department Q's past cases. He had been shot in his car in the carpark outside Slagelse, but why had he been there in the first place? From the computer found in his lap it was clear he'd been surveilling the remand center and the fire station pretty closely. But to what end?

Bente opened the window, lit a cigarette, and stared at the glowing end while she tried to piece it all together. Hell of a mess, and it hadn't gotten any easier since she'd lost contact with Eddie Jansen. Now the whole thing had been dumped onto her plate.

Kenneth might have been part of the assassination plot, if he'd had some kind of PTSD-induced grudge against Carl, but he could also have been a sentry, posted to inform or warn Carl about any funny goings-on near his cell. Was he working alone, or had somebody put him up to it? She'd love to know. Maybe the doctors at the hospital would allow her to question him tomorrow, if he was in a fit state for it.

And if not, maybe Carl could give her the answers himself. But where was he?

Bente opened her laptop and watched Carl's video for a few minutes. The background was neutral, probably just a living room wall, but at the top of the screen she could just make out the edges of the original stuccoed border running around the ceiling. Bente recognized it as a style common in luxurious houses from around the nineteenth century or a little later. But where was this stuccoed room?

Gordon had said that an unidentified individual handed over two bags to a taxi driver, whom the police had already been able to contact, since Gordon had had the presence of mind to note his registration number. The Moroccan taxi driver had confirmed everything. He would never normally drive bags without passengers, he insisted, but he'd been given the name of a policeman, Gordon Taylor, who worked at the Investigation Unit at no. 1 Teglholm Allé, so he didn't think he could say no.

Stupid man, thought Bente. The bags could have contained powerful explosives. Stupid too because he had only a vague recollection of what the man who gave them to him looked like. It certainly wasn't Carl Mørck, he'd said, when they showed him a photograph. He was, however, absolutely sure he'd been hailed on Jernbane Allé in Vanløse, because he'd been driving up and down it all day.

Bente took a few drags of her cigarette before tossing it out the window. Mørck had been close to the gray Mercedes. What if he had driven in it, cleared out all the items that now lay in front of her? But then who had he given them to? Had he given instructions for them to be delivered to Department Q? Most probably he had. Did he think turning everything over to the police would exonerate him? Or was it someone else entirely who'd taken them from the Mercedes?

Bente was confused, and she didn't like that. More or less since childhood she had preferred dead certainty, preferred getting her teeth into something and pursuing it to the bitter end.

She picked up the satellite phone, weighing it in her hand. An Iridium 9575 Extreme like this would have cost a fortune. It weighed half a pound, she'd read. Why hadn't the gunmen kept it on them when it was so handy? Pair of idiots.

She opened it, and with a little difficulty she eased out the SIM card and put it in her pocket. Then she leaned over the table of guns and took up a Heckler & Koch pistol almost identical to their own service weapons. Whatever was coming, she had to be ready to give as good as she got.

• • •

"I think you should stay here for a couple of days, Carl," said Assad. "There's too much furo around you right now to risk leaving the house."

"It's furor, Assad, but I get what you mean."

"Does the word have anything to do with 'roar'? Anyway, that way you can get your injuries treated too. Your face still looks terrible," he added emphatically.

"And what are you going to do?"

"I need to think through everything we've talked about. It makes me very sad. And I'd really like to go home to my family and sleep in my own bed." He could have kicked himself at the sight of Carl's miserable face. "Sorry, Carl, I wasn't thinking." He gave him a gentle pat on the arm. "We'll be out of this nightmare before you know it, and you'll be back home with Mona and Lucia."

Carl smiled lopsidedly, but he didn't look like he dared to hope.

After two buses and a train, Assad was standing outside the apartment complex where he lived. Bright yellow windows a few stories above welcomed him in.

He sighed heavily. Carl was now more or less certain it was Bente Hansen who was behind the attempts on his life. It was just so difficult to believe. And what were they going to do about it? There were plenty of hints, but they had no conclusive proof, and they couldn't tell anybody without her finding out. And if they were right, she would rapidly be able to cover her tracks. The only way of catching her would be to lure her into revealing herself. But how? They had agreed to sleep on it before they got anyone else involved.

As he walked toward the main door, a car whizzed by on the street behind him, making him whirl around. No sudden movements were welcome these days. When the car had passed, he glimpsed the grayish outline of a man standing on the path in the park opposite. He narrowed his eyes, preparing for the worst, because there was no doubt the man was keeping watch on him. Had he been standing there in the freezing cold all day, hoping Assad would eventually show up?

Now the man was taking out his phone—or was it a gun? It was hard to tell in the dusk.

Shoving his hand into his pocket, Assad gripped the pistol they had found in Kenneth's car. And when the man opposite didn't move, Assad strode across the street and made directly toward him, as the man hurriedly broke off his conversation.

"Hands up," cried Assad, doing his due diligence—he had no intention of becoming the next victim—but the man spun around and began to run as though he had the devil at his heels. Only then did Assad realize he had seen him before. It was the way he ran. Knees lifted high, long strides on the balls of his feet.

There was no question: it was the man from the field. The man who had stood in the tower and fired a missile at Slagelse Remand Center, the man who had given him the middle finger in the getaway car. And was he also Bente's hired goon? It was mind-boggling.

Assad picked up speed, knowing that if he shot the man in the back it could have serious legal consequences, assuming he even managed to hit him.

But he shot anyway and missed, because the man dodged sideways into the gloom of the trees and disappeared from view.

The shot made dogs bark and electric lights switch on in windows all around him. The police would be there soon, so he'd have to act fast.

Grabbing his phone, he called Merete Lynggaard, who said, "I'll call Ploug right now and send my own people to the area around where you live, Assad. We need to launch a manhunt."

Assad thanked her, then paused for a moment to gaze up at his family's apartment once more.

What did that guy want with me? he wondered. *To kill me? Then why didn't he shoot? I'm not exactly hard to fucking spot.*

Assad ran through the last couple of minutes in his mind. Pictured himself walking toward the apartment, but from the man's point of view. The lampposts were roughly a hundred feet apart, so the man might not have been able to identify him properly until he was standing under the streetlamp opposite the path.

But then why not shoot instead of taking out his phone? he thought, and realized in a flash that the nightmare was far from over.

They wanted him alive so they could track his movements. They wanted him to lead them to Carl.

Assad was under no illusions. If they had to, they'd do it by force.

He smiled for a moment, moving toward the door of his building.

By force?

He'd like to see them try.

68

BENTE

Saturday, January 9, 2021

Friday night had been uneasy and full of interruptions, because today was the day she had to put an end to the current state of affairs. For twenty years, Bente Hansen had avoided suspicion. Her job as a detective had provided a golden opportunity and perfect cover for her side hustle, and by now she had accumulated so much money in Caribbean banks that, in hindsight, she probably should have gotten out of the game at least ten years ago, because by then she already had enough to sustain a life of luxury until the end of her days.

But she also knew it wasn't really about that. It was the thrill she lived for. The thrill, and the ambition that drove her to be the best at everything she did, no matter what it was. In that sense she was already living the perfect life, balanced on the edge of the abyss.

A double life on both sides of the law—two ambitious careers, one in the police and one in the drug trade—had been a near-inexhaustible source of hair-raising suspense, throwing up challenges that demanded bold, lightning-fast decisions. Bente Hansen wasn't fearless, but it was often fear that triggered the biggest endorphin rush when the high-stakes game paid off. Almost from the moment Rasmus Bruhn and his friend Gérard Gaillard had recruited her, she'd hatched the idea of a coup in the ranks, and she pursued this doggedly in the years to come.

Bente had waited patiently for the right moment to strike. Part of the plan had been to build her own team outside of the drug world, and she had singled out two of her slightly older, married colleagues on the force as potential recruits: Anker and Carl.

She had let herself be "tempted" by the company of her two older colleagues but was outwardly careful to maintain the hard-won respect she'd earned from the others. Carl turned out to be a bit too Jutish, his feet a bit too solidly planted on the ground, but Anker took the bait. She got him hooked on coke and made him think she was crazy about him. It turned into a secret affair, which she started to enjoy for its own sake. Her drug of choice was thrills—any and all kinds. She recruited Anker into the drug business and as the secret partner in her planned coup.

At first Anker had approached it almost like a game, and they felt like an undercover Bonnie and Clyde. But after the bosses came down hard on Anker and Bruhn for fighting in public and making fools of themselves, things got serious. That con man Gérard had pulled one con too many, and Anker was ordered to beat him to a pulp in front of Bruhn before Gérard was killed with a nail gun. The incident broke something in Anker, and Bente realized she would have to hedge her bets. Bruhn was tasked with getting rid of the body, and Bente made sure the crate contained compromising material against Anker and Carl before it was buried under the dealer Georg Madsen's shed. That gave her something to fall back on, if things went south. When the crate was found several years later, she also called in an anonymous tip that put Bruhn on the scene at the time.

In the final days of 2006, Bruhn was responsible for a large shipment of drugs and currency from Rotterdam. Bente decided to strike. With Anker's assistance, she played decoy, "intervening" with the transport in the middle of Zealand one cold December night. The coup had succeeded without leaving a trace.

She and Anker agreed to stay away from each other until the dust had settled, and they went their separate ways. Bente packed the loot into a special suitcase, adding in some euros with Anker's and Carl's fingerprints, notes she'd got hold of previously just in case they came in handy. Without Anker's knowledge she put the locked suitcase at the back of his messy locker at the station. Nobody would dream of looking there.

Over the following days they both kept up the façade and their agreement. But gradually paranoia crept in. What if Anker cracked and pinned it all on her? The police she could handle, but she couldn't let the bosses suspect a thing. She decided to move the suitcase but discovered it was gone. Anker had given no sign of even knowing it was there, which further fed her paranoia. Was he plotting a coup of his own? She didn't really believe it, but the idea rankled. The same thing was probably happening to Anker: mutual paranoia.

Still, Bente continued to follow the script, allowing a suitable "delay" to pass before contacting their employers to complain about the undelivered shipment. The theft was discovered, but where in the chain had it occurred? The bosses were furious, more that it could happen at all than because of the lost money and drugs. They demanded punishment, striking and severe.

That same day, a Dutch contract killer with two different-colored eyes appeared in Copenhagen. Suspicion came to rest on Bruhn, but initially he managed to blame it on Georg Madsen's nephew, Jake, although he insisted they couldn't let Jake suspect anything until Bruhn had found out where the stolen shipment had got to.

To set an example for both Nick and Jake, the hit man had shot a nail through the head of Jake's uncle Georg, left the nail gun behind, and gone back home.

When the nail gun crime still hadn't been discovered after ten days, Bente was ordered to get the wheels moving. That night she went to examine Georg Madsen, noticed the stench, and got the lawyer, Mandrup, to call in Jake to meet with her at Uncle Georg's the next day.

In the morning she made an anonymous call to Georg Madsen's new neighbor and complained about the smell. The neighbor had just moved in and said he didn't think the smell was coming from his place, but he'd try to find the source of it outside.

Not long after that, he reported the body to the police, and Bente sent a message to Anker: his team was to go and investigate, and he was to give the neighbor a dose of their "sedative" medication.

Explanation to follow, she promised. It was time they started talking again, and Anker seemed both relieved and uneasy at the same time. Everything would be all right.

Bente's actual plan had been that Anker would arrest the "killer"—Jake—and put the case into the hands of the police, where she could manage the cleanup. But then Jake and his buddy shot Anker's team and took off. It wasn't how Bente had pictured it, because Anker was the only person who knew where the suitcase was, and now of course he was dead.

Their employers, on the other hand, were pleased with the ensuing commotion. It was a message that would be understood by the person in question.

They appointed Bente to run the Danish division by herself from then on, and in particular to make sure that Bruhn found the missing loot and executed the culprits in suitably spectacular fashion. So something came of it after all.

Time passed, and eventually even her double life showed signs of becoming routine. But then, two weeks ago, the missing suitcase turned up in Carl's attic, containing drugs and cash and both Anker's and Carl's prints.

And all hell broke loose.

Bente knew her employers would want revenge, so in order to maintain control of the situation and her position, she devoted all her efforts to compromising and eliminating Carl, although she thought it unlikely he knew anything about the stolen drugs. If she killed him, any doubts as to her loyalty would be erased, and her role in the whole hazardous game would remain unknown.

Yet Carl was still alive, and her employers had sent their top hit men, Gustaaf Mulder and Thom Loos—two killing machines—to Denmark. The very interference she had been trying to avoid. But even they couldn't take Carl out. All they had done was wreak havoc and worsen her situation. Mulder was dead, while Loos had escaped by the skin of his teeth. Fortunately, he had at least contacted her on a Danish phone outside the bosses' network. He couldn't go home or escape liquidation if he didn't complete the mission and kill Carl.

So where could Carl have gone? Bente would love to know that too. Their best bet right now was to wait for Assad to show up, then somehow make him lead them to Carl. Loos had already reported that he'd been spotted and temporarily had to abort the surveillance, so it was clearly not his main skill set. He had no choice but to return to his post, she told him. Meanwhile, she would see what she could find out, and she promised Loos she'd be back in touch shortly.

Bente called the members of her team on the weekend shift and explained that she thought she might have caught COVID again and that they should just keep going through the items received from Gordon Taylor—and call her if they found anything useful.

She stared at the blank sheet of paper on the desk in front of her, then began to write in thick marker pen:

Where is Carl Mørck?

Close to where the bags were handed over in Vanløse?

Somewhere with stucco from the late 1800s?

Does anyone in Department Q know where?

The taxi driver who brought the bags, who did he talk to? Someone close to Carl?

And what don't we know yet?

Will Carl reveal anything onscreen? Does he actually know anything compromising?

Will Jess Larsen talk? Is he a security risk?

Peter "Loudmouth" Joensen—has he made a deal?

She dialed Terje Ploug's number.

"Hey, sorry, Terje, we're still analyzing the equipment from Gordon Taylor. Do you have a minute for some questions?"

Although it was obvious he was at home, and there was a lot of cheery laughter and conversation in the background, his voice was as bright as ever.

"Ask away, Bente. I'm just glad someone's putting in the work this weekend!"

"Thanks! Do you have the number of that taxi driver, the one who was given the bags? I have a few additional questions for him."

"Not a mobile number, because it was a different department that spoke to him. But I have the registration number of the taxi he was driving. I'll send it to you, and you can look it up yourself. Was there anything else?"

Good, she thought. She'd see if her colleagues could get anything else out of it.

"Yeah, I was wondering if Peter Joensen has made any kind of deal? I can see on Pol-Intel that he's been charged and remanded into custody in Vestre."

She noted a tiny pause on the other end.

"We haven't made a deal with him. We're just letting the case take its course," he said.

Right. So Loudmouth wasn't at the top of Ploug's agenda, she thought.

"And what about Jess Larsen?" she went on. "Has he started talking? I know you've been doing your best to crack him."

Again, that hesitation. Bente didn't like it, but that was just how Terje Ploug was sometimes.

"Hmmm. Well, I think we're getting there," he said at last. "It's clear that his lawyer's violent death had an effect on him."

Bente smiled to herself. Ploug was so transparent, the boring old fart. He was probably being cagey because he didn't want to let slip any information that might give her an advantage when it came to finding Marcus's successor.

Which will hopefully be soon, she thought.

At any rate, Jess Larsen wasn't Ploug's top priority, which meant he wasn't hers either.

She thanked him and hung up with a smile. When all this was over, she'd most likely be in Marcus's hot seat. Chief of homicide. Poor, stupid, sensitive Marcus. If he hadn't got his feelings all hurt over what he thought Carl had done, he could have given him ironclad protection. Now the wedge between them had made Marcus pull back, leaving Carl a sitting duck. Leaving him out in the open, where he could be hunted down.

The taxi driver's name was Abdella Alami, and he was precisely what Bente had imagined. Thin, sinewy, dark, and bearded. A not particularly dazzling smile that bared large, lavishly gold-plated front teeth.

Oh yes, he remembered it very well. The man on Jernbane Allé had been pleasant and given him a generous tip—which he would of course be reporting on his tax return. He underscored this point with sloping brows that clearly meant the opposite.

"The man you spoke to, did he say what was in the bags?"

"No, no, we didn't talk about that. They were for the police, so it was none of my business," he replied.

"It didn't occur to you they might contain bombs that could blow up the police station?"

From his wide eyes it was obvious this hadn't crossed his mind. "Haram Allah, no, no!" he exclaimed, gazing entreatingly at Bente. "You don't think I am a bad guy?"

Bente smiled indulgently, not least because of his strong accent.

"Was the man old or young?"

He shrugged. "Not very gray hair, I guess!"

"You called him pleasant. Because of the tip, or what?"

"We understood each other very well, it was nice."

"What do you mean, understood?"

"He spoke French!" The man smiled broadly. "I come from Morocco, so I do too."

Bente paused. "But you also spoke Danish together, right?"

"No, we didn't. He couldn't."

"And you told this to Gordon Taylor when you gave him the bags?"

"No, no, he didn't ask."

"And the police? Did you tell them he spoke French?"

He shrugged, and his eyes drifted vaguely to one side. "Mmm, no, I don't think so. I think I just said we spoke the same language."

"But not that the language was French?"

"I don't think we mentioned that."

She shook her head, thanked him, and said she might be back, if that was all right.

He said yes several times. Probably he didn't dare do otherwise.

69

MONA / MERETE

Saturday, January 9, 2021

The last few days had been devastating for Mona, to such an extent that she had asked for time off work.

Everybody understood, although not much was said about her husband at the station. It was as though all terrible things that had happened had been placed on Carl's shoulders.

Clips of the inmates' grieving relatives were played on TV, blaming Correctional Services for not taking better care of the prisoners' safety. On the other hand, the staff at Slagelse were still in shock, explaining gray-faced how unfair this was and how vulnerable they had been.

It was something that was never supposed to happen.

In the immediate aftermath of the attack, Mona got a call at work from Merete Lynggaard to tell her Carl was missing, which meant there was hope.

She wept, prayed to God, and cast her rage in all directions. It wasn't until she saw Carl's face in the drone footage on TV an hour later that she collapsed.

She'd been waiting for a message from Carl ever since. She had a hunch that more than a few of the people around her knew more about where he was, but nobody would tell her anything. Every once in a while she glanced out the window and was met by a chain reaction of blinding flashbulbs. Several news vans were waiting on the road, as journalists wandered to and fro in down jackets. What the hell did they think they were going to get out of her? She didn't know anything.

When Carl appeared on TV the first time, she tried to hold it together while Lucia pointed at her dad. It was an enormous relief to hear his voice, although he was pale and had deep lacerations on his face. He was obviously somewhere safe.

On Saturday morning, thirty-six hours after the attack, Merete called and told her to turn on the TV. The plan was that Carl would be making another statement. It would probably be no more than twenty minutes before one of the stations picked up his video message—most likely *News* would be first, she thought.

Once more, Mona tried to coax Merete into revealing Carl's whereabouts, but she insisted yet again that she didn't know.

Thank god Lucia was asleep when Carl appeared onscreen.

He was still pale, but he seemed more controlled, and the wounds on his face were scabbing over.

"My name is Carl Mørck, and I am still a free man," he began, explaining that for him freedom meant being able to speak freely. He was appealing for understanding: he couldn't surrender himself to the authorities as long as his life was still in jeopardy.

"Who wants me dead? That's what I've been asking myself. On the one hand, the state is accusing me of some very serious offenses, and on the other, an unknown criminal organization is trying to shut me up. Somebody believes I know something damaging to them. Maybe they're afraid I can identify them. But why would I hold back something that could stop them? All I'd have to do would be to open my mouth. Look into my eyes." He paused for impact. "If I knew what to say to stop these people, I could just do it now. On the other hand, that would confirm the police's suspicion that I've been holding back information all along. Information that would reveal me as a criminal in league with the people trying to kill me. Do you see the paradox here?"

Mona could tell that although he was trying to go on the offensive, he didn't really believe it would work. It was brutal to see her big, strong, upstanding husband looking so disillusioned and lost.

"Anyway, today I'm mainly here to send a special message to a very special person," Carl went on. He leaned closer to the camera.

"Mona," he said, so intimately that it sent a jolt through her body. "I love you, and I miss you. I never stop thinking about you and Lucia, and I want you to know that I'm okay. Happy birthday for tomorrow. I hope we'll be together again soon." Then he blew her a kiss, but as he sent it off with a sweep of his hand, he accidentally bumped the screen, knocking it momentarily away from his face. He pulled it immediately back and smiled broadly. "You'll be hearing from me again soon, love," he finished.

• • •

Most of Merete's staff were glued to the screen.

"He's doing great," one of them said, but Merete wasn't so sure. If there wasn't a breakthrough soon, she was afraid Carl, Rose, and the other two members of Department Q would take matters into their own hands. Was that, she wondered, what Carl's enemies at the central station were hoping would happen?

"There's plenty of data on the satellite phone's SIM card, but so far we can't decode it," said one of the techs. "Do you think you could get Ploug to ask Bente Hansen if her team has made any progress?"

"I'll try," she said. "He's at Vestre Prison right now, with Gordon from Department Q, to see what Larsen has to say. But I'll call him for an update in an hour or two."

"We also checked the fingerprints on the phone, but unfortunately there aren't any matches in Denmark."

Merete had thought as much. They'd have to ask the Dutch, she said. "We suspected Leif Lassen's twelve million kroner might be tangled up in this—do we know any more about that?"

Her expert in the area looked sheepish. "Well, we can see that Lassen has been working hard for years, renovating the houses his family lives in, then flipping them, buying a new one, and renovating that. So the money's all aboveboard. He originally trained as a carpenter before going into the military, then joining the police. So nothing suspicious to report there. We can see he was working as a detective in Viborg during the years this case got started, so chances are the Sniffer Dog is just an ordinary cop."

Merete frowned. "Then what's left to get our teeth into?"

"Not a lot," said one of them. "They released some information on TV about the escaped hit man, so that might get us somewhere. But the composite sketch Assad did with Ploug's team isn't much help, really. I could name at least five tall guys with pencil mustaches and shadows under their blue eyes off the top of my head.

"We just have to hope that Carl Mørck and whoever's hiding him saw the announcement too, and that they're keeping an eye out for someone fitting the description."

"Eddie Jansen's account on the Rotterdam police intranet is still active, even though he's been confirmed dead, so we're monitoring that—discreetly, of course, as usual," said someone else. "But I doubt we'll find many useful clues. We're also checking the dark web, but the chances there are even smaller, so don't get your expectations up too much."

Easier said than done, when they were pretty much at rock bottom.

70

BENTE

Saturday, January 9, 2021

Bente Hansen's appearance at the Rigshospital's Trauma Center did not go down well.

"What made you think we'd let you waltz in and interrogate someone with life-threatening injuries?" asked the doctor on duty.

She apologized repeatedly, saying she knew it wasn't an easy decision but it meant life or death to people besides Kenneth. Perhaps this softened the doctor a little, because he told her rather grudgingly that the patient had woken up that morning in an improved condition and had now been transferred to intensive care. She could try her luck up there. She thanked him and was about to leave when he said brusquely that she'd have a tough time getting anything out of him anyway, because his vocal cords had been so badly damaged by the gunshot.

The hectic, intense atmosphere in the unit was intimately familiar to Bente, so she hung back a little and waited. After a bit of a palaver she was kitted out with a mask and a sterile gown and led past the team outside Kenneth's room, who were monitoring all his vital signs. In the room itself, Kenneth was hooked up to dozens of tubes and electrodes, and bandages were visible covering his whole chest and throat.

His eyes were alert, following her movements like a guard dog from the moment she was ushered through the door until she was standing as close as the nurses would allow.

She introduced herself as a senior detective with the Copenhagen Police and mentioned her close relationship with Department Q and Carl Mørck.

"I've been told you're not able to speak yet, unfortunately. I'm really sorry to hear that. But maybe we can communicate another way," she said, forcing a smile into her eyes.

"I'm working as hard as I can to get Carl's situation sorted out, but I'm also hoping things stabilize a bit in the meantime and that the trial will be scheduled soon."

Kenneth blinked. Did that mean they were on the same wavelength?

"You were surveilling him, and I'm sure you had good reason, but it seems you weren't the only one. I believe you were working with someone who wants and believes the same thing I do, and right now we really need to coordinate our efforts. So I've come here today to ask for your help."

Again the same blink. It felt like a good sign.

"Can you tell me who I should talk to next?"

He lay there for a long time, staring at her. Was he trying to figure out the best way to communicate without words?

Then he grinned, closed his eyes, and turned his head gingerly from side to side on the pillow.

"Does that mean you don't know?"

Again, his head turned on the pillow.

"But you're not going to tell me?"

He opened his eyes, narrowed them, then mouthed something as clearly as the tube down his throat allowed: a resounding NO!

Bente tried to signal disappointment and sadness, but the guy was cool as ice.

Back in her apartment, she sat down and examined her checklist.

Her contract killer was currently wandering around near Assad's block. The news on the TV had just put up a composite sketch of him that made her smile. For one thing, he was hardly six foot three, and for another, the description of his clothing, hair color, and pencil mustache were already history.

The man was skillful, professional, and vigilant. His dimpled cheeks might make him look innocent and harmless, but she knew the man could kill without hesitation, and the murders he committed—whether with nail guns, silenced pistols, or knives—were always quick and discreet. If she couldn't find Mørck herself, then he certainly could, and that would be case closed, even if it did mean the ever-faithful Assad would have to go as well.

She looked again at the screen, watching for a moment as one of the retired detectives from the Mobile Task Force offered his analysis of the best way to catch the killer before they cut to the next feature.

Bente's eyes widened as Mørck began his second TV appearance. She clenched her fists as he explained his situation. He made no direct reference to her, thank god, but when he appealed to unnamed colleagues to come forward if they had noticed any of their fellow officers behaving strangely around his case, she knew there was no mistaking it: he meant her. Was this his final warning? She was supposed to let him be?

She had no intention of doing so, now less than ever. *You're finished, Carl. I'll find you!* she thought. Then Carl switched tracks entirely and began declaring his love for his wife. In his circumstances it felt a little pitiful. He ended by blowing her a kiss, accidentally joggling the screen. In the split second before he turned it back to him, Bente glimpsed something unexpected outside the camera's normal field of view. It was hard to tell exactly what it was, but it looked like a hairdresser's dryer hood or a *Star Wars* costume. White, hard, rounded plastic.

She looked up the same video online—it had already been shared hundreds of times—and fast-forwarded to the point where Carl bumped the screen. She had been hoping for a sharper, less shaky image, but one small detail did catch her eye. Was that a strap?

Bente closed her eyes, trying to recall where she'd seen something similar before. Was it something linked to Carl's network of friends?

Probably not Mona, because then he wouldn't have sent that pathetic message. What about Rose, Gordon, or his old friend Hardy, maybe they . . . ?

Her train of thought ground to a halt, and she sat staring briefly into space. Then she started browsing. *Hardy Henningsen and Carl Mørck*, she typed. First checking Pol-Intel, then Google.

The first hit that popped up on Google was, luckily, the one she'd remembered seeing before. An interview in *Gossip* where Hardy's miraculous transformation from paralysis to mobility was immortalized in both text and images. Bente stared for ages at Hardy's white exoskeleton. She brought up the still from the video, then looked back at the article in *Gossip*.

A rare chill ran up her spine.

Quickly skimming the feature, she reached a phrase that stood out to her as clearly as if it had been printed in letters three feet high: "Hardy Henningsen's Belgian carer." Beside it was a photo of the carer and Hardy.

"Despite the language barrier, communication is possible with only a few words of French," read the caption.

This was the man with the bags in Vanløse, she was certain of it, and he was Hardy's French-speaking carer. Carl had been with Hardy when that video was recorded, but as far as she could remember, he still lived at Carl's old place in Allerød. Did that have stuccoed ceilings? Not likely! That house was modern, all slabs of concrete slapped one on top of another, one among scores of totally identical homes. Which meant Hardy was somewhere else, not where he usually lived.

"It's a good thing you survived that shooting, Hardy," she said aloud to herself. With his help, she was sure she could find out where Carl was hiding.

71

WAYNE

Saturday, January 9, 2021

Wayne Peters hadn't heard from Cees Pauwels in a couple of days, and after their last messages, that didn't surprise him. As instructed, Pauwels had arranged the death of Wilbert de Groot, the detective, and was then going to take a well-deserved holiday with his family.

He'll have a nice few final days at least, thought Wayne. Cees himself was facing imminent execution—it would happen as soon as his contract killer Thom Loos was back from Denmark, having completed his mission there.

But on this particular day, everything was unexpectedly flipped on its head.

As in previous days, he'd been baking cakes for the children running and whooping in his garden. All was peace and serenity in his home when he opened his computer and went to check the news on the Rotterdam police intranet, which he could log in to using Eddie Jansen's access code. Once in a while, having this unauthorized access to information had warned him about something important, but usually there wasn't anything useful to be gleaned. He was just about to log off when he noticed Eddie Jansen's name. The investigation into his death was in full swing. A team had spoken to his wife, Femke Jansen, who had been assaulted by a burglar. They suspected a possible connection between

Eddie's death and this break-in, so they had decided to check Eddie's summer cabin in Bergen aan Zee.

That was the moment Wayne Peters realized a nightmare might be coming his way.

The detectives had found the cabin locked and deserted when they arrived. But when they peered in through the windows, they thought they could see blood on the floor. And since they couldn't get hold of Femke Jansen, Eddie's widow, for permission to enter, they simply let themselves in.

There was a worrying odor inside. Like burned hair and flesh, and in the middle of one of two bloodstains on the floor they found a projectile lodged in the floorboard.

The corpse they found rolled up in a carpet in a bathroom. It was badly burned and had two bullet holes in the torso, the same distance apart as the bloodstains on the floor.

The description of the body was brief, given the burns, but the estimated age and record of the dead man's height and weight were enough for Wayne to feel sure. There was every chance this was Cees Pauwels, and Wayne had no idea how that had happened. He felt rage simmering. But he had to keep a cool head.

The authorities had begun working hard to find Femke Jansen, he read, so the woman was evidently missing, and that wasn't good, considering the information she was almost certainly carrying.

Wayne leaned back and took stock of the last two days. Two people were currently in Vestre Prison, Christian Mandrup was dead, as was Wilbert de Groot, and Niels B and Femke Jansen were missing. As for the two hit men he had sent to Denmark, Gustaaf Mulder was dead and Thom Loos was a wanted man. They had failed to kill Carl Mørck, and now Mørck was at large and uploading video recordings of himself to the internet.

"Chaos" was the right word, if he was going to describe the overall situation in both Denmark and Holland, and Wayne knew better than anybody that if his organization showed the least sign of weakness, there were plenty of others waiting to step into the breach.

He was about to log out of Eddie's account when he realized he wasn't the only one active on it.

It was rare for Wayne to sweat, but at that moment he felt damp patches spreading in both armpits. Did that mean somebody else had had free access to his computer and secret network while he'd been logged on?

He yanked the LAN cable out of the computer and considered his position for a moment. The sense of being compromised lingered. That was the worst-case scenario, especially right now, when things were already beginning to slip.

Who was it? he wondered. And why?

He had heard stories of how brutally his rival drug cartels pursued their business. He had no doubt that the rumors of torture containers at the docks were true. Lately, many of his most trusted people had shown signs of weakness and disloyalty. Was this a final attempt to take him down so that they could take over his business? Or was it the accumulation of cases in Denmark that was threatening him?

He gazed blankly into the garden, where the kids were running around shrieking. A couple of adults had arrived now too, smiling and chatting, as though his front garden was the most natural meeting place on the whole street. Wayne smiled briefly, but he knew this was the end of an era and that today would be his last in this place, now that so many arrows seemed to be pointing straight to it.

The flare of rage subsided as abruptly as it had come, superseded by a deep, icy calm.

Today would be the day he put into action the plan to wind down his organization and his current life, the plan so carefully prepared in every detail over many years. It would shut everything down, burn any bridge that might be traceable to the place where he would rise from the ashes, the place already waiting for him five thousand miles away.

Not long afterward he stopped the car on a hill just outside of the town he had called home for decades. It had reached the time of day when the neighborhood mothers were calling their children and their men inside for dinner. The camera pointed at the front garden showed that all the activity going on merely thirty minutes ago had now ceased. The street was empty and the lawn deserted, only a few crows hopping around and pecking up the cake crumbs. The world would just have to do without them.

Taking a deep breath, he sent up a silent vote of thanks for the time he'd lived among those people and in that house. Then his thumb pressed a button on the remote control, detonating an explosion meant to look like a gas leak. The roof of his house shot skyward on a colossal sea of flames, followed by a bang that set car alarms howling all throughout the neighborhood.

He programmed his GPS for the airport in Amsterdam and started the engine with a diabolical smile.

It was a wistful feeling, but also good.

He was still the invisible power behind it all.

72

BENTE

Saturday, January 9, 2021

Bente spoke with the confidence-inspiring dependability of an angel when she got Morten Holland on the line. A gullible, good-hearted man who—along with his partner—had helped Hardy get back on his feet, Morten had always been a sucker for praise and a kind word or two. Bente spent several minutes gushing with boundless admiration for him and Mika, and when he was sufficiently softened up and weepy with emotion, she asked very gently if she could speak to her former colleague Hardy Henningsen. She wanted him to know how delighted all his ex-colleagues were that he had been given another chance at life.

"Ahh," said Morten. She could hear him swallowing the lump in his throat. "I'm afraid Hardy doesn't live here anymore."

She did her best to sound ostentatiously surprised. "Oh really? But how can he manage without you? Has he moved into sheltered accommodation?"

At this she noticed a slight hesitation, although Morten had been happily gabbling away moments earlier.

"Is there anyone else you could ask? Hardy made it very clear we weren't allowed to say anything."

So Morten did know where Hardy was. Bente could have jumped for joy.

"I understand, of course. I'm sure you're being mobbed by journalists and all sorts, wanting his story."

You're going to tell me, Morten, she thought. *Otherwise I'll come around there and drag it out of you, and you won't survive that.*

"Oh yeah, we've had loads of calls. But I can't say anything."

"Because he's with Carl in that lovely old house?" she asked.

This time there was total silence on the other end, and then the line went dead.

Shit. She had pushed too hard. Now he'd go blabbing to Carl the first chance he got. Fuck's sake. Was she under more pressure than she'd realized? She didn't usually make these kinds of blunders. Almost never, really.

She paused for a moment, analyzing the conversation. Obviously Morten wouldn't call from his phone: that was bound to be tapped as part of the search for Carl, same as everybody else with close connections to the wanted man.

If she wasn't much mistaken, Morten would currently be rushing around to a neighbor's house to call Carl from their phone. And Carl would say it was odd that Bente Hansen knew about the house and that Morten should steer clear of his place until Carl called back.

But what exactly did Carl believe? Probably that she had been enlisted into the force-wide manhunt for him, almost certainly at Jacobsen's instigation. It wasn't likely he suspected her directly. Then, within a very short span of time, his sharp brain would realize why she had referred to his hiding place as "that lovely old house." He would kick himself for allowing the stuccowork in the living room to appear in his videos, but that was all. You could find stucco like that everywhere in old Copenhagen.

Combing through everything she could find on Henningsen's current and former life, she learned that Hardy was a man with a very small social circle.

Which brought her right back to the key question: Where was Hardy?

Then her phone lit up, and Terje Ploug's number appeared on the display.

Thank god, here's someone who can help, she thought, answering the call in the same bright voice she had used on Morten.

"It's good to hear from you, Terje. How are things going on your end?"

"Hi, Bente. Just wanted to let you know that Gordon and I finished questioning Jess Larsen, and it paid off—I reckon we can get him a good deal. Gordon showed him a passport photo of Gustaaf Mulder yesterday, and it was obvious he recognized him. He was the one driving the car that killed Adam Bang."

Bente frowned. *Does Larsen know anything about me?* she wondered.

"Okay, great work—but how did he know that?"

"Because Jess was threatened into handing over the keys to Gustaaf Mulder. It was the day after his partner had killed Hannes Theis, while Mulder was holding him. And Jess—"

"Hang on, Terje, I'm not keeping up. Why did Theis have to die?" she asked, as if she didn't already know.

"They'd argued because Theis wanted out. He didn't want to keep doing the shipments to Holland. So they got rid of him.

"But Jess heard everything, is what I was just about to say, so he was terrified and very aware these guys were not to be trifled with. That's why he gave them the keys to the DKNL carpark and the car. He didn't dare go to the police because he felt complicit, not just because he'd given them the keys but also because he'd been working for the organization for a long time, packing up furniture for Holland, then unpacking the defective furniture that came back with the drugs. Instead, he confided in his lawyer when he was arrested."

"Christian Mandrup?" She did her best to sound puzzled. "Wow. Now the penny's dropping, eh?"

Terje laughed. That was how he sounded when he was feeling smug.

"I was calling about something else, actually. What have you guys found on the satellite phone? Do we know what communication was happening between the hit men and the people giving the orders?"

She took a deep breath. Due diligence, that had always been her calling card.

"I'm afraid that's a dead end, Terje. My people found that calls were only registered on the SIM card, but that had been removed. So, nothing. It's too bad."

He swore at the other end.

"Have you heard from Carl, Terje?" she asked in a worried tone of voice.

"Yeah, he's all right. Haven't you seen his videos?"

"Sure, and it's great to see he's somewhere safe and warm. Hardy's come up trumps, it looks like."

"Yeah, Minna's a redoubtable woman, you've got to hand it to her."

Bente held her breath. Had he really said that? Minna?

She had scarcely hung up before she checked Hardy's file. Minna Henningsen was his ex-wife.

Was she providing a house?

Bente looked her up in the Yellow Pages, checked the address, then searched for the house on Street View. Holy shit. Her luck had turned. The style, the size, the location—everything fit with the way she'd imagined the house.

She called her Dutch hit man, giving him the address and thorough instructions. She preferred to stay behind the scenes until it was all over.

She smiled. At long last, she was going to end this game with Carl Mørck. Over the years she had often wanted to try to lure him onto her side. It was a challenge she would have relished, because his rebellious nature had potential she knew could be guided in directions other than its current one. And she could easily have persuaded her employers that Carl would be the ideal partner for her in Denmark.

Now it was far too late for overtures of that kind. In a few hours, Bente would be finished with that part of the story.

Still, she would be happy to attend the funerals. It would be quite a show.

73

ASSAD / MERETE / CARL

Saturday, January 9, 2021

Assad only budged from his post by the living room curtains for a few minutes at a time. If he was careful, he could keep watch on both the network of paths and the park opposite, a full 180 degrees, without being seen.

Marwa had been bemused to find him standing there for so long. Assad didn't want to worry her, so he explained he had to keep an eye on things as long as Carl was out and about. What if his partner showed up and someone was lying in wait?

Marwa wasn't best pleased with the idea of having a wanted man in their home. The chief of homicide had, after all, fixed things so that Assad's family didn't have to undergo the same security checks that relatives of other police officers did. What would happen if the authorities found out they were harboring an escaped prisoner?

If they covered for Carl, especially when Jacobsen disliked him so much, he wouldn't help them a second time.

Assad replied tersely that they owed Carl. Without him, their lives would have turned out very differently—and not for the better.

She nodded anxiously, withdrawing to make sure that Afif didn't go up and pull aside the curtains so that he could watch as well. Nella did come in every now and then, though. If anybody other than him knew how to make a cup of coffee that blew the cobwebs off your taste buds, it was Nella. It was like sitting in a village café in some faraway country, and Assad loved it. Very discreetly, a tiny glass with a sugary mocha appeared out of nowhere, nudging his instincts for self-preservation. When she came in for the third time, she could no longer hold back.

"Are you watching what the police are doing?" she asked.

"The police?" he said. "What do you mean?"

"Ever since the shooting in the park yesterday they've had a car parked on the corner. You can see it from the kitchen window."

Assad shook his head in confusion. "Shooting? I didn't hear any shots."

Nella looked at him, disappointed. "Dad. I grew up with gunshots going off around me. You don't think I know what they sound like?"

"Maybe I wasn't home when it happened, because I don't remember," he lied.

She shrugged. She didn't care, but Assad did. Whether it was the hit man or the police in that car, it amounted to the same thing. If he left the apartment, Carl was screwed.

Assad hated it. If he didn't take action, didn't do something, he'd go out of his mind. Yesterday's breakthrough in the case had shaken them all deeply, and now they had to figure out where to go from here. But what could *he* do? Where could he start?

I wonder if Merete has anything on Bente Hansen? he thought, dialing her number.

"I've actually just spoken to Terje Ploug, so you've picked the right moment to call, Assad," she said. In the background was a rumble of indistinct voices cutting across one another.

"Terje had a chat with Bente a little earlier today, and there was one detail in the conversation that genuinely alarmed me, to put it mildly."

"Spit it out!" Assad crossed his fingers. *Please let it be something we can use to take her down*, he thought.

"Bente told Terje there was no SIM card in the satellite phone. But I've got a few colleagues next to me working on the data right now. It's encrypted, Assad, but it's there."

"Hafizna Allah, Almighty God!" Assad was beside himself. "Then she's given herself away—and I think she's destroying the evidence." Assad clenched his fists and told Merete that he, Hardy, and Carl also suspected her but couldn't prove anything.

"That's not all," Merete went on, before detonating the next bomb. "Terje is on his way to tell Carl that he also mentioned Minna's name to Bente. I don't think it struck him as much of a problem, to be honest."

Assad stiffened. It would take her exactly ten seconds to get the address. "Where is Bente Hansen now?" he asked.

"At her apartment. We had a man check to see if she responded, and he'll be keeping an eye on her if she goes out."

"Merete, listen! Bente won't risk doing anything that obvious. Ten to one she's got someone else to do her dirty work."

"The surviving contract killer, yes. Larsen identified him as the man who killed Hannes Theis."

"I need to get over there right now. Tell Terje to tread *very* carefully. That man is extremely dangerous."

• • •

Minna walked into the living room. "Here's the prepaid card from the corner shop, Carl. There are plenty more where that came from," she said. For some reason she was in high spirits—rather oddly, given the generally downcast mood.

He put the SIM card in, called Rose, and asked her to phone back, also on a prepaid card.

Five minutes later, Rose called back. Carl could hear the relief she felt at finally talking to him. It was a touching moment, all smiles, but it passed in a flash.

"NOOOOO, there's no way!" cried Rose down the telephone. "Not her, it can't be. Not Bente, that just can't be true!"

Carl gave her a brief summary of their thinking but added that they didn't yet have the evidence to bring her down.

"I need to confront Bente by unmasking her, and I can't do that without you and Gordon," Carl said. "Can you get hold of him and come out here?"

There was a creak and heavy footsteps from Hardy's room, so Carl put the phone down. He'd been thinking about calling Mona. God, how he needed her by his side.

"I think it was a mistake to send my carer, Gaston, to give the bags to the taxi driver," said Hardy as he came in.

"Why's that, Hardy?"

"I told him to speak English to the driver, but he says he spoke French. The driver was Moroccan, so it seemed natural."

"Where is Gaston right now?" asked Carl.

"At the pharmacy."

Carl deliberated. "The bags were handed over to Gordon at the Investigation Unit, right?"

Hardy took a clunking step forward. "Yes. Terje says Marcus asked Gordon for more information, and he'd noted down the taxi's registration number."

"The contents of the bags were pretty incendiary, so the police must have been sent to question the driver, right?"

"Yeah. Bit of a screwup, admittedly."

Carl looked out the window. "Isn't that Terje's car headed our way?"

Hardy bent and peered out the window. He smiled.

"There's a taxi outside too," he said. "Might be Gaston coming back." He shook his head. "No. It went past the driveway."

"I hope Terje has good news for us," said Carl, getting to his feet. "I'll answer the door. It's been bloody ages since I've been able to open a door from the inside."

Finally, something to bump up the mood a notch or two.

To be on the safe side, he hid behind the door so that he couldn't be seen from the outside and opened it.

"Jesus, Carl," said Terje, with a strange expression in his eyes, when he caught sight of him. Far from the stoic Terje he was used to.

"I've got bad news, Carl, I—"

There was a muffled pop, and Terje's face changed within a milli-second. It was as though the connection to his facial muscles was cut, and he slumped forward into the hall, toppling face-first on the carpet.

Without stopping to think, Carl bent down and grabbed Terje's arm, pulling him away from the door before he slammed it shut and locked it.

"Get away from the windows, Hardy!" he yelled at the top of his lungs.

Beneath him, Terje moaned. He'd been struck in the back at the edge of the shoulder blade—it might have punctured a lung.

"Minna, get down here, quickly!" he shouted, but she was already on her way. She halted for a second on the stairs and clapped a hand to her mouth, but took the final steps in a single bound.

"Lay him on his side so he doesn't choke on his own blood." The words were racing out of him. "And stay away from the windows and this door, and call the emergency services," he said firmly.

"That means the police will be coming too, Carl," she said.

As if he didn't know.

"Are there any doors or windows open in the house?"

She shook her head, but then he saw a moment's doubt. "Maybe in the kitchen?"

Carl ran. The kitchen directly overlooked the garden—perhaps the attack would come from there—but the windows were closed.

He drew a medium-size knife out of the block and tucked it into his belt.

"What do we have to defend ourselves with?" he shouted to Hardy from the hall, where Minna was on the phone with the dispatcher. She was trying to stay calm, stroking Terje's back and cheeks with trembling hands.

He heard dull footsteps in the living room.

"I'm sorry, Carl," said Hardy from the doorway, brandishing a poker. "This is all I've got."

"And Assad's got the gun we found in Kenneth's glove box. *Fuck*."

"Do we know how many of them are out there?" asked Hardy. He sounded cool as ice, but his brow was a maze of furrows.

Carl shook his head. "Might just be one, I don't know." He turned to
Minna. "Do you have anything we could use to defend ourselves, Minna?"

Terje's legs were beginning to shake convulsively, and the pool of
blood beneath him was growing.

The real urgency of the situation suddenly seemed to dawn on Minna.
Holding a hand over her phone, she tried tearfully to explain where the
pepper spray she'd had for several years might be kept.

It was hopeless.

"Mads and the kids will be home soon," she stammered, holding the
phone to her ear.

"Then stop them, Minna," said Carl. "Hang up on emergency
services—they've already got the address—and call your son."

For the next few minutes they all held their breath. Where were the
police cars? Where was the ambulance? Were they hanging back because
of the fraught circumstances?

The attack came from somewhere they did not expect.

Carl had barely registered the tinkle of glass shattering on the floor
above before he grabbed Minna and pulled her into Hardy's living room.

"Help me drag this sofa across the door, Minna," he commanded,
while she cried and said they couldn't just leave Terje Ploug to die in
the hall.

Carl was distraught, but he knew he had no choice. Otherwise it
would be Hardy and Minna who paid the price for sheltering him. The
nightmare felt unending.

"Do you know where the guy got in, Minna? Anything you've forgotten?"

She shook her head. Maybe he'd taken a ladder from the garden and
climbed up onto the bedroom balcony, she said.

Again, they waited. Carl assumed the man would finish Terje, who lay
prone on the hall floor, but there wasn't a sound.

Protected behind Hardy's bulky frame, Minna was trying desperately to get hold of their son. She cried, talking frantically about how small and defenseless the grandchildren were.

Hardy looked sorrowfully at Carl. "This is how it all began, Carl. Is this how it's going to end as well?"

"I'm so sorry you two got dragged into this. I'm so sorry."

Hardy shook his head and turned to Minna, who glared at him accusingly. Carl knew exactly what she was thinking. Hardy should never have brought Carl into this house and made everybody else a hostage.

Hardy drew her in close. "I'm sorry, Minna," he said quietly, but she pushed him away and leaned forward into the mobile phone as though she wanted to attack it.

"Mads, thank god you picked up!" she cried. "Stay away, there's a killer in the house. Keep your distance. We've called the police." Then she hung up.

"Where are they?" asked Hardy.

"They'd just gotten to the end of the road. He said everything seems normal."

"Give me the phone, Minna. Gaston might be on his way," said Hardy.

He dialed the number, and ten seconds later a phone began to ring in the hall.

Hardy clenched his fists. "Dammit! He's always doing that. Putting his phone down in the hall when he's putting on his coat, then forgetting it."

Then the ringing stopped. "Yes," said a stranger's voice.

Hardy held up a hand to the others, put the phone on speaker, and pointed to the hall.

"It's very simple. I get Carl Mørck, and you and this guy on the floor get to live," said the voice in English.

Hardy's face went gray. "No way," he replied after five seconds.

The man in the hall didn't like that answer, responding by thudding his body against the door. When it didn't give way, he fired several shots through it. The bullets slammed across the room and into the far wall.

Minna was sobbing loudly.

"Move over beside the door," Carl whispered. "We can't let him see us through the holes."

Minna obeyed, while Hardy squeezed himself back against the wall by the fireplace and held out the poker to Carl. He pointed eloquently at the bullet holes in the door.

Was Hardy really suggesting he ram the poker through the holes into the man's eyes? Carl shook his head. Surely Hardy didn't think the man would be stupid enough to stand that close?

The front door creaked, then they heard it slam.

There was no doubt in Carl's mind. "The bastard's plan was that we'd lock ourselves in here, so just wait! He'll be coming from that way any minute, Hardy."

Carl pointed at the living room windows. Beautiful, wood-framed windows made up of smaller panes, quality construction, arranged around one larger pane of glass.

"He'll put the ladder up against the window and fire down at us through the glass."

"Oh my god!" Minna gasped. She looked around the room. Where could she hide?

"Idiotischer dummer Schweinehund!" Carl yelled as loudly as he could— he thought the guy would understand that, but there was no reaction.

"Okay, so he's probably not still in the hall," he went on. "Help me push the sofa out of the way; I've got to get out before he comes back with the ladder."

There was no point protesting. What other choice did they have?

Carl went out and drew back the catch without a sound. If he'd miscalculated, the guy would be waiting for him outside.

He poked his nose toward the crack in the door. He couldn't see the guy anywhere: all he had to do was get through the door, away from the gravel path, and across the lawn.

He leaped out, running until he was behind some laurels, evergreens, quivering in the bed among some bare bushes. From there it was roughly thirty feet to the window, so the bastard could easily turn and fire before Carl got to him, but he had to take the chance.

Then he heard the crunch of gravel. As the man rounded the corner of the house, carrying the ladder on his shoulder, Carl saw him close up for the first time. If they'd met under ordinary circumstances, they might have struck up a conversation, because the impression he gave with those very blue eyes and dimpled cheeks was of friendliness and reliability. Mona would probably say the young man was very good-looking, and Carl would agree. How did someone like him become this monster, killing for money without a second thought?

Just as Carl had predicted, the man rested the ladder against the wall next to the large window, put his nose to the glass, and looked around the room. Then he smashed the window with the butt of the gun, and Minna screamed.

Carl sensed the man pause. Had he noticed the sofa had been pulled away from the door?

Carl heard him spit a few incomprehensible swear words as he climbed down the ladder. When he was on the bottom rung, Carl launched himself into a run, but the man heard and leaped down the final step, spinning around so that they were face-to-face ten feet apart. With a serene smile, he aimed the gun at Carl at the very moment Carl threw the knife. The shot was fired, and the sharp blade bored into the man's thigh.

Carl tumbled to the frozen soil in agony. Had the bullet gone straight into his broken ribs?

Carl lay wheezing for breath as the man recovered and pulled out the knife. If Carl had hit a major artery, the man must know he could collapse from loss of blood at any moment. But his dimples only deepened, and he limped toward Carl with the silencer aimed directly at his head.

Carl was suddenly overwhelmed by the sense that most of his life had been in vain. Why go through all this if he was going to die so miserably? He closed his eyes and thought of Lucia and Mona.

"You said *Schweinehund*!" the man repeated, laughing.

Carl said goodbye to the world. But the shot that inevitably rang out was anything but silent.

Carl opened his eyes and watched as the man limped hurriedly out of the front garden and into the bushes leading to the neighbor's house.

Propping himself up on his elbows, Carl turned his head. At the far end of the driveway stood Assad. He fired a couple more shots into the undergrowth, and as the sound of emergency vehicles came screeching toward them, Carl sank back to the ground.

He heard Assad direct the sprinting officers toward the bushes that had swallowed the man. Then Assad ran past him, headed in the same direction, and shot him his characteristic warm grin.

"Hang in there, Carl. The cavalry's arrived. I'll catch that bastard."

Then he was gone, and seconds later Rose was crouching down beside him.

"How serious is it, do you think?" she asked, but didn't wait for an answer. "If you can get up, come with me."

An ambulance was pulling into the driveway, and two men came rushing toward them but stopped when Rose waved them off.

"Go in there first," Carl shouted. "A man's badly injured. Hurry."

Carl caught a brief glimpse of Minna in the doorway, waving to her doctor son and grandchildren, then Rose hauled him to his feet and half carried him toward the road, where Gordon was waiting.

74

CARL / BENTE

Saturday, January 9, 2021

"**Nope, you're not** making me do that, Carl, no fucking way," Gordon said with a sniffle as he maneuvered the car through rush-hour traffic, his movements slightly too frantic. Darkness was falling, and the lights of the city were mirrored everywhere in the wet surfaces. "There is absolutely no way I'm talking to Bente Hansen right now, okay, I'm still in shock that our Bente . . ."

He tried to compose himself and sighed. "I just didn't see *that* coming, Carl, all right? That she's as rotten to the core as a person can be. Jesus Christ, man! It's a tragedy!"

Carl was clutching the wound in his side, trying to ignore it.

"I'm really sorry, Gordon," he said, "but you're the best person to do it, and Bente listens to you, I know she does."

"I don't know. Right now I'm in no state to say anything to her without breaking down."

"I haven't forgotten what you've been through these last few weeks, Gordon." Carl gave his shoulder a squeeze. "Look, just take a moment to get yourself together. We . . . no, *I* need you so that we can put an end to this nightmare, okay?"

"You're bleeding on his car, Carl," came a dry voice from the back seat, as Rose switched off her phone's display and put it down.

Carl glanced down. Yes, there was a small stain. She didn't miss a trick, that woman.

"I appreciate your concern, Rose. And now that you mention it, it's nice to see you two again as well."

"Don't start," she said. She had bottled up the storm raging inside her, Carl could tell.

"I've been in touch with Merete and she's on board," she went on. "We'll be meeting with her shortly just around the corner, near where Bente lives. She's just told me her people are in position, and they're ready to cover our backs, come what may. So let's just take it from there."

Apart from Merete, Carl didn't know any of the four people who got out of her four-wheel drive, but they were calm and looked up to the task.

Carl gave them a nod, then went straight up to Merete and hugged her.

He took a step back and scrutinized her closely. It was a near miracle to see her so strong and standing so tall. It was impossible to put into words how infinitely grateful he was to be standing in front of her right now.

Carl remembered helping her out of the pressure chamber and felt his eyes grow damp.

She smiled back, moved. She was obviously going through the same emotions. Then she noticed the blood on the right side of Carl's torso and signaled one of the men to check the extent of the damage.

He carefully lifted up Carl's jacket and shirt.

"Ouch, that hurts, I can tell. Probably still does," said the man. "The bullet grazed you, and it took a pretty decent chunk of flesh with it. I can see a bit of the rib, so you'll have a nice scar. I'm going to put a compress on it, then we'll carefully put some gauze around your torso. We'll have to get you examined at the hospital later."

Carl gritted his teeth, trying to take a deep breath and hold it. He was really hoping they could lay their hands on the bastard who'd shot him.

• • •

"I've been waiting for you to call, Thom. Give me the good news."

Bente stared. *You've got to be kidding!*

"I want you to weigh your words carefully now, Loos. You're telling me you shot a man, but it wasn't Carl Mørck."

He confirmed, apologizing, and told her where he was and that he'd given his pursuers the slip.

Bente was confused. How had a pair of bunglers like him and Gustaaf Mulder earned a reputation as ruthless killing machines? Or did Carl just have the world's most badass guardian angel?

She really was in a temper now, because her situation hadn't changed in the slightest. Carl Mørck was still breathing, and she very much begrudged him that.

"You have a serious problem now, Thom, you do realize that?"

He said he'd give as good as he'd got. He had a reputation to protect.

"I'm afraid you're down to your last chance," she said coldly, before her attention was grabbed by an incoming call from Gordon Taylor.

"Give me a minute, Thom. Stay on the line. I'll come back to you, but I need to take another call."

He was about to protest, but she put him on hold.

Gordon sounded deeply shaken—he was stammering to get his words out. "Just moments ago Carl survived another assassination attempt, and it was a close call," he said. "Terje Ploug, however, was shot in the back and is fighting for his life. You've never seen Carl this upset, and now he wants to hand himself in before anybody else gets hurt."

Don't screw this up now, Bente, she told herself, mind racing furiously.

"Oh my gosh, Gordon, that's awful. But thank you for telling me." She paused for effect, sniffling loudly. "What happened?" she asked at last.

"The guy just came out of nowhere. Shot Terje in the back and tried to get into the house. Hardy and Minna were in there too. All I know is that the assailant was chased off by the police."

"Poor Terje! A shot in the back can be fatal." She sighed noisily enough that she knew Gordon would definitely hear it. "Carl was with Hardy and Minna, you said? So where is he now?"

Tell me, Gordon, so that Thom Loos can prove his value! The words were a roar inside her head. Perhaps she could snatch victory from the jaws of defeat after all.

"Carl says he'll only hand himself in to you personally. He can't think of anybody else who would be so neutral and who has enough weight to hold their own against Marcus."

Bente held her breath. "I just need a minute, Gordon." She went over to the sink and turned on the tap, so it sounded like she was pouring herself a glass of water. Then she opened a kitchen drawer, which contained another, secret drawer underneath the countertop. The drawer where she kept keys, sharp knives, and a gun she had confiscated years ago and for which she had later obtained a certificate.

She took the safety off and tucked it into the back of her waistband. Now she was ready.

"I'm all right now, Gordon. Just needed something cold to drink. This really is terrible news, but Carl has made a wise decision. Of course I'm happy to bring him in. Will you be coming with him?"

"Yes, me and Rose. He's badly injured, so h—"

"How soon can you be here?"

"Soon, I think."

"Okay, give me ten minutes. And if it's just you guys, and Carl agrees that you'll bring him in handcuffs, then I'm happy to arrest him here, then call some additional officers without going through Marcus."

"Handcuffs? But he's coming of his own free will, Bente, and he's in pretty bad shape, like I said, so you have nothing to fear from him. Plus we're there too, all right?"

"Okay, fine. And thanks! I'd say that's a job well done, Gordon. Was it you who talked him around?"

"No, it was Rose."

"You guys are amazing. But you do sound a little shaky. Must have been tough, I can imagine."

"It . . . yeah, it's all tough. We just can't get our heads around it.

We've been working so closely with Carl for so many years. Plus all that
Sisle Park stuff is getting to me, I think."

"When all this is over, we'll make sure you get a well-deserved holiday, Gordon. And I think a bit of a promotion might be in order too."

Gordon did not reply.

"Be here in ten, all right?"

Gordon agreed and hung up. Bente was breathing heavily. All at once,
everything seemed to be going her way. This could not have turned out
better.

Bente returned to Thom Loos, giving him one last earful for his recent
failure and repeating that he was getting one final chance.

"I'm giving you Carl Mørck on a silver platter. All you have to do is
not screw up."

She texted him a code and explained how he could get into her apartment unseen from the neighboring street via the basement bike storage,
which was shared by the whole block, then up the back stairs.

"Don't smoke down there, because then the fire doors will close auto-
matically," she said. "When you enter my kitchen, Mørck will be sitting
there, and this time don't hesitate. Kill him before anybody can react.
Got it?"

"Roger and over," he said tonelessly, then hung up.

She would kill him afterward, of course, so that Carl would look like
the victim of an internal gangland dispute and she'd be the hero coming
to her two colleagues' rescue. If they ended up getting caught in the cross
fire, then so be it.

75

ASSAD / ROSE

Saturday, January 9, 2021

On the other side of the bushes, there were several private gardens, and beyond those were a welter of shortcuts and bends and myriad possibilities. Assad went to stand on a street corner, peering around. *Why didn't they bring a canine unit to help with the chase?* The officers were simply gazing bemusedly in all directions. The trail was cold.

When they returned to their patrol cars, Assad lingered.

It was the faint ping of a text arriving on a phone somewhere across the road that caught his attention. Assad tried to localize the sound but saw only trees and blackberry bushes.

He withdrew behind some stray maple trees by a rusty wrought iron fence and waited. Then he heard a faint voice growing gradually clearer, and after a minute the man emerged from the thicket of blackberries, his skin cut and scratched everywhere it wasn't covered. Perhaps the man had been born without a pain threshold, because he paid no attention to his injuries or made any complaint about them, although several of them looked pretty deep.

"Roger and over," he said, switching off the display and limping in the direction of the ring road.

The bloodstain on his trousers was only slightly bigger than when

Carl had first thrown the knife into his thigh, but the wound was slowing him down.

You're not getting away from me this time, thought Assad, who wasn't too hampered by his injured calf. Right now they were only a few hundred yards apart. Assad tried to decide whether he should try to stop him now or if this game of cat and mouse might be the ideal opportunity to get the man to lead him to the people behind it all. It was clear he had a destination and that he was trying to get there quickly. Several times he raised his phone, looked at it, then at the street signs, then continued on down the road.

What am I going to do if he jumps in a taxi? thought Assad.

There weren't a lot of taxis available on the bypass at this time of day. But like the man he was following, Assad kept glancing regularly over his shoulder, and when the first taxi with a green light approached he hailed it.

He showed the driver his badge. "It's a bit unorthodox, this, but I'm on duty, and we can't lose sight of that man walking ahead of us down the pavement. Drive as slowly as you need, and if he hails a taxi as well, we'll follow it. Does that work for you?"

The man nodded, looking almost delighted, as though he finally had something to tell his wife when he got home.

Only a couple of minutes passed before the expected happened, and the two taxis drove through the city, tethered via an invisible string.

• • •

Bente gave a welcoming smile as she opened the door to them. "Despite the circumstances, it's good to see you, Carl!" She nodded to Gordon and Rose. "Come inside. We'll grab a beer in the kitchen so we can relax for a minute while we wait for the officers."

Rose gave a friendly smile back, but it took all her willpower not to pounce with claws bared, ready to scratch the fake grin off Bente's face. How could this colleague of theirs, admirable in so many ways, have taken them all in for so long? Suddenly she understood Marcus's reaction a little better, if he'd genuinely been convinced of Carl's guilt.

Careful, Rose, she admonished herself. She couldn't allow herself to betray the rage seething inside her.

Carl could cover for his stiffness and emotions by dropping his head in shame and playing up his pain. Gordon had the general situation and Sisle Park's torture to explain away his agitation. But Rose didn't have a similar excuse. She had to pretend to be upset about the situation and stay on her guard. As far as they knew, Bente had never resorted to violence herself, but you could never be too vigilant.

She offered them seats on three kitchen chairs while she leaned against the edge of the kitchen table.

The mood took a turn when Carl sat down heavily and pinned her with his gaze. "Bente, I've come here to persuade you to turn yourself in and confess your part in this case."

She seemed genuinely taken aback. "What are you talking about? Where has this come from?" She scrutinized Carl's face with a smile, as though testing to see if it was some bad joke, but Carl's heavy-hearted expression was unmistakable. He meant it.

"Carl, honestly, what a load of nonsense!" She tried to force a hint of levity back into her voice. "I know you're under pressure, but accusing me of something this serious isn't going to help matters."

She turned to Rose and Gordon. "I mean, it wasn't my attic where they found the suitcase covered in your fingerprints and Anker's, was it?"

"It's the suitcase, among other things, that's your downfall, Bente," Carl said dryly.

She smiled crookedly and shook her head, but Carl went on, unmoved.

"Anker brought the suitcase, but I didn't know what was in it. Otherwise it probably wouldn't have been left untouched for so many years, would it? As it happened, I forgot all about it and assumed it was junk my ex-wife or her son, Jesper, had never got around to clearing out.

"The suitcase testified to my close friendship with Anker, I'll admit that, and it even convinced our chief of homicide that Anker and I were in league."

"Your fingerprints were on the banknotes, Carl; you can't get around that," said Bente.

"They were planted in the suitcase, and that would have required somebody close to us both. That person was you, Bente. You and Anker were together."

"Apart from his wife, that was no secret to anybody, I'd imagine. You're being pathetic right now, Carl. If this wasn't so pathetic, I'd be angry." She turned to Rose and Gordon. "Has he tried persuading you two as well?" she asked, and they nodded cautiously.

"You might be pleased to hear what I'm about to say, then. Like you, I've been doing my own little investigation into the case. I've often wondered why it remained unsolved for so many years. And the simplest explanation is that Terje Ploug is behind it. He's had the case from day one, and he's used his position to cover his tracks.

"He planted the banknotes with the fingerprints in the suitcase and the prints in the crate in Amager. It's true that Anker and I had a brief affair, which is how I was close enough to know that he and Terje were into some dodgy business together. That was one of the reasons why the affair stopped."

"What evidence do you have against Terje, Bente?" asked Rose.

"I mean, Terje comes across as very trustworthy, I know that. But just this morning he tried to cast suspicion on your escape, Carl, and almost 'accidentally' revealed where you were. I expressed skepticism, and then he tried to do the same to me and my investigation into the evidence you gave me. Something about a SIM card, I think it was." She looked inquiringly at Gordon, who nodded again.

Rose could see Gordon's mind was in tumult. Bente was so convincing that even she couldn't rid herself of nagging doubts.

Then Carl began to clap loudly from the sidelines. "Brava, Bente! Cheap shot to pin the blame on Terje, who's currently fighting for his life, but otherwise that was a magnificent performance. Tanto di cappello!"

She didn't turn a hair. "Thanks, but I'm not finished following the lead yet, so why don't we coordinate our investigations? I don't think you're guilty either, Carl." Her eyes darted to the clock on the oven. Was she wondering how long it would take the officers to arrive?

"Good Lord, Bente, you're taking home one Oscar after another. But now I'm going to tell you something you don't know," he said gravely. "Terje Ploug records all his conversations. Including the one in which you told him there was no SIM card in the satellite phone. Not to mention that Merete's people are currently in the process of decrypting that very SIM card, which Gordon was quick-thinking enough to copy before the phone was handed over to you—*with* the SIM card, mind you." He looked directly into her eyes. "That SIM card is going to reveal the conversations you had with your hired killer."

She shook her head. "I take it back that you're innocent, Carl. You're a sly one, aren't you? So it's you who's in cahoots with Terje after all. You think I don't know how easy it is to make digital copies?"

Carl smiled. "You're tough, Bente, but then you have to be, when you've done as many terrible things as you have. Yes, Terje and I are very close. That's why I'm so pleased to be able to say, again, that Terje recorded his conversations with you. Among other things, it's very clear that you coaxed my address out of him, and not the other way around. We have given the phone to our best people in the police. So that means you're screwed, Bente."

"Wow, Carl, you've spun quite a tale here, but I'm actually pretty close to a—"

There was a shattering, crunching bang as something slammed hard into the back door, making them all leap to their feet. As the unlocked door flew open, Rose noticed that Bente Hansen had drawn a gun out of her waistband. A young man with a bloodied face and an outstretched pistol tumbled forward into the kitchen. He tried desperately to keep his balance, twisting around toward the figure on the steps outside. At that moment Assad leaped through the doorway and fired a shot that pierced his shoulder, but the guy was still clutching the gun.

"He's going to shoot," yelled Rose, and Gordon, standing next to him, swung one very long leg and kicked the gun out of his hand.

Assad charged the swearing man to the ground and held him in a grip of iron.

"We've got the evidence against Bente lying right here," he cried loudly.

As though in slow motion, Rose saw Bente raise the gun she was holding and take aim at Assad. Rose threw herself at Bente's arm at the very moment the shot was fired. And no more than ten seconds later, the kitchen was filled with Merete's security people.

There was a howling whine in Rose's ears as Carl grabbed Bente Hansen and twisted her arm behind her back.

Bente's shot had assassinated her kitchen bin but barely grazed Assad. The only other injuries were to the gunman.

"Sorry, Assad," said Bente, as Carl handed her over to the security people. She nodded at the man on the floor. "It was him I was trying to hit. It looked like he had a knife as well."

Carl helped Assad to his feet.

"That's what you'd like me to believe, Bente." Assad smiled broadly. "I heard that guy talking on his phone and receiving a text, then I followed the bastard all over town without him even realizing. He was making a beeline for your neighborhood. So I called Merete and asked her to let him pass through."

"I know absolutely nothing about that man," Bente protested.

"Fascinating, because you know I actually watched him let himself in with a code from his mobile phone, then I sneaked in after him through the basement and up the back stairs. He was in a bit of pain thanks to that stab wound in his thigh, courtesy of Carl, so he was groaning loudly enough that he didn't hear me following him all the way up to your back door. When he pulled out his gun, I cracked him over the head with my own pistol. It's out there in the hall."

"I don't know him," said Bente furiously.

"Well, then maybe we should check his phone. I took it off him just a minute ago. I think we can safely assume it's been in contact with your phone several times in the last half hour, Bente, and I'm equally sure we'll find a text from you with the code."

Rose went up very close to her. All her pent-up resentment and fury had been replaced now with disgust and pity. "I don't think there's any doubt about who just ordered a hit man, since you've got Carl here."

"Fuck you all—this whole thing is one big conspiracy," she snarled.

"Is it indeed?" said Merete, taking a step forward. "I wonder if you've heard enough now, Mr. Jacobsen?" she added, turning toward the hallway.

Marcus appeared in the doorway, pale as a corpse and visibly shaken.

Rose smiled sheepishly at Carl. "Sorry, Carl. It was me who invited him to listen in. Merete's people smuggled him in here."

Carl nodded. "Great. He's arrived just in time to give me an apology."

Marcus swayed on the spot for a moment—it looked almost as though he was about to lose his balance. Slowly his eyes drifted up to meet Carl's. He reached out a hand and grabbed Merete's sleeve. Then he took a tiny step forward and said in an undertone: "Carl!"

His voice was shaking, but he got it under control. "If you can find a way to accept it, then here it is: I'm sorry, my friend. Sorry, sorry, sorry."

Carl's head gave a tiny jerk. He could feel the others staring at him.

"Come on, Carl!" he heard Rose say.

Then he stepped forward and drew Marcus in close.

They stood like that for a moment. Jacobsen didn't say a word, but he nodded at Carl with eyes that shone.

Then he stepped to one side and arrested Bente Hansen.

Once they'd gone, and only Rose, Carl, and Assad remained in the kitchen, Rose opened the beers that had been waiting on the kitchen table.

Assad sat down on the chair next to Carl. "They're taking you to the Rigshospital. The ambulance is already on its way. But first, tell me: How did you know Terje Ploug records his conversations?"

Carl looked into his brown eyes with a smile. "Does he?" he inquired.

76

CARL

Sunday, January 10, 2021

The Sunday ritual had become a reality. Mona was sitting on the edge of Carl's hospital bed, reading him the news headlines while Lucia tried to poke yet another freshly baked bread roll into his mouth.

"It's quite a story these journalists have got," said Mona, wiping her eyes. She looked at Carl and put her hand on the front page that had touched her most deeply.

"Carl Mørck Is a Free Man," it read in huge type, as though announcing the end of a war.

"A free man!"

Carl grabbed Mona's hand and squeezed it.

"You've got a visitor, Carl," said a nurse from the doorway. "I also wanted to let you know that the doctors have examined the X-rays, and you've broken four ribs, but the breaks are clean and the bones are in the right place, so there's not much else we can do for you. You can get dressed and go home now. Come back on Tuesday to get the wound cleaned, if you don't want to do it yourself."

She moved away, revealing Merete Lynggaard and Assad standing right behind her.

Carl maneuvered himself effortlessly into a sitting position on the edge of the bed and hugged them, and Lucia laughed as only a delighted child could.

Mona went up to Merete, took her hands, and sobbed until Merete was crying too. They both laughed with relief, embracing first each other, then Assad.

"This is a wonderful day," said Merete. "But I think there are a couple more people in this hospital we ought to visit, now that we're here."

"Yes, we've had Malthe Bøgegård transferred to one of our units," said the doctor in the ward next to Carl's. "Correctional Services brought him in handcuffs, but we've been told we can remove those. After everything he's been through, a judge said this morning that when we discharge him, he'll be going to an open prison. His lawyer is with him now."

His lawyer? Mona smiled—what did she know about that?

"Congratulations, Carl," said Molise Sjögren from a chair next to Malthe's bed. Of course it was her.

Carl barely recognized Malthe, lying there all dressed in white, on a white bed, with one leg up in a sling.

"Hello there, my friend. How are you feeling?"

He threw out his arms. He could barely speak.

Carl leaned over him and gave him a hug. "We did it, Malthe!"

He nodded and reached for Molise Sjögren's hand. "She told me my brother has had the operation. That he's doing okay, so now we're just hoping for the best."

Carl bent his head and sighed deeply.

Then he pointed at Merete, standing behind him with lips clamped shut and glistening eyes. "She's the one who paid to get your brother down there, Malthe. She's been your guardian angel, and mine, and your brother's."

Malthe propped himself up on his elbows and reached out a hand. He could barely get a word out—but words weren't necessary.

When they left Malthe's room, the doctors told them his injuries had been quite extensive but that the broken bones would most likely heal within a few months. There was a good chance they'd be discharging him in March.

Carl promised to be there, that he'd accompany Malthe on his way to the new prison. He wanted to see him off properly.

For as long as Malthe wanted, Carl would always be there for him. He'd earned it.

Terje and Kenneth were both in intensive care, but Carl and Merete were allowed to stand in the doorway of Kenneth's room.

Merete gave him a thumbs-up. "You'll be out in two or three weeks, Kenneth," she said. "Then we'll soon have you and your voice back on your feet." She laughed at the clumsy choice of words, and Kenneth's eyes creased into a smile.

Carl nodded. "If it hadn't been for you, I'd be a dead man today. So thank you for my life, Kenneth. I'm eternally grateful, and I wish you the speediest possible recovery. Give my best to Mia when you see her."

Kenneth raised a thumb to them in reply, smiling as widely as the tube in his mouth would allow, and Assad stepped forward and returned the gesture.

Terje had just come out of surgery, so they couldn't speak to him, but they were told the operation had been a success, despite the hemorrhaging in both lungs and the surrounding tissue. Their prognosis was another couple of weeks in hospital, then he'd be as good as new.

Carl and Assad were both very relieved.

"When do you expect him to wake up?"

"Sometime this afternoon, I think," said the doctor on shift.

"Do you mind if I leave him a note?" asked Carl, and when the doctor nodded, he wrote:

Dear Terje, The case is closed. Congratulations, Mr. Chief of Homicide, haha!

Best wishes, Carl, a Free Man.

77

DEPARTMENT Q / CARL

Monday, January 11, 2021

Despite the safety of his surroundings and the doors open throughout their apartment, despite the wide mattress and Mona by his side, Carl didn't sleep much that night.

His ribs throbbed at the slightest turn, and his thoughts were more confused and uncontrolled than they had been since he was very young and his first crushes had knocked him off his feet. One moment his cheeks were burning with rage at the wickedness of humankind, and the next they were pouring with tears of emotion at the thought of the boundless loyalty and love he had been shown.

Get your mind right, Carl, he said to himself.

After everything he'd been through, there had to be some kind of resolution drawn from it all. Mona had told him to take at least two weeks off before he started looking to the future. But for a fifty-five-year-old veteran officer and busy detective who had just been through the greatest crisis of his life, it didn't feel like much of a solution.

He had to go back to the Investigation Unit in Sydhavnen. Hug Gordon, Rose, and Assad and thank them for helping him in every possible and impossible way. He had to look his other colleagues in the eyes, and he had to see whether the fire was there, or if it had finally been put out.

And if it had, then he would need to figure out if there was a way to make it flare up again.

Last night he'd been more inclined to think this chapter of his life would have to end, but then the doubt and unease returned.

Because what then?

Even as he stood outside the building, he knew he'd been sleepless for a reason.

What the hell was left for him in there? Despite the solid walls and all the windows, it felt as though the whole façade had been peeled back. He pictured the teeming offices behind it. All the many people striving at their many desks to catch those who lived outside the law and society's norms. Even though the vast majority of criminals deserved to be hunted and required a line of defense, the last fortnight had revised and nuanced his perspective on who was trapped in the system—like his colleagues inside the building—and who was on the outside. Over the course of the night, Carl had been thinking about the confrontations he'd been through during his career as a policeman, and he could tell right now he'd entirely lost his taste for it. The boundaries between guilt and innocence, good and evil, had grown porous. How could he possibly hope to navigate that reality?

He greeted the receptionist as though he'd never seen her before, and the faces that passed him as he headed toward Department Q were blurred. He didn't doubt that some of them were welcoming him back, nor that just as many wished he were a million miles away. Several teams had lost members in the last twenty-four hours, so nobody was in particularly good spirits. Terje Ploug was in hospital, Bente Hansen was in jail, and Marcus Jacobsen hadn't turned up yet. The whole floor felt burned out, much like Carl himself.

His faithful colleagues in Department Q were ready to receive him. Gordon, arms and legs swinging, pulled him into a hug so painfully tight that Carl finally understood Gordon had grown up. Assad was gentler.

He'd also been involved throughout the whole thing and was exhausted, but his smile and his stubble were the same as ever.

It was Rose who was the most surprising of the three.

"Welcome back, Carl. We're over the moon about how this ended, although we never doubted it for a minute," she said, but her face was pale and her eyes watchful.

"How are you doing, really?" she asked, gathering herself.

The question was inevitable, of course, and of course there was an answer. Only, he still hadn't committed himself to it, so he couldn't tell her. He was simply speechless, fumbling for words that wouldn't come.

"I thought so," she said. "That's what I was afraid of."

The other two looked on, brows furrowed, first at her and then at Carl, who sat down heavily in the chair by his desk and began to shake his head.

There was a lump in his throat that thwarted all answers.

"Let's get you a nice cup of coffee," said Assad, already starting to pour fluid as black as pitch.

"Sugar?" he asked, not waiting for an answer.

Carl accepted the cup reluctantly and raised it to his lips. It was so strong his mouth began to burn.

"Jeez," he rasped. There, that was a start.

He wiped his eyes and the corners of his mouth. "Thanks, Assad," he said, knowing it would be a long time before he let himself make that mistake again.

Carl took out his wallet and opened it. Then he placed it on the table so that all three could see the photograph inside.

"I think it might be time for another kind of life. I have to be there for Lucia."

Only Gordon still failed to catch on. "So you're cutting down your hours? That's going to be tough, Carl," he said.

But Rose and Assad nodded.

"He's quitting, Gordon!" said Rose, and she didn't look happy to be saying it out loud. Then she turned to Carl. "When?"

Carl shrugged. "I don't think Jacobsen intends to carry on, not after this case. Once Terje is back we'll have a new chief of homicide, if you ask me. There will be a lot of changes in the months to come. New team leaders, new procedures, new political decisions. Why stick around for all that?"

"So, now?" said Rose.

He nodded warily.

"What then? What are you going to do? Can you both live off Mona's income?" she asked.

He nodded again. "We can. But I still don't know what I'm going to do with myself." He smiled at them, reaching out across the table and inviting all three of them to take his hands.

The warmth of them almost made him reconsider. This really was a difficult decision.

"Department Q will always be here; you're indispensable. And you each have to decide for yourselves how much you want to put into it."

Assad was clearly shaken. "If you're not going to be here, Carl, then nor will I."

Carl gripped his wrist. "You'll have as much freedom as you need, I'll make sure Terje promises. And remember, Assad, all you have to do is pick up the phone and I'll be at the other end. The same goes for all three of you; I could never fall out of touch with you. So I want you to think this through very carefully, Assad. There's also your pension to think of—don't turn your nose up at that."

"Think it through carefully," Assad repeated a couple of times, shaking his head. "I think you should do the same, Carl."

"Okay, Assad, I will," said Carl, resting a hand on his shoulder.

Rose nodded. "If you really want to do something to help us, Carl, you should write about our department. That way we might get a bit more respect and positive attention."

"Write? I don't think I can."

Quite unexpectedly, Rose shrieked with laughter. "You've got to be kidding me! I know you hate writing reports, but honestly, you've always been really fucking good at it."

Then it was Gordon's turn. He wasn't happy, but then again, he could never resist the urge to make suggestions. "There are lots of prominent detectives who make a living doing talks and consulting for TV channels after they leave the force. You could do that too, although you'd probably have to be a bit less surly than usual." He grinned. "But yeah."

It was too much information in too short a span of time, but Carl thanked them. It had been easier to get it off his chest than he'd feared.

He was just on his way out the door when Gordon stopped him.

"By the way, do you remember when those important documents went missing in the Palle Rasmussen case? Well, here they are!"

Carl paused and took the sheets. It hardly mattered.

"Yeah, they were at the bottom of a pile on your desk when I was clearing up. Whatever you decide to write in the future, you should probably keep better track of your papers."

They all laughed, and for a moment the mood in the room was light and relieved, but only for a moment.

Carl looked mournfully at his comrades. How could he ever turn his back on them? On this?

Worst of all was the final moment when he had to leave. His friends stood very close to him, hugging him as though they never wanted to let go.

EPILOGUE

CARL

Monday, January 11, 2021

It was a few hours before he could bring himself to tell Mona what had happened.

Until she brought Lucia home after work, his mind had been focused on the future. If he didn't have something concrete to do, he'd judder to a halt.

His mother would be happy about the news, but he wouldn't be returning to Brønderslev and running the farm with his older brother. He could do it when Bent was going on holiday, but that was all.

Nor would he be appearing on TV like some sort of performing monkey. There were already retired officers who did a much better job of that than he ever could. He'd just start arguing with the other police or politicians, and he'd hate having to put on a jacket and a nice blue shirt to sit on some morning TV show.

Then there was Rose's suggestion. If he did that, he could drop Lucia off at nursery and pick her up again, taking the burden off Mona. Maybe he could even learn to cook.

Carl began chuckling to himself. He'd made an omelet the other day that Mona had described as a brown flying saucer.

Mona, in her own way, was relieved to hear what he'd been thinking. The last fourteen days had been awful for her, but even before that, she'd often found herself staring blankly into space because of Carl's job. For a man of fifty-five, despite the sweet little paunch, he was in pretty good shape, she'd always said. But his body had been through an ordeal, and many of the wounds had been deep, some life-threatening—a millimeter or two to either side would have killed or disabled him. In fact, it was one major reason why she had originally resisted his advances for so long.

She saw no appeal in being a widow.

"Listen to this." He smiled widely enough to play the next bit off as a joke. "Rose suggested I start writing. She was thinking maybe some 'true crime' stories drawing on cases from my own life."

Mona beamed from ear to ear. Was she making fun of him? Couldn't she see him sitting patiently hour after hour in front of the computer, was that it?

"No? You don't think I could do it?"

She sat down on the sofa next to him and placed her hand on his. "You can do whatever you want. And you've certainly got enough material for it." She pointed at the adjoining room. "There's a computer in there. Why don't you sit down and try to write a couple of sentences? Then I'll tell you what I think."

She got up and went into the kitchen. It was the briefest discussion of his future he had ever heard. When his father had advised him not to go to high school but start at the farm instead, while there were still dairy cows in the barn, the conversation had lasted two hours. Certainly that had seemed very different.

"Does *she* believe I can do it?" he grunted, sitting in front of the computer.

He mulled it over. If he was going to write, then he wanted to write about his own cases and preferably in his own way. But how?

He tapped at the keys for a bit, but after a minute he looked up, staring off into space, and thought about something else.

Maybe it would be better to be a consultant or a speaker after all. As a consultant he could travel the country, help out the local police a bit. He imagined how good he would be at it, and immediately had second thoughts. He'd have to listen to a load of nonsense and gossip, take them seriously when they'd already bungled their investigations. Sit in some hotel room in East Nowhere and watch regional TV! He shuddered at the thought. Rushing around giving talks would probably be no more thrilling either. Standing in front of a crowd who were really only there to gawp at the man who'd escaped from Slagelse and were mostly looking forward to the coffee afterward. Carl stared again at the computer. He liked sitting in his own desk chair, which he'd acquired in the days before that kind of stuff tended to break a month or two after the warranty ran out.

Warily, taking a deep breath, he began.

"Thirty years ago, the way we investigated cases was very different from today . . ." he wrote, then rapidly deleted it.

He snorted, then got up and went into the kitchen, grabbed the first beer that came to hand in the fridge, and downed it in one gulp.

It quenched his thirst but made him no readier for the task.

How do you start something when you'd rather be taking a nap? he asked himself. Perhaps it was better after all to go to work and nap there until his pension kicked in after God knew how many years.

"Honestly, Carl, aren't you too old to be thinking that way?" he said out loud to himself as he passed the mirror in the hall. Funnily enough, it made no reply.

He sat down again at the keyboard.

"My Life as a Detective" was the heading of his next draft. But no matter how much he puzzled over the words, Carl had no idea where the hell they could possibly lead. What did they mean, fundamentally? That he was the most hated man at the station, so they'd stuck him in a dull-as-dishwater basement with an immigrant who pottered around cleaning up the place in green rubber gloves. Or that they'd later added a totally unhinged woman who had quickly sorted out who called what shots down there.

Again he deleted what he'd written and stared for a while at the blank screen.

What did he even know about what was interesting and how to write it?

What cases would he find satisfying to write about?

He thought back to the early days of Department Q. When the cleaner had turned out to be an accomplished detective. When the whole thing really began to get off the ground.

He would miss it. He would miss Assad and his piss-poor coffee. He would miss Rose's big mouth and fiery eyes. And he would miss Gordon too, the pallid ghost who had proven he was able to cope through even the worst moments.

Perhaps there was a middle way. Perhaps they'd call him all the time, asking for advice.

He took an extra-deep breath. Put all ten fingers on the keyboard, even though he could only type with four. Then he tried to think of a way to write about his three colleagues in Department Q that still allowed him to feel close to them. Perhaps he should simply try to describe how it had all started in that basement at the station sixteen years ago and write about a woman trapped in a pressure chamber.

He smiled at the thought. It would be a tribute to the strongest woman he had ever met.

If he could have lit a cigarette, he would have, but he knew Mona would throw a fit. He'd have to air the place out for a week, then repaint the entire apartment. Dammit.

Carl sank back into his chair and closed his eyes, and after thinking for a minute or two, he wrote:

"How Department Q solved the Merete Lynggaard case."

He reread the sentence a couple of times. It triggered something, he could feel it, but then Mona came in and put her hands on his shoulders.

"Hmm, yeees," she said, after chewing it over for a minute. "Something along those lines might work. But maybe shift the point of view. What if you started by really digging into your characters? Put yourself in the victim's shoes; it'll be more engaging for both you and the reader that way, I think."

Then she withdrew, leaving him to ponder.

But Carl thought she was onto something. Mona was no fool. In fact, she had touched on something profound about him as a detective. *Dig into the characters, put yourself in the victim's shoes,* she had said. And wasn't that what he'd always done? Not just with the victims but with the aggressors as well. Now that he'd been a victim himself, he knew it might be worth another try.

Lingering for a moment, scratching a fingernail along the edge of the desk, he felt the scene take shape.

And when he could picture it in its entirety, he wrote:

The Keeper of Lost Causes

She scratched her fingertips on the smooth walls until they bled, and pounded her fists on the thick panes until she could no longer feel her hands.

And Carl's four fingers danced lightly across the keys. It was almost like the words flowed of their own accord.

ACKNOWLEDGMENTS

A big thank-you to my wife and soulmate, Hanne, for her loving support and indispensable comments on the very first draft.

A warm and special thank-you to Henning Kure for his lightning-fast, razor-sharp, utterly invaluable, and brilliant work.

Thank you to my assistant, Elisabeth Ahlefeldt Laurvig, for her unwavering support, research, and meticulous organizational skills.

Thanks are also due to Elisabeth Wæhrens, Eddie Kiran, Micha Schmalstieg, Leif Christensen, Jesper Helbo, and Karlo Andersen for their insightful early proofreading and suggestions.

Thank you to Line Holm for her unerringly sharp eye. Thank you to Stine Bolther and retired detective and chief of homicide Jens Møller Jensen for crucial interventions regarding police procedure and factual accuracy. Thank you to corrections officers Ulrik Thorsen and Christian Dines Paulsen at Slagelse Remand Center for their thorough proofreading, amendments, and forgiveness. Thank you to J. "J" Nielsen for a few sobering truths about life as an inmate.

Thank you to my conscientious editor, Charlotte Weiss, for her great patience and lifelong friendship.

Thank you to publisher Lene Juul, that extraordinary creative powerhouse, and again to Charlotte Weiss for her support and our many years of fruitful collaboration. Without you, I would certainly never have ended up becoming a writer. Thank you to Charlotte Fournias for her professional coordination of anything and everything. Thank you to Tomas Henriksen for staying cool, calm, and collected and keeping the production side running smoothly. Thank you to Rudi Urban Rasmussen and Sigrid Stavnem for their charm and for keeping the whole world on tenterhooks. Thank you to Per Nørhaven for being on standby.

Thank you to Daniel Struer for his invaluable assistance with Old Norse. Thank you to Kenneth Schultz and Thomas Thorhauge for creating beautiful covers.

Thank you to the rest of the team at Politikens Forlag who have persevered with me so magnificently throughout Q10: Pernille Engelbert Weil, Magnus Thielsen, and everybody else in the Politikens Forlag marketing department; Christina Zemanova, Camilla Wahlgreen, and the rest of the press team; Anette Whitt and the entire finance department; the multitalented Jakob Harden; junior editor Magnus Kruse Lykke; and multitasker extraordinaire Louise Kønig.

Thank you to Tine Harden for once again giving me an utterly unique photograph to start the campaign.

Thank you to Githa Lehrmann for lending her wonderful voice to all the audiobooks.

Thank you to my Dutch translator, Kor de Vries, for his sharp-eyed proofreading and for passing on his insights to many of my other translators. Thank you to all my translators—you must have worked incredibly hard.

Thank you to Stella Løkkegaard, Anders Fisker Caspersen, and Rasmus Markussen for ensuring that the day-to-day accounting, administration, and auditing remain seamless.

A big shout-out to everyone I've worked so closely with in previous years: Karsten Blauert, Anne Christine Andersen, Lene Wissing, Lene Børresen, Helle Schou Wacher, Nya Guldberg, Lise Ringhof, Sofie Voller, Thomas Szøke, and the ever-omnipresent Camilla Høy.

Thank you also to my considerate bosses at Politiken over the years: Lars Munch, Stig Ørskov, and Jørgen Ejbøl.

Thank you to Sandra and Kes for inviting us to be near you and the grandchildren.

Thank you to my sisters and brothers-in-law and all the members of our beloved family.

Thank you to Gitte and Peter Q. Rannes for another few rewarding and hospitable stays at the Center for Danish Authors and Translators at Hald Hovedgaard.

Thank you to Søren Pilmark for sharing a writing room with me in Barcelona and at Hald Hovedgaard.

Thank you to Olaf Slott-Petersen, Michael Kirkegaard, Annette Merrild, and Arne M. Bertelsen, my indispensable families in Barcelona.

Thank you to Stine Bolther for putting me in touch with the immensely obliging and professional individuals who allowed me to interview them in 2020–21: superintendent Dannie Riese; defense counsel Mette Grith Stage; detective and lead investigator at the Police Complaints Authority, Niels Raasted; prosecuting counsel Jesper Rubow; defense counsel Jakob Buch-Jepsen; and public prosecutor Lise-Lotte Nilas.

Thanks again to Stine Bolther for the fantastic course she arranged in autumn 2020, which helped to put me on the right track and was helpful for many different aspects of this novel. A list of lecturers can be found at the back of the book.

Thank you to the Slagelse Remand Center for allowing me to visit, and to Tine Vigild, chief of staff at the Danish Correctional Services, for our fruitful conversations, as well as to Helle Sejersen, Heidi Hovgaard Rasmussen, Morten Lauridsen, Knud Erik Kristiansen, Pia Bosse, Palle Svendsson, Jytte Bredahl Pedersen, Christian Dines Paulsen, and Ulrik Thorsen. Thank you to Lea Bryld and Frederikke Siert, Preben Schunck, Henrik Jacobsen, Britt Rhymer, and Helle Østergaard for an invaluable visit to Vestre Prison.

Thank you to the doctors and nurses at Vestre Prison.

Huge thanks to former sergeant Mikkel Bredgaard, former corrections officer Per Laustsen, and police officer and dog handler Thomas Meedom for giving me interviews and for being so open about their own experiences when things got a little off track.

Thank you to Just Kamp and Ole Drost for my visit to the courthouse.

And finally, special thanks to Ellie and Louie for keeping Hanne and the undersigned going.

LECTURERS

Thank you for the inspiration and expertise regarding research and courses, 2020.

Dannie Rise—chief superintendent, Bornholm Police

Brian Belling—deputy chief superintendent, Copenhagen Police

Anne Birgitte Stürup—former prosecuting counsel and public prosecutor in Copenhagen

Bo Samson—superintendent, Rigspolitiet

Lars Mortensen—superintendent, Special Crime Unit

Henrik Sønderby—chief superintendent, Special Crime Unit

Claus Birkelyng—superintendent, Copenhagen Police

Lisbeth Fried—chief superintendent, Rigspolitiet

Mikael Henrik Wern—chief superintendent, Special Crime Unit

Thomas Kristensen—head of communications, Central and West Zealand Police

Jens Bech Stausbøll—judge, Copenhagen City Court

Lise-Lotte Nilas—public prosecutor in Copenhagen

Jens Fuglsang Edelholt—press officer, Rigspolitiet

Trine Møller—superintendent, Copenhagen Police

Mai-Brit Storm Thygesen—defense counsel, Storm Thygesen Advokatfirma

Lea Bryld—acting deputy head of branch, Correctional Services

Sabrina Ejstrup Vig—press consultant, Correctional Services

Frederikke Siert—section leader, HR Jura og Forhandling, Correctional Services

Paw Lauridsen—section leader, Correctional Services

Steen Holger Hansen—deputy state coroner, Institute of Forensic Medicine, University of Copenhagen

Jørgen Andersen—head of financial intelligence unit, Special Crime Unit

Christian Jeppesen—former inmate

ABOUT THE AUTHOR

Jussi Adler-Olsen is Denmark's #1 crime writer and a *New York Times* bestselling author. His books routinely top the bestseller lists in Europe and have sold more than twenty-seven million copies around the world. His many prestigious worldwide crime-writing awards include the Barry Award and the Glass Key Award, also won by Henning Mankell, Jo Nesbø, and Stieg Larsson.